The Wolf and the Highlander

ALSO BY JESSI GAGE

Highland Wishes Series

Wishing for a Highlander

Blue Collar Boyfriends

Reckless

COMING SOON

Jade's Spirit

Cole in My Stocking

The Highlander's Witch

The Wolf and the Highlander

A HIGHLAND WISHES NOVEL

Jessi Gage

To my mom

Acknowledgements

Thank you to Julie Brannagh and Amy Raby, my faithful friends and critique partners. I look forward to seeing you both each and every week. Thank you to Shane for your love and support. I couldn't do this without you. That goes for you too, Mom. Between babysitting, brainstorming, help with the housework, and just listening when I need to talk, you make it possible for me to follow my dream. Thank you to Kim Killion for your beautiful cover art. Thank you to Joanne Wadsworth, Shiboney Dumo, Kate Day, and Mary Merrell my wonderful beta readers. And thank you to Piper Denna for editing this manuscript. You all helped me make this finished product the best it can be.

Chapter 1

FRIGID WIND WHIPPED the mist. Icy particles scraped Anya's cheeks like a demon's kiss as she gazed across the wide valley of farmland toward the village she'd been exiled from more than a year ago. Ackergill. Another hour's ride and she'd be home. By sunrise, she'd most likely be dead.

"Best get it over with," she muttered to Leah, the pony Gravois had given her.

"*Chi-Yuen tells me your legs are fully healed,*" the leader of the tinker camp had told her two days ago near Inverness. "*There is no more she can do for you.*"

"*Are ye trying to get rid of me?*" She'd made light of Gravois' not so subtle hint, but in truth, her stomach had shriveled with fear at his words. After five months of traveling with his camp, she'd come to feel a mild sort of belonging with the mysterious tink and his magical misfits.

"*Never, mademoiselle. But your destiny lies elsewhere.*"

She'd learned not to argue with him when he claimed to ken such impossible things. Spurning the impossible seemed to be a specialty of Gravois'. She should have died after she'd fallen into a crevice in a remote patch of rocky terrain and broken both her legs, but Gravois, a stranger at the time, had miraculously found her. She should never have been able to walk again, but Chi-Yuen's medicines had healed her to the point she could bear her own weight for short periods. If he thought she had a destiny waiting for her, mayhap she ought to listen.

"Take this," Gravois had said, holding out a polished amethyst gemstone the likes of which a common lass like her would never dream of possessing. *"It will guide you to the place you are meant to go. Embrace your destiny, and I will consider your debt for the last five months paid."*

She'd grudgingly taken the gemstone and ridden Leah to Inverness, despairing over having nowhere to go and intending to sell both pony and gemstone. If she were lucky, she'd make enough off them to eke out a few years' miserly existence. But, curse the barmy tink, he'd been right again. Over the course of the ride, she'd recognized a restlessness in herself. Once she paid it heed, she'd realized where she must ride. And now here she was.

She touched her heels to Leah's sides, and the pony started down the gentle slope into Ackergill's farming valley. Hooves clopped over the hard ground as they followed the wagon-rutted road. In the distance, Big Darcy's windmills stood atop the cliffs like pieces on a chessboard. To the left of the mills, squat and brooding, hunkered Ackergill Keep. Crofters' cottages dotted the slope rising from the valley to the cliffs. At the familiar sight of her clan's land, her restlessness lifted. She felt peace.

'Twas right she should come home. She'd done much wrong to her clan. She'd heard Big Darcy walked with a limp because of her, and he likely would forevermore. Fortunately no lasting harm had come to Ginneleah, the wife Laird Steafan had chosen over her. In her jealousy, Anya had sent Ginneleah doctored oils under a false name. She'd claimed the oils would aid conception when in truth the mixture was one Anya herself used to prevent catching a bairn. Big Darcy's wife had been the one to discover Anya's plot. Aodhan had exiled her for her treachery, and shortly after, she'd heard Ginneleah had gotten with child, the child Anya had wanted to give her laird. Hearing the news had so enraged her, she'd slipped Darcy and his wife an apple sack with a poisonous viper inside. The viper had bitten Darcy's foot. He'd nearly died.

That very day, she'd fallen from her horse and into the rocky crevice.

She'd thought being scarred and utterly broken from her fall were just deserts for the treachery she'd dealt. But no. She bore her punishment in dishonor, having never faced those she'd wronged. 'Twas not the Keith way. It had taken a meddling tinker to make her realize it. Whether Gravois' gemstone or her conscience had led her here, she was grateful. 'Twas time to balance the scales in full.

Leah started up the slope into the village. Anya rode her to the stables, which were thankfully abandoned for the evening. She groomed the pony and gave her grain and a pat on the neck for her work. That done, she pulled the hood of her cloak over her head and hobbled off in search of Aodhan. As war chieftain to the Keith, he would most likely be found at the keep.

The November cold nipped her nose. Wind buffeted her cloak. Her legs ached like someone was jabbing needles into her joints. The walk from the village to the keep had never taken her so long.

As she approached the fortress-like building, the sounds of a gathering filtered around from behind. She followed the fiddle and bagpipe music to the bailey behind the keep.

The oak doors from the great hall were thrown open to the chilly night. A bonfire in the center of the bailey threw sparks into the dark sky. Men sang loudly and sloshed their tankards. Women danced and laughed. A table strewn with scraps from a feast sat near the fire. In the center of the table was a carved out log. Without looking inside, she kent what that log would contain. At one end would be a pile of dirt, at the other a pile of salt. The Keith were celebrating the life of a clansman or woman with a salt and earth ceremony.

Too bad someone had died, but bloody convenient for her

since she needed to find Aodhan and he would certainly be in attendance. Steafan too. She hobbled into the shadow cast by the keep door and looked over the gathering, searching for their faces.

Across the bailey, a head of honey blond hair peeked above the rest. Big Darcy. Her stomach turned over. He wasn't dancing but standing beyond the table, sipping ale and talking with another warrior. Could he dance anymore? Was it difficult for him to run his mills with his damaged leg? *Och,* if she'd never set upon her foolish course of vengeance, Darcy would be hale. She'd never have been exiled, never have fallen and become this twisted, broken wretch of a woman.

The musicians stopped as a broad shouldered man made his dignified way to the head of the table. Laird Steafan. She waited for the tug on her heart she always used to feel upon seeing him. It didn't come. Strange. She'd always loved Steafan, ever since she was a wee ane. At least she'd thought so. Mayhap she'd only loved the position and privilege she'd hoped to find as his lady, or his mistress. At one time, she'd done everything in her power to secure a place in his bed. Tonight, she would go to his dungeon. If she was lucky, she wouldn't remain there long before he ended her misery. But if her laird chose to make her end slow, she'd not complain. She'd earned whatever punishment he rained down upon her.

Steafan waited for the revelers to attend to him. He smiled, showing his even teeth. 'Twas time to honor the dead by tossing the earth and salt into the fire, the earth to represent mortal flesh, the salt to represent eternal life.

Vaguely, she wondered who'd died, but mainly, she searched for Aodhan's dark head. She didn't see him. Mayhap she'd find him in the keep. She turned to go inside.

"Tonight, we gather to honor the passing of Fergus Douglass MacDougal Keith." Steafan's voice hit her in the chest like a sledgehammer.

Da.

The salt and earth ceremony was for her da.

"To Fergus," one man shouted.

"To Fergus," the revelers answered.

Her legs became weak. She leaned on the door. *Gone. They're all gone.*

Her mother had left when she and Seona had been small. Seona, her elder sister and dearest friend, had disappeared from the bawdyhouse in Thurson shortly before Anya had taken up a post there after her exile. She'd never stopped searching for Seona, not even after her fall. Everywhere Gravois brought the tinker camp, Anya would ask about to see if anyone had seen her sister. Nothing ever came of it.

Now her da was gone too. She hadn't seen him since her exile, and they had never gotten on well, but he was still her da. Her heart recognized the lost connection with a deep pang of sadness.

Her courage fled. She no longer wanted to find Aodhan, no longer wished to pay for her sins. She wanted to climb on Leah and ride away and weep for all she'd lost. Was it too late to go back to Gravois and beg for a place in his camp?

Sniffing back tears, she limped from the keep. Behind her, she heard the hiss as Steafan threw the contents of the log on the fire. Her chest constricted. Her da's spirit would have heard the hiss too and departed for Heaven's peace.

He was really gone.

Christ, she felt so alone.

The crowd cheered. Their singing followed her all the way down to the cottages. Her feet led her to the dark alley she kent like the back of her hand. The cottage she'd shared with her da was just ahead, there beyond the hedgerow where the widow McAllister kept her ewes.

The slope of the thatched roof greeted her like an old friend.

She limped to the front door. It was cracked open. A band of golden light peeked through the crack.

She stopped short.

Someone was inside.

How dare someone pillage her da's cottage while his bonfire was still burning? She pushed open the creaky door to find a dark-haired man bent over her da's shelf of knickknacks, poking through the creations of seashells and driftwood her da had cobbled together to amuse himself.

The man straightened and spun around, nearly dropping the box he'd just lifted from the shelf. A lantern on a nearby table lit his features. Aodhan.

§

RIGGS'S THIGHS BURNED as he raced through the forest. He pushed harder. Faster. He would not lose the quarry he'd tracked all night, all the way into the wilds of Larna. For one thing and one thing alone would he risk crossing paths with the barbarians who lived across the border from Marann. Marbled boar.

He could already taste the sow's sweet meat melting on his tongue. Her hindquarters would make a fine breakfast. Then he'd make a bedcover from her hide to sell to a noble in Chroina. Over the years, he'd saved up enough coin to buy ten lottery tickets. Now he needed to pad his purse enough that he could pamper the lady if he should happen to win one for a season. The take from a single marbled boar skin would bring him up to his goal.

The sow disappeared into a gully then reappeared as she made for a line of evergreens. He leapt the gully, gaining ground on her, but his boot skidded in the slick leaves on the far side. He windmilled his arms and had to put one hand to the ground to keep from falling. The boar disappeared past the line of trees.

He lowered his head and plowed on. Nothing would stop him

from catching her. This was his lucky year. He could feel it in his bones.

The scent of pine burst over him as he tore a hole through the line of trees. He didn't see the sow at first. A scrabbling noise to his right drew his gaze just in time to see that beautiful mottled hide disappear into the bracken. She was tan and black with just enough white to make her stand out against the autumn-brown forest.

Come on, sweetheart. You know you're mine. Stop fighting it.

From the way her sides heaved and her pace had slowed, he could tell she was tiring. He was tired too after running full-out most of the night, but once he caught her, the exhaustion would be worth it. Oh, would it be worth it.

There! She tried to jump a fallen log and caught her hoof in the rotted wood.

He lunged and fell on her. His nails dug into her hide like daggers, holding her bucking body. He opened his mouth wide, ready to tear out her throat.

"What's that racket?" A rumble of a voice coming from a nearby copse of trees made him freeze.

"I'll go check."

Shite. Larnians.

The sow took advantage of his distraction. She twisted around and gored his thigh. Pain ripped through his leg. Worse, the sow slithered out of his grasp. She tore off in the direction of the voices. Smart girl. She knew he'd come from Marann's side of the border and wouldn't risk becoming outnumbered by enemies.

She dashed into the copse of trees. Yells erupted.

"A marbled boar!"

"Get her!"

"Where's my dagger?"

"Don't just stand there with your thumb up your ass! Go after her!"

"We'll mind the trap. Hurry! Don't let her get away!"

Riggs made out four voices. Must be a hunting party. Only reason Larnians tolerated their own company was to hunt or make war. Rest of the time, they'd just as soon slaughter each other as work together.

There were sounds of men shucking their clothes and giving chase. Two sets of running feet took off into the forest. Two men stayed behind.

If he wanted to pursue the boar, he'd have to kill the Larnians for her, because now that they'd spotted her, they wouldn't give up until they had her.

He didn't mind killing Larnians, but couldn't countenance it for a quarry, even a marbled boar. Shite. He punched the ground.

He sat with his back to the rotted log to catch his breath. The bark scratched his skin with a refreshing bite. The scent of the marbled boar lingered like a taunt in his nostrils.

Only thing worse than losing such a rare quarry was the thought of her fine hide being sullied by Larnian filth.

Run, sweetheart. Run like the wind.

He let his head fall back on the log and gazed past the treetops. By the moon, he was tired. And hungry. And bleeding. He needed breakfast. Best if he snuck away quietly and hunted on Marann's side of the border.

He started to get up to go when murmuring from the copse of trees caught his attention. "We could play with her," one man said. "Give her a taste of what's in store for her once we get back to Saroc. Huh, beautiful? How'd you like to come out and play?" The sound of a wooden cage being rattled.

A growl. Then the sounds of an irritated animal thrashing.

Ah, shite. They'd caught a she-wolf. Riggs had heard rumors about the Larnians that had turned his stomach. He'd hoped they were just rumors, but now he knew there was some truth to them. Despicable. And not something he would stand by and let happen.

Looked like he might get to kill some Larnians this morning after all.

"You got a muzzle in your pack?" one of the men said.

"Yeah, here." Silence while Riggs crept closer. Then, "Come on, beautiful, hold still."

He'd gotten close enough to see the men through the boughs of a pine. They were shirtless but wore faded blue war kilts. Soldiers, like most of the remaining Larnians. And like most remaining Larnians, they were older than Riggs, their beards streaked with gray. One had stuck a pole collar through the bars of the trap-cage. He got the loop around the neck of a snarling she-wolf and tightened the collar. "Got her. Go on. Open the cage."

The other man held a muzzle and lifted the door of the trap. "Not as pretty as the little females Bantus likes to flaunt, but she'll do for a quick rut while the others are distracted with the boar."

King Bantus flaunting females? Did they mean she-wolves? They must, because Riggs's king, Magnus, had evacuated the remaining women from Larna in the last war. Since then, Larna's King, Bantus, had been ruling a dying country of men with no hope of living on through their young. Some claimed that justified the Larnians' interest in she-wolves. Riggs disagreed. No creature deserved to be rutted against their will.

The man holding the pole struggled to keep the wolf still while the other extended his arm into the cage, muzzle first.

"Feisty little female," the one holding the pole said. "She'll do. She'll do just fine."

"The fuck she will," Riggs said, stepping around the pine.

The men jumped to their feet. Snarling, they turned to face him. They had to look up—way up—to meet his eyes. They were well muscled and had to be tough since they'd survived the war, but like most everyone, they were smaller than him.

He showed his teeth in challenge.

Their snarls died on their faces. He never got tired of seeing the fight go out of men when they realized they were outmatched.

The she-wolf tore into the forest with the pole around her neck. Riggs noted which way she went.

Unsurprisingly, the men turned tail and ran too. Cowards.

He wanted to give chase. It had been a long time since he'd had just cause to kill Larnians. But if the she-wolf couldn't free herself from the pole collar, it would hinder her ability to hunt. Probably wouldn't be fatal, but he sure wouldn't want to go through life with a pole collar stuck around his neck.

He took off into the forest after the she-wolf.

When he'd scented marbled boar yesterday, he'd anticipated a fine meal and week of tanning a beautiful hide. Guess he'd be limping around Larna after a pissed off she-wolf instead. So much for feeling lucky.

Chapter 2

"WHAT ARE YOU doing here?" Anya blurted.

Aodhan's ice-blue eyes widened. "Me? What are *you* doing here? You're dead." His face paled as he looked her up and down.

She snorted. "I'm no ghost, if that's what you're thinking. I'm alive as you are, though no' for long I suspect since I recall your warning last time we met in this cottage." He had just returned from Dornoch, where Darcy and his wife had revealed Anya's plot to keep Ginneleah from catching a bairn. Ever true to his laird, Aodhan had told her to leave Ackergill and never return. If she did, he'd hand her over to Steafan along with a list of her sins. Steafan was not known for his mercy. Looked like she was going to meet her justice tonight after all.

Aodhan's color returned. *Och,* nothing rattled the war chieftain for long. He'd probably have recovered just as quickly if she really had been a ghost.

"Before ye bring me to Steafan, I have somat to say." She stepped closer to him, letting him see her jarring gait. "Tell Darcy I am sorry for what I did. And tell Ginneleah I deeply regret the pain I've caused her." Her throat felt tight. She cleared it. *Courage, Anya. Make your da proud.* "And I'm sorry, Aodhan. I'm sorry for betraying you by plotting against your daughter and your laird. Our laird. I'm ready to face him now. Go on. Take me to Steafan."

She lifted her chin and squared her shoulders. She'd learned not to expect Mercy from Aodhan merely because they'd been lovers. He'd cured her of that misconception when he'd exiled her and then left her for dead when he'd found her in that cleft.

His brow creased. "Christ, lass. What happened to you?"

Did he mean her limp? Her scars? "Ye ken what happened. I fell."

"I recall," he said gravely.

He was likely also recalling how she'd pleaded with him to rescue her, and how he'd refused because she'd failed to show concern for those she'd harmed with her plotting. What would he think if he kent how she'd changed these last months? *Och*, it didn't matter. Feeling sorry didn't change the wickedness she'd committed, especially when it had taken her near death to make her realize the depth of her own depravity.

"How did you get out?" he asked.

"A Rom rescued me."

He shifted on his feet, and the light of his lantern reflected off the box he held. It looked about the size of a shaving kit. Rich rosewood inlaid with white metal peeked out from between his fingers. The box looked familiar, but she couldn't place where she'd seen it before.

"Is that my da's? What are you doing with it?" Anger lit a fire in her breast. "Are you thieving from him now that he's gone? Why, ye bloody—"

"It's the box Steafan tried to destroy. The one Darcy's wife said brought her from a future time."

The breath froze in her lungs. No wonder it looked familiar. She'd handled the bloody thing once, even read for herself the impossible date beside the maker's mark. It had been springtime in the year 1517 when she'd last seen that box, yet it claimed to have been made in 1542.

Her encounter with that box had been the start of her troubles. If she'd never laid eyes on it, would she be hale today? Would she be up at the keep, celebrating her da's life with her clan?

She took a step back. "Keep it away from me. It's evil."

"Mayhap," Aodhan agreed. "I watched Steafan take every weapon in the keep's armory to it trying to destroy it. Even put it under the grinding stone in Darcy's mill. Not even that did the trick. Last time I saw this, 'twas flying over the cliffs. Steafan shrieked like a banshee when he threw it. Look." He rotated the box. "Not even a scratch."

Anya refused to get close enough to confirm it.

"Your da must have found it while culling seaweed for market. Must be why he kept it with this rubbish." He motioned toward the shelves.

"'Tis no' rubbish. Those trinkets made him happy."

"Whiskey made your da happy. These things kept him busy until the pub opened each night."

He was right, curse him. "Ye shouldna speak ill of the dead. How did he go? Do you ken?" Pain swelled in her chest and brought tears to her eyes. She didn't let them fall. She wouldn't let Aodhan see her cry. Her da *had* been a drunk, and a mean one more often than not, but he'd been her drunk to care for. Because of Aodhan, she hadn't been able to comfort him at his death. *Och,* no. Because of her. *Her.* She was the wicked one.

"Auld age, An. I suppose." His eyes went soft on her when he used the shortened version of her name. "Or too much drink. Took about a week. He suffered some, but went bravely, like a Keith. I came to inventory his possessions," he went on, the softness lifting. "Everything belongs to the laird now, since your da has no surviving near kin."

He leveled a look at her, letting the statement penetrate. Since he'd exiled her she was no longer considered clan. She didn't count as her da's heir. She hadn't expected any different, but hearing it said aloud still stung.

"Well," she snapped. "What are ye waiting for? Take me to Steafan."

Aodhan shook his head. "Nay. I doona think I will. Nor will I pass along your apologies to Darcy and Ginnie. If you turn around and walk out that door, and I never see you again, I'll tell myself the box made your spirit manifest to me tonight. By morning I may even believe it."

She shook her head. "I came here for a reason. You must see me punished. You must." Her da had died bravely. So would she.

"Seems to me you've suffered enough. Go on with you, lass." He lifted his chin toward the door.

This couldn't be happening. Once again a man was telling her to leave when she had nowhere to go. She'd made peace with coming back to Ackergill. Her conscience felt light for the first time in ages.

"Go on," Aodhan said again, and he turned his back to her, pretending interest in her da's knickknacks.

He was showing her mercy, but it was the last thing she wanted. She'd felt so strongly she was meant to come here. She'd hoped to belong somewhere again, even if only for a few precious moments.

A song one of Gravois' travelers used to sing filled her mind like a prayer:

When I had a home, I could not wait to leave it.
When I had none, I longed for a hearth of my own.
Lord, if you have not found me lacking,
Open up your gates; I'm coming home.

She was home. Or nearly so. She wouldn't limp away like a coward. "Take me to Steafan," she said, but a faint clinking sound coming from Aodhan's direction interrupted her. The cottage began spinning around her, quicker and quicker, as if she'd been caught up in a waterspout. Dizziness dragged her to her hands and knees.

"What the bloody hell?" Aodhan said.

Somat clattered to the floor. Amidst the spinning, she glimpsed what had made the noise. The box. Though stationary on the floor, it streaked past, leaving a trail in her vision like a shooting star. Its lid was open.

The whirling floor changed from dust-streaked wood to dried leaves. The lantern-lit dimness of her da's cottage changed to the gray light of either dusk or dawn.

"Anya! What's happening, lass?" Aodhan's voice was distant.

"It's the bloody box!" she cried. But the cabin was gone. Aodhan was gone. The spinning stopped as abruptly as it had begun.

She was surrounded by a thick gray forest. Cautiously, she sat up and searched her memory for clues as to where she might be. There were no forests this dense near Ackergill. The vines of ivy hanging from the mossy trees were like nothing she'd ever seen.

"Bloody hell." The bloody meddling box. It had sent her who kent where. Mayhap across oceans. Mayhap across time, as Big Darcy's wife had claimed.

Did that mean she was trapped here? Wherever here was?

A rusting noise drew her gaze around. A beast burst through some bracken and ran straight at her. A boar! A giant one! All great tusks and slobbering snout.

She screamed and scurried out of its path.

It charged past, grunting, its brown eyes glazed with panic.

Thank the good Lord it ignored her. Rolling to her side, she watched its hindquarters as it raced into the trees. She'd never seen anything like it before. Its coat was mottled like that of the calico cat she and Seona had kept as children. She doubted anyone would welcome *that* beast on their lap while they darned near the fire.

No sooner had the boar disappeared than more rustling made

her look in the direction the boar had come. Two naked men crashed through the bracken, running at high speed. They were hairier than any man she'd ever seen before. And wilder. Their eyes fairly glowed with animal alertness.

Upon spying her, they skidded to a stop, both panting. One of them bent to brace his hands on his knees. They gaped at her for long seconds.

"The boar went that way," she told them, pointing. Obviously, they were after the thing. She was eager to see them on their way. They did not appear the helpful sort.

One of them grinned at her. His teeth were bulky in his mouth, his eyeteeth especially. They were like daggers of bone. "Think we found something even better than marbled boar, yeah?" He nudged the other with his elbow.

"Must have escaped Bantus's harem and walked here from Saroc," said the other. That one had eyes the color of blood. These were men, but they weren't like any men she'd ever seen before. "And she must have been there a long time to know our tongue."

What were they blethering on about? Her escaping from some man's harem? Made no sense. She'd only just arrived here.

The first man grunted in agreement. "Let the others have the marbled boar. If they can catch her. I'm more than happy to make use of our king's leavings." He cupped his cock and bollocks, leaving no doubt about his meaning.

They moved toward her as one.

Fear pounded through her veins. She struggled to get to her feet. Pain ripped through her left knee.

Saints above, she'd never be able to flee these men on her pathetic excuses for legs. She dug under her skirts for the dirk she kept strapped to her calf. *Och,* that's right. She'd left it on her cot as meager payment for Gravois' pony and gemstone.

She had nothing with which to defend herself.

The men towered over her. One of them reached for her, and

his hand was tipped with black, pointed fingernails.

She screamed.

§

RIGGS TRIED NOT to think about the two measly foxes he'd had for breakfast instead of sweet marbled boar. Instead, he remained alert for signs left by the she-wolf. She wasn't hard to track. All he had to do was follow the distinctive line the pole collar drew in the earth. She was taking him on a southerly route. At least she hadn't turned west, taking him deeper into Larna.

A patch of hair on a thorn bush caught his eye. Several strands of white, a few of tan. He rubbed them between his fingers. The color and coarseness could mean only one thing. The marbled boar had crossed paths with the wolf. His spirits lifted. Maybe he'd catch the sow after all. That is, if she'd managed to elude the Larnians.

A few minutes more brought him to a moist creek bed, nearly dried up. The she-wolf's prints stood out clearly, as did two sets of footprints that must belong to the Larnians chasing the boar. Unsurprisingly, the she-wolf changed direction, heading east out of the creek bed, toward Marann and his cabin. He followed the wolf prints.

A minute's run brought him to a formation of boulders. Wedged between two rocks was the pole collar. The she-wolf was nowhere to be seen. She had managed to free herself.

Good. He squatted to rest. Should he continue east to home, or pursue the boar and risk running into a number of Larnians he couldn't defeat?

A shrill cry to the south interrupted his thoughts.

What in the low realm? That wasn't the cry of either a boar or a wolf.

Curiosity piqued, he ran toward the sound. Before long, the

low rumble of men's voices touched his ears. He slowed, moving silently, cocking his head to listen.

"What are you doing?" one man said. "Stop toying with her."

"I want to chase her," another man said.

He heard a pained whimper. The she-wolf? No. She wouldn't have let herself be caught a second time. Must be some other poor creature they were toying with. But no animal he knew of made a sound like that.

"She can hardly walk, you idiot. Look at that crippled gait."

"Get up, you ugly cow," one of the men said.

There was another pained cry. Then, "Ugly cow? At least I'm no' a mangy cur! Get your filthy paws off me! Help! Help!"

By the moon. That is no animal.

It was something more valuable than a whole cart packed with marbled boar skins. A woman.

Snarling, he plowed through bracken and sailed over a formation of boulders. He rounded a thicket and found one Larnian standing by while another tried to mount a small woman in a faded blue dress struggling on hands and knees to get away.

The woman reared up, crashing her head into the nose of the pig atop her. It gave with a crunch.

"Aaargh!" The man shoved her down with a hand on the back of her neck, mashing her face into the leaves. "Broke my nose, the bitch did!" He struck the side of her head.

Riggs's vision went red with rage.

He knocked the Larnian off the woman's still form and tore out his throat before the pig could so much as raise a hand to defend himself. The foul taste of enemy blood filled his mouth.

Jumping to his feet, he faced the other Larnian. He bared his teeth in challenge.

The man was big and appeared fairly young for a Larnian. But Riggs was bigger and younger. Nevertheless, the Larnian didn't run like the ones he'd found with the she-wolf. A woman was worth fighting a losing battle for.

They circled, sizing each other up. The Larnian had defeat in his blood-red eyes, but he kept his chin up, his gaze defiant. "We could both use her," he said. "No one else needs to know."

"You'll touch her over my dead body," Riggs growled. He made the first move, getting in quick and delivering a blow to the man's side. He tried for a follow-up to the stomach, but the man danced away on fast feet. Riggs's fist hit nothing but air.

They circled again. His opponent hunched around where Riggs had connected with that first punch. A few more of those, and he'd have the maggot beat.

"You kill me and take her, the others'll track you," the Larnian wheezed. "Think they'll let a woman's scent go unfollowed? You won't get far."

"I'm not afraid of a few Larnians." Riggs went in for a punch to the face.

The man dodged, turning the blow into little more than a graze. He was fast. But Riggs could be fast too, when he needed to be.

"Not a few, yeah," the man said. "I can see that. You're a fucking beast. But there's more than a few of us camped out here. We make good money catching she-wolves and selling them up in Saroc. We're well supplied. Got horses and tracking wolves who'd be more than happy to cross into Marann and tear you limb from limb for such a prize. But enjoy the woman with me for a few days then walk away, and I'll swear on my mother's grave to keep it secret. No one will ever know a Maranner was poaching on Larnian soil today."

Yeah, right. Likely, this maggot thought to offer him the woman first and attack his back while he was distracted. As if he'd give him the chance.

He flicked a glance at the woman. She lay face down on the ground, too still. Enough of this. She needed help, and he was wasting time.

He charged the Larnian, a surprise move.

The man grunted at the impact and went down hard. Riggs slammed his fist into the maggot's face, stunning him. Then he grabbed his head with both hands and gave a fierce twist.

It was over.

He rushed to the woman's side. Instantly, her scent overwhelmed him. Sweet flowers, hyssop, and woman's musk. She also smelled of horses and leather tack, of damp wool and mist. Glossy chestnut hair fell across her face, obscuring it.

Don't be dead.

He crouched and reached a hand toward her. Pulled it back. She was so small. He was afraid to touch her.

He observed her instead, his gaze going to her back. It rose and fell with steady breaths. She was alive.

By the moon. He was in custody of a woman.

The tight coil of fury in his chest turned to wonder. It lasted only a moment before turning into a heavy weight of responsibility.

Shite. He was in custody of a woman.

"Where did you come from?" he asked. Of course she didn't answer.

Gently as he could manage, he curled a finger around the silky strands of her hair and lifted them off her face. By the moon, her ear! It was rounded like a clam shell!

His heart pounded as he studied it, as he transferred his scrutiny to what he could see of her face. Her eyes were closed, her lips parted to reveal oddly blunt teeth, like a ewe's. The graceful arch of her cheekbone looked as delicate as finely crafted porcelain. She wasn't wolfkind.

"Where did you come from?" he asked again. She didn't stir.

He touched a fingertip to her perfect eggshell cheek, careful not to scratch her. When she didn't respond, he patted her cheek.

"Wake up."

Still nothing.

Careful of his hands, so large compared to her thin arms, he rolled her onto her back. She went over limp as a freshly slaughtered doe. Her face turned up to the sky. Her loveliness froze the breath in his throat. Not even the old claw marks furrowing her left cheek could ruin such beauty.

Her eyelids appeared thin as vellum. He could make out the spider web network of vessels in the skin. Her cheeks looked like sunset, pale pink against her ivory-cloud paleness. Her lips were dark pink and full as dripping heart blooms.

His gaze roved downward, over the high neckline of her dress, over the mouthwatering swell of breasts beneath faded blue fabric. His whole body thrummed with sudden desire, which he resolutely ignored as he fixed his attention on those claw marks. Had this stunning creature been a plaything for the Larnians? Had some man marked her as his in this barbaric way?

No. He would smell mating on her if any man had had her recently. The Larnians must have found her moments before he'd heard her cries.

Shite. Larnians. In his shock over finding this treasure, he'd forgotten he was still in Larna.

He had to get her away from here. If the second maggot he'd killed had told the truth about this forest being populated by trappers with access to horses and tracking wolves, he'd better hurry. It took time to organize a tracking party. That would give him a head start. He'd need it.

He started to scoop the woman into his arms.

Her eyes opened. Her pupils contracted as she focused on him. She screamed.

He pressed a hand over her mouth. "Hush. Hush, now. Quiet."

She continued to scream. Her tiny fingers with their blunt nails grasped at his arm. Her heels dug in the ground as she tried to get away from him.

"Hush, now! I won't hurt you. I won't hurt you! I'm not like them."

The last made her stop screaming. Her eyes, dark brown, like the wary eyes of a doe, darted to the dead Larnians.

He released her mouth. "Easy, easy now. I killed them for you."

She looked down the line of his crouched body, her gaze stopping on the evidence of his attraction to her. Her eyes grew wide, panicked. Shite, she was going to scream again.

He pressed a hand over her mouth again just in time. "Stop it," he said over her muffled squealing. "There are more of them out here. If they hear you, it'll be both our necks."

That gave her pause.

"I can't help this." He motioned to his prick. "But I won't hurt you. I promise. I won't hurt you."

She narrowed her eyes on him. She looked like she wanted to speak.

He took his hand away.

"Why are you naked?" Her voice rolled with a burr that pleased his ear.

"I was hunting."

"You hunt naked?"

"Doesn't everybody?"

She frowned. "What are you?"

He felt himself grin. "I was just wondering the same about you. We can discuss it later. For now, we have to fly." He offered her his hand.

She stared at it. Then she swallowed and took it.

At her touch, his chest gave an unsettling lurch. He ignored it and tugged her to her feet.

She got them under her with difficulty. A wince pulled taut her lovely mouth.

"Look at that crippled gait," the soldier had said.

"You're wounded." He scooped her into his arms. With her bird-light bones, she weighed next to nothing.

She swatted his chest. "Put me down, you brute! I can walk."

"But can you run?"

She glared at him. It was answer enough. He tucked her close to his chest and sped toward the border.

"You mentioned there are more of them," the woman said, winding an arm around his neck and peering over his shoulder. A thrill shot through him at the trusting gesture. He almost lost his footing. "How many more?" Her voice was steel. Brave lady.

"I don't plan to find out."

Chapter 3

IF ANYA EVER saw that blasted box again, she was going to chop it into a million bits. Laird Steafan hadn't been able to manage it, but there was no force on Earth as powerful as an irate Highland lass. How dare that bloody thing interfere with her plans to face her laird and pay for her sins? How dare it thrust its magic upon her and cast her into a world of great mottled boars and enormous naked men?

Och, make that a single enormous naked man. The other two she'd seen had been naked but not enormous. That hadn't made them any less terrifying when they'd been trying to rape her.

The one now running through the forest at alarming speed while cradling her in the brawniest pair of arms she'd ever seen ought to terrify her too. He clearly wasn't human. Not with those bulky teeth and animal eyes, those pointed fingernails and that luxurious body hair covering his chest and stomach and growing thick and tempting between his legs. But for some reason she wasn't afraid. Mayhap 'twas the way the skin of his cheeks above his thick black beard had turned a shy shade of pink when she'd noticed his cock-stand. Or the way his eyes had crinkled at the corners when she'd asked how many men might be after them. Or the way his scent of pine and clean, dusty dog made her think of home and happiness and safety.

Or mayhap she was merely addled from when the other man had hit her in the head. *Och,* it felt like someone had flayed her skull open upon the blacksmith's anvil and pounded away at it with the Devil's own hammer.

Furthermore, it seemed to be morning wherever *here* happened to be, yet to her weary bones and heavy eyelids, it felt like the middle of the night. The rocking motion of the man's loping stride tempted her toward slumber. A great yawn stretched her mouth. After it passed, she asked, "Where are you taking me?"

"To my home."

Such guileless eyes. She could hardly look away from their captivating color. A brown as bright and pure as hardened tree sap glinting in the sun.

Content he hadn't said, "torture chamber" or "slave house," she rested her cheek on his firm shoulder and let sleep claim her.

A change in the soothing rocking motion woke her. She opened her eyes to bright sunlight. Her headache assaulted her afresh, as did other aches and pains, too numerous to count. But she didn't fash about any of that. Somat was wrong. She recognized this *dip-rise-pause* sort of walk. Her rescuer—or was he her captor?—was limping.

While she'd been asleep, they'd passed into a narrow meadow of fluttering wheat-colored grass. He skirted the meadow, keeping close to the crumbling stone wall at the tree line. The sun kissed her face, but its warmth was a mere flicker of a candle compared to the raging bonfire of the man's chest, which heaved with exertion and heated her through her dress and shift like a bed warmer. He'd been carrying her for what felt like hours. He'd slowed to a walk, but still, his arms didn't tremble.

She let her head fall back on his shoulder to study his face. Tension pinched the skin at the corners of his eyes. "How long did I sleep?"

He startled, and suddenly his gait became smoother. "A while," he said, avoiding her gaze. He did not wish for her to find weakness in him.

She understood that. "How far to your home?"

His gaze swept the path before them, alert, though his eyelids drooped with weariness. His skin had taken on an ashy pallor. "Not far."

"How. Far."

His lips twitched. He didn't answer.

"Put me down."

"No."

"You're weary." And injured, if his complexion was any indication. When she'd first seen him, he'd been crouching over her with splatters of blood on his face, chest, and legs. She'd assumed it was because he'd just killed two men to save her, but what if some of the blood was his?

He shrugged, a powerful bunching of muscle beneath her cheek, as though the fact of his weariness was barely worth considering. Stubborn man.

"I can walk. I can certainly keep up with a wounded man."

"You're wounded as well." He didn't deny he was hurt. *Och,* and he'd carried her who kent how far while she'd slept like a lazy cur.

"Mine are old wounds. I can walk." She wiggled, trying to get free.

His arms didn't budge. He glanced at her skirted legs. "The Larnians didn't hurt you?"

Larnians? He must mean the other two men. "Gave me a bloody headache. But no, they didna hurt me much." Thanks to him. "Put me down. I'd like to walk." Chi Yuen hadn't made her walk every day the last few weeks simply for the joy of watching Anya grimace, like she'd assumed at first. The movement eased her aches and loosened her knotted muscles. She could use some easing of her pain now, even if initially she would suffer.

"These old wounds. They still pain you." He was stalling. Why he'd want to continue carrying her when she'd given him an excuse not to, she couldn't fathom.

"They'll pain me less if I move about."

His brow pinched with distress she didn't understand. "I can't put you down. But I'll do what I can for you soon enough."

If he thought that tone of gruff finality would dissuade her from arguing, he was sorely mistaken.

"My wounds pain me much less than yours. Put me down."

"How did you get them?"

Stalling again.

"I'll tell you about my wounds if you put me down."

"Be easy," he answered, his gaze soft on her in a way that made her stomach flutter. "Not long, and we'll be there."

"Unless ye keel over on the way. You're pale as a sheet. Put me down. I won't ask again."

"Good. I'm growing tired of the request."

Irritating rascal. "That was supposed to be a threat, not acquiescence. Put me down, you great oaf!"

He had the gall to grin. And that grin had the gall to worm its way into her chest and lodge there like it belonged. "Don't worry. I'm strong." He squeezed her, demonstrating the truth of the statement. His grin grew cocky, as though he challenged her to find him lacking in any way.

Clearly, arguing with him wasn't working. She tried honesty. "If anything happens to you, I'll be lost. If you must carry me like a thick-skulled fool, at least tell me how to find this home of yours so I can fetch supplies and come tend you when you drop like a stone." She might be smarter to leave his carcass where it lay, given she had no assurance his intentions were decent, but she wouldn't. If he fell, she'd do what she could for him. If only to repay his rescuing her.

His cocksure grin melted away. He met her gaze and held it. "Don't worry, lady. I will make it. For you, I would walk a hundred times as far with wounds a hundred times worse."

Because she didn't ken what to say to that, she said simply, "I am no lady. Call me Anya."

§

ANYA. A LOVELY, unique name for a lovely, unique woman.

Dark had fallen, and with the setting of the sun, the night-rich scents of the forest rose up to meet his nose. Damp moss, rotting bark, and decaying leaves. Not long now, and they'd be at his cabin. He'd be able to care for her like the lady she was, even if she didn't consider herself one.

Why she didn't, he could not imagine. There wasn't a woman alive in Marann who wasn't revered as a lady. But she wasn't wolfkind, which meant not only was she not Maranner or Larnian, but she was from no place on Earth he had ever heard of. She had to have come from somewhere, though, since women didn't just appear out of thin air.

It was a problem for later. For now, he had a potential party of trackers to elude. Turning against the night breeze, he headed for the creek that bordered his land. His thigh hurt with each step, but the muscle was still strong. The bleeding had slowed to a trickle. With a good dressing and plenty of bread and tea, he'd be mended enough to hunt by morning.

He smelled the fertile mud of the creek and the musk of the creatures that came to it for drink long before its musical babble reached his ears. Coming to the water's edge, he loped down the bank, squeezing Anya tight to protect her from his jerky movements.

She'd slept much of the journey but stirred as he climbed the opposite bank. "Water?" She spoke with her eyes closed. When she opened them, her pupils were large black disks. Even in the darkness, he could tell her gaze was unfocused. She needed to drink, but he dared not stop. Lingering, even for a moment, would make their scents thicker in the air. If trackers were coming for her, he needed to delay their discovery of his cabin as long as possible. And get Anya well away by the time they found it.

"Soon," he told her. "We're nearly there." He changed direction, doubling back to confuse the trail. Another half-hour's walk brought him to the branch of the creek that led to his cabin. He stepped into the creek and made the rest of the journey with water lapping at his knees.

The scent of freshly-chopped wood met his nose as he stepped from the brook into the clearing where his sire had built their log and stone cabin long ago. He strode past where his maul lay propped against the chopping block, ready for him to split more wood for the coming winter. Before he split any more, he had a precious treasure to see to safety. Unfortunately, he could think of only one place to take her where she'd be safe. And once he got her there, he'd have to leave her.

He would know but a few days in this woman's presence. The thought sent a stab of disappointment through him. Ignoring it, he shouldered his cabin door open and laid her on the furs covering his pallet. After lighting a lantern and pulling on his shirt and trousers, he filled his finest cup, a pewter tankard, with water from the rain barrel and brought it to her. With an arm at her back, he helped her sit up.

"Drink, lady."

She did, deeply, cupping her hands around his and draining the cup in several swallows. He filled the cup again, and she drank that too, this time sitting under her own power while he sat beside her on the edge of his pallet. She'd been in his home less than five minutes, and her scent already permeated the air. His bed would smell like her for weeks if he didn't wash his bedcovers.

He swallowed hard as he watched her throat work. The smooth column looked like bronze in the lantern light. He wanted to feel its smoothness with his fingers, his nose, his lips.

She finished the water, and her tongue darted out to catch what moisture clung to her lips.

He felt that lick like she'd done it over the skin of his neck. A shiver passed through him. Shite. He'd have to get his reaction to her under control if he was going to walk across the country with her. Or he'd have to put up with tented trousers the whole way. "More?"

Thankfully, she didn't look at his lap, only shook her head in answer. "But I'm hungry."

"I have bread." The wrapped loaf on his hearth was two days old, but it would do. He would bake some fresh later tonight, and they could take it with them when they left in the morning. He crossed the cabin and got the loaf. Before putting it in her delicate hands, he broke its grainy bulk in half, easier for her to manage.

She tore into the first half with her blunt little teeth. Her eyes rolled back in her head as she chewed. A deep moan came from her throat.

With burning cheeks, he turned from her and busied himself tearing strips of linen to dress his wound with. He set the strips and his medicinal salve on the workbench, relieved when the moist, rhythmic sound of her chewing and swallowing stopped.

He'd gotten himself under control enough to face her again. "Where are you hurt?"

She blinked. "I told you. I'm no' injured."

"You said the Larnians didn't hurt you *much*. That means they hurt you some." She had old wounds that affected her legs as well. "And you never told me how you got hurt before."

She shifted and put a dainty foot on the floor, smoothing her skirt as she moved to keep her legs hidden. The other foot followed more slowly. She pushed off the pallet frame and stood, wincing. Her mouth made a hard line, masking her reaction to the pain. She liked showing weakness about as much as he did.

"Broke my legs months ago in a bad fall. As for the Larnians, they didn't do anything to me that can't be mended with a wee bit of this." She reached a hand into the gathered linen at the neck of her dress and pulled out a leather flask.

His mouth went dry at the thought of what delights that object had been nestled near all this time. Would the liquid inside be as warm as her skin?

She uncorked the top and lifted the flask, as if toasting him. "To Fergus." She took a gulp that made her hiss. "Christ, that's good. Now it's your turn." Her eyes went to where the boar's tusk had gotten him. "Strip off those trews and get on the bed. Let me tend you." She came at him with her limping gait and shoved the flask into his hand. "Where do you keep your vinegar?"

"Name's not Fergus," he said. "It's Riggs. Some call me the trapper."

"Well, Riggs the trapper, I'll reserve judgment on whether 'tis my pleasure to make your acquaintance until I ken what ye plan to do with me. Fergus was my da. He's dead. I never got a chance to toast him." She nodded at the flask. "Drink."

His name rolling off her tongue stole his breath. He'd never heard any woman other than his mother speak his name before. Then he realized what she'd said. Her *da*, her sire, was dead, gone to Danu's breast, like his. Wherever she had come from, she currently had no source of protection. Except him. And she didn't know whether she could trust him.

"I'll never hurt you," he vowed.

"We'll see. Drink." She left him to the flask and hobbled to the cabinet. Positioning the lantern nearby, she began searching through his medicinal supplies.

He wrapped his mouth around the opening of the flask, more so his tongue could search out her taste than because he needed distraction from his pain. The sharp bite of whiskey overwhelmed his nose, but beneath it he found a hint of salt from her skin and the hearty sweetness of his barley bread. He took a healthy swallow. Fire burned a path to his stomach.

The drink was good, just as she'd said. The surprising flavor of wood smoke thickened on his palate as the heat from the spirits melded with the heat of Anya's body and slid down his throat. Such an intoxicating cocktail!

He was tempted to drain the flask and take as much of her warmth into him as he could, but he capped it instead. He needed his wits about him. Already with one gulp of whiskey making his lips tingle, he entertained thoughts of wooing and keeping Anya. Not here, of course. At least not until the danger of trackers had passed. But there was an even more remote place he could live in secret with her, take her as his mate. Breed with her.

And what then? Remain hidden for their entire lives? If they bore a child together, would he keep that secret as well? What if it was a girl child?

"Here we are." Her voice yanked him from his thoughts. She came at him with his jar of vinegar in one hand. "Bed." She pointed for emphasis. "Trews." She pinched his trousers at his hip and gave a firm tug that zinged him in the worst possible place.

By the moon, he wanted to plant himself deep between her thighs. He wanted it so bad it hurt. Leaning a hip on his workbench, he gritted his teeth against the pleasurable ache and shifted the pile of bandages to hide the tent in his lap.

She put her fists on her hips. "What are ye waiting for? On the bed with you."

"I can clean my own wound," he said more harshly than he'd meant to. "But first, I'll see yours cleaned and dressed."

She was standing close. He could see tears in the sleeves of her dress and pink scratches beneath. *Fucking Larnians.* He'd be worse than those barbarians if he let his painful arousal keep him from caring for her. "Give me the vinegar." He wrapped his hand around the jar. His fingers covered hers.

She didn't let it go. "My injuries are practically nonexistent. Your wound is far more serious." She tugged the jar toward her bosom.

He should let go. He didn't. Not even when his knuckles brushed the laced-up front of her woolen dress. A drab thing it was—nothing like the bright silks favored by the ladies in Chroina—but it fit her curved body like a glove. The gathered linen around her neck invited a man's nose to search among the folds until he found her warm, fragrant skin beneath. His thumb left the jar to stroke the fabric over her breast.

She sucked in a breath.

Their gazes met and locked. Her pupils dilated. She licked her lips.

Something wild grew inside of him, filling him near to the point of agony. Relief could only come by joining his body with hers. His hands shook with the necessity of claiming her flesh, branding her with his scent until no other male would mistake her as a woman available for breeding.

He'd known bodily urges before and never failed to relieve them with his own hand. This was more than that. Much more.

Was this what happened to a man when he got a cock-stand near a flesh and blood woman? Is this what the lottery winners experienced when taking ladies to their beds?

He closed the small distance between them until the only thing keeping their bodies from fitting tight together was the jar with both their hands wrapped around it. He was going to take her. Danu help him, he would not be able to stop himself. He bent his head to hers, needing to put his mouth on her skin, needing to rub his scent on her.

She turned her face away. Her eyes dulled. She stepped back, relinquishing the jar.

"You'll no' get what you're after," she said, her voice as flat as her expression. "I'll repay you for your kindness, but no' with my body. My service is only as good as a crippled maid's, but it's all I have to offer. You'll settle for that pittance or you'll get nothing at all." She raised her chin. "Now will you permit me to tend your wound or no'?"

She thought he wanted her body for payment? Or to keep her as a servant?

What had he almost done?

The vinegar slipped from his numb fingers. He lunged and caught the jar the instant before it would have shattered on the floor. The move sent a shard of pain through his thigh. He deserved it. He'd taken a liberty with her that would have earned him a lashing in Chroina. That rogue touch had started something he almost hadn't been able to stop. Ashamed, he settled onto his knees before her, head bowed, holding the stupid jar.

"Forgive me, lady. I seek no payment, especially not...of that nature." He risked a peek up at her.

Her lips were pinched in a line. Her brow furrowed, as if she found his apology confusing.

How could he make his meaning more clear? "I won't touch you again. You have my word."

Much as he craved her hands on him, he'd never keep his word if he let her tend his injury. He stood, welcoming the pain ripping through his leg. "Rest, lady. I'll wrap my wound in my preservation hut. But first I'll fetch you water to bathe with."

"You'll do no such thing. Get on the bed."

He headed for the door.

"If you want my forgiveness, you'll take off your bloody trews and get on the bloody bed. Now."

He could not resist glancing at her, not when her voice held such fire and strength.

Her eyes blazed. Her beauty shone like the moon. She captivated him utterly and completely.

He was helpless to look away. His tongue felt glued to the

roof of his mouth, so instead of responding, he merely shook his head and forced himself to leave.

Outside, he took his time filling the water bucket, hoping the crisp night air would cool his lust. It didn't.

When he returned, he found Anya at the workbench, coating bandages with salve and muttering about "bloody thick-skulled fools." Even angry, she made him want to wrap her in his arms and never let go.

He cleared his throat before approaching the workbench and setting the bucket on the floor. "I'll give you privacy," he said as he collected the bandages and vinegar. "Wash yourself and set your dress on the hearth. You can find a clean shirt to sleep in under my pallet."

He turned to go, but felt something catch on his sleeve. He looked down to see her hand curled in the fabric.

"Stop being stubborn. I'm decent at healing. Let me do this. To thank you for rescuing me."

He wasn't the only one being stubborn. Purple circles under her eyes spoke of her need for sleep, and yet she worried about him. He gently uncurled her hand from his shirt, keeping the touch as brief as possible. But when he spoke, he made his voice hard. "I've dealt with far worse than this on my own. I don't need you to care for me. Now, let me lick my wounds in peace."

She flinched at his pretended impatience. It was for her own good. For the good of them both.

He walked out, leaving her to the quiet cabin and his comfortable pallet.

If he'd had any doubts before, they were gone now. He needed to take her to Chroina. She'd be safe in Marann's capital. From the Larnians. And from him. Unfortunately, it was a long walk, and he had a sinking feeling the longer he kept company with her, the harder it would be to keep his word.

He'd never been one to pray. The goddess, if she existed, had forsaken his people long ago. But if a little faith would benefit Anya, he had to try.

Danu, don't let me fail her.

Chapter 4

HANDS ON HER hips, Anya watched the door close on the cold autumn night and an enormous, stubborn fool. If the wound turned, it would serve him right.

She considered following and getting him out of those trews by fair means or foul, but didn't much care for the tone he'd used with her and was glad to be rid of him for a time. No matter what the pang behind her breastbone suggested.

Sighing, she turned in a circle to survey his home. The single room with walls of log and mud was about the size of the front room of her da's cottage, roughly ten paces square. Two stone pillars kept the roof from sagging, and between the pillars a rug of roan animal hide covered the floor. Mortared stone framed the door Riggs had just left through, as well as the two shuttered windows sharing the wall with the door. The next wall was dominated by a great sooty fireplace and a stone hearth cluttered with cooking things. Above the fireplace hung five sets of mounted antlers, all fierce looking and huge. Had he felled those stags with a party of hunters? By himself? She could almost believe it, given his size.

He was taller than the largest man she'd ever met, Big Darcy. And his nether regions were comparably awe-inspiring. Years ago, she'd ridiculed Darcy for his size to humiliate him for refusing her offered virginity, but deep down, she'd found him pleasing. Until Riggs, she'd never seen a match to the weapon Darcy carried under his kilt. What would it feel like to have a lover so large, so powerful?

Och, bloody waste of time, such idle ponderings. She was through with men. No good ever came from bestowing affection upon them, and no decent one would have her the way she was now. Riggs might want her for a tup, but she'd stake her flask he'd leave off with wanting her once he saw her mangled legs. Better not to encourage his affections, or heed her growing affections for him.

Besides, he wasn't even human. What he was, she didn't ken, but she'd be finding out before long.

In the meantime, she forced her attention back to her surroundings. After all, this might be her new home.

Though small, Riggs's home was cozy in a den like way. It contained everything a body needed in an arrangement that pleased her. She could see herself rolling dough on the workbench, which sheltered an assortment of tools and grain sacks. It would require a good cleaning first, since the surface was only slightly less dusty and disheveled than the recess beneath. Mayhap that would be her first project, once she'd slept off her headache. Riggs may not have accepted her offer to do his cooking and cleaning, but if he was going to keep her here, she was bloody well going to make herself useful.

And if he doesn't keep you here?

What if he intended to sell her to the highest bidder? Selling one's self was one matter. Being sold, without choice or dignity, was another. If Riggs thought to do that to her, she'd snip off his bollocks in his sleep.

Speaking of sleep, the bed took up most of one wall. As long and wide as Riggs, framed in beveled wood, and piled high with fawn-colored animal skins, it practically begged her to burrow into its soft, warm depths.

She bathed with the water he'd left her first, and found a linen shirt in one of the two finely-crafted drawers beneath the bed.

When she put it on, it draped around her like a sheet. Tying the laces as tight as they would go ensured the garment wouldn't fall off her shoulders, but she had to roll the sleeves four times to expose her hands. There was nothing to be done about the hem. On him, it would fall to his knees. On her, it reached her ankles like a nightgown. As far as the width of the garment, three of her could have easily fit in the space Riggs normally took up with his upper body alone.

Refusing to dwell on the excited flutter in her stomach, she turned down his bed and climbed beneath the animal hides. Their weight settled on top of her. Odd, but with Riggs's scent of pine and loyal, dusty dog surrounded her, she found herself not fashing over returning to Ackergill. In fact, she was curious about Riggs and his world. What was he? Were all the people in this place like him? Could she possibly belong here?

Sleep beckoned. Her questions would wait for the morrow.

The scent of baking bread woke her. It felt as though mere moments had passed, but morning light peeked from behind the closed shutters. Across the cabin, Riggs crouched near the workbench, stuffing supplies into a large leather sack with more straps and buckles than she'd ken what to do with. He was working quickly, almost hurriedly.

"Are you going somewhere?" she asked around a yawn.

He stopped and looked at her. He didn't answer.

"Going somewhere?" she repeated.

His brows pinched until a hard line appeared between them. He rose from his crouch, and his head came nearly to the roof of the cabin. The sight of him before her so large and virile made her toes curl beneath the animal skins.

He said somat, but she didn't understand.

"Pardon?" she said.

He said it again, this time with a shake of his head. She still couldn't make sense of it. 'Twas no more than a lilting rumble of meaningless syllables.

She sat up, clutching the skins around her. "I must be half asleep. Could you say it again?"

He spoke again, this time more urgently, and it made as little sense as what he'd said a moment ago. He kept trying to tell her things, and she kept not understanding.

They stared at each other. Outside one of the windows, a pair of squirrels chattered, having a meaningful conversation while she and Riggs stared at each other with furrowed brows.

Before her nap, they'd understood each other perfectly. Now, it seemed, they spoke different languages. What had changed?

Riggs looked all around the cabin, as if he'd had a similar thought. His gaze landed on the fire dancing happily in the grate. His eyes widened with alarm.

Muttering unintelligible things, he dashed to the hearth and grabbed a set of tongs. A quick reach into the flames produced somat that looked like charred fabric. The blackened heap dropped to the hearth. Riggs poked through it with the tongs, then with his fingers as the fabric cooled. Odd, some bits were faded blue, like her overdress. And a scrap of sooty linen looked suspiciously like her linen shift.

She searched the hearth for the bundle of clothing he'd instructed her to leave there, finding nothing but the flask and flint box she never traveled without. *Och,* he didn't. He wouldn't.

"You burned my dress!" She threw off the skins and hoisted herself out of bed. Her legs cramped. Cursing them, she fell back on the furs.

Using the tongs, Riggs plunked something he'd pulled from the fabric into a bucket of water, which emitted a hiss. After a moment, he reached into the water and withdrew the object. His large hand obscured her view, so she couldn't identify it. Whatever 'twas, it caused a look of wonder to pass over his face.

"What is it?" Her voice sounded angry, betraying the pain she was trying to ease with her kneading hands. Damn her legs.

Riggs met her eyes, then looked down to her massaging hands. His gaze darkened. "Let me," he said, and she understood him.

He knelt by the bed, took one of her hands, and placed in it the amethyst gem Gravois had given her. It was hot as a cake from the oven. She rolled it between her fingers so no one bit of her skin got burned. It must magically allow people of different tongues to understand each other.

"That barmy tink."

"What's a barmy tink?"

She became aware of Riggs's strong fingers kneading her most painful spot, below her left knee. He was touching her beneath the nightshirt. Learning how deformed she was.

She swatted his hand away and tucked the shirt tight around her legs. "You vowed you wouldna touch me."

Hurt flashed in his eyes. He hid it by rising with a grunt and turning away.

She remembered his tusk wound, now hidden by fresh trews, and regretted her harsh words. He'd only been trying to help, not taking liberties as he had before. Though to be fair, she'd been the one to bring that jar close to her breasts, kenning full well his hand had still been holding it.

"A barmy tink is an interfering, mysterious man who gives magical stones to maidens in distress and fills their heads with foolish talk of destinies. I'm sorry. You were only trying to help. But I doona like my legs being touched."

He inclined his head in a nod, not looking at her. His face was in profile. He had a strong nose, straight and masculine in its broadness. Firelight danced over his beard, making it shine like the richest sable. Saints above, he was an attractive man.

"My apologies," he said.

"Best you keep to your word and no' touch me at all."

"Of course, lady."

"And cease calling me lady."

His eyes glinted at that. It seemed there was one command he didn't intend to obey.

§

RIGGS STOKED THE fire and glanced at Anya over his shoulder. She sat on his pallet, pale and small in his shirt. She'd bathed and washed her hair, which had dried in thick, chestnut waves that shone in the firelight like silk. He couldn't look full at her. It hurt too much. She was too beautiful. Too precious.

Even more precious now that he understood just who she was. Anya was so much more than he'd first assumed.

His mind went back many years, to when he'd been little more than a pup and King Magnus had been newly crowned.

He followed his sire into the pub in Figcroft feeling like a man, carrying his very own axe and standing as tall as any other in the place, taller even than some.

His sire thumped him on the back while he addressed the barkeep. "A full draught for my son, and another for me. Your reward for a hard day's work," he said to Riggs.

The barkeep slid two tankards their way. "Heard about the king's latest scandal? News just come from Chroina by way of a traveler last night."

His sire lifted the tankard to take a sip, eyeing the barkeep coolly.

Riggs mirrored him, sucking down the foamy beer. Behind them were the sounds of men conversing at the tables. A boy sang with the voice of a lark and strummed a lute by the fire.

Licking his lips and setting the drink down, his sire said, "I prefer to get my news from the messengers who bring the monthly reports."

The barkeep made a dismissive noise. "A little gossip keeps things interesting, don't it?"

His sire's friend, Vorish, appeared at their backs, dropping a token onto the bar. "Usual," he said to the barkeep. Then he greeted Riggs and his sire with slaps on their shoulders. "Let Rolf have his fun. He only feels important when he's got rumors to distribute."

"He'd do better to distribute booze," his sire grumbled, but he did so with a grin.

Rolf pushed out his lower lip, pretending offense, but his eyes gleamed with whatever news he couldn't wait to share. Leaning over the bar, as if the news were for their ears only, he scratched his beard and said, "Apparently, Glerick's finished the portrait the king commissioned. His Majesty unveiled it two nights ago at a big to-do at the palace. Get this. When the curtain parts to reveal the long-awaited portrait, the ladies and gentlemen gathered in the great hall gasp as one. The subject, it's not Himself, as tradition holds. It's a lady." Rolf's eyes went wide. He looked between the three of them, waiting for a reaction.

Riggs failed to see how this was interesting. Everyone knew King Magnus honored the ladies. It was probably a portrait of Diana or something. He drank some more and turned his attention to the boy, wondering how close they were in age and who his mother might be.

He caught snippets of the conversation at the bar, but was trying to listen to the boy's lyrics. He sang about a world where women ruled and men fought each other to the death for the right to breed with their queen. Riggs lost himself in the fantasy, imagining himself a full-grown warrior, wielding a battle axe, wearing a breastplate and armor on his arms and legs, winning exclusive breeding rights to his queen.

"But not just any lady, I heard," Vorish said.

"A dark-haired beauty," Rolf piped in. "Visited the king's

dreams the night of his coronation, I heard."

Riggs's ears perked up. His mother had dark hair, like him. And she was lovely enough to dream about.

"Not overly dark," Vorish said. "The color of roasted chestnuts. If you're going to gossip, be specific, man."

Not Hilda then. Riggs tried to return to his fantasy. His queen welcomed him into her bedchamber. She waited for him on her bed of fine furs, naked and glorious.

"Yes, yes. Chestnut hair," Rolf was saying. "But that's hardly as notable as the fact her breasts were hairless. Pink little nipples in the center of smooth ivory orbs, like twin moons."

Riggs abandoned the fantasy. Hairless breasts deserved his undivided attention. He turned back to the bar to find Rolf cupping his hands before his apron.

"She's not wolfkind," Vorish said.

Rolf slapped his dishrag on the bar. "Who's telling the story?"

"Sorry. Go on. What else was remarkable about the lady?" Vorish exchanged grins with his sire while Rolf recovered his rag and tucked it into his belt.

"Tell us more about her breasts," Riggs said.

His sire smacked the back of his head to the laughter of the other men.

"Fine, round, succulent things, I heard," Rolf said, showing his yellow teeth. "Smooth and tasting of honey."

"Tasting of paint, more like," his sire said.

They all laughed at that.

"Tell them about her markings," Vorish said.

Rolf leaned in again, conspiratorial. "On her cheek, the lady in the painting bears the brand of the goddess, the paw-print of Danu in her wolf form. And around her neck she wears a gemstone. King Magnus says it's a gift from the goddess, a sign that she'll be the savior of our people."

Riggs rolled his eyes and pushed away from the bar. Nonsense. Either the king was as batty as half the country seemed to think, or Rolf got his news from Chroina's most imaginative drunks.

Before joining a table of men to listen to the boy's next song, he heard his sire say, "When is this savior supposed to come?"

"No one knows," Vorish said. "Not even His Majesty."

He'd scoffed at the barkeep's gossip then, but over the years, he'd wondered. His sire had always believed Danu would not forsake them. He'd scolded Riggs for suggesting King Magnus was mad for the vision he'd claimed to have.

Now the king's vision sat on his pallet, claw marks like a paw print on her cheek, and a magical gemstone that could very well be a gift from the goddess in her hand. Beneath his shirt, her breasts would be bare. He could tell from how smooth her arms and legs were. The hairs there were as fine as wood dust.

He'd fantasized about bare-breasted women for years after that visit to Figcroft. Never in his wildest imaginings had he imagined his own shirt would conceal such rare treasures.

He'd known he would need to take her to Chroina because it wasn't safe for females outside the city gates. But now he understood just what had been entrusted to his care. Anya was the king's lady. The one whose portrait the king had hung in the throne room and commanded Marann to anticipate. Each report from the palace ended with the charge: *Hope is alive. Danu has not forgotten her people. A savior comes.*

Apparently, he would be the one to bring that savior to the place where she belonged. Not just Chroina, but the palace.

King Magnus had never taken a queen or a concubine, claiming he waited for his special lady. He attempted to breed, of course, not discounting the possibility of creating an heir with one of Chroina's fine ladies. But he claimed no woman for his own, denied no woman access to other men, other chances to conceive.

The king would take Anya as his pledgemate, his queen. Of all women, she alone would belong to one man. Why should that burn a hole through his chest?

"Why did ye burn it?"

He looked sharply at her. Did her gemstone give her the power to read minds as well as speak his tongue?

She widened her eyes impatiently. "My dress. Why did ye burn it? I could have mended the tears. Did it occur to you 'twas all I had to wear?" She spread her arms, indicating herself in his shirt.

His chest swelled with pride. The king's lady wore *his* shirt. When he delivered her to the palace, she would smell like *him*.

"Had to destroy it. It carried your scent."

Her jaw dropped. "Aye, it needed washing, but to burn it? Must you insult me as well as hold me prisoner?"

He spun to face her. "Prisoner?" Is that what she thought?

"What else am I to think? You carry me away to your cottage. You take away my clothes. You doona bother telling me what ye plan to do with me." She gestured with her arms as she ranted. Her voice rose along with the color in her cheeks. But when she stopped, her shoulders sagged. Her doe-eyes turned down to the floor. "What's to become of me?"

He went to her and sat on the pallet beside her. He started to reach for her, but remembering his vow, stopped before he touched her.

She lifted her gaze to his, and it felt like a thread went taut between them. It pulled at his stomach, unsettling him even as it seemed to anchor him. She felt like *his*. But she wasn't. She belonged to the king.

"You are not my prisoner," he told her. "I am your servant."

She frowned. "I should be *your* servant. I owe you my life."

"You'll serve no one. Not ever again. You will want for nothing. This I swear. But first, I must take you to Chroina. It's

48

not safe for you anywhere else. It's a long journey, and we should leave soon. There may be Larnians tracking us. That's why I burned your dress. Less scent for them to follow."

She searched his eyes and must have found what she'd been looking for, because she nodded. "Well, I canna go in naught but your shirt. What am I to wear, o' servant of mine?"

His heart turned over. She was so brave. Crippled and lost, she had nothing left to her, not even the clothes on her back. Nothing but the magical gemstone curled in her fist. Yet she gave him her trust.

He would not fail her. He could not. Not when the survival of his people depended on her womb.

Chapter 5

ANYA SAT ON the bed and watched Riggs paw through the large chest in the corner near the fireplace. He was looking for clothing he'd worn as a lad, he'd told her. While he searched, she uncurled her fist and studied the smooth amethyst gem Gravois had given her. When she held it, she and Riggs could understand each other. Like magic. Had Gravois known what would happen to her?

"Your destiny lies elsewhere," he'd told her. *"There is a place for you. Perhaps you will find it if you take a leap of faith."*

Or if a meddling magic box gave her a push.

Did her destiny lie here with this man? She looked around his cabin, feeling quite at home already. She could be content standing at that broad, stone hearth to boil coney stew. She could be content in this pallet beneath the brawny body of the most powerfully built man she'd ever met. Aye. She could belong in this place.

But he'd said they had to leave. He intended to take her to a place called Chroina that was far from here. For her safety, he claimed. Likely 'twas because he didn't want her. She didn't blame him, but that didn't keep his rejection from stinging.

A thumping sound made her look up. Riggs had dropped a pair of heavy-looking boots at her feet.

"Here." He set a stack of folded clothing on the bed and toed the boots closer. He was taking great care not to touch her again. That stung too. She liked it better when he was gazing fondly at her and stealing private caresses, however brief.

He opened the door to the sound of chirping birds greeting the day with enthusiasm. Only a mild ache remained from the knock to her head yesterday, thank the saints. A night of rest had done her well.

"There's bread and tea over there." He indicated the hearth. "I'll be gone a while. When I return, we leave for Chroina." He left, closing the door behind him.

"Man of bloody few words." At least she could understand them now.

She grabbed the clothing he'd left her and shook out a pair of trews cut from heavy canvas, then a sturdy linen shirt. Both smelled like cedar and clean dog. Thankfully, they were sized much smaller than the shirt she currently wore. She stripped and put on Riggs's old clothes, tucking in the shirt. The fit was reasonable, though the trews were wide in the waist and required rolling at the ankle. Not to mention, it felt odd sheathing her legs like a man from the Lowlands. The seams scratched her skin and felt thick between her thighs. The deep pocket on her right hip provided a safe home for the gemstone. Now, if only she had a belt to help hold them up. She looked under Riggs's bed, not finding anything to use as such. When he returned, she'd have to ask him where he kept his rope.

A pair of woolen socks darned many times over had been rolled together and stuffed into the right boot. Just looking at the boots, she kent they'd be too big. But beggars should not be choosers. At least they fastened with leather laces, so they wouldn't fall off. She supposed she should be thankful he had spare boots from when he'd been a child.

While she imagined Riggs as a child—all boundless energy and wild black curls—she put on the boots and tied them up nice and secure. She took a few jarring steps. Might as well have bags of sand strapped to her legs, they were so heavy. But the thick soles, like cork seasoned with pitch, would protect her feet. 'Twas definitely different from walking in her doeskin shoes, but she'd get used to it. Had to, since he'd burned her shoes along with her dress.

Riggs was, in fact, gone "a while." She ate the half-loaf of warm bread he'd left her, sipped some strong tea, swept up the ashes from the fire, tidied his workbench, and fetched fresh water from the brook that ran near the cabin. She'd just thrown open the shutters for fresh air when she caught sight of a towering dark form loping out of the forest and splashing into the brook.

She gasped with fear until she realized it was Riggs. In all his naked glory, like he'd been when she'd first laid eyes on him. Only then, he'd been too close for her to notice the animal grace infusing each of his movements, the beauty of his coat of masculine hair as it grew thick on his chest, forearms and lower legs and thinned on his shoulders, thighs and flank. Her eye went immediately to where that coat was thickest, between his legs. Her cheeks warmed as she stared. She had yet to look her fill before he turned his back and bent to wash himself.

He scooped up great handfuls of clean water and let them trickle down his powerful hips, across his broad back, over his head, turning his black hair blue with a wet sheen.

As the water returned to the brook, it was pink. His skin grew fairer, as though the water carried away something dark. Not dirt. Blood.

He was covered in it. Especially his hands, beard, and neck. She hadn't noticed before, so enthralled was she with his form.

A pang of worry struck her. She looked at the bandage around his thigh, relieved to see the blood that had seeped through made a spot no larger than a thumbprint. Searching his fine body for other wounds, she found none. 'Twas not his blood. That meant it belonged to someone or somat else.

"I was hunting," he'd said when they'd first met.

"You hunt naked?"

"Doesn't everybody?"

He'd hunted this morning. That's where he'd gone. And he hadn't brought anything back with him, which meant he'd already eaten whatever creature whose blood he was washing off. He'd eaten it raw. After catching and killing it with his bare hands. And those large teeth.

A chill swept through her.

He was not human. She'd kent it before now, but the reality of it struck her anew.

Riggs stepped from the brook and raised his chin, looking toward the cabin.

She ducked away from the window, heart thundering.

She'd instinctively trusted him, but she'd done so without truly understanding what he was. He hunted and ate like an animal. But he also baked bread and heated water for tea. He was built like a beast, but he slept on a beautifully crafted bed in a cozy cabin. Were all the people in this place like him?

The sound of a door closing made her return to the window and look toward the shed twenty paces from the cabin. He must have slept there last night. Was he changing the bandages on his tusk wound? Clothing that powerful body? *Och,* none of her business.

Forcing her attention to matters that concerned her directly, she moved toward the workbench to wipe out her teacup. Her trews inched down her hips with each step. This wouldn't do. She looked under the workbench for rope or somat else to use as a belt. *Och,* the chest by the fireplace. That's where he'd gotten her new clothes. If he had a belt her size, it would be in there.

She hobbled over and lifted the heavy lid. There may have been clothes folded underneath, but resting on top of a linen sheet was an axe so shiny and fancy, she doubted it had ever been used for anything as mundane as chopping down trees. Its head flared in a wide arc, the tips tapering to sharp points. The back of the blade narrowed to a wicked spike. It gleamed from black handle to steel blade, and it was probably worth more than the half-dozen sheathed knives lining the lid combined.

The door banged open.

The lid slipped from her hand and crashed closed, nearly taking her hand with it. She pulled it back just in time.

Riggs rushed toward her, fully clothed, his hair shining with moisture. His eyes were wild. Was he angry she'd been snooping? Her heart stopped with fear.

"Are you all right?" He grabbed her hands, inspecting them. His worried gaze jumped to her face. "I thought—" He closed his eyes and released a great breath. "I thought you'd caught your hand in the lid."

He wasn't angry. Her shoulders began to unwind. He'd promised he wouldn't hurt her, but she had no assurance he'd keep the promise. He'd also said he wouldn't touch her, but he kept doing so. She slipped her hands out of his. "Well, you can see I am unharmed," she said shortly.

His face hardened, but not quickly enough to hide his hurt from her. He stomped to the pack on the floor and fiddled with its straps.

"What did you have to break your fast?" she asked.

He looked up from the pack. "Found a lynx in the valley south of here."

"And you caught it with your bare hands and ate it out in the forest?"

His brow furrowed like the answer should be obvious. "Yes."

Saints above. She didn't ken whether to be impressed or disgusted. "You ate it raw?"

"Of course," he said as if there was no other reasonable way to eat meat. He stood and pulled the pack onto his back, buckling a belt-like extension low around his hips. Which reminded her what she'd been about before he'd come in.

55

"Do you have a belt I can use to keep these trews up?" she asked in a meek voice quite unusual for her.

He went to the chest and lifted the axe out as easily as if it were a quill. After propping it beside the hearth, he dug in the chest and came up with a leather belt. "Here." He held it out.

Her feet couldn't decide whether to go to him to take it or not. Part of her was afraid of him. Part of her still tingled with warmth over the memory of his naked form.

His eyebrows, straight, thick sweeps of black hair, lowered to shadow his eyes. A soft growl came from him. He looked dangerous, but oddly, that look dispelled her fear rather than heighten it. It also turned the tingling warmth inside her to flaming heat.

He tossed the belt on the bed. Then he took a sheathed hunting knife from the lid of the chest and tossed that on the bed too. Grabbing up the axe, he said, "Time to go," and stalked outside.

She'd upset him. That shouldn't bother her. But it did.

Cursing herself, she put on the belt, slipping it through the knife sheath, and followed him outside, closing the door behind her.

He was already across the rough-hewn bridge spanning the brook, trudging into the forest.

She hobbled after him as fast as her legs could carry her. It bloody well hurt, but she gritted her teeth and pressed on, doing her best to match his stride. When ten minutes had passed and he was still a stone's throw ahead of her, she shouted, "Humans doona eat raw meat."

He stopped and looked back. Even from this distance, she could see his hurt feelings in the narrowing of his eyes.

"*I* doona eat raw meat," she explained as she gained ground. When she got near him, she stepped closer than propriety dictated, wishing to remove the hurt from his eyes by showing him she didn't fear him. She put a hand on his brawny forearm.

He had his shirtsleeves rolled up to expose the powerful muscles. Touching this gentle beast sent a thrill through her.

He looked at her hand, then at her. The anger melted from his features. "Of course you don't eat meat."

"What do ye mean, *of course?*"

"You're not built to hunt, even if your legs were right. Your hands are too small. Your teeth are too blunt."

She scoffed. "My teeth do just fine, thank you, and even cripples can buy meat from the butcher and cook it to their liking."

"Cooked meat," he murmured. He made a small noise of consideration, as if he'd never thought of such a thing.

"Aye," she laughed. "Like your bread. Cooked. I adore meat when it's cooked."

After a moment of thought, he nodded. "I can cook meat for you." Then he started walking again, this time keeping his pace slower so she could remain alongside him. "You're human?" he asked after a while.

"Aye. And you are?"

"Other than your servant and protector?" he asked with a grin that made her stomach flutter pleasantly.

She rolled her eyes. "Aye, other than that."

He smiled full at her, and the sight of his eyes crinkling with warm affection turned the flutters in her stomach to shivers that raced over her whole body. "We are wolfkind," he said.

"Wolfkind." The term seemed to fit him. His animal grace, his teeth, his eyes that practically glowed with ferocity when he was angry. "I've never met a...wolf-man before. Have you ever met a human?"

"No."

She must seem as unusual to him as he did to her. Mayhap that explained some of his gruffness.

They were of different peoples. Different lands. 'Twas only

by the magic of Gravois' gift they could understand each other.

She took in the forest around them. The trees were bigger around and taller than in Scotia. The air was scented more richly with moss and loam. But the differences weren't so pronounced she felt as though she were in a different world. Yet she must be. She'd always assumed talk of mythical peoples and places was nonsense. She couldn't have been more wrong.

"Barmy tink."

§

ARE YOU ALL right? Does it hurt to walk? Should I carry you?

Riggs bit back the questions as they came to him. Anya would not appreciate them. He hardly knew her, but he knew that much. The woman had as much pride as any man.

For most of the morning, he'd let her set the pace and had remained by her side as they followed the creek northward. This route, which would take them through Marann's northern foothills, was not the quickest to Chroina, but it was the most secluded. And if they were being pursued, the trackers would not expect it. As long as they made it to the lake by nightfall tomorrow, they would elude any trackers.

Given Anya's pace, that was not guaranteed.

He walked five paces in front of her, keeping his steps short, his speed almost painfully slow so as not to tax her. He'd moved ahead of her when the sight of her upper body weaving with her stride had become too much to bear. It had to be hell on her back. He could no longer see her, but he still heard her. Her breathing was heavy but regular, her steps uneven but rhythmic, like a lilting tune.

And he smelled her. Even after bathing with his lye soap and putting on his old clothes, she still smelled like flowers and hyssop. And woman. Another benefit to being in front of her was that she couldn't glimpse his half-hard prick. Would it ever fully relax in her presence?

"How far is this Chroina?" she asked.

He directed his voice over his shoulder. "By horse, we could comfortably ride there in four days. A man can make it from border to coast in two with frequent changes of mount." Though, not by the route they were taking.

"So it'll take us a week or more, walking." She was no stranger to traveling.

"At least." He could do it by himself in five days, even with a uniwheel cart laden with skins for Chroina's market. But with the rest Anya would need, taking the time to cook meat for her, with her limp... They'd need to find horses along the way to make it in a week. But horses could only be rented in well-populated villages. Going to one would make it harder for him to keep her secret.

The sooner they got to Chroina, the safer she would be, but to get there quickly would draw unwanted attention. Protecting a female was becoming more complicated by the minute.

"Tell me about these Larnians who might be after us. You didna seem to lose any sleep over slaying two of them. Are they an enemy clan?"

He huffed a humorless laugh. "'Enemies' is putting it mildly. Larna and Marann have hated each other for nearly the entire history of Eire."

"Eire? Is that what you call this land?"

He nodded. "It is an island of two nations. Marann to the east. Larna to the west."

"So we're in Marann, I take it, but not far from Larna, since you're fashing about Larnians tracking us."

"I won't let them get you," he vowed.

"I ken it," she said, as if she felt completely safe with him. Her confidence made his chest swell. "But who are they? Why is

Marann at odds with them? Do they steal your livestock? Pillage your stores? Rape your women?" She rattled off offenses as casually as items on a shopping list. Were these things common where she came from? These days, Maranners and Larnians lived far enough apart that such trespasses were almost unheard of.

"Nothing like that, at least not since the last war. Their blood is corrupt."

"But they doona harm your people or your land?"

"Not anymore."

"Then why do you pay them heed? Why hate them when you could simply ignore them? No good ever comes from hating." Her tone turned bitter at the end, as if she spoke from experience.

"Who have you hated, Lady Anya?"

"Doona call me lady. And we werena talking about me."

"We are now. If you won't tell me who you hated, tell my why you don't consider yourself a lady."

She made that snorting noise she liked to do, like a mix between a laugh and a scoff. Why should such a brash sound make his blood heat every time he heard it?

"Doona expect me to tell stories if you willna."

He smothered the chuckle that rose in his chest. "It's not that I don't want to. It's just...my sire was the storyteller, not me."

"No' hard to tell a story," she said. "You start at the beginning, pass through the middle, and stop when you reach the end. What's the beginning? When did Marann and Larna first become enemies?"

He thought about how his sire would start. He would have gone all the way back. *"You can't understand the present unless you look to the past. And our past begins..."* "Long ago," Riggs said, "legends were told of Danu, our goddess. She traveled the threads of time and searched every realm for beings with uncommon strength, loyalty, ingenuity, and beauty."

The words came easily. He could practically hear his sire's

voice in his head. Maybe it wasn't so hard to tell a story. He'd just never tried it before.

"But no one race had all these qualities to her liking. So she took the seed of a fey prince and placed it in the womb of the wolf queen to create a people superior to those of any other god."

He glanced down and found Anya's eyes round with interest.

She waved a hand at him. "Go on. You're doing fine. 'Tis a fascinating tale."

Her encouragement filled him with confidence. "A Larnian king, Jilken, tried to improve on Danu's creation. He wanted fiercer warriors for his army and tried to get them by breeding men with the most ferocious she-wolves he could find. When he couldn't get the wolves to conceive, he summoned magic from the low realm to aid him. Eventually, Jilken got offspring from the wolves. Soon, Larna was filled with people who had more wolf in them than Danu intended. They were savage and ruthless and constantly attacked Marann. They tried to dominate the whole of Eire. But where they gained strength from their unnatural breeding, they lost their cunning. Our kings set traps and used spies to out-maneuver them. Marann held her borders, as she always will."

Anya wrinkled her nose. "Men bred with wolves? Disgusting. Though mayhap less so if your people come from wolves, at least in part. Still. I doona like to consider such a thing."

Neither did he. Which was why he didn't put much stock in the legend of their creation: a fey bred with a mythical wolf by a goddess. Yeah, he had some things in common with wolves and with the fabled fey, but he was *wolfkind*, not immortal, not an animal. He certainly didn't condone mating with animals. The Larnians, on the other hand...

"More disgusting is what they did to the offspring Jilken didn't find pleasing. Any whelps who appeared weak or didn't have the desired traits were thrown out like threadbare rags, especially the females, since they didn't have as much value on the battle field."

Some thought that's when the curse began. Children were treated like refuse, so the goddess made children rare, especially female children. If there was a goddess, he didn't think she cared about them enough to curse them, but he could see the logic in the assumption.

Anya was silent. What was she thinking behind those somber brown eyes?

"I have told you a story," he said as they came upon a fast moving stream spanned by a log with its bark rotted away. He didn't trust Anya to cross it on her own. Stepping onto it, he held out his hand and said, "Your turn. Talk."

She looked at his hand, then at the log, then back at his hand, no doubt remembering his vow not to touch her.

"Take it," he said. "If you do it, I won't be breaking my word."

"I doona ken if I should trust a man who claims to be part wolf and part fey." She narrowed her eyes, but a smile played at her lips. "Wolves are bloodthirsty and the legends I've heard about the fey claim they're mischievous trouble-makers. Not to be trusted."

"Guess you'll have to take your chances. A bloodthirsty trouble-maker or the possibility of wet socks for the rest of the day."

She harrumphed, but slipped her hand into his with a sparkle in her eye that made his trousers feel too tight. Luck help him if she looked down.

Her skin was cool and softer than lily petals. When he closed his fingers over hers, her delicate bones pressed together. He relaxed his grip, worried he'd hurt her.

"You won't break me," she said, grasping his hand more firmly as she followed him up onto the log. "I doona particularly wish to fall in. I suppose I can tolerate your touch to keep myself dry." Her eyes danced with her own human brand of mischief. "Shall I tell you how I came to be here, then?" Ah, she would tell him a story now. A fair one, his lady. Lady...

He slid his feet over the wet wood, holding fast to her hand, adjusting his balance when she wobbled this way or that, ready to sweep her into his arms if she started to fall. "No. If I'm to get just one story from you, I want to know why you don't consider yourself a lady."

Her lips compressed in a hard line.

They finished crossing the log, and he helped her onto the bank. He thought she wasn't going to answer, but at last she said, "Whores cannot be ladies."

He froze in place.

She hobbled past him. "If you expect me to lead the way, I'm afraid it may take us more than a week to get to Chroina." She said it without looking back.

"You're a whore?" he blurted out. He thought of the young men who sold themselves in some of the villages. He'd never thought poorly of them. What they did wasn't very different from what Marann's esteemed ladies did: attempting to breed with lottery winners in exchange for a sizeable share of the lottery pot. A veneer of respectability and necessity didn't change the fact that the ladies mated with men chosen for them by chance in exchange for money.

He didn't think poorly of Anya, but the thought of her selling her body caused a burn behind his breastbone.

"Aye," she said, her tone flat. "Used to be, anyway."

He forced his feet to move and caught up to her.

She glanced at him briefly, her expression impassive, hiding what she felt.

"Is it because you came here that you're no longer...a whore?"

She shook her head. A thick lock of hair tumbled free from the knot at the back of her neck. It curled under her chin, snaking into the collar of her shirt. The sight of that shiny tress tickling the tops of her hidden breasts made him ache to touch her. He ignored his desire, more concerned with the melancholy that had settled over her.

"I'm finished with that life." As they passed under the sparse canopy of late-autumn leaves, spots of sunlight made her hair wink with gold. Like her eyes, her hair would be almost dull one moment and shining with life the next, depending on the light. "When my body was worth somat, I didna mind selling it. Now—Christ, why am I telling you this?"

She was distressed. He wanted to touch her. A caress on her shoulder. A brush of his hand over her sleek locks. But he remembered his vow. "Now what?" he prompted.

"*Och,* I suppose it doesna matter." She blew out a breath that billowed her cheeks. "I'm no' going back there." They walked several strides in silence. Then she said, "They would put me on the ground floor now. With my legs the way they are. With my face the way it is. I'd earn half the coin for twice the service, and I wouldna even have the privilege of earning it in a private upper room." She shivered. "'Tis no' difficult to be a beautiful whore, to have your pick of the men who come through, to have a man want you because you're the most bonny of the lot. But when you're a last resort, when ye have no choice but to go to a man, no matter who he is, no matter if ye want to or no'..."

He felt the ache behind her words. She was the most beautiful thing he'd ever laid eyes on, lovelier and more valuable than a whole herd of marbled boar, maybe even more valuable than all the ladies cosseted in Chroina's safe houses put together. But she thought herself ugly, ruined.

Then the implication of her words penetrated his mind. *"When you're a last resort, when ye have no choice but to go to a man."* She valued her choice.

And he was taking her to Chroina to give her to the king, knowing he would take her as his queen. He was taking away her choice.

But without her, his people would die. Her going to King Magnus had been predestined. The king himself had seen it, seen *her*. Riggs hadn't believed it until he'd seen her gemstone and felt its magic, or rather the loss of its magic.

It wasn't him taking away her choice. It was fate. Or Danu, if he was willing to believe the goddess still gave a shite about them.

Still, uneasiness stirred within him. How would Anya react when he told her the truth? Would she hate him? It shouldn't matter. He was not the one she would need to breed with.

If only he could convince his body that was the case. To borrow a curse from Anya, he was getting bloody tired of walking with a hard-on.

Chapter 6

TALL BIRCHES SOARED over Anya's head. The woodsy scents of moist bark and dried leaves filled her lungs. All around were the sounds of scurrying creatures and chirping birds who had not yet headed for warmer climes in preparation for winter's chill. Alive. The forest was alive. And it made her feel alive too. She almost didn't notice the pain in her legs or the way her back and side had started to burn with her labored gait.

Several paces in front of her, Riggs led the way to Chroina, this city that would apparently be her new home, where he claimed she would not have to be a servant and would want for nothing. She believed him about as far as she could throw him. Nothing in this life came free, especially not luxury.

She didn't fash overmuch about it. Riggs gave her bread to eat and clothes to wear, and he treated her well. He seemed concerned with her safety. He might be part wolf and part fey, but he was all man, and she'd known precious few men in her life as trustworthy as Riggs seemed.

Things could be much worse. Especially if she'd never come to this place. She'd probably be dead by now, at Steafan's hands, and rightfully so since she'd betrayed him and nearly murdered his nephew. 'Twas by the grace of the saints the viper she'd handed Darcy in that bag of apples hadn't killed him. Or his wife. Or the wee bairn on his wife's lap.

"Any whelps who appeared weak or didn't have the desired traits were thrown out like threadbare rags."

The venom in his voice when he'd spoken of the abominable Larnians applied equally well to her. She'd taken a foolish risk with the life of a child who'd done no wrong to her or anybody else. Vengeance had blinded her to the kind of morality respectable women took for granted.

There was somat broken inside of her, and it had been broken long before her fall. 'Twas almost a relief to have her outside match her inside. And 'twas why she didn't fash about Riggs's plans for her. Mayhap they were innocent—he didn't seem the type to lead a lass into harm's way intentionally. But mayhap they weren't so innocent. Sometimes he got a secretive glint in his eye, and he liked to dodge certain questions, like what she might expect when they reached Chroina. She didn't press. If she came to harm by trusting Riggs, 'twould be no more than she deserved.

In the meantime, she focused her energy on moving forward in her trews and clunky boots, and she drank in the sight of the stunning wolfkind male cutting a confident path through the forest. If she walked herself to a damning fate, at least she'd enjoy the view along the way.

The enormous pack obscured most of his back, but she had a lovely view of other parts of him. His dark hair shining with health and curling over his ears and collar. His powerful thighs as they flexed beneath his trews. His arms. She loved the way his muscles appeared as if they'd been chiseled from stone and then dusted with dark hairs. Her fingers would have been eager to stroke those hairs if she weren't too broken to ever again entertain such fantasies.

And just like that, her pleasure at appreciating this specimen of brawn and wild grace evaporated into the cool autumn air. "Where's the nearest village?" she asked to give herself somat to think about other than how loathsome he must find her now that he kent she was beneath even whoring. "Where do you buy your grain, get news from Chroina?" Where did he go for his tupping?

Surely he had one or more women he visited on occasion. Probably not whores. A fine looking man like him probably had plenty of women willing to give him what he required for free.

Unbidden images assaulted her: Riggs atop a sturdy wolfkind woman with broad shoulders and bulky teeth to match his, moving over her, lifting her thigh to move inside her. Riggs poised behind a lass of his own kind, taking her like an animal, like they were both animals.

Pain in her palms made her look down. Her hands had curled into fists until the nails bit into her skin.

"Used to be Figcroft," he said, and it took her a moment to remember she'd asked about the nearest village. "Half a day's walk from my cabin. Now..." He shrugged and muttered somat she couldn't make out.

"What's that?"

"It changes all the time." Was that resignation she heard in his voice?

"What does that mean?" Were wolfkind a travelling people, like the Rom? Riggs did not strike her as a nomad. His cabin was most definitely a home that had been lived in for many years. And once he brought her to Chroina, he would likely return to it. Without her.

"It means, I'm not sure. If Baileyrock still has the Farworth brothers running the inn, then that's likely the nearest village. A day's journey due east."

"When did you go there last?" How often did these villages "change"?

"Early summer I went over to trade skins for supplies."

So it had been months. Did that mean he hadn't had a lover in months? Why should that make her glad?

Silly lass. Get your head out of the clouds. He's taking you away from his home, and it doesna sound as though he intends to bring you back. What more proof did she need that he didn't view her as a potential bedmate? Why did she even care, when she'd made up her mind never to tup again?

They walked in silence a while. Her legs began to ache. Her lower back burned. She hadn't walked this far in one go since before her fall. Chi-Yuen had gradually increased the length of their walks, but none had lasted more than two hours. It had been at least four since they'd left Riggs's cabin, and he showed no signs of needing rest.

After another agonizing hour, the sun was well past its zenith and her stomach began to growl. She needed rest and food, but she said nothing, pushing her body through the pain. If she complained, Riggs would insist on carrying her. If he put his brawny arms around her, she'd start contemplating tupping again.

After another hour, she spotted a patch of mushrooms that looked like an edible variety she'd picked countless times. They grew near the base of a fir tree, fat and happy in the dark, shaded soil. She broke from the trail Riggs made and stopped before them. Her mouth watered.

With her knees swollen, there was no graceful way to kneel, so she bent at the waist to pick them. Losing her balance in her overlarge boots, she toppled forward. Her knees bent, and shards of agony stabbed her like swords all up and down her legs. She cried out and instantly despised herself for it. She would despise Riggs too, if he showed her pity.

She fell to her side, her shoulder hitting the soft earth. Tears sprang to her eyes as much from mortification as from pain. She refused to let them fall.

Riggs appeared over her, eyes wide. His pack hit the ground with a thud. Then he was on his knees lifting her into his arms. The sudden change in the position of her knees made her gasp with renewed pain.

"What happened? Did you trip?" He held her with one arm while his other hand roamed down her hip and paused over her left knee. The tightness of the skin there and the coolness of his hand through the canvas meant the joint was even more swollen than she'd assumed. Chi-Yuen would have scolded her for letting herself come to such a state. Then she would have thrust one of her hempen rolls into Anya's mouth and kneaded and stretched her legs, heedless of her screams and threats of violence.

Riggs's alert demeanor softened as his fingers explored her leg. His shoulders rounded, and his eyebrows pinched. "Lady," he said, and he drew her tighter to his chest. "Why didn't you tell me?"

Pity. She shoved at his immovable chest. "Doona call me lady."

"I'll call you what I damn well please." Gold flecks in his eyes crackled against the brown in his eyes. She'd never been close enough to notice them before. Or mayhap they only came out when he was angry. "You let yourself become lame," he practically bellowed. "It'll be days before you'll walk again." He jabbed a thick finger in the direction they'd come. "If we're being followed, we may not even have a full day's advantage. I could have carried you and gone twice as far. We've wasted half a moon-cursed day!"

"Cease yelling at me!" Was fury better than pity? She couldn't decide. She only kent she wanted to get away from this growling, furrow-browed beast. She struggled to break free of his hold, with no success. "Bloody ungrateful cur! I walked today to spare you having to carry me. And what do I get? No' thanks. *Noooo.* I get an earful of grumbling." Her fists hitting his shoulders might as well have been feathers hurled at a stone wall.

Her aching body could take no more. She collapsed against him, hating her crippled form, hating him, hating everything. The tears she'd been holding back slid over her cheeks. Damn them to bloody hell. She swatted at them, and at least *they* had the grace to react to her touch.

"By Danu, forgive me." He bowed his head over her and pressed his cheek to her forehead. He rubbed his face on her there, once, twice, his coarse beard lightly scratching. "Forgive me, lady." He spoke against her skin, his breath fogging her brow.

Her tears fell faster. When had her arm wrapped around his neck? When had the fingers of her other hand curled into the rough fabric of his shirt? When had her body curved around him as though seeking comfort from the worst of her pain?

"Nay. You're a cocksure, thick-skulled, overbearing brute, and you doona deserve forgiveness. And doona call me lady." She spoke into his shoulder, too embarrassed to meet his gaze.

A soft huff from his nose might have been a chuckle. "You're a proud, stubborn female. I've driven mules more amenable than you."

She gasped. How dare he insult her further?

"And you're fair as the winter's first snowfall," he went on, "delicate as a rose, and braver than the fiercest soldiers I've fought beside."

Her tears stopped.

"Do you have any idea what will happen if trackers are after us, if they find us?"

She shook her head, unable to look away from the grim set of his mouth.

"Let's not find out, yeah?" He stood with a powerful thrust of his legs and not so much as a flinch due to his healing wound. Cradling her first in one arm then the other, he hoisted his pack into place and secured the straps. He picked up his axe and hooked it through the strap that fitted low across his hips, all the while treating her like a sack of grain.

"So, I'm to lie here like a useless slug and let you carry me until nightfall?" How would she bear the indignity? Curse her legs.

"You could tell me stories while I walk," he said. "Or sing me songs. Or keep playing with my hair like you're doing."

Och, she was twisting his curls around and around her fingers like a bloody child with her mother's apron strings. She made herself stop, but not before giving those silky strands a sharp tug.

A chuckle rumbled from his chest. His lips tilted in a grin that suggested he had more than protecting her on his mind.

Mayhap the decision never to tup again had been made in haste.

§

ANYA HAD AVOIDED Riggs's gaze all afternoon. She also seemed disinclined to touch him any more than necessary. She'd crossed her arms over her breasts, barring their generous swell from his view, and kept them like that until she'd fallen asleep. Now, with her eyes closed and her face soft and peaceful, she'd nuzzled into his shoulder and threaded one arm around his neck, where her fingers dipped into his collar to cool his heated skin. Every time they twitched, tingles raced up and down his spine.

"I walked today to spare you having to carry me."

Like carrying her was a chore. She fit in his arms like she was meant to be there. In fact, having her slight weight in front pleasantly stretched the muscles in his shoulders beginning to ache from his pack. With her snug to his chest, he felt balanced. And since he didn't have to worry about her comfort, he'd managed a much quicker pace than they'd averaged that morning.

He hoped it was enough.

Soon it would be too dark to walk so briskly. He could keep going at a slower pace or he could stop and rest. Care for Anya's painful legs. When he'd felt her left knee earlier, he'd found it swollen to twice its natural size. She had to be in agony.

If he stopped, they risked leaving a stronger scent trail for any trackers. If he kept walking, he could reach the lake—and the logboat he kept moored at the southern tip—by dawn. Their trail would be lost once they pushed off into the lake, thus buying time for Anya's legs to heal before they continued to Chroina.

He could go without sleep until they reached the cave, but one thing he could not go without was food. He needed to hunt to keep himself strong for her, even if he just found a fox or two. It was unavoidable. They'd have to stop. Just for a short rest. And he knew the perfect spot.

By the time dark had fallen, the pounding rush of Aine's Falls filled his ears, and the fresh scent of mist in the air tickled his nose. He followed his senses to the edge of the pool where the falls splashed down into the great river that fed the forest. The black-blue of a moonless night shaded the tall conifers surrounding the pool. Above, the clouds made a gray canopy.

"Wake up, lady." He lowered Anya to the ground near the bank.

She stirred and stretched then winced.

"Easy. Here." He put his water skin in her hands and helped her sit up so she could drink. Feeling down the line of her left leg, he found the knee nearly as swollen and hot as it had been earlier. "We'll rest here. I'm going to hunt. While I'm gone, take off your trousers and soak yourself in the pool. The cold water will ease the swelling."

She nodded and handed the water skin back. It was nearly empty. "You're hunting meat?" She had a hopeful lift to her tone.

He hated to disappoint her, but... "It's too dangerous to have a fire." If trackers were anywhere nearby, the scent of burning wood and meat would draw them like a beacon.

"No fire?" she said in a small voice.

"I'll cook meat for you when we reach my cave. For now, this will have to do." He held out a half-loaf of bread to her.

She didn't look at it.

"Take it," he said, dropping it in her lap.

She touched it and said, "More bread."

"You like my bread." He would never forget her throaty moan when she'd taken that first bite.

"Aye, but it's all I've had to eat for two days. A lass likes some variety." She turned her face in his direction as she spoke but didn't look higher than his chin. Would she ever look him in the eye again?

"I'll cook meat for you as soon as I can." Had she not heard him the first time?

Sighing, she lifted the half loaf to her mouth. Her blunt teeth tore through it, unlocking the aromas of tangy grains, flour, and the honey butter he liked to spread on top just before sliding the bread stone into the oven. After swallowing, she muttered, "Should have picked those mushrooms while I had the chance." Then she tore off another chunk.

"Mushrooms?" She ate vegetation? He wished he'd known. They'd passed a field of autumn-ripe pitberries while she'd been sleeping. He could have picked some for her.

She looked up, startled, as though she'd forgotten he was there.

He leaned forward, crowding her body with his so she wouldn't forget again.

"Aye, mushrooms," she snapped, pushing herself backward with her free hand and her right leg.

Amidst the scents of bread and saliva, he smelled something spicier and headier, something he'd smelled on her before, something that called to instincts he struggled to deny. Instincts he must deny or betray his king.

"The ones growing beneath that fir tree," she continued. "That's why I fell down. I was going to pick them, but my legs had other ideas." She rubbed her left knee with one hand while she brought the bread to her mouth for another bite.

By the moon, his lady had wanted something to eat hours ago

but hadn't been able to have it. She blamed her legs, but the mushrooms had been growing all around where she'd landed. It was because he'd scolded her and then insisted they keep moving that she hadn't gotten to pick them. He was an ass for not realizing she'd been hungry then.

"I'll find you some mushrooms." He stood and checked the hunting knife at his hip. A fox or a rabbit for himself would be welcome if he could find one quickly, but he would not return without a bounty of mushrooms for his lady.

"Ye doona have to do that," she said too quickly, her voice pitched too high. Did she fear being alone?

"I won't be gone long." He'd skip hunting for himself so he could hurry back to her. He'd make do with bread tonight. "Do you need help getting to the pool?"

"Nay. I can hear it."

"You can't see it?"

"It's bloody night time. Of course I canna see it."

She couldn't see in the dark? Even enough to make out the falls and the pool? His delicate creature was night blind. He could not leave her to find her own way into the pool. She might drown herself.

Caring for the king's lady was more involved than he'd been prepared for. Hopefully, King Magnus would know better than him what Anya needed. Until then, she'd have to put up with a bumbling trapper.

He crouched by her side. "I will help you get in." He reached for her belt.

She swatted his hands away. "I can undress myself. Stop crowding me."

That quick temper of hers never failed to bring a smile to his lips. "I thought you couldn't see."

"I doona have to see to know where you're looming. You blot out what meager light there is like a bloody mountain. And you smell like...you."

The spicy scent coming from her intensified. Mystifying. Tempting. It sent his body a completely different message than her brisk tone.

Best not dwell on what that message might be. She belonged to the king. Once he saw her safe to the palace, he would return to his cabin and resume his life. He couldn't do that if he was locked away in Chroina's prison for mating with a lady outside a breeding contract.

Anya lay back and raised her hips off the ground to push her trousers down. The instant she did, her scent rolled over him stronger than before. Despite his best intentions, every drop of blood in his body surged between his legs. How easy it would be to lie atop her, to wrap her in his arms and revel in that fragrance all night long.

He stood and stalked away from her, which didn't do him any favors since the distance between them now offered him a view he couldn't look away from no matter how hard he tried. From beneath the hem of her shirt, her bare legs stretched across the rocky earth like two graceful, shapely columns. In the dark, he couldn't see the swelling or the way her left leg bent differently than the right. In the dark she didn't look crippled. She looked beautiful as she flexed her tiny toes in the pebbles.

Distracted by those wiggling toes, he almost missed it when her lithe fingers pulled at the laces of her collar. He held his breath as she lifted the shirt over her head and laid it on the ground beside her trousers. There was nothing between her skin and his hands except a few pitiful shreds of restraint.

Her breasts were as hairless as he'd imagined, but the reality of them was a thousand times more potent than even his most illicit fantasy. He'd seen the trading cards men collected, showing painted images of ladies in various states of undress. There wasn't a man alive who hadn't fantasized about stroking his hands over the luxurious coats covering the breasts of Marann's esteemed ladies. But these breasts were far superior to any image he'd ever seen. Lacking hair, they seemed so much more accessible to a man's hands, so much more inviting. Needing to heed that invitation, he took one step toward her, then two. He started a third before he managed to stop himself.

Her head whipped in his direction. She hugged herself, covering her breasts. She wrapped her arms around her shins, spreading her fingers over the unnatural curve of her lower left leg.

She spoke, but he didn't understand her.

"Your gemstone," he told her.

She likely didn't understand the words, but her eyes widened with comprehension. She fumbled in her trouser pockets and came away with her fist clenched tightly, protecting her treasure.

"How well can you see me?" she said.

"I can make out your shape," he said, though truthfully he could do much more than that. He could see the whites of her eyes as she searched the darkness for him. He could see the play of tendons beneath the skin of her neck as her shoulders relaxed.

She rubbed her arms once against the cold then dropped them, accepting his vague answer.

Guilt made him shift on his feet.

With the hand not clutching her gemstone, she reached out blindly in his direction. "Are you helping me or do I have to crawl to the water?"

Gritting his teeth against the pain in his groin, he closed the distance between them and took her hand.

She latched onto it and pulled herself to her feet with a long, low groan. It softened the edges of his need, remembering how badly she was hurting. He was despicable for wanting her like this.

She leaned heavily on his arm as he directed her down the

bank. At the edge of the water, he said, "Will you trust me to hold your gemstone? I'm worried you'll lose it in the water."

"Aye. We'll understand each other just as well if you keep it." She transferred it to his hand.

He tucked it deep in a pocket and moved his hands to her waist. "Careful now. There's the water."

She hissed. "So cold." Her skin pebbled beneath his hands.

How shameful that he found even that arousing! She was suffering because *he'd* failed to read the signs she was hurting and hungry.

He cleared his throat. "It'll be good for the swelling. Just go in far enough to sit and have your legs covered." He stood watch while she made her shivering, moaning way into the water, inch by torturous inch. He wanted to go with her and warm her with his body so her teeth didn't chatter, but she'd never allow it. "I'll spread my cloak for you. You can use it to dry yourself when you climb out."

"Y—ye have a c—cloak?"

"In my pack. The nights will be cold. It'll keep you warm."

She gave a jerky nod and started to lower herself into the water. She didn't get far before she cried out and started to fall.

He lunged and caught her, held her tight against him. Cold water spilled into his boots. He didn't care. Not when his lady gasped in pain in his arms. Under his hands, the skin of her back and arms was rough as a sanding stone with goose bumps.

It should not be this way for her. She deserved the best doctors and luxuries Chroina had to offer, not to freeze half to death to treat her painful legs. But there was no help for it. Half an hour from now, she'd be out and warm in his cloak, and her legs would feel better. He'd even rub them for her if she'd let him. All night, if that's what it took to soothe her pain. Trackers be damned. He'd tear out the throats of anyone who thought to take her from him.

"Easy. Easy does it." He scooped her up and lowered her into the water, soaking himself to the knees and elbows. Once she'd settled herself, he crouched behind her in the shallow water. His senses told him there were no predators nearby. She would be safe if he left to hunt. But he didn't want to go. He didn't want to leave her for even a second.

"I k—ken this is what my legs n—need, but a d—dip in this poo—ool would be m—more pleasurable in s—summer. And d—daylight." Her voice shook less as she adjusted to the water's cold embrace.

Her strength of spirit warmed him. He hoped she found some warmth in it too. "I'll go find you some mushrooms while you soak."

"The b—bread was fine. If we see some tomorrow, we can pick them. B—but you should hunt. You must be hungry after carrying me all day."

He couldn't help himself. He stroked a hand over her hair. The knot she'd had it tied in earlier had come loose. Her waist-length strands were warm and dry above the water line, cold and clinging to each other beneath. Her arms tightened in a violent shiver, and he wondered if his touch had done that to her. She did worse to him, just by being near him.

"Go on with you," she said, looking over her shoulder. "I'll be fine."

"If you need anything, call out for me. I won't go out of earshot."

Longing rent him to pieces as he left the pool and stalked into the forest.

Chapter 7

A LONE BIRD trilled high above. Anya opened her eyes to a forest a shade brighter than full dark. Another bird answered the first. Within minutes, the forest was gray with morning light and awake with the music of life.

'Twas an oddly optimistic thought. Mayhap she owed it to the juicy, filling mushrooms Riggs had brought her last night, even though she'd told him not to bother. Mayhap she owed her buoyant mood to waking for the first time in three months to the sounds of birds and not the fire of cramping muscles in her legs. That was because of Riggs as well, since he'd ignored her demand to leave her be and used those strong fingers of his to knead her legs through her trews and work out deeper knots than she had ever been able to reach on her own. Mayhap she owed it to the solid warmth of him as they lay back to back on the forest floor, the security of his protection more certain than anything she'd ever known.

His deep breathing changed. His back tensed. Power and readiness seeped from him, sudden and heavy enough to penetrate the thick wool cloak she was bundled in. He held his breath and remained utterly motionless for several heartbeats. He was listening.

She held her breath, too, and strained her ears. She heard nothing beyond the expected forest noises.

Riggs inhaled a great gulp of air and sprang up with animal quickness. Apparently, his ears were better than hers. He'd heard something.

She rolled over to find him crouched with one hand on the ground and one on the axe he'd slept beside. His gaze was fixed to the south, the direction they'd come from.

"Trackers?" she asked, her heart thumping her to wakefulness.

She'd barely uttered the question before he scooped her up and began running. Just like that. Running. Faster than she'd ever felt him go before. Everything but his axe and the clothes on their backs was left behind.

He slung her over his shoulder and held her with an arm around her thighs. His other arm pumped, axe in his fist.

The forest whipped past, gray trunks, dark firs, dead leaves on the ground. Riggs's boots pounding, pounding, pounding. And yet his gait was smooth, like a horse's gallop, even when he darted left or right, presumably to avoid obstacles.

Hanging upside down and backward was bloody disorienting, but she resisted the urge to close her eyes. Instead, she lifted her head to search for signs of whoever might be following. She saw nothing. But then, the forest grew even thicker here than near Riggs's cabin.

"How close?" she asked.

"Too close."

"How many men?"

"Not men," he answered between heavy breaths. "Wolves."

"Wolves!"

"Tracking wolves. Four. Maybe five."

Terror thrummed through her. She kent better than to distract him with any more questions. Gripping his shirt, she curled around his shoulder as best she could so she didn't flop like a bloody fish.

The forest opened into a meadow, tinted with golden, early-morning light. She hoped they lived to appreciate the sun's warmth today.

The tree line behind them grew farther away as Riggs's stride lengthened in the wide open space. 'Twas a mixed blessing, the open space. Riggs could move faster, but if the wolves broke through that tree line, they'd move faster too. Could he possibly outrun a pack of wolves? What would a pack of wolves do to them if they were caught?

She held her head up to watch the trees. *Please, no wolves. No wolves.*

There. A gray beast burst into the meadow. The thing was as tall as a cart pony, bigger than any wolf she'd ever heard of, more like a Wolfhound, but with even more bulk. It dropped its head and drove forward on long legs that ate up the distance between them. Two more wolves emerged from the forest.

"They're coming," she said.

"I hear them. How many?"

"Three. No, four, five. Christ, six. The sixth is smaller." Their long-haired coats varied from gray to brown. Each one flashed deadly-looking fangs. And they were gaining.

Riggs plunged them back into the forest.

The light dimmed. 'Twas eerily quiet save for his pounding footsteps until the wolves entered the trees. The tattoo of dozens of swift paws multiplied in her ears like brittle thunder.

Riggs skidded to a stop.

This was it. She didn't mind dying, but the thought of Riggs going with her rent a gash in her soul.

"Just throw me to them!" she cried. He'd be able to run faster without her. Better only one of them get killed than both. "Get away with you! Run!"

Riggs hefted her into the air. "Grab on!" he shouted.

A sturdy tree limb appeared above her head. She grabbed for it with both hands and hooked her good leg around. The moment she was free of Riggs's hold, the enormous gray wolf lunged for him.

Riggs spun with his axe at the ready. He was going to die fighting. Her protector. Her brave, brave wolf-man.

He swung his mighty axe while he threw himself to the side to dodge the leader's fangs. The axe missed the beast's haunches by a breath. Riggs hit the ground with a grunt but bounded to his feet in time to swing his axe at a second attacking wolf. His blade lifted the beast off the ground with a sickening crack to the ribs. Blood sprayed.

At least he would take one of the wolves with them into the afterlife. But there was no way he could survive the five remaining.

Four of them skidded into a snarling, writhing circle around him. The smaller wolf was nowhere to be seen. From her upside-down perch, she watched Riggs adopt a wide stance. He swiveled his head from wolf to wolf, assessing. Which would attack first?

She didn't have to wait long to find out. A large brown one flattened its ears. Riggs drew his hunting knife, doubly arming himself. The wolf crouched, ready to pounce.

A sharp pain tugged at her throat.

Och, Riggs's cloak! She'd forgotten she was still wearing it. Something had grabbed the heavy wool as it dangled beneath her.

She clutched at the ties, trying to undo them one-handed while she clung to the branch.

There! The ties gave. The cloak jerked from her neck. She twisted to see the small wolf trying to shake the garment from its head. It was blinded, but not for long.

She released the branch and fell.

The ground knocked the wind from her and rattled her teeth. While she was still too numb to feel any pain, she drew the hunting knife Riggs had given her.

The small wolf stood over her, looking much larger from this angle. It shook the cloak free.

She didn't give it a chance to attack her, or worse, to attack Riggs. She swung her arm in an arc. The blade ripped across the wolf's throat. Blood gushed down its chest. Wide eyed, it stood over her. Would it attack while it bled to death?

She held the knife ready, but didn't need to land another blow. The animal stumbled and went down.

A thud sounded behind her. Then a whimper.

She rolled over to find Riggs striding to her, breathing heavy, covered in blood. He crouched and cupped her face in his hand.

"It's over," he said. "Come."

Disbelief plowed over her. How could it be over? Could he have really slain five monstrous wolves while she'd fought the smallest one?

He scooped her up and tucked the rumpled cloak in her arms then picked up his axe. His powerful legs launched them into a run. She craned her neck to look back. Gray and brown carcasses covered the ground.

He'd done it. And he'd come out of it in good enough shape to run.

Her heart lifted with hope. And filled with somat warmer than relief and fiercer than mere affection. It went beyond gratefulness. Beyond lust. And it scared her more than a pack of wolves.

§

RIGGS HELD ANYA tight to his chest as he cut through the forest, glad he lived to do so. It had been a near thing. Very near. Damn him for giving in to the temptation to lie down beside her last night. He should have let her rest in his arms while he pressed on through the night, but she'd looked so beautiful in the moonlight, and he'd been so exhausted after his hunt. He'd meant only to rest his body for an hour.

Fool.

He wouldn't make that mistake again. Even if he had to stay awake until he got her to Chroina.

"What happened?" she asked, her voice trembling. "How did you kill them all? Are you hurt?"

He flicked his gaze to her, assuring himself she was uninjured, then went back to picking out the path ahead—it would all be for nothing if he crashed into an obstacle and killed her. The glimpse revealed she was searching his face, her eyebrows pinched with worry. For him. His tight chest relaxed a fraction.

"I'll be fine," he told her. "You? You fell far."

His heart had nearly exploded out of his chest when he'd seen her fall from the tree out of the corner of his eye. He'd turned to help her, but one of the damn tracking wolves took the opportunity to sink its teeth into his calf and another had taken a chunk out of his axe arm. Something had snapped to life inside him then, some wild instinct he'd felt prowling deep within him when he'd been at his cabin with Anya. *Kill!* It had commanded, and the world had seemed to slow down around him. Strength had surged into his limbs. The pain from his wounds had all but disappeared.

His axe and hunting knife found their marks with unprecedented accuracy. Never before had he fought with such purpose, such focus. It had been exhilarating.

When it had all been over, that instinct had shouted, *run!* Where there were tracking wolves, trackers would not be far behind. He'd snatched her up and ran, and he wouldn't stop until he reached the lake. He would not fail his lady.

No, not his. The king's lady.

That inner instinct growled.

Anya rubbed the back of her head. "I'm fine. I expect I'll have a headache soon enough, but it could have been worse."

Worse, indeed. He held her tighter. So precious. And so brave. A warrior, this woman. She wore the blood of her victim on her knife arm like a badge of honor. That sixth wolf might have made the difference between his victory and defeat. Anya very well might have saved his life.

"Well, what happened?" Anya demanded. "How did you best five wolves? Why are you running like the hounds of hell are after us?"

He hadn't answered her questions. Partly because he still couldn't believe what had happened. Partly because he needed to mind his footing.

"I fought well," he said, conserving his breath. "You helped. Trackers not far behind."

Her brow pinched with distress. "Why? Why are they after you?"

They weren't after him. It was her they wanted. The wolves had proved it when they'd fought to kill. Tracking wolves were trained to corner the prey whose scent their masters gave them. And kill whatever got in their way. It was her scent they followed. The trackers must have gotten it from where he'd found her, where he'd abandoned the bodies of the Larnians who had attacked her. A female's scent in the middle of the forest would stand out. A female's scent anywhere but in Chroina would stand out.

He didn't have the breath to tell her all that now. "Later," he said, ignoring the knives of pain stabbing his lungs and the fire of his fresh wounds.

She started to ask something else, but he shushed her. "I won't let them get you. No more questions."

She fell silent. But she didn't stay that way for long. "Your arm," she said, and he felt her touch the shredded linen over his bicep. The wound would need a tight binding, but they couldn't afford to do it now.

"I'll be fine."

"It's your axe arm."

"I can fight with either." When she didn't look convinced, he added, "I'll keep you safe. We just need to stay ahead of the trackers."

"Can we? Stay ahead of them? Are they on foot? Horses? How many? *Och,* never mind. I can see ye struggling no' to keel over. And you're limping besides. Save your strength. But you'll be answering my questions soon."

He grinned at her trust and how she held her curiosity in check. Her brave spirit took his mind off the pain.

Wind whistled in his ear. The scents of pine and loam and musty leaves filled his nose, layering over the hyssop-laced musk that had stamped itself on his consciousness since he'd found Anya. He kept to the landmarks he'd learned as a pup, when he used to follow his sire to the lake to fish and trap the long-haired goats that lived in the northern foothills. Sweet meat, those goats had, and beautiful coats that brought fine sums at market.

The lake was his home away from home. He could walk its northern inlets and valleys with his eyes closed and know where each rock and fallen tree lay. Once there, the trackers would not find them easily, especially without their wolves. He and Anya would be able to rest safely for at least a day and a night. He'd be able to hunt and cook meat for her. He'd rub her sore legs and sleep beside her for as long as they both needed.

When they were rested and well fed, they'd take the northern route to Chroina. Where he would transfer her custody to King Magnus. A hollow burn flared in his gut, and it stayed there all the way to the lake.

§

ANYA ACHED ALL over. The arm she'd had wrapped around

Riggs's neck all day felt fixed in its curled position. Her legs cramped with the day's inactivity. Her neck and shoulders ached from the fall. And her stomach was so empty it made an angry fist inside her. But she was alive. And relatively unhurt.

Not bad for a skirmish with a pack of oversized wolves. Too bad she couldn't say the same for Riggs. Well, he was alive, thank the saints. But the sharp, coppery smell of blood stung her nostrils, reminding her of the open wound in his right arm. And his limp was becoming more pronounced by the hour. He must be even hungrier than she, and thirstier after running from dawn 'til dusk.

His pace had slowed from his powerful lope to a shuffling jog, but he persevered. Never had she known a man more capable and determined. He'd fought wolves for her. He'd carried her for leagues without complaint. She'd never been in more danger. And she'd never felt safer.

She was beginning to hate the idea of Chroina. Riggs spoke about the city with obvious admiration, but she still didn't understand why he felt he must bring her there. Why couldn't he keep her in his cabin? A lass could do far worse than caring for a gruff wolf-man who lived in a cozy hut in the woods. Aye, there was the problem of the trackers. But Riggs struck her as a man who kent the forest as well as his own home. Surely he could hide her away someplace and bring her back to his cabin when there were no longer men after him.

That was another thing she'd be asking him soon. Why was he being pursued? Might it be for killing those Larnians?

Riggs slowed to a walk. Ahead of them the trees thinned in the way of a forest yielding to a loch. Beyond lay a vast expanse of hyacinth-blue evening sky. Far in the distance, lavender tinted, white-tipped mountains stretched to majestic heights. Her chest compressed with longing for her Highlands.

This place is just as wild. Just as lovely.

But it was not her home. She had no home. And Riggs carried her ever farther from the one place she wouldn't have minded calling home.

Would Chroina ever feel like home? What would a city of wolf-people be like? Why was he bringing her there? She sensed he was hiding somat from her, but she couldn't bring herself to demand answers now. Not when her fingers itched to bind the seeping wound in his arm. Not when they both needed food, drink, and rest.

Riggs walked through the last of the trees and down a mild slope. His boots crunched over small pebbles and damp sand. Glassy water stretched for leagues. A grand loch curved around a hill rising to the east. The surface reflected the mountains and the ghost of a nearly full moon visible in the twilit sky.

"Drop the cloak here," he said.

She did, glad to be rid of its warm weight. Between the cloak and the heat coming off Riggs, she was sweating rather profusely. A *thud-slap* must have been his axe hitting the pebbles, head first, then handle. Barely slowing, he walked into the water.

"What are ye doing?" She clung to him tighter than ever, inching up to avoid the surface rising up in churning whorls around his legs.

He didn't answer, but lowered her in. Much too quickly. She hissed as the icy water billowed her trews and soaked her to her waist. He must figure her legs needed another cold soaking. Well, the man might have warned her first!

She was about to berate him, but he surrounded her with his body, with all of his body, giving her some of his weight, burying his nose in her hair.

Shock made her go stock still as he wrapped a big, hot hand around her head. The other scooped her so tightly to him he had her bending backward. But she didn't fall. His strong arms wouldn't permit it.

Against her breasts, his stomach heaved. He was catching his breath after the strenuous journey. His breathing slowly returned to normal. For some reason, her breathing had quickened.

His hand moved over her hair, rubbing her head round and round, the gesture clumsy and yet oddly reassuring. Her stomach tightened, recognizing tenderness. Protectiveness.

No. She couldn't tolerate this from him. She already desired him too much, considering he planned to abandon her in some strange city, considering how broken she was. His tenderness would surely turn to pity once he saw her unclothed by the light of day, a crooked shell of a woman. She'd rather be alone than pitied.

"Riggs." She warned him with her voice.

He straightened enough to look at her with liquid brown eyes. The flecks of gold melted her in places she did not wish to be melted. Then he expelled a breath and lowered his cheek to hers. He rubbed his beard over her skin. He moved to the other side and rubbed her there, too. It chafed, but in a way she didn't mind. It made her feel alive, like hard kisses, the kind that bruised lips against teeth, the kind that left her panting.

She was panting.

So was he, but not like he was still out of breath. She was no stranger to this sort of heavy breathing. He was aroused.

She ought to push him away. But her hands wouldn't work properly. Her arms had wound themselves up and around his sweaty neck. The heat pouring off him stole the chill from the water. She was warm all over. Wet and warm. And warmest of all was the place where his arousal pressed against her abdomen in a hard ridge that burned through their layers of clothing.

When he nuzzled into the hair at her nape, she nuzzled the black curls behind his ear. *Och,* his scent there! Woods and perspiration. Warmth and loyalty.

They could tup here, quickly on the shore. They could serve

each other and then continue their flight. But no. If he meant to keep her at his cabin as his companion, perhaps she could let him close enough to feel her legs wrapped around him. But he did not wish to keep her. She would not risk her pride only to have him deposit her in a strange city, strut away with a sated smile on his face, and forget about her. Not when she didn't think she could ever forget about him.

"We shouldn't stop for long," he said into her neck, interrupting her thoughts. "Can you wait another few hours to eat? I'll cook you meat when we get to my cave."

Her mouth instantly watered at the thought of meat. And at the thought of Riggs providing it for her and bedding down with her in a cave. But he should not be the one caring for her, not when he stood before her exhausted and bleeding.

"Look at you, foolish man. You're in no shape to hunt." She ran a hand across his broad shoulder and down to the tear in his shirt. The linen was destroyed. The tear is his arm looked even worse. "What am I to mend this with? We have no sewing things."

"It's just a shirt."

She swatted his chest. "I meant your arm."

"I know."

Och, that grin of his would be her undoing.

"It just needs binding. I'll take care of it soon enough." He acted like he'd gotten a splinter, not had vicious teeth rend his skin and muscle. And he made it clear, as he'd done at his cabin, he didn't need her doting on him.

She felt bloody useless. "Fine." She pushed out of his arms and began scooping up handfuls of water to quench her thirst.

Riggs did the same. When they'd both had their fill, he said, "Stay here," and waded parallel to the shore several paces before disappearing behind a rocky outcropping.

"Riggs?" Curse her for sounding frightened.

"I'm not leaving you." His voice carried over the loch's surface. "Just retrieving something we need."

He reappeared a few minutes later, guiding a logboat silently though the water. The thing was nearly as long as his cabin, and at its middle, the width appeared twice that of a man's shoulders. The sides reflected the meager light, showing it had been pitched and polished for durability. A sound vessel, it appeared, at least as far as navigating a peaceful loch.

"Man of miracles, you are. Where did ye get that?"

"Made it. With my sire. Use it to fish. Fine trout to be had here." He lifted his chin, indicating the loch. "We'll row to the northern tip under cover of dark. The trackers will lose our scents. Should buy us some time to rest." He left her with the logboat and waded to the shore to retrieve his axe and cloak. Holding them above the water, he brought them to the logboat.

"In you go," he said, and he lifted her up and over the side.

Water drained off her trews as she scrambled onto a bench. The cool night air made her teeth clack.

"Take off your trousers and wrap yourself in the cloak," he said. The logboat tipped dangerously as he hefted himself over the side and climbed in.

She leaned in the opposite direction to balance the narrow craft. While Riggs arranged himself on the other bench, she peeled off her clinging trews and tucked the dry cloak around her legs. From her ribs down, her shirt was soaked, but it would dry under the cloak with her. There were worse things than being wet.

Like bleeding. She looked up to find Riggs dipping an oar into the water. They began to move.

"What do you think you're doing?"

"Rowing."

"With a wounded arm? After you've been running under a load all day?"

"I'll manage." His voice was tight as he worked the oar in

another powerful stroke.

"Give me the oar." She could never match his speed on land, but she could row at least as well as a wounded man. Her arms had always been strong.

He made no response.

She secured the cloak around her waist and made her way to him, hands sliding along the edges of the boat.

He tensed at her approach.

"Give. Me. The. Oar."

"No. Rest, lady."

She knelt between his spread knees. The water that had dripped from his clothing dampened her knees through the cloak.

His eyes went wide, but he kept rowing and wouldn't look at her. His expression seemed almost shy. Her massive, strong wolf-man was acting shy after he'd rubbed his face all over hers. After he'd held her like a drowning man clinging to a bit of driftwood.

She put her hands on his thighs. His muscles jumped under her fingers.

"Lady." A growl rode under his speech, a warning like the one she'd given him earlier.

Ignoring it, she squeezed her hands along the line of his firm muscles, around his knees, down to his calves. There it was, the reason for his limp. A hot, swollen wound, slick with congealed blood beneath torn canvas. She probed the wound, measuring its severity. It wasn't terribly deep, but it should be bound now and cleaned well when they had supplies and light. "You're wounded here." She rose up on her knees, interrupting his rowing. "And here." She touched his arm above the ragged hole in his shirt. "Bind your wounds, Riggs. I can row."

He shook his head in one sharp jerk. "When I get you to safety. For now, I will serve you."

"*Och,* you've done nothing but serve me. You've done

everything for me for days. *Everything*. I feel useless. I'm tired of being a burden. I need to *do* somat. Can you understand that?" What was it about this man that made her appeal to him from her heart rather than belittle or badger him until she got her way? She hadn't spoken this honestly with anyone since Seona. 'Twas almost as if she'd found a friend in him.

Foolish lass. 'Twas merely the strain of the day twisting her judgment. Emotion after danger could never be trusted.

She cleared her throat and wrapped her hands around the oar. The smooth wood met her palm and brought to mind carefree summer afternoons fishing on the lochs between Ackergill and Wick.

Riggs released the oar.

She smothered her smile of triumph. "Up with you. This is my place tonight."

Chapter 8

THE LOGBOAT ROCKED beneath his feet as Riggs squeezed past Anya and shuffled to the opposite bench. He sat down with a sigh. By the moon, he was weary. He'd had too little food and sleep the last two days. And he'd lost too much blood.

At least Anya was in better shape. It should shame him to have her serve him this way, but the shame didn't come. Instead, as he watched her dip the oar into the water and propel them northward, he reveled in the sight of her serene brow, her relaxed smile. Her beauty shone brighter than the waxing moon above and tugged at his spirit with a pull a thousand times as strong. This was Anya at peace, and she found peace in being useful. He'd ensure she felt this way often.

She switched sides every few strokes, keeping them straight. Amazing that a lady knew how to row. She'd clearly done it before. Someone had taught her. Her sire? Mother? A lover?

His stomach contracted at the thought of another man instructing her. He did his best to ignore the discomfort. Wasn't his place to be jealous of the men who had touched her, interacted with her, loved her. If any man had the right to be jealous for Anya, it was King Magnus.

A growl started in his chest.

"What are you fashing about? Are your wounds bothering you?"

"No."

"Well it's a wonder. You're sitting there like an oaf, bleeding all over your fine boat. Those wounds arena going to bind themselves."

A different sound rumbled from him. A chuckle. The sound was foreign in his ears. And most welcome. "What do you suggest I bind them with? There are fishing nets beneath my bench, but I doubt they'd hold the blood in."

"Use your shirt. Cut strips from the bottom."

"That'll ruin my shirt."

She grinned. "Where I come from, many fine warriors choose to go without shirts. They get caught on the bracken and provide a handhold for the enemy."

"Don't they grow cold in winter?"

"Aye. Verra cold, indeed. But when the day's work and skirmishing is done, they go home to their wives or mistresses and get verra, verra warm." Her saucy grin spoke of experience warming such men.

By the moon, this woman had taken many lovers. It infuriated him. And it excited him. Heat and energy spun in his gut at the thought of her vast experience.

Judging by the gleam in her eye, both wicked and gleeful, she knew what she did to him.

He pictured her nude amidst bedfurs, her glorious breasts rising and falling with her needy pants as he covered her with his body and his scent. The primary reason to resist mating with her was growing distant and insubstantial: imprisonment.

He had not won the lottery. He had not paid for a breeding contract. Thus he could not mate with her according to Marann's Breeding Law. To plant his seed in her womb would earn him a ten-year sentence. Ten years away from his cabin and his trapping. Ten years to do nothing but sit on a cold stone floor, eat bread and vermin, and relive the memory of her body beneath his, her heat surrounding him, her breath stirring the hair behind his ear, as it had done a few minutes ago when they'd been standing in the water.

If that were the only consequence, he'd do it. He'd mate with her. Tonight. In his cave. After feeding her with cooked meat and laying her down on the soft bed he kept there. He'd fill her with his seed and take pleasure from her and give her pleasure in return, the way he'd always dreamed. They'd be one for this night. And the next, and the next, and the next, until they reached Chroina. He'd hold her soft, lily-cool body tight to his while they slept, instead of settling for the press of her back against his. She'd be his, even if just for a short time. It would be worth it. He'd walk proud and smiling into his cell because no man would be able to take the memories from him.

But giving in to his urges would bring more than imprisonment down on his head. It would bring the shame of knowing he'd betrayed his king. Magnus was a good king, from a line of good kings and queens. He deserved Riggs's loyalty. If he did what he wanted with Anya, it would be a betrayal of the most personal kind. She was not just another female his king would mate with in hopes of breeding. Anya was special. The king had publicly claimed her in faith long before Riggs had found her. By doing so, he had invited the mockery of half the country, including Riggs. But he'd given hope to the other half.

Of course, most of the ones who had taken heart at the king's proclamation had gone to Danu's breast like his sire, but maybe once Riggs brought Anya safe to Chroina, the ones who still mocked King Magnus would change their minds.

All of Marann would hear how she'd appeared in their midst like magic. Like Riggs, they'd have no choice but to consider that maybe, just maybe, Danu had not forgotten them. Maybe King Magnus wasn't mad. Maybe new life would come to the world through this miracle lady.

So much depended on the next few days. He must resist the urges of his body. He must focus on keeping her safe. Hidden. He must not fail.

"Are you going to bind that arm, or do I have to do everything for you?" Anya's voice eased the weight of responsibility threatening to suffocate him. "I doona mind. I've undressed many men. Doctored some, too. But I canna do it and row at the same time. I only have two hands."

He felt his mouth turn up at the corner. She was flirting with him. He could flirt too. "I'm fond of this shirt. Maybe I should use yours. You have the cloak to wear, after all."

Anya's laughter filled the night with joyous harmony. "*Och,* you'd like that, would you? Well, too bad. I plan on keeping my shirt on around you."

Smart lady.

"Cut strips from the hem," she said, growing serious. "You'll still be able to tuck it into your trews. No one will suspect."

And wise.

He loosened the laces and tugged the shirt from his trousers, undoing his belt to ease the way. "Keep the moon to your left," he told her as he drew his hunting knife and smoothed his shirt over his knees. He poked the blade through the fabric. "And point the bow at that jutting copse of trees." He jabbed a thumb over his shoulder to indicate the far-off marker for the hidden inlet that led to his cave.

"I canna see it. It's dark as pitch. But I can keep the boat straight by keeping an eye on the moon. Just tell me if I drift." Only she wasn't looking at the moon. She was looking directly at his naked chest.

He bound his wounds, smiling to himself while the king's lady, not nearly as night blind as she pretended, blushed beneath the three-quarters moon.

§

ANYA GAZED AT the moon as Riggs carried her up a steep slope. The cool white orb was high and bright and would reach its fullness in another two or three nights. Pebbles crunched beneath his boots, and the sound of his breathing filled her ears. The air smelled of fresh water and pine, and it nipped her face with the crisp bite of an autumn night. But she was warm against Riggs's chest and bundled in his heavy cloak.

It wasn't so bad, really, being carried about. Undignified, aye, but she'd trade a wee bit of dignity for the privilege of having such hard working arms around her and such a reliable shoulder to rest her cheek on. At least she'd been able to serve him tonight instead of him doing everything for her.

"We're almost there," he said. His voice was smaller than usual, as though he lacked his usual amount of breath. He must be beyond exhausted. He better not be thinking about seeing to her needs before his own. A few hours of rowing was nothing compared to his day of running and fighting.

The sound of his steps and his breathing grew louder and took on a faint echo. They'd entered a cave. His cave. He'd told her about it as she'd paddled. He'd been coming here with his da since he was a child. Even though his da was gone, like hers, he still came every spring and summer for the fish and the fine furs of the animals that lived in this place and no other on the island.

Pitch blackness settled over her like a second cloak.

"I'm starving," he said as he lowered her onto a soft bed.

Leaves crackled as her weight compressed a welcoming padding of animal skins atop bracken. She settled in with a sigh, surrounded by the scent of clean bedfurs and Riggs. *Och,* she would be content to lie here for a week and not move.

"I'm going to hunt for myself first." His voice was close to her. She could see nothing but felt the warmth and substance of him wonderfully near. "Then I'll cook for you. Can you wait a little longer?"

Good. He would see to himself first. As a good protector should. One could not protect if one did not keep strong.

"I've gone longer than a day without food before. I'll survive. But you've fought and bled today. You need fresh blood to replace what you've lost."

Earlier, it had disturbed her to see Riggs return from hunting covered in blood. Tonight, she craved blood for him. She'd noticed the moon reflecting glassy hunger in his eyes as he'd dragged the logboat into its hiding place and the way his skin stretched tight over his cheekbones. He needed fresh meat. Blood. Viscera. Whatever a wolf-man consumed. She wanted him to have all he needed. Always.

"Go. Take as long as you need. I'll likely be asleep before you set foot out of the cave, I'm so weary."

She squeezed the burning muscle between her neck and shoulder. The rowing had been a welcome activity, but she'd pay for it tomorrow with soreness. At least they'd have the next day to rest—Riggs had assured her they'd be safe for at least that long.

"I'll return as soon as I can." She heard his clothing rub as he shifted. "I might go far to find what I need. Keep your knife in your hand. And use this if you need to." A clunking sound must have been his axe meeting the stone floor. "Do not make any noise. And do not leave the cave for any reason."

"You said the trackers wouldn't find this place. Not so soon."

"I'm not worried about the trackers. There are wolves and lynxes in this area. I've seen bear not far from here. I won't lose you to a wild animal."

She reached out until her hand cupped his cheek. His beard was cool and coarse, so terribly masculine. She stroked her thumb up and over the skin of his cheekbones. Even to her blind touch, the bone felt more prominent than it should. "Go on with you. I'll be fine."

Riggs put his hand over hers, molding her hand tighter to his face. He wasn't leaving. He nuzzled into her hand and leaned closer.

She threaded her fingers into his hair and lifted her face to his. Inviting his affection was as natural as breathing. It shouldn't be, kenning he planned to leave her in less than a week. But *och*, it was.

He rubbed his beard over her forehead. A gentle, lingering caress. "You did well today, lady." He spoke against her skin.

"As did you."

She heard him swallow. He shifted even closer until he was over her, pressing her into the furs with his presence rather than his weight.

If she arched her back, her breasts would touch his chest. She didn't. He needed to hunt. But she couldn't seem to stop touching his beard, his cheeks, his strong jaw, his mouth. His lips were soft and warm in that luxurious nest of tidy hair.

He was a wolf-man who lived secluded in the wilderness, but he kept his beard trimmed. He kept himself clean. He was gruff, but he was a gentleman in every way. He might slaughter his own meat and eat it raw, but his cleanliness and civil behavior put many a Highlander to shame.

She wanted to kiss those lips, wanted that mouth on her body. She craved him in every way a woman could. They could make a life together. Here in this cave. They could hide from the trackers, and when they were no longer hunted, return to his cabin.

"Why must ye take me to Chroina?" she blurted.

"I told you. You won't be safe anywhere else."

She remembered him telling her that. Safe from what? From whom? What did Riggs fear when he was capable of fending off wolves to protect her? "I don't believe that. You've kept me safe thus far." She cupped his neck, just below his jaw, let her thumb rub over his ear. "Don't take me to Chroina."

He remained silent and motionless, except for his breathing.

She felt his pulse beating in his neck, felt the movement of his chest when his shirt brushed her cloak with each inhalation.

"Keep me here. With you."

Och, what was she doing? Asking a man to keep her had never turned out well before. She'd asked Aodhan, and he'd jested and distracted her from her talk of marriage with his wicked mouth. She'd asked Steafan, and he'd called her a whore when she hadn't even worked at the bawdyhouse as yet. Now she asked Riggs. Would he crush her hopes like the others? She held her breath.

"I'd love nothing more."

Her breath rushed out with relief. She wrapped her arms around his neck and tried to draw him down on top of her. Was she actually considering having him tup her? Could she do so and enjoy it without fearing his reaction to her twisted leg? Yes. Here in the dark, where he wouldn't see, yes. *Och,* yes.

Riggs didn't budge, but remained inches above her. His neck tensed. "But I can't."

The words hit her chest so hard, she felt like she'd been kicked by a mule. How had she let herself come to a state where his rejection should hurt as it did? She shoved at his shoulders, needing to get away.

He was immovable as a boulder.

"Lady," he whispered. "Sweet lady." He rubbed his cheek on hers as he had at dusk. First one side, then the other. The warm friction at her cheek ignited a matching heat low in her belly.

Curse her body for clinging to hope when his words had stamped it out. He didn't want her. The one man she thought mayhap she could trust not to recoil from her brokenness, and he wanted nothing to do with her. She should scorn him, unman him with her words. That had always been the penalty for any who dared refuse her before.

But she couldn't. Not when he'd bled for her today. She bit her tongue to keep silent.

"I need to hunt." The words sounded forced. His arm trembled as he braced over her, demonstrating how hungry he must be.

Silence throbbed between them.

"Go. Eat." She rolled away, giving him her back.

He rose to stand by the bed, saying nothing. But she heard him there, breathing.

"I'll be fine. Go." She made her voice airy, as though she weren't aching inside.

Without a word, he left.

Chapter 9

RIGGS STALKED FROM the cave, leaving Anya warm and welcoming and flooding his bed with her fragrant musk. And it nearly killed him.

He skidded down the rocky incline he'd climbed a few minutes ago. When he reached level ground, he kicked off his boots. His hands shook as he unlaced his shirt. His body was strung so tight with desire it caused him pain to push down his trousers.

It was more than physical longing. Yeah, his body roused to her, but his full response went so much deeper. Being with Anya pulled tight strings that reached way down to the core of his person. Being away from her made it feel like someone plucked too hard at those strings and made them discordant.

He felt connected to her. The power of the connection terrified him.

The urge to claim her was a living thing, an instinct arising from the same place that had given him the strength to defeat the wolves today. But she'd already been claimed. She was a treasure fit for a king. He needed to protect that treasure, not plunder it.

Snarling, he tore across the river and into the forest. The undergrowth was thicker here than near his home. Thorny bushes and reaching branches scratched at his skin with stings that distracted him from his hopeless predicament. His feet beat against the hard ground, hitting sticks and rocks with flares of dull pain that faded all too fast.

He pulled the fresh air into his lungs, searching through the scents of pine, cedar, and moss for the spicy bite of game. There. He veered to the right, following the nose-ruffling scent trail of a young buck.

The air changed. A barely audible flutter in his ears meant the buck had heard him and taken flight. He forced his attention to the hunt. His feet flew as he closed the distance between him and his prey.

He rounded a copse of pine and saw the white tail disappear into the trees. He pushed himself to run faster, ignoring the burn in his muscles and the pain from his wounds.

The buck had speed and grace, but Riggs had strength and endurance. And hunger. Deep hunger. He let the empty ache in his gut summon his instinct to the surface. His thoughts reduced down to their simplest form. *Catch. Kill. Feed.*

Provide.

§

ANYA TOSSED AND turned on Riggs's bedfurs, but she couldn't sleep. Not when he'd given her proof of her worthlessness. Not when humiliation heated her belly and made her want to slink away into the darkness, never to bother Riggs again.

But she wouldn't slink away. He might not want her like she wanted him, but the thought of leaving and never seeing him again hurt worse than breaking bones. She'd cling to him despite their apparent imbalance of desire, because she could. Because even though he'd just hurt her, being near him would provide a measure of comfort. Until they reached bloody Chroina.

She was pathetic.

But she'd known that already. She'd get over it. In the meantime, she'd make herself as useful as she could. Riggs already had to carry her and provide meat for her. The least she could do was forage for her own greens and make a fire so she could cook the meat herself when he returned.

She got up and made her way to the half circle of blue night beyond the black cavern. Thanks to the moon, she could see well enough to make out the winding river below and the densely wooded hills all around, making of this place a hidden valley. Far in the distance, the loch sparkled like a dark gem.

Somewhere out there were men intent on finding Riggs. Were they anything like the brutes who had first found her? Would they try to arrest him for murder?

She'd vouch for him that the deaths of the Larnians had been justified, but who kent what a woman's word was worth in this place, especially a crippled woman. Speaking on Riggs's behalf might do more harm than good.

Stop borrowing trouble, lass.

She turned her attention to the task at hand. Pulling the cloak tight for warmth, she hobbled down the hill in search of firewood. Riggs had warned her not to leave the cave because of dangerous animals, but she was no stranger to spotting wolf and bear sign. She'd ventured into equally wild areas in search of kindling for Gravois' camp and managed to avoid predators well enough. Besides, she had the hunting knife at her hip. The axe, she'd left in the cave. 'Twas far too large for her to wield effectively.

The narrow patch of earth between the river and the forest would make a nice bed for the fire. She began collecting twigs and arranging them in a conical shape. Venturing into the dark forest but never going so far she couldn't hear the river, she let her hands and feet guide her search for logs small enough to carry. After an hour's work, she had a decent woodpile she could light with her flint box once Riggs returned.

Having worked up a hearty thirst, she lowered herself to her elbows on the pebbly bank. Several groans came forth, and she was glad Riggs hadn't been there to hear them. Reaching down to the water, she scooped up a few handfuls.

Ah. Cold, crisp. Wonderful.

The chill of the water on her skin made goose bumps sprout up and down her arms. It left an icy trail down her throat to her empty stomach. Meat would be very welcome after nothing to eat all day.

Rustling in the foliage across the river made her look up sharply. An enormous black form appeared out of the trees. 'Twas too large to be Riggs. She sucked her breath and scrambled back from the bank. Pain shot up her legs. *Och,* she couldn't get them under her to flee!

When she tried to draw the knife at her hip, the blade caught in the sheath. In her panic, she struggled with it and managed to slice the webbing between finger and thumb.

She hissed with the pain and made a second attempt, bringing the knife out and brandishing it toward the giant now wading through the hip-deep water. It was coming straight for her.

"What are you doing out here?" came a booming, growling voice. Riggs's voice.

He came up the bank like a Norse conqueror, moonlight reflecting off his wet muscles, thunderclouds gathering behind his eyes. As he approached, she saw his already substantial size was exaggerated by the partially eaten carcass of a buck draped across his shoulders. He slung the carcass to the bank with a wet thud. Water drained off him, making puddles around his feet.

She exhaled with relief. He might be angry, but at least he wasn't a hungry bear or a Larnian tracker.

"I told you not to leave the cave. You could have been eaten. You could have been taken! By the moon, I can't even leave you alone for an hour!" His voice rose until it echoed around the valley.

"Cease your caterwauling!" She sucked the wound on her hand, embarrassed. He was right. If he'd been a wild animal, she wouldn't have been able to defend herself. She was too slow, too crippled. "I'm no wee ane in need of constant care. I doona even want your care. Just tell me which way Chroina lies and I'll find my own bloody way. I've had enough of you, you—you big brute."

"You're not going anywhere on your own." He'd ceased his yelling as she'd asked. He was quiet now. Dangerously so.

After all his bellowing, hearing him like this filled her with dread. Or mayhap he only seemed more dangerous because he smelled like blood from his hunt. Whatever the reason, she'd lost her appetite.

Foolish lass. She should have slunk away while she had the chance.

§

ANGER SURGED THROUGH Riggs. Anger at Anya for disobeying him. Anger at himself for leaving her alone. Images of wild animals tearing her apart or Larnian trackers capturing her flashed before his eyes and tied knots around his heart. *Protect!* his instinct roared. It was his ultimate duty, and it was pure luck that he hadn't failed in it tonight.

His lungs tightened with the urge to yell at her some more, but he stopped when she uttered a cry. She was trying to get up off the ground, and causing herself pain in the process.

"Here." He went to her and wrapped a hand around her slender arm.

She shook him off. "Doona touch me!"

"I'm trying to help you."

"I doona require your help." She managed to get her feet under her and rose with a grimace. Without casting him a glance, she limped off toward the incline.

He followed her with his eyes, afraid he'd shake her

senseless—or nuzzle her senseless—if he went after her.

She passed a pile of wood that hadn't been there when he'd gone hunting. It was half as tall as she was and as big around as a uniwheel cart. It would burn more than long enough to cook the hindquarters he'd brought her. And the clothes he'd left in a heap were folded neatly atop a flat boulder. His boots sat perfectly straight, side by side like soldiers in a line.

He was a royal shite.

She hadn't been challenging his order when she'd come down here. Disregarding it, maybe, but with the intent to help him. She was hungry and weary and probably sore from rowing all that way, yet she'd worked to save him time and effort and to do what she could to take care of herself.

He wiped a hand down his face.

Anya was unlike any lady he'd ever heard of. Independent, hard working, surprisingly capable for someone so small and so damaged. She liked to be active and make decisions for herself. Much as he hated to admit it, her logic was sound given what he'd told her, which wasn't much. How could he expect her to steward her own safety if she didn't understand the threat?

It was time to tell her everything.

He yanked his trousers on and went after her. She was just entering the cave when he stopped her with a hand on her shoulder. The coppery scent of fresh blood stung his nostrils. His stomach dropped.

"You're bleeding." He hadn't realized it when she'd been near the buck.

She shrugged his hand off. "It's no concern of yours."

He stepped around her, halting her progress. "Lady." He put both hands on her shoulders.

She wouldn't look at him.

"I'm sorry. I shouldn't have raised my voice." Good thing he didn't plan on keeping her for himself. A heartless clod like him didn't deserve such a delicate treasure. He would only hurt her again and again, like tonight, like yesterday when she'd fallen near those mushrooms. King Magnus would know how to treat a lady. King Magnus wouldn't make her hide her face and shy from his touch.

"I doona wish to talk about it. Leave me in peace. I'm tired." She tried to shake him off again, but this time he held fast to her graceful shoulders. The muscles there were overly warm through her shirt and cloak. He swept the heavy wool of the cloak aside to explore that heat with his fingers. He found knots and started rubbing them like he'd done for her legs last night at Aine's Falls.

The tense line of her shoulders relaxed ever so slightly.

"Where are you bleeding from? What happened?"

"If you must ken, I thought you were a bear, and I cut myself trying to draw your bloody hunting knife."

Curse him. "I'm sorry." He felt down her arms until he had both her hands in his.

"You said that already."

"I'll say it a thousand times if that's what it takes to earn your forgiveness." He lifted her hands. There. The right one had a gash in the tender place between finger and thumb. He put the wound to his mouth and licked it, like he'd do for himself if he were bleeding. Her blood tasted sweet and salty and clean. The flavor made his eyes roll back in his head.

She hissed in a breath and went completely still. "Only a thousand?" she said on a wavering breath. She cleared her throat. "*Och,* it would serve you right if I demanded ten times that number."

He continued to lap her wound gently. It wasn't deep, wouldn't need sewing. The bleeding had nearly stopped already. "Ten thousand apologies?" he murmured, his lips brushing her hand. "I can do that. I might get them all said by the time we reach Chroina."

She stiffened at his mention of their journey and slipped her hand out of his grasp.

He let it go with a pang of loss. "It's time I tell you why I'm bringing you there. And what's at stake if I fail."

In the ensuing silence, it felt like the weight of the world settled on his shoulders. Maybe it had. His world would die without her. She needed to know it. He couldn't be with her at all times. She needed to know how important she was, how vulnerable.

She would probably hate him once he told her the truth. His proud lady would not like being told she must provide an heir for his king. Then again, maybe her hating him would be for the best. His scent already wafted off her from when he'd nuzzled her earlier tonight. He couldn't seem to stop touching her, layering more of his scent on her. Instinct demanded he make her smell like *his*.

But she wasn't his. The instinct was wrong.

He needed her to hate him so she wouldn't let him touch her again, but not so much she'd refuse to do what his people needed.

Shite. Women were complicated.

He held out his hand to her. "Come. I have no idea how to cook your dinner. You show me what to do, and I'll tell you all about King Magnus."

Anya eyed him suspiciously. Then she put her hand in his and let him lead her from the cave. "You're right," she said. "'Tis about bloody time."

Chapter 10

RIGGS CROUCHED ON the bank and skinned the buck's hindquarters.

Standing by the woodpile, Anya drew a flint box from her pocket. Smart lady to have kept it on her person. The one he used to make campfires for tea was still in the abandoned pack the trackers would have confiscated by now.

When she knelt, she didn't make a peep, but her pain was written in the pinching of the corners of her eye.

He moved to help, but her glare warned him not to go near her. He resumed skinning the buck and pretended not to be entranced by her proud yet vulnerable beauty.

She had the inner cone glowing with embers in no time. As the fire crackled to life, it made angry red slashes of her scars. He wanted to caress them with his hands, his lips. He wanted to show this woman no part of her was unlovely to him.

But it wasn't his place. If anyone showed her such things, it would be King Magnus.

He stripped the last of the hide away, feeling lost. Where did he stick the knife to begin cutting meat to a human's liking? How did he begin carving out the truth for her? Like the buck's hindquarters, he couldn't possibly give her the whole truth in one chunk. It would be too much.

"Here, let me." She got up from working on the fire, hiding her wince behind a mask of impatience. She came to stand over where he squatted. Her gaze raked him from crown to toe.

He hadn't put his shirt back on. Hadn't even washed himself from the hunt. The buck's blood streaked his shoulders. Dirt and dried blood made his arms gritty. When he lifted his chin to look her in the eye, the remnants of his meal cracked on his neck and flaked away.

Her lips parted, looking like soft pillows. Then they pressed in a hard line. She held out her hand for his knife, and he gave it over. Without a word, she lowered herself beside him and began cutting the meat into cubes with swift movements, like she'd done this hundreds of times before.

"The trackers are after *you*," he blurted, "not me." It was a terrible place to start, but at least he'd stuck the blade in somewhere.

She looked up. "What? How do you ken?"

Now to shape the truth into manageable chunks. "The wolves. They were prepared to kill me. That means it's your scent they were following, not mine."

Her brows drew together. "So they wouldn't have killed me?"

"No. They'd have cornered you and held you until their masters arrived."

On her exhale, her chest stuttered. "Why me? I'm nothing to them. A trespasser, a foreigner." She resumed her cutting and piled the cubes onto the hide to protect them from the sand. "Get me some sticks to slide these onto."

He helped her arrange the meat for cooking.

She seemed intent on the task and didn't rush his answer, which was good since he didn't know what to say. He didn't want her thinking he would take her choice from her, even though that's exactly what he would have to do unless she chose for herself to help his people. Could he tell her the truth in a way that would encourage her to choose what he wanted?

His insides squirmed. He didn't want to manipulate her. He wanted her happy, and that was the core of the truth. But he also wanted his people to survive.

"Why me?" she asked again, once they'd laid the sticks around the base of the fire.

Her attention was a weight on his skin. He suddenly felt the need to wash himself. While the savory scent of cooking meat billowed around them, he stripped off his trousers and stepped into the river, going far enough for the water to cover the evidence of his desire before he half-turned to keep her in sight. Maybe he was a coward. Or maybe he just needed a moment to gather his thoughts.

He rubbed his palms up and down his arms and over his chest. Water trickled over his neck and back, carrying away the scents of game and forest. She'd seen him do this before, although she pretended she hadn't. She pretended not to watch him now, but out of the corner of his eye he saw the truth. When he cocked his head to look directly at her, she glanced away and busied herself with turning the sticks of meat.

"You should soak your legs while it cooks," he said.

She shook her head. "The venison will be done sooner than I could get out of my trews. Besides, I'm in fair shape. I've hardly walked at all today."

Fair shape, his ass. She was in agony. He saw it in her stiff movements, in her taut face. Maybe after she ate, he could coax her into the water for a few minutes like he'd done at Aine's Falls.

Aine.

Of course!

He suddenly knew where to begin.

He finished washing and returned to the bank.

Anya didn't look his way as he put his trousers back on, but her cheeks darkened with a rosy hue. Her reaction to his naked form made him proud. Even if he couldn't have her, he liked knowing he affected her. By the moon, she affected him.

How would he return to his cabin without her after bringing

her to Chroina? How would he stay sane knowing she was in another man's bed? Shite. He no longer wanted to buy lottery tickets. If he couldn't have Anya, he wanted no woman.

His limbs felt like lead as he finished dressing and sat beside her near the fire.

"Well," she said. "Are you going to answer me or no'?"

"I'll answer. But first, I have a story to tell."

"I thought you didna like to tell stories."

The savory scent of cooking meat turned sharp and sooty. It was starting to burn. Was it still edible after being charred like that?

"I never said I didn't like telling them. I said my sire was the storyteller. This is one he told many times. Rescue your meat and I'll try to do it justice."

§

ANYA BLEW ON a stick to cool the venison. She loved meat like this, charred on the outside, hopefully still tender on the inside. She took a bite. *Och.* Heaven. Tangy and gamy with a slight crust that would probably leave unsightly black flecks on her lips. She licked them between bites, just in case.

Riggs's gaze fixed on her mouth. There was hunger in his eyes, but not the sort sated with meat. That look made her squirm in her trews. She shouldn't want him at all. He was of another race. He ate his meat raw. He yelled at her when she didn't do as he commanded.

He'd told her he didn't want her.

Why did he look at her that way when he'd made it clear she was unsuitable for him? Men could be so bloody confusing. They weren't always. Sometimes they were as straightforward as an arrow shot from a bow. Other times...*och,* she'd never understand them.

She forced her attention to the venison, determined to eat as much as she could hold. Who kent when she might get meat again.

Meanwhile, Riggs leaned back on an elbow and watched her. The dying fire made the gold flecks in his eyes dance. He absently twirled her discarded stick between his fingers as he began, "There once lived a man named Gregor."

A change came over him, a sort of contemplative soberness in place of his usual self-assured gruffness. The lines around his eyes seemed deeper. He looked older to her in the firelight. For the first time, she wondered about his age.

"He was governor of Figcroft," Riggs continued. "Which was at that time a thriving town. He and three other men shared a woman named Aine. The falls we stopped at are named after her."

"Wait," she interrupted. "Shared? What do ye mean?" Polishing off one stick, she reached for another.

Riggs plucked one of the remaining sticks from the log where she'd laid them and sniffed the venison, wrinkling his nose. Setting down the stick again, he exchanged it for a long, smooth stone from the rocky sand. He began flipping it over and under his fingers in a trick she couldn't look away from. How could such large fingers be so flexible, so quick? How did he not drop the stone when he wasn't even looking at it?

His eyes were on her when he answered. "In those days, it was common for several men to share a single woman." He shrugged and stuck out his lower lip, as if this were the least astonishing bit of information to ever be spoken. "Back to Gregor—"

"Why did several men share a single woman?"

"If you keep asking questions, it'll take all night to tell the story." He winked, and her foolish body fluttered with pleasure.

"Fine. Tell your bloody story. I won't interrupt." She took an enormous bite to finish the second stick.

"Good." He handed her the stick he'd sniffed. "Centuries

before Gregor's time, the birthrate tipped toward males. By the time Gregor became governor of Figcroft, the only chance most men had of breeding was if a female invited him to enter a breeding pact. Every female was obligated to enter into one with at least three men of her choosing within a year of reaching breeding age."

She took another big mouthful to keep herself from barraging him with questions. Like, how few women were there for such a practice to be common? How could young lasses be expected to choose three men to share a bed with so soon after becoming young women? Were these pacts like marriages? Could a lass get a divorce if one or more of the men treated her poorly, as any Highland wife could if her clan was led by a just laird?

Riggs tossed the pebble into the fire and chose another to roll between his fingers. "Aine chose her three, but then she met Gregor. She chose him as well. Nothing wrong there. There was no law restricting a woman to only three men. In fact, there was no upper limit, as long as the female shared herself fairly between her pactmates.

"But Aine did not share fairly. As governor, Gregor had his own home, a fine home. Aine spent more time there than in the house she'd shared with her other pactmates. They soon became jealous, but recognizing her great affection for Gregor, they held their tongues. They didn't want to upset her. Until two whole seasons passed and she didn't return to the communal house. The three went to the governor's home to demand he send Aine to them. It was more than their turn to try and breed with her.

"The whole town stood behind the three outside the governor's gates, outraged at their leader's selfishness. How was he to rule in breeding pact disputes when he himself didn't respect the rights of his pactmates?"

Anya felt herself nodding, angry with Gregor on behalf of the pactmates. "What happened?" She picked at the third stick with her fingers, too fascinated with Riggs's tale to eat.

He began carving into the sand with the stone, etching deep, straight lines. "Gregor came to the gate to meet the townspeople. He claimed Aine was ill and could not come out. The pactmates forced their way inside. They found Aine inside, smelling strongly of Gregor's mating scent and something else, something more pungent and much, much more rare. Every man there understood what the scent meant, even though they'd never smelled anything like it before. Gregor had taken Aine as his lifemate."

Riggs had gouged into the earth the shape of a box.

"Lifemate?" The stick dangled in her hand.

The fire was burning low. Riggs's face was half in shadow, half in wavering light. "Legend says that when Danu made us, she put a bit of the moon's power in our souls. On rare occasion, a man would recognize within a woman a piece of moonsoul that perfectly matched his own. If he petitioned the goddess and received her blessing, he could mate with his chosen female under the full moon and the goddess would permanently and irrevocably unite their souls. They would become lifemates.

"It was said of lifemates they were inseparable, even in death. Every time they mated, the male would mark his female with a special scent that would strengthen their bond and repel other males."

She snorted at that. "I doona ken of a single man who would let somat like the way a woman smells discourage him from tumbling her if he wanted to. There's no' bloody much that can come between a man's cock-stand and his pleasure."

Riggs went still, all except for his right hand. He began flipping the stone over and under his fingers again, slower than before. While he did it, he watched her with a strange intensity in his eyes.

"Furthermore, the female would not be receptive to any other male," he continued as if she hadn't interrupted. "It was said none except her lifemate would be able to breed on her, that her womb would open for his seed alone."

She rolled her eyes. The story had captured her attention until he'd brought up this moonsoul nonsense. "I suppose you wish me to conclude Gregor acted selfishly by taking Aine as his lifemate."

This lifemate business sounded like the kind of story men told their wives to frighten them into being faithful. Those same men would visit a bawdyhouse without compunction. She hated men like that. If a husband was going to be unfaithful, he ought to have the decency to look the other way when his wife repaid him in kind.

"Selfishly, yes. And illegally." Riggs returned his attention to his drawing. He was adding vertical lines to the front of the box. "Exclusive pairings of any kind were outlawed when breeding pacts were established. Women of breeding age were too rare to be kept by one man alone. The law applied mainly to pledgemates, an old practice where a pair would pledge themselves to each other for life. It was understood this went for lifemates too, though lifemates were so rare no one had bothered to pen it into law at that time.

"Gregor claimed he hadn't petitioned Danu to make Aine his lifemate. He hadn't even pledged himself to her. The bond simply happened. Aine vowed the same. They hadn't done it intentionally. But no one could argue that for the first time in generations, it *had* been done.

"Furious, the people of Figcroft deposed Gregor and brought him to Chroina for the king's judgment. The king heard the case and ruled that Gregor could not have made Aine his lifemate unintentionally. A new law was penned, and Gregor was sentenced accordingly. Life in prison for violating Aine's pact with the other three." He tapped a finger on the sand. The box had become a cage.

"But that wouldn't help the pactmates," she said. "If they couldn't get her with child, what would be the point of continuing the pact?"

Riggs inclined his head, agreeing with her point. "There would be no point, if that were the end of it. But some thought with separation, the lifemate scent might wear off. Apart from Gregor, Aine might eventually become receptive to her pactmates, even conceive for them."

"Some *thought*? Didna they ken for cert? If this is how things were, why did the people nay understand how it worked?"

"By Gregor's time, there were no lifemates left to offer advice. Not even pledgemates. Exclusive pairs were a thing of the past. They only had a handful of historical records to guide them."

How strange. What must it have been like to live in such a world? "Well, doona keep me waiting. Did Gregor's scent fade from Aine? Did she welcome her pactmates to her bed eventually?"

"It took a single moon cycle for Gregor's scent to fade, but that wasn't all that faded." Riggs began drawing another picture beside the first. "The very substance of life seemed to drain out of Aine. Her skin became dull. Her hair became limp. Sadness snuffed the glow in her eyes. She would not eat or drink and began wasting away.

"Her pactmates were distraught. They did everything they could to please her. They made her gifts with their own hands, showered her with affection, sang her songs, and saw to her every comfort. Nothing worked. She simply stopped thriving. Eventually, she stopped speaking and just lay in her bed, staring at the wall."

With a pang of sympathy, Anya remembered lying in her cot in the ladies' cart after her fall. She would stare at the wall for hours on end. She'd refused to speak, to eat. Parted from her beauty, strung tight with pain, and kenning how badly she was bound to be crippled, she'd wanted to die. She'd cursed Gravois every hour for rescuing her.

How much of Aine's state was due to this mystical lifemate connection, and how much was due to plain old self-pity?

"Not knowing what else to do, they brought her to Chroina. They thought, if she could visit Gregor in prison, she might improve. But when they arrived, the jailor told them Gregor had hanged himself in his cell weeks before. He'd written on the wall with his own blood, *My life, my Aine.*"

The fire went out. The only light came from the moon and a handful of embers. It was enough to make out the dark shape he'd drawn beside the cage. A noose.

She brought her hand to her throat. "What happened when Aine learned of it?"

"She showed no reaction. Some say she'd known somehow. They say when Gregor died, he took her soul with him to Danu's breast, where they could finally be together with the goddess's blessing." He raked his fingers through the sand, ruining his pictures. "She died on the way back to Figcroft. Just stopped breathing one night while she slept in the cart between her pactmates."

"How awful." She shivered, suddenly cold. The meat was cold too. Just as well. She was no longer hungry. The extra would keep and make a fine breakfast. She wrapped it a swath of hide and drew the cloak tight around her. It felt late. She should go to the cave to lie down, but sleep would come reluctantly after Riggs's story. "Why did ye tell me all that?"

"You asked why the trackers were after you and not me." His voice rumbled softly in the night. Staring at the ashes of the fire, he sighed like he was steeling himself to remove an arrow lodged in his flesh. "Aine and Gregor lived almost a thousand years ago," he said, slowly turning his head to meet her gaze. "Females have become more scarce ever since. Only one hundred and fifty-three remain. They all live in Chroina, under the protection of King Magnus. None has birthed a child in eleven years. It's the longest period in our history without a birth. Some say it's the end of the world. I'm just someone who killed a few Larnians who were up to no good. You're a female. A miracle."

Chapter 11

ANYA KEPT WAITING for Riggs to dissolve into laughter and say, "I'm jesting, of course." He didn't. He stopped talking, and silence settled over her like a blanket of ice.

Since he wouldn't laugh, she did it for him. She cackled like a mad hyena. She laughed so hard she had to steady herself with a hand on the ground. She laughed until tears leaked from her eyes.

When the laughter died, she straightened to see Riggs looming close beside her. He'd scooted close enough for the heat pouring off him to penetrate her cloak better than any fire. The wash of moonlight made his expression appear hard. Instead of warm gold flecks in his eyes, she saw silver shards.

"End of the world?" she said on a chuckle. "Truly? You think the end of the world is at hand?"

He remained silent.

"The world canna just *end*. 'Tis impossible! Things will always go on."

"Not without females."

"Well of course females are necessary. But surely, you're mistaken about the number."

"The only way I'm mistaken is if a female has gone to Danu's breast since the last report from Chroina."

He meant if a female had died. If he was wrong about the number, 'twas because he'd overestimated, not underestimated it.

"One hundred and fifty-three?" An oddly specific number. If there were truly so few women, it would make sense to ken the exact number. Each one would be precious. Each death tragically mourned.

"One hundred and fifty-three," he confirmed.

There were more women than that in residence between Ackergill and Wick. To have so few for a whole country of men? Impossible. Unless Marann was a wee country, though it didn't feel so wee considering how far they'd gone, and they weren't even half way to Chroina yet. "How many men are there?"

"About six thousand at the last census."

That wasn't very many men. She'd heard of armies ten times that size. "Six thousand," she repeated. "In all of Marann?"

He scoffed. "No."

Something in her gut relaxed. He was going to explain what he truly meant and put her mind at ease. 'Twas merely a misunderstanding they were having.

"In the world."

A chill made the skin on her neck prickle.

Riggs had never struck her as a mad man before, but she feared for his sanity now. She scooted away from him and said in her gentlest tone, "That canna be true. What about Larna? What about beyond the sea?"

"Twelve of the females in Chroina were among the ones rescued from Larna in the last war. They're all old now. There hasn't been a female in Larna since our soldiers brought them out. There are no females left across the sea."

"How can you be certain? Have you looked?"

"Of course we've looked." He sounded like he'd just rolled his eyes at her.

"Well, how am I to ken? Mayhap wolf-men have never heard of boats."

After a stretch of silence, Riggs began to chuckle.

Then she started up again.

Soon they were both chortling like fools, releasing the weight of all he'd just told her. Could it be true? Could that blasted box have brought her to a place where females were rarer than diamonds?

"You've been in my boat," he said, wiping a tear from his eye. "You know at least one wolf-man can cross water."

"Mayhap you're the only one. Mayhap your king ought to hire you to teach the rest of them how to go about it."

"A pitiful armada that would be, if the king's vessels were nothing but hollowed out logs."

They both chuckled some more.

"How did it happen? Where did all the women go?" She couldn't imagine a world like Riggs described. Her mind darted from one implication to the next. No women meant the men did everything, the cooking, cleaning, sewing. The tupping. Without warm cunnies, men would turn to each other.

Had Riggs ever been with a man? She wouldn't blame him if he had. Urges were urges. One thing was clear to her now, though. He'd never had a woman.

He'd inched closer while she lost herself in thought. She felt his warmth again, and despite a mild wariness—because after all, he still might be quite mad and have made all this up—his nearness comforted her.

"There were fewer and fewer girl children born," he said. "It happened slowly. Some think it started around Jilken's time, because of his atrocities. Eventually, a full year went by without a female birth. Then ten. Then..." He looked into the banked fire. "The youngest female is eighty-three years old. Her name is Diana. She is one of only thirty-five females still young enough to breed. But time is running out. Even Diana may have only ten or twelve years left to breed."

"Eighty-three?" she interrupted. "No woman that auld has conceived since Abraham and Sarah. If wolfkind's hope rests on an eighty-three year old woman, then you're all dead."

He frowned. "Eighty-three is not old. Women breed well into their nineties, sometimes even to a hundred. And our hope no longer rests on Diana and the others of breeding age. It now rests on you."

Cold sluiced her neck and chest. It felt as if he'd just dumped a great bucket of river water on her. She wanted to slap her hands over her ears and unhear what he'd just said.

He took her hands in his and squeezed them. She tried to pull away, but he didn't let her. He captured her gaze as well. She'd never seen him look so serious. "King Magnus needs an heir. None of the females have conceived for him. You will. I know you will. You'll bring life to Marann. To the whole world. That's why I'm bringing you to Chroina. So you can save us all."

She shook her head. "Nay. I canna." She tried harder to pull away from him, but his arms went around her and sucked her in, pulling her tight to his chest.

"Please," he said softly. "Do this for me. For my people. We need you."

His plea snared her heart. She curled her fists in his shirt. Damn him. Damn him to bloody hell.

She should be furious with him for keeping his true intentions from her for so long. She should hate him for making her care about him when all the while he'd intended to give her to another man.

She should be elated because after years of pining for an honored place in the laird's bed, she was now being handed something even better, a king's bed.

But she didn't feel any of the things she should. Anger and hatred burned like twin fires behind her breastbone, but their heat was directed solely at herself. Anger because if she had pieced it all together sooner, she never would have let herself grow so fond of this gruff wolf-man, and then his plan for her wouldn't feel like a betrayal. Hatred because even if she wanted to do what Riggs asked, even if she wished to lend her womb to his king for the survival of his people, she couldn't. Her legs had not been the only things damaged in her fall. In the five months since, she'd not once had her courses. Her womb was damaged. She could not have bairns.

"Let me go," she told him. She released his shirt and tried to push out of his arms.

"No." He held her fast and stroked her hair. The dull points of his fingernails gently grazed her scalp. "Not until we get to Chroina."

Despite his speaking them tenderly, his words were a slap to her face. "I hate you."

"I know," he said, and he held her even tighter.

§

"YOU WANT ME to do what?" Anya shrieked. Her voice echoed around the wee valley. They'd rested a full day and night. It was the second morning since they'd reached the cave, and Riggs was squatting near the river with his back to her.

"Climb on. I'll carry you on my back today."

She shook her head, but it was wasted on him, since he wasn't facing her. "How would I stay on?"

"You'll hold on around my neck, and I'll support your legs." He wiggled his fingers beside his hips. "Didn't your sire ever carry you like this?"

"Nay. He didna." She folded her arms across her chest.

Riggs peered at her, turning partway. He wore a smirk. Bloody infuriating, handsome man.

After his full confession the night before last, she'd wanted nothing more than to get away from him. She'd thought to escape this foolhardy plan of his and take her chances in the wilderness of Marann, but he'd refused to leave her side.

"I don't expect your forgiveness," he'd told her as he lay down behind her on the bed and tucked her tight against his body. *"But please, lady, let me enjoy you. I may never know the company of another female. I'll remember these days the rest of my life. They'll be the best of my life."* How did a lass run away from a man who said such things? How did she tell him she couldn't possibly be what he needed her to be?

"Are you afraid I'll drop you?" he said.

"I'm afraid of being mistaken for a bloody monkey."

"If anyone sees us, it's not comparison to a monkey I'd worry about."

They'd done nothing but rest and talk yesterday. He'd told her his plan to walk to a nearby village by the name of Valeworth where they could rent horses. Riding the rest of the way to Chroina would be quicker and safer, since it would give them the only fair chance to outpace the trackers, who were likely on horseback as well. While she was in no hurry to get to Riggs's bloody king, she didn't particularly want to meet the men who had set those wolves on them. Unfortunately, obtaining horses would mean entering a village where they must keep her identity as a woman secret lest the men in residence decide to make off with her.

"Would they nay bring me to your king like you're doing?" she'd asked while eating her cold venison.

"I would like to hope so," had been Riggs's reply. *"But I'm not willing to take any chances with you."*

"There really are no women outside of Chroina," she'd said in a tone as grim as the expression on Riggs's face.

"Only you."

Desperate men made for dangerous men. It was by the grace of the saints she'd wound up with a decent one.

As much as she hated to admit it, from all Riggs had told her, Chroina really did seem the safest place for her. And if she was going to Chroina, she might as well live in luxury at the palace. 'Twould be the highest price she'd yet earned for her body: privilege and possession in exchange for becoming the bedmate of a king. 'Twas a far better price than she'd thought any man would pay for her again.

Of course, the king could very well take one look at her limping gait and scarred face and refuse her. In that case, mayhap Riggs would keep her after all.

"Come on," he said. "We have a lot of ground to cover. I want to arrive with enough strength to flee with you if things go badly."

Her neck prickled with the foreboding in his tone. "If any man tries to steal me from you, I'll stab him in the eye."

"Good." He wiggled his fingers again, inviting her to climb on. "It'll be best if we arrive soon after the men come in from their day's work. They'll be too weary and too intent on their beer to look twice at a man and his son traveling to Haletown for a doctor."

She scrambled onto Riggs's back, hugging his muscular hips between her thighs. He wrapped his hands under her knees. With her arms locked in front of his throat, she felt fairly secure.

The position might be undignified but 'twas not without its merits. Warmth from his back seeped into her stomach and breasts. Her nose dipped into the curls brushing his collar. His woodsy scent would make her drunk if she let it. But what she appreciated most was the way she'd be able to use the strength in her arms to support some of her own weight, saving Riggs from having to work so hard. It made her feel useful, clinging to him instead of lazing about in his arms. Speaking of arms...

She eyed the tear in his shirt, beneath which, his blood-stained bandage could be seen. His wounds were healing remarkably quickly, but they were still tender. "Does it hurt, holding me like this?"

"No. Hold on." A powerful thrust of his legs brought him to

standing. Axe tucked in his belt, he set off to the east, following a branch of the valley that wound between two wooded hills. He wasn't even limping from the wound in his calf. Either Riggs was exceptionally hearty or there really was fey blood in him. 'Twould also explain how his people lived so long if they'd been made from immortals.

"Tell me more about your people," she said. "You mentioned the youngest female is eighty-three. And she's still within breeding age. I canna imagine such a thing. And how is it your wounds heal so quickly? Is it your fey blood?"

"I don't heal quicker than anyone else."

She snorted. "Three days ago, you were gored in the thigh. Two days ago, you were ravaged by wolves. Today, you're walking about as if you'd never been injured at all. A human would be limping from those wounds at best, lying in bed with blood fever at worst, especially since you've not had the bites cleaned properly."

He shrugged a beefy shoulder. "They are minor wounds."

"Not to one of my kind, they wouldn't be."

He grunted, a sound of mild interest.

"How auld are you?" she asked.

"Sixty-three."

"What?" she shrieked.

Riggs flinched. "Not so loud, lady, your mouth is right by my ear."

"Sorry. But sixty-three? My da was only fifty-three when he died, and no person in their right mind would have considered him young. You canna be sixty-three. 'Tis impossible."

He turned his head enough that she could brush his cheek with her lips if she'd wanted to. His hair had become damp with perspiration, and a bit of his ear showed through the silky black strands. The tip was pointed.

She had an urge to stroke the hair away so she could trace the shape with her finger. Why didn't it bother her, that foreign shape?

"How old do I seem to you?" he asked, drawing her attention from his ear to his cocksure grin.

How sad that he'd never had a woman. A man like him, handsome, virile, kind and capable, should be fending them off with sticks. "I wouldn't put you a day over thirty-five."

"A pup becomes a man at twenty-five. A thirty-five-year-old man is barely into his beard. Do you know how old King Magnus is?"

"I'm afraid to ask."

"Seventy-five."

"Most humans are considered blessed by the saints if they live to seventy-five," she said quietly. Riggs's people were much different from hers. "I take it, King Magnus isna auld."

"He's in his prime. He's strong and fit and wise. He's a fine ruler, and a fine man. You'll like him."

She scoffed.

"You will. All the ladies like King Magnus."

"I'm sure they do. He's a king." Wealth and position used to draw her eye too. Not anymore. She'd be happy to live out her measly short human life in a cozy cabin in the woods with a hearty, rugged wolf-man. Too bad the one she'd had her eye on didn't want her.

"A *good* king," Riggs insisted.

"Have you met him?"

"No. But in the fifty years he's sat the throne, he's led fairly and done much for Marann. He revised the lottery so almost any man could afford a ticket. He's brought Larna under submission. No other king or queen before him has been able to do that. And he's expanded the archives started by his mother, Queen Abigail. With so few people left, many trades were in danger of being lost, but King Magnus has collected a vast library of records so all trades can be relearned. He's never given up hope."

She harrumphed noncommittally. Of course Riggs would want her to like his king, so he'd talk the man up. She'd reserve judgment until she met him. "You mentioned the lottery yesterday as well. How does it work?"

"Every season men can buy tickets representing each of the thirty-five women of breeding age. Drawings determine which men get the honor of trying to breed. Before King Magnus, tickets used to be priced too high for most men to be able to afford them. My sire saved for twenty years to buy a single one. He got lucky. He won Hilda, my mother, for a season, and they conceived me. I'm one of the few men born to a commoner during that time. Now, thanks to King Magnus, almost any man can afford a ticket every season, and no one is permitted to buy more than ten per drawing. It means just about every man has a chance to breed."

How many tickets had Riggs bought over the years? How many times had he hoped to become as lucky as his da? She wanted to ask, but didn't.

He headed down a gentle slope. Heat poured off his neck as he kept up a brisk walk. Soreness lingered in her arms from rowing two nights ago. Now they were doubly sore from holding on around his neck, but 'twas a welcome ache.

She considered the breeding lottery. It made sense given the state of the population, though it sounded a lot like whoring to her. Only in Marann's lottery, men paid for a woman not for a few hours but for a whole "season."

"A season," she said, "Is that what you call a woman's fertile time?"

"It's just a season," he said. "You know, spring, summer, fall, winter. The drawing for winter will be soon. We may get to Chroina before it happens."

"Ah, so the men who are chosen have two or three chances to breed in a season."

Riggs cocked his head then shook it. "One chance. Women tend to have one fertile time per season."

Another difference between wolfkind and humans. "For human women, it's more," she said.

He craned his neck to meet her eyes briefly. "Two or three?"

She nodded. "Many women have a chance each month to catch a bairn." Made it bloody difficult on whores who didn't wish to do so. She'd never had a scare. Most weren't so lucky, even the very fastidious. It had made her wonder sometimes if mayhap she didn't work right down there, even before her fall.

Riggs looked straight ahead. His back went stiff. "Have you ever...caught a child?"

"No."

His shoulders relaxed. "You will," he said. "For King Magnus, you will." He nodded with certainty.

She didn't ken how to tell him he was wrong.

"How old are you?" he asked, dragging her thoughts away from breeding lotteries and kings in need of heirs.

"Twenty-five. That's well into womanhood if you're wondering. Humans are considered grown at fifteen or sixteen."

"So young." He splashed across a narrow brook and headed up the bank into the trees. It amazed her he could tell where he was going. It all looked like wilderness to her. "How long do humans live?"

"I told you, seventy-five is a ripe auld age. I've kent men and women to live into their eighties, but it's rare."

He walked in silence a long time. Then he said, "You have about fifty years left. So does King Magnus. You'll be well matched."

Likely the king would discard her once it became apparent her womb was worthless as a mule without a cart. Her only consolation was that Riggs wouldn't be around to see her inevitable dishonor. He'd be living out his life at his cabin, trapping, hunting, baking his honey-sweetened bread and eating it at his workbench, alone.

"Tell me about Larna," she said to take her mind off the sad thought. Yesterday, he'd told her about the war twenty years ago. At King Magnus's command, Marann's army had brought Larna under submission. "What started the last war?"

"Our spies found out Bantus, Larna's pathetic excuse for a king, had been hording women for himself and treating them like dirt."

Bantus. That name sounded familiar. *"Must have escaped Bantus's harem and walked here from Saroc,"* the men she'd first encountered here had said. Her skin erupted in goose bumps.

"He had a harem of wolf-women?" she asked.

"Wolfkind women," Riggs corrected. "But yeah. You could call it a harem. Refused to let other men try to breed with them until one of them gave him an heir. Only, none of them ever did."

"This was twenty years ago?"

"Yeah."

Then why would those men have assumed she'd escaped from King Bantus? "You're sure all the women got out?"

"Positive. King Magnus appointed his cousin and second in line for the throne to govern Larna. Bantus still holds the title of king, but he can't so much as wipe his ass without Ari reporting it back to King Magnus. Ari would have found out if there were any women remaining, and King Magnus sent spies besides. No evidence of women being held in Saroc was ever found."

"How long were the spies active?"

"A few years," he said with a shrug.

"So no spies have been to Larna recently?"

"No, but Ari's there keeping an eye on things. Why?"

"The Larnians you saved me from mentioned Bantus. They assumed I'd escaped from his harem, and that I'd been there a long time because I could speak their tongue. Of course, I could speak and understand them because of the gemstone. I'd only just arrived. But according to what you've told me, they should have been surprised to find a woman in Larna. They didn't seem surprised. They seemed delighted, like they couldn't believe their luck."

Riggs's back went stiff. His hands tightened under her knees.

"You doona suppose there are women in Larna?" she wondered out loud.

He shook his head. "Impossible." Only, he didn't sound convinced.

Chapter 12

RIGGS HIKED EVER deeper into the northern foothills carrying Anya on his back. Where the western forest near his home smelled of old growth and dried leaves, the northern forest smelled of moss and clean moisture. It rained more up here. Good game up here. But there was no time to hunt today. He needed to get to Valeworth, get horses, and get out. Once he had Anya well away from the village, he'd think about leaving her to hunt. Or maybe he'd just stock up on bread in Valeworth and survive on that.

She was precious. She was worth skipping meat for.

But was she as rare as he thought? *"You doona suppose there are women in Larna?"*

Impossible. Wasn't it?

He should know. He was one of the spies who'd snuck into Saroc a year after the war ended to confirm no scent trace of any woman could be found. His uncle Neil, King Magnus's war chieftain, had led the large-scale, clandestine effort. They'd even brought a pair of King Magnus's finest tracking wolves, who'd been given the scents of the evacuated Larnian women. Between the wolves and the spies, every room, passageway, and outbuilding of Castle Blackrock had been searched.

Riggs had done the dungeons himself and had been mortified to find evidence of past habitation by women, beds that were little more than piles of moldy hay, grooming combs lying forgotten on the floor, strands of long hair clinging like spider webs to rough patches on the stone walls. But no fresh scents. There had been no women in Saroc.

With all the remaining women accounted for and safe in Chroina, there would have been no place to get women, so no more searches had been done. But Anya had come by magic from another world. She wasn't wolfkind. The fact that the Larnians he'd killed hadn't been surprised at finding her didn't bode well.

What if there were other women in Larna, gotten through magical means? Women like Anya? *"Not as pretty as the little females Bantus likes to flaunt,"* he'd heard one of the Larnians say. Riggs had assumed he had been referring to she-wolves, but he could have meant women like Anya.

He hated to think it, but it was possible. By the time he shouldered through the pines atop the ridge overlooking Valeworth, he knew what he had to do.

Clouds covered the moon, stealing most of her light. Below, darkened huts huddled loosely around the log and mud buildings that housed the pub, the inn, and the trade center of the small village. He hadn't been to Valeworth in more than a year and wasn't sure he'd find anyone here, but the central buildings glowed with light. How many men held the village? Thirty? Twenty? Fewer? Were they a law-abiding bunch, or had they grown desperate enough to cheat each other and unsuspecting travelers?

He hoped there were enough men to justify keeping a few horses on hand to rent. He'd have to be careful how he asked. If he seemed desperate, they'd charge him an eyetooth. If he paid what they asked, they'd assume he had more, and they might attempt to rob him. It would be a balancing act, this trip to Valeworth.

He gave Anya's knees a squeeze. "Ready to walk?"

He felt it against his shoulder when she nodded. "Aye. My arms feel like soggy rope, they're so weary."

He crouched to let her to the ground, missing the warmth of her weight against his back the second she let go.

"*Och,* I canna even straighten them. I look like a bloody praying mantis."

He set down his axe and took up her arms one at a time to loosen the tight muscles with his rubbing fingers. "Better?"

She nodded, not looking at him. Ever since he'd told her the truth about what he intended for her, she'd been different, more reserved, not quite mistrustful, but no longer as open as she'd been. He missed the full measure of Anya.

Just as well. It was easier this way. She'd find solace from whatever hurt he'd caused her in King Magnus's arms.

His molars ground together, making his jaw ache. "Put up your hood," he growled. "And keep it up no matter what. Keep your hands hidden."

She fluffed up the hood. Her bright eyes disappeared in shadow. He saw nothing of her face. The thick wool of the cloak hid the delicate line of her shoulders. Its folds hid her beautifully curved shape. Where he'd cut off the hem so it wouldn't drag on the ground, her boots peeked out, overly large on her, just right for her height if she'd been a boy. His boy.

His chest compressed at the thought of having a child of his own. A daughter would be far too much to even long for, but a son... He still had enough to buy those ten lottery tickets when they arrived in Chroina. He no longer wanted to do so. If he couldn't have Anya, he wanted no woman. Guess that meant he was giving up hope of ever siring a child of his own.

"Why are you staring like that? Can you see me or no'?"

He cleared his throat. "You're well hidden. Keep your chin tipped down. All the men will be taller than you. It'll make it impossible for them to glimpse you."

He leaned down to sniff her.

She tucked her chin to avoid having their faces come close,

but he didn't miss how her body leaned toward his ever so slightly. "What are you doing?" she asked, voice breathy.

"You still smell like you. If anyone gets a good whiff, they might suspect. Come here. I need to cover you with my scent."

"I'm surprised I doona smell like you from riding on your back all day."

"Not enough. Come here."

She didn't come. So he dragged her into his arms and held her still while he rubbed his beard and neck all over the hood of her cloak. He squeezed her even closer and made sure the wool around her shoulders tucked into his armpits. He bent around her, surrounding her with himself.

She didn't protest as he layered his scent over hers. In fact, her arms went around his waist. She curled her hands in his shirt and buried her nose in his neck. "Are you done, yet?" she asked, but her voice was free from impatience. Her breath tickled his skin, made him hot all over.

He lowered one hand to the gentle slope below her waist. Holding her to him, he pressed forward with his hips. He did it without thought, craving pressure just there, where he was so hard for her, but needing to be closer to her as well.

A thrill of blissful sensation surged in his blood. Everything in him urged him to continue, to rub against her until pleasure wiped out his dread over a future without her.

Her woman's musk billowed up to tease him. That scent begged him to keep on like this. It also made his blood run cold. They were about to go down into a village of men who could very well be a law unto themselves. It was the worst possible time for her to release that musky scent.

"Lady," he said. His voice had gone husky. He made himself ease her away from him. It was the hardest thing he'd ever done. Even after taking two steps back, he still smelled that heavenly musk. The men in Valeworth would smell it too. "Shite. I can't take you down there smelling like you're in heat."

Anya's hands curled into fists at her sides. "Why, you bloody cur. I canna believe you! This is your fault, you and your—your manhandling."

He hurried to put a hand over her mouth. "Hush. You want to be heard?" He pointed down at the village. "By the moon, I must be out of mind to consider bringing you down there. You're going to get me killed and yourself stolen. Can't you control yourself?"

Within the shadow of the hood, her eyes blazed. Her musky scent began to fade, replaced by an almost masculine spice.

"Good. That's better. You smell like a furious warrior. Keep it up."

She made a noise of disgust. With a final glare in his direction, she set off into the trees, limping down the hill and muttering about wolf-men and their blasted noses.

Despite the possible danger awaiting them, his mouth curled into a grin as he followed.

§

ANYA KEPT CLOSE by Riggs's side as he stepped up onto a narrow, wheel-rutted road. Never in her life had she been forced to depend so thoroughly on someone so infuriating. Her arousal wasn't her own to attend to or not as she saw fit. *Noooo.* It was every bloody wolf-man's business, apparently, so long as he had a nose to sniff her with.

Och, at least she didn't smell like a dusty, wild mongrel. Wait, she did, thanks to Riggs rubbing practically every inch of himself over practically every inch of her.

How was a lass to keep from becoming aroused when an enormous, panting wolf-man handled her with such roughness and passion? How else was she to react when he tugged her snug against his ready body?

He didn't even intend to *do* anything about his readiness...or hers. *Noooo.* He planned to give her to his precious king.

"Mangy cur," she muttered as she trod the dark road.

Riggs stalked beside her, gripping his axe and scanning from side to side, watching for danger. His alert posture reminded her how precarious their situation was. She shut her mouth and hoped she smelled as angry as she felt.

Pines towered over the road. The forest was thicker than near Riggs's cabin, and the terrain was hillier. Above, the sky was black except for a haze of blue that showed where the nearly full moon tried to shine through the clouds. From the ridge where Riggs had stopped to rest, she'd seen a few wee lights burning in the village, but now that she was on a level with it, she saw nothing. Heard nothing. The place felt utterly deserted. But Riggs was on his guard, as if he sensed danger.

Her fingers twitched near her hunting knife. *Doona fash, lass. He'll keep you safe.* She might be furious with him, but she kent he would allow no harm to come to her.

The trees thinned. Large, dark mounds of earth loomed like massive anthills encroaching on the road. Long grass grew around them. Moss and weeds climbed their sides. "What are these things?" she asked, keeping her voice low.

"Cottages. Long abandoned."

"People used to live in them? What are they made of?"

"Sticks and mud."

"I like your cabin better." She glanced at Riggs and found him looking straight ahead, but his eyes had crinkled in that warm way of his that was almost like a smile. Curse her for giving him aught to smile about. She kept forgetting to be angry with him.

The steady rhythm of a trotting horse sounded behind them. A rider approached. She tensed and started to look over her shoulder, fearing trackers.

Riggs cleared his throat in a sharp warning.

She caught herself and ducked her head, staring at the ground as the horse and rider passed. Only after the rider was several paces in front of them did she risk looking up. The rider was tall and cloaked, but his hood was down, revealing black, curling hair a little shorter than Riggs's. The horse was black as well, and as big as a Percheron. Never had she seen a horse so large used for aught but pulling carts and plowing fields.

"Tracker?" she asked once the rider was out of earshot.

Riggs shook his head. "Just a traveler. Or a messenger. Trackers'll be in a group."

The mud cottages gave way to dreary buildings with crooked porches and dark interiors. She strained her ears for signs of life, hearing nothing but their footsteps and the stirring of tall grass in the breeze.

She followed Riggs around a turn in the road, and the horse from earlier came into view. It stood tied to a post outside another dilapidated building. The tip of its hind hoof dented the dirt. It paid them no heed as they approached.

Across the road was a two-story log and stone building in better repair than the rest of the village. Lantern light glowed behind the partially-opened shutters. As they drew closer, the sounds of murmured conversation floated out.

Her pulse sped. Besides the Larnians and Riggs, these were the first men she'd been near in this world.

"The Pub," Riggs said. "We'll get a meal and rent a room for the night." He nodded at the upper floor. Leaning close, he said softly, "If we don't attract attention, no one should bother us."

She swallowed and tried not to be frightened at the prospect of entering a room full of wolf-men.

A set of rickety steps led up to the porch. With a death grip on the railing, she hauled herself up, step by painful step with Riggs hovering close by her side. Once she made it to the plank-wood landing, the voices inside became clearer. There was no music.

No laughter, just a few voices murmuring quietly.

Riggs pulled open the creaky door and held it while she limped through. Past the edges of her hood, she glimpsed four long wooden tables in the low-ceilinged room. Five men clustered around the table nearest the flickering fireplace. One of them was the dark haired rider. Each had a tankard in his hands and a gleaming axe on his hip. Whether it was the fine weapon she'd grown so familiar with or the man holding it, she wasn't sure, but the axe in Riggs's hand looked more dangerous. She breathed a little easier for its proximity to her.

The conversation at the table stopped. All five heads turned their way.

She instantly looked at her boots.

Riggs steered her toward the bar with a firm hand on her shoulder.

A gravelly voice asked what he wanted.

"A room for me and the boy. And dinner." Coins jingled as Riggs plunked them on the bar.

Gradually, the murmuring across the room resumed. Riggs kept a hand on her shoulder. She felt the tension in him as snippets of the conversation behind them reached her ears.

"How old, you think... Who's the mother... Lottery winner... Lucky bastard... Not as lucky as all that. Did you see the pup's limp? Injured or lame, you think?"

After a minute, gnarled hands pushed two trenchers across the bar at them. Each held a loaf of bread and a beheaded ferret. These were followed by two tankards and a big iron key. "Room twelve," the gravelly voice said. "How old's the pup?"

"Nineteen," Riggs answered without missing a beat. "You got horses in the stables? The quicker we can get to Haletown the better."

"My cousin, Len, has two mares he could rent you. They're not shod, but they'll get you where you need to go. You'll find him in the trade center."

A pause where Riggs might have nodded his understanding. "You got a tray so we can take our dinner to our room? And how often do messengers come through?"

Those knobby fingers fidgeted on the bar. "Who's the mother?"

"Hilda," Riggs said promptly, as if he'd anticipated the question. "A tray before morning would be nice."

The barkeep grunted and went away. While he was gone, Riggs passed her his axe so he could have both his hands free.

She slipped it under her cloak, careful not to expose her hands for more than a second.

Riggs nodded his approval, and she ducked her head again when she heard the barkeep coming back.

A wooden tray clattered onto the bar beside their food. The barkeep hollered, "Bilkes! This man's got a job for you."

The murmuring behind them stopped. A bench scraped against the floorboards, as though one of the men had risen from the table.

"You need a delivery?" A big man with a tenor lilt came up beside her and set his tankard on the bar. Must be Bilkes. He spoke to Riggs over her head. She felt his gaze on her and resisted the impulse to look up.

Riggs said, "I've got a message to get to Chroina."

The man sipped his ale. "I wasn't planning on heading back that way 'til day after tomorrow. How fast were you thinking?"

"Tomorrow night. No later."

Bilkes whistled. "That'll cost you. Who you want it to go to?"

"Neil at the armory."

"The war chieftain?" Bilkes asked, surprised. "That'll cost you even more, and I'll be needing your guarantee the ornery brute won't slit my throat when I find him."

"Give him my name, and he won't. Riggs the trapper."

149

She wondered how he knew Marann's war chieftain. She'd remember to ask when they were safe in their room.

"Seven crowns," Bilkes said.

Riggs's loose fist opened and closed on the bar. "I can't afford seven. I can do five and a half. I'll bring you the message after my son and I have had our dinner."

"Wouldn't be worth my time for less than six and a half." By the nearness of his voice, she could tell Bilkes was staring at the top of her hooded head. He inhaled long and deep.

Angry. Be angry. Think about wolf-men and their bloody noses.

"Never mind. I'll go to Chroina myself after Haletown."

"Now, now," said the messenger. "Maybe I could do it for six even. Have your dinner. I'll be here to take the message in an hour." He started to move away. His knuckles brushed her arm.

She tensed but didn't permit herself to shy from the touch.

Riggs snagged Bilkes's elbow. Had he seen the touch? Had he noticed Bilkes sniffing her? Were they about to be exposed? She braced herself for Riggs's reaction.

"Can you get me paper and a quill?" he asked.

"Not very prepared, for a man needing to send a message, are you? That'll cost you another quarter crown."

Riggs growled low in his throat. "Six and a tenth, and not a kernel more. And for that price, I want wax to seal it too."

Bilkes huffed a short laugh. "All right. What's your room? I'll find what you need and leave it outside your door."

Riggs told him their room number and herded her up the stairs.

Their cramped room smelled musty with disuse until the aromas of warm bread, fragrant ale and lantern oil filled the space. She laid Riggs's axe on the patchy furs covering the bed and stared at the tray of food he set on an uneven table. The bread looked good, but the blood oozing from the ferrets' necks chased her appetite away.

"You take both loaves," Riggs said. "I'll eat the meat." He took a long drink from his tankard. A fine sheen of sweat coated his cheeks. He looked like he'd just run a gauntlet.

Thank the saints she'd found some dandelion leaves and mayweed to nibble on this afternoon. It appeared wolf-men didn't eat vegetation of any sort. Just meat and bread. Letting down her hood, she rescued the loaf from the trencher with less blood pooled on it. When she held the bread at an angle, blood dripped off the bottom. She picked away the soggy parts then perched on the edge of the bed to eat. The furs were stiff and matted and smelled of crumbling leather and moth-eaten bedding. They were nothing like the soft furs Riggs had all over his cabin and on the bed in his cave. Wrinkling her nose at the shoddy craftsmanship, she tore into her bread.

Riggs turned the chair at the desk to face the bed. He sat down and ran both hands through his hair, ignoring the ferrets.

"No one suspects, do they?" she asked around a mouthful.

"I don't think so. The messenger sniffed you, but didn't seem overly curious. You don't smell female. Maybe he wondered why you smelled so much like me, but if you're my son, you would, wouldn't you?"

She shrugged. "Mayhap he wondered why you want to send a message to the war chieftain." She ate more bread and washed it down with some ale. "Why do you?"

His gaze darted to the door. He raked his hands through his hair again until his curls stood on end. "Neil is my uncle. If anything happens to me before we reach Chroina, I need someone I trust to know about you."

She paused in her chewing. Riggs carried a heavy burden. He carried it alone.

She swallowed her last bite and shook her head. "No," she said gently. "Doona send a message. Anything you write, the messenger can read."

"He won't. I'll seal it. It's a crime for a third party to break a seal."

She snorted. "Aye, you'll seal it. With wax and a seal he brings you. Who's to say he won't have a duplicate in his pocket so he can replace it?"

Riggs pulled somat from his pocket and held it out to her.

She took it. A ring. It was made of heavy brass and sized for a man with large hands. Across the top was a seal portraying a scythe beside a sheaf of wheat and a sickle moon surrounded by several stars.

"When I came of age, my mother gave it to me. Said she wished she could have been more of a mother to me, but she was proud of the job my sire did. This and another just like it belonged to her sire. He gave this one to her on his deathbed, and he gave the other to his son, my uncle Neil. I use this to seal all me letters. If the messenger tampers with it or replaces it, my uncle will cut him down before he's finished handing the thing over."

The metal was warm from being in Riggs's pocket. She treasured the feel of it in her palm and stroked her fingers over the seal. 'Twas an honor to hold such a personal item of his. Reluctantly, she handed it back.

"It's lovely. Truly. But it still won't ensure your letter is secure. There's nothing to stop the messenger from simply reading the letter and destroying it."

Riggs looked at her uncertainly. "A dishonest messenger doesn't remain a messenger very long. Most are honest. I use them often without issue."

She harrumphed. "You told me the villages are descending more and more into lawlessness. Mayhap he's been honest up until now. But you've told him you ken the war chieftain and because you want the message to get to him quickly, he'll ken it's important. What if he thinks to take credit for whatever news ye have to share then learns you have custody of a woman?" She spread her palms.

"Shite. You're right." He ran his hands through his hair again.

"I'm no' saying doona write to your uncle. I just think you should be careful what you say. You must assume other eyes will read it. And you shouldna rely on the message reaching its destination."

Riggs leaned forward and settled his head into his hands. He rubbed his temples with the pads of his fingers and cast her a sheepish glance. "How did you get to be so wise? You think so many steps ahead."

She laughed without mirth. "I'm no' wise. I'm a devious woman who has done much evil. No' hard to predict wickedness in others when one's own heart is wicked." Memories of the ill she'd done to her laird and clan, to Darcy, assaulted her. *I might have murdered a wee ane like the Larnians Riggs so despises.*

He frowned at her. "I don't believe that."

She didn't have the energy to argue. She said only, "'Tis true. I've done many vile things." Just as well that he planned to give her to his king. With her head for plotting, she'd fit in well with a royal court. Bitterness twisted in her stomach. She'd been a silly lass to think she might merit a decent man like Riggs after the things she'd done.

He got up from his chair and knelt in front of her. He put his hands on her knees. His thumbs gently stroked, sending tingles racing over her skin. She ought to push them off. She didn't deserve his comfort. But selfish hag that she was, she absorbed every detail of the moment so she could cherish it later, when Riggs was gone and she was naked in the arms of a stranger. The warm weight of his hands, his woodsy scent, his charmingly tousled hair, the earnest regard in his gaze.

"I've seen wickedness," he said. "I've looked it in the eye, and I've fought it. I know it well enough to recognize it, and I promise there's no wickedness in you."

She shook her head. He was wrong.

"There isn't," he insisted. "I would know it if so. If you were wicked, I wouldn't lo—"

A knock came at the door, making them both start.

He whispered a curse. Her own heart echoed it. Whatever he'd been about to say, the loss of those words rattled around in her chest like dried peas in a bowl.

"The messenger," Riggs said. He picked up his axe from the bed and cracked the door. After a moment, he opened it, squatted to pick up somat off the floor and closed the door again. "My paper and quill." He shook his head. Humor quirked his mouth, but he wouldn't quite meet her eyes. "Useless now. I have much to tell my uncle, but nothing I'd risk having another lay eyes on." He was back to running his hand through his hair. He began pacing, restless.

"Eat your meal," she told him. "Then see about the horses." Activity would soothe him. She could use some activity too, but she kent better than to leave this room.

He nodded and sat down to eat the ferrets. When he finished, he took up the quill and began writing on the paper.

"I thought you decided no' to chance a message."

"I'm not going to mention you," he said without looking at her. "But I need to write something after hiring the messenger. It'll look strange if I don't bring him something to deliver. I'll be careful what I say."

Och, he was right. If he didn't bring down a message, it might raise suspicions.

He scratched out a few lines then paused in thought and wrote some more.

"How often do you write?" she asked. She rarely had need of writing and was slow at it when she did. She usually reserved the skill for copying perfume recipes or methods of harvesting and preparing herbs.

"I send a letter to my mother every season, and receive one in return." He glanced at her with a proud smile before returning to the letter. "And I correspond with my uncle occasionally. When my sire was alive, he made me write out an entire volume about trapping and tanning for the king's archives. Had me write the damn thing so many times until it was just so." His huff of humor belied the grumbling words.

Riggs was decent, capable, and literate. He could fight when necessary and fight well. Better that she warm the bed of a man who would never love her than attempt to earn the affections of a man as fine as this one. She sighed as she watched his powerful arm move with practiced quill strokes.

After filling half the page, he folded the letter and set the pot of green wax the messenger had left atop the oil lamp to melt it.

"What did you write?"

He half turned in the chair to face her. "Just that I tracked a marbled boar into Larna and overheard some things that might concern the king. And that I would come for a visit after bringing my son to Haletown to see a doctor." He smiled crookedly. "I made up some nonsense about how his legs pain him and with winter coming, we hope to find some better medicine."

"Good. That's clever. He'll ken ye have no son, so he'll understand you're traveling with someone. But if the messenger reads it, he willna think anything of it, especially since he's seen how I walk."

He poured a spot of hot wax and pressed his da's ring into it. Holding it there, he said, "And if we don't make it to Chroina, Neil will know I intended to come, and that I had news too important to put in a letter. At least I hope he'll realize it. He might think I had too much Firebrand and was half out of my mind when I wrote it."

"We'll make it," she said.

He turned a soft, weary gaze on her as he stood to leave. That look said so many things. *I hope you're right. I appreciate your faith. I wish I could keep you for myself.* She might have imagined that last.

"I'll be right back." He stepped out, and she heard the key in the lock as he left to find the messenger.

Taking advantage of her momentary privacy, she found a dented pan under the bed that she supposed was meant to be a chamber pot and quickly relieved herself. She went to the window to dump it but thought twice about opening the shutters. She might be seen. But it wouldn't do to spend the night in a cramped room with a full chamber pot, especially with Riggs's sharp sense of smell.

Ah, the cloak. She shrugged into it and pulled the hood around her head. Thus hidden, she opened the shutters. Their room overlooked the road they'd walked in on. The large black horse still stood across from the pub. While she threw the contents of the pan down to the gutters, the front door opened.

Angry men's voices rose to her ears, preceding a jumble of bodies pouring out of the pub and down the steps. At the center of the brawling knot of men was a tall head of curly black hair. The messenger? She couldn't see his face.

The man threw a punch, knocking another of the men to the ground. He whipped his head around and searched the side of the building until he spotted her in the window. Brown eyes flecked with molten gold blazed up at her.

Riggs!

Her heart turned into a pounding drum as four of the men from the pub made a circle around him and drew their axes. *Och,* had Riggs taken his axe with him when he'd left? She couldn't remember. She turned to scan the room, relieved when she didn't see the weapon.

She started to turn back to the brawl, but heard the faint

clicking of a key fitting into the lock. The lock tumbled. The door opened.

A pair of men shouldered into the room. One was jowly and gray with age, and he gaped at her as if he'd seen a ghost. The other had to be the messenger, Bilkes. He had sharp features, like an eagle, and darting green eyes. "Poor little lamb," he said in his tenor lilt. "I've got some medicine to take your mind off your legs." He cupped his cock and bollocks through his trews with one hand and pitched Riggs's crumpled missive onto the bed with the other.

The gray-haired man slapped the back of Bilkes's head. "Show the lady some respect." She recognized the voice of the barkeep. He squinted at her and licked his lips. She got the distinctive impression he saw currency when he looked at her.

Beneath her cloak, she inched her hand toward her hunting knife.

"Thought you were mad, when you said you smelled a female downstairs." The barkeep nudged Bilkes with his elbow. "Guess your nose is better than mine." He thumbed the bulbous appendage in question.

"Told you," Bilkes said with a smirk. "Hard to mistake the scent of a woman. Even harder to mistake the scent of a human, no matter that a dumb trapper tried to cover it with his own."

She gasped. Bilkes had been around humans. That had to mean somat, but what? She couldn't think. Her mind was numb with terror.

"Quickly," the barkeep said. "Get her away before the others finish with the trapper. I'll meet you at Ferndell in the morning and we can discuss what to do with her."

She found the knife and curled her hand around the hilt. Her heart hammered at the thought of men outside trying to "finish" Riggs.

The messenger advanced on her.

She took a breath and let loose the biggest, loudest scream she could muster.

Chapter 13

JUST AS ANYA had hoped, both men clapped their hands over their sensitive wolf-man ears.

"By Danu! Make her stop!" Bilkes shouted.

The barkeep lumbered around the bed toward her, sneering to show bulky, yellow teeth. He fluttered his hands around his head as though he could swat away her screams. She kept it up, even though she felt like a crazed banshee.

She drew her knife and dodged the barkeep as he reached for her. Her legs gave out and she fell onto the bed. Bilkes scooped her up. Curse it!

She screamed some more, aiming her voice right at the side of his head.

He bellowed and bent his neck to press his ear to his shoulder. "Shut it! Shut it!"

She didn't "shut it." She kept screaming while she wriggled free from his hold. On her way to landing in a heap on the floor, she stuck him in the stomach with the knife. He groaned and bent forward around the wound.

Saints above. She'd stabbed a man.

She didn't give herself time to think on it. On hands and knees, she scurried out the door, cursing her legs for being so bloody worthless she couldn't even flee from these bastards on foot.

At the end of the hall, she came to the stairs. How would she get down them? What was happening to Riggs? Could he hold his own against those men? She had to get to him.

Grabbing onto the banister, she hauled herself up and started down the steps on her feet, clutching the rail.

A cruel arm banded around her chest and yanked her back against a hard body.

She screamed again.

"Shut it, I say! You'll raise the low realm with all that racket!" Bilkes. The stabbing hadn't taken. Looked like she'd have to do it again.

She kept screaming, hoping to distract him from the blade still in her hand until she could position herself for a better attack, but luck was not on her side. A gnarled hand seized her wrist and squeezed until pain made her drop the knife. The barkeep.

Together, they manhandled her down the stairs.

"Shut her up," the barkeep said. "She'll alert the whole damn village."

"For Danu's sake, lady, I'm not going to hurt you!" Bilkes said when they reached the empty barroom. On the heels of that promise, he soundly slapped her. And it bloody damn well hurt.

He hauled her up so her face was an inch from his. His green eyes sparked with heated warning. She'd seen men look at each other like that—it was a look a man gave to someone he wouldn't mind hurting very badly. His face was red, and veins popped in his neck. "You listen and you listen good. There are twenty men in the trade center down the lane. If they hear a female bleating like a ewe, they'll all come this way with their pricks out. Now, we can leave nice and tidy without a pack of randy men on our trail or you can keep up that fucking screaming and draw them all straight to you."

She shut it. Escaping two men was definitely preferable to escaping twenty.

He dragged her out into the road.

She made a dead weight of her body, forcing him to do all the work.

Unfortunately, he seemed more than up to the task. Bloody durable, these wolf-men. When they were on her side, that was a boon. When she needed to hurt one, it was unfortunate.

She craned her neck toward the knot of fighting men. One form lay motionless on the ground.

Don't be Riggs.

The men shuffled around. There he was! Still standing, tall and broad shouldered, feet spread, muscles straining against his shirt. But he still faced three men. He had his axe clashed with one, and the other two gripped their axes like they'd step in if their friend needed help.

Saints above, it was just a matter of time before he fell. He couldn't keep this up.

She had to do somat to help him. But what? What could a cripple whore do without creating a fuss?

Och, there was one skill she'd once employed to accomplish whatever she desired. She hadn't tried it since her fall, but if there was ever a time to attempt it again, 'twas now.

Bilkes lugged her to his big black horse.

"You all right to ride tonight?" the barkeep asked. He stood with the reins in his hand.

"I'll be fine." Bilkes shoved her into the barkeep's stale-smelling arms and mounted. "Barely a scratch. Hand her up and make sure no one follows us."

"I'll hold 'em off. Best hurry, though. They'll be done with the trapper soon." The barkeep grabbed her under her arms and thrust her up in the air. "Make sure she doesn't come to harm. She'll be worth more if she's untouched. Hurry, now."

They meant to sell her to the highest bidder. Mangy curs. Not if she could bloody help it. She wound her arm around Bilkes's neck and snuggled up to him, sitting sideways on his lap.

His posture went stiff. She didn't blame him for being

suspicious after she'd stabbed him.

"I'm sorry I hurt you," she said as he yanked the horse's head around and kicked it into a trot. "I was frightened. I can see now I'm better off, though. The trapper can't even hold his own against four drunkards. Thank heaven I've found a strong protector." The lie tasted bitter on her tongue, but it would be worth it if she could find a knife on this man and stab him proper.

While she cooed in his ear, she watched the fight over his shoulder. A man advanced at Riggs's back, making her cringe. Riggs ducked forward to dodge the axe of the man in front while kicking backward to send the man behind him flying. Pride sealed her determination. *Hang on, love.*

Bilkes's shoulders relaxed. "If he had any wits, he wouldn't have let you say a word up in your room. Downstairs, I'd suspected from your scent, but it was your voice that gave you away."

Och, how stupid of her. She should have kept to whispers. This was her fault. *I'll make it right.* "How fortunate for me you heard." She inched her hand around his side, looking for a sheath or a hilt.

"What are you doing?"

"I'm checking your wound. Where is it? Thank heaven it's just a scratch. I hope you'll let me tend it when we get where we're going." Her pinkie brushed the rough edge of a sheath. He had a knife on him.

He moved her fingers to the oozing wound a few inches away. "It's the least you can do. Maybe I'll let you serve me in other ways too, to make amends."

Not bloody likely. He hissed as she gently prodded the wound.

"Mmm. Sore, aye? Fear no'. I shall make amends, indeed." She prepared to jab her fingers into the torn flesh and slip his hunting knife free with her other hand.

A sudden change in the horse's direction threw her off balance as Bilkes steered the horse around a corner. She had to grab his shirt to hang on. Damn. She'd have to get into position again.

He heeled their mount into a canter. They were about to pass a building that would block her view of the fight. She strained for one last glimpse of Riggs and found him standing in the road with fallen villagers all around him. His eyes flashed in the darkness, watching her go. He didn't see the man staggering to his feet behind him or the axe the man raised and brought swinging down.

The sight was wiped away by the dark wood of an abandoned building. Her heart lunged into her throat. She cried out to warn Riggs, but the sound of a horse screaming drowned out all else.

Bilkes cursed and jerked the reins. Several dark shapes crowded the road. Horses with riders.

Bilkes's horse reared. He tumbled backward, taking her with him.

Her gut thrummed in that moment of weightlessness before the fall grabbed her and threw her to the ground. *Och,* she hated falling!

She hit hard. Her bones rattled. Her breath whooshed out.

Hooves pounded all around her. Too close! She'd be trampled! She covered her head and curled into a ball.

Equine grunts and whinnies exploded into the night. Men shouted.

"There she is! Get her!"

"Mind your horse! Don't trample her!"

She cowered like a bloody tortoise. If she was to be trampled, she'd bloody well see it coming like the Keith she was. She rolled and looked up. A pair of great hooves flashed above her. Bilkes's black horse, riderless and rearing.

A body covered hers.

"Look out!"

Bilkes. Protecting her. He rolled them.

She could see nothing past his broad shoulders, but she felt it when the hooves came down. They struck Bilkes, who had moved her out of the way. He jerked and grunted. His arms convulsed around her.

He'd taken the blow in her place.

She screamed.

A pair of boots slammed to the ground. A hand with black, pointed fingernails reached for her and grabbed her by the back of her cloak. She was hauled up against the chest of a bearded man with eyes pale as ice. Aodhan had eyes like that, but there had often been warmth in the Keith war chieftain's eyes when he'd looked at her. There had never been an ounce of warmth in these eyes. Never.

"Been looking for you." His voice was so deep it was part growl.

The trackers.

Fear froze her veins.

Riggs was surely dead, and she was in the hands of the trackers he'd worked so hard to keep her from.

§

DAWN BROKE COLD and misty. Anya sat astride the tallest and broadest horse she'd ever been on in front of the tracker she surmised to be the leader, the one who had yanked her up from the road. The other three deferred to him, and he carried himself like an important man, with absolute confidence and disdain. Even though she had yet to get a clear look at him, his air of command came through in the relaxed way his hips swiveled with the horse's gait and the unconcerned way he rested his wrists on her thighs with the reins loose in his fists. An expert horseman without a care in the world as he stole a woman away from an enemy village. His manner alone told her he did not expect anyone to challenge them for her.

She should have been repulsed by her proximity to such men, especially when they were the very ones Riggs had worked so hard to keep her from. She should have wanted to shove his hands off her lap and leap from their mount. She should have wanted to get away at any cost. But she was too empty to feel anything. Too soul-weary to do anything.

Her wolf-man was gone.

Dead. Killed by his countrymen while trying to protect her. Would anyone bury him? Would anyone but her mourn him? 'Twas a pity he couldn't have died doing somat much more honorable, like protecting a woman worthy of his affection and his hope.

Her body ached from her fall, but the hole in her chest left by Riggs's loss hurt immeasurably worse. Without his presence to anchor her, she felt lost. Adrift.

Vaguely, she took in her surroundings. A familiar boulder here, a remembered pasture with a crumbling wall there. The trackers were covering the same ground Riggs had trod yesterday with her on his back. Which meant they were taking her in the opposite direction from Chroina.

Riggs had wanted her to go to Chroina, to King Magnus. Mayhap he'd believed in error she might be able to help his people, but it had been his dying wish to deliver her safely to his king. What kind of ungrateful shrew was she if she didn't do everything in her power to see it through for him?

King Magnus wouldn't want her, not when she confessed to being barren on top of her scarred and broken appearance. But mayhap he'd protect her since Riggs had seemed to think so highly of him. Protection was more than she suspected she'd get from these men.

There was also the news Riggs had wanted to tell his uncle

about there possibly being more women in Larna. Yet more reason for her to get to Chroina.

She'd do it or die trying. Her wolf-man deserved no less.

Resolve burned behind her breastbone, urging her to action. Each step the trackers' horses took away from Marann's capital was like a stick poking a hornets' nest, stirring her anger more and more. She needed to escape these men, and soon if she had any hope of finding her way to the city that was a three-day ride east from Valeworth.

She began to study the trackers with an eye for their readiness. What would it take to escape them?

One man rode up ahead. Two behind. Each carried a broadsword and had a sheathed dagger strapped to his calf. They wore drab cloaks over plaids that might have once been dyed a rich blue but were now faded to dull gray. Just yesterday, she'd listened to Riggs talk about how there had been no trade to speak of in decades. Luxuries like fancy silks and dyes from foreign lands were things of the past. The pleated wool covering the thighs of the man she rode with was less threadbare than what the other men wore, but not by much.

The men carried themselves like soldiers. They would be well acquainted with their weapons. She would not be able to fight them. Mayhap she could take one man by surprise, steal his dagger, and slit his throat, but the other three would not give her another chance to surprise them. Seduction might earn her a chance at killing a second man, but again, 'twould only work once.

If they were smart, and she suspected they were, they'd sleep in shifts. She would not be able to sneak away in the night, especially considering she'd need one of their horses if she were to have any chance of outrunning them. If by some miracle she managed to get away on foot, they'd merely track her down again.

Where did that leave her?

She'd have to kill them, all four of them, to stand a chance of reaching Chroina.

A cold pit of dread sank in her stomach like a stone. Stabbing Bilkes was one thing, but even if she had the means to kill four men, she didn't think she had the cods to do it.

Och, *Riggs, why did you leave me? What should I do?*

Mayhap if she learned more, a solution would present itself. "Where are you taking me?" she asked the leader.

His hands tensed on her thighs. "You shouldn't be able to speak our language."

"Well I can. Where are you taking me? What'll you do with me?"

Leaning around her, he grabbed her chin and tilted her face to his scrutiny. "You're not an escapee. How did you learn our tongue?"

"I'm gifted with languages," she lied. "Where are you taking me?"

"How long have you been in our realm?"

Our realm? He wouldn't use that word unless he kent there were other "realms." Not to mention, he'd studied her face and would see she was no wolf-woman. And just like the Larnians who'd first found her, he wasn't surprised. He must ken of other human women. Had he seen them? Where were they? She had to learn more and bring this information to Riggs's uncle.

"A long time," she lied again. Lying was easy for her. Always had been. "Who says I'm no' an escapee? Mayhap we all worked together to get me out. Amazing what women can do when they work together."

"Liar. I'd recognize you. If you were from Bantus's harem, I'd have had you. I've had all his pets."

"Good to be the lieutenant," the soldier behind them muttered. "Rest of us settle for wolf cunt."

"Silence," the leader barked.

Saints above. These were evil men to speak of women like pets to be passed around and used. To speak of bestiality. At least she'd learned somat. He'd mentioned Bantus's harem and hadn't batted an eye when she'd used the plural "women." That meant there *were* human women in Larna. How horrible for them.

"Hmm, I wonder if our little Maranner weasel has been keeping you secret from King Bantus. Are you Ari's pet? Is that how you learned our tongue?"

Ari. That was the name of King Magnus's second in command. He was the one Riggs had told her kept an eye on King Bantus.

"Aye. You caught me. I belong to Ari." If she could find this Ari, mayhap they could discover a way to help the other women. Mayhap Ari would help her get to Chroina and King Magnus. "If you return me to him, he'll give you a great reward."

"Oh, I'll get my reward all right," he said, and he shifted in the saddle so she felt his hard cock behind her. "I'll get it soon as we get you back to Saroc."

"Ari doesna like to share," she said coolly.

"Another lie. He most definitely likes to share. And he likes to watch. He and Bantus both."

Och, no. He made it sound as though Ari was in on whatever was going on in Larna. Best not end up in his hands then.

She'd have to make her escape soon. Nothing but horrors upon horrors awaited her in Larna. It tripled her determination to get the news of the other women to King Magnus and his war chieftain.

"A lass can try," she said lightly, pretending to cooperate.

The leader huffed what might have been a chuckle. Even his laugh seemed cold and superior. "No harm in trying. I like a cunning woman. So does Bantus. More fun to break."

She gulped. If her resolve were an entity within her, 'twould be nodding resolutely. To avoid the fate these men carried her toward, she'd be more than happy to kill them all. Then she'd see about doing somat for the women trapped in Larna. She could think of no better way to honor Riggs's memory.

Pretending to drift to sleep, she bided her time. Her opportunity would come, and when it did, she'd show this horse's arse what a cunning woman could do.

Chapter 14

HUNGER GNAWED AT Riggs's stomach as he shuffled through the darkening forest on the trail of the men who had ridden away with Anya. His legs burned from running. His arms ached from the fight with the villagers in the road. His stomach cramped with the need to feed. Those two ferrets at the pub had barely sated him, and that had been nearly a full day ago. He should hunt and then rest before continuing on. But he didn't stop. He wouldn't stop as long as Anya was in danger.

Back in Valeworth, he'd been distracted from the attacking villagers by the sight of the messenger riding away with her. One of the villagers had taken advantage and tried to decapitate him from behind like a coward. The telltale whistle of steel through the air was almost the last thing he'd ever heard, but he'd managed to dodge the blow. With urgency to get to Anya thrumming through his veins, he'd cut down the last attacker and run after the messenger only to find the man limping off the road with the help of the barkeep. Anya was nowhere to be seen. But in the distance, four horsemen disappeared around a bend in the road. The trackers.

He'd given chase on foot, keeping to the shadows and remaining far enough back not to alert the riders. He'd glimpsed Anya sitting in the saddle in front of one of the men. Before long, it had become clear where they were headed. His cave. Good. They'd likely make camp there tonight. He'd have the advantage of knowing the land. He'd need every advantage he could get.

Another hour of jogging brought him near the familiar river that wound through the valley in the shadow of his cave. He slowed to a silent walk as he neared the spot where Anya had built the fire two nights ago. He would kill the trackers either way, but if he found one hair out of place on her head when he arrived, he'd make sure they suffered.

It was full dark when he crept up to a thicket that shielded him from the clearing. He cocked his head to listen. Two voices murmuring low, both of them male. The sounds of wood being piled.

"By the moon," one man said, his voice placing him the distance of a cast fishing line away. "How long does it take a woman to empty her bladder?"

Riggs found a narrow cleft through the thicket that gave him a view of the clearing and the river beyond. The speaker leaned on a tree with his back to him. He had on a faded blue Larnian war kilt. And he was fully armed with a sword and dagger to Riggs's axe and hunting knife. For all the Larnians' faults, lack of readiness wasn't typically one of them. These soldiers would be as well-trained in using their weapons as Riggs was with his. They wouldn't go down as easily as the villagers had. He settled in to rest from his run and gather intelligence. If he could confirm the other two were off hunting, he'd take the odds of two against one and attack now.

"Not as long as she's taking," said the one making the woodpile. "Go put an eye on her. Make sure she's not trying to escape."

"Of course I'm no' trying to escape. What kind of fool do you take me for?" Anya.

His heart skipped a beat. Her voice came from the tree line. He had to shift to see her through the thicket. She limped toward the woodpile, unharmed and lovely as ever. The fist that had closed around his heart on the road in Valeworth relaxed a fraction.

"Not going anywhere on those legs, yeah?" said the man leaning on the tree.

"Bet they spread just fine though," the other said.

Riggs swallowed the growl that rumbled in his throat.

"Wouldn't you like to find out?" Anya said. "You'll have to wait your bloody turn, though. Bantus gets me first. Isn't that right? Then Ari. Then your lovely commander. Then the lowly soldiers can have their go. I've got a bloody parade of Larnians and one traitorous Maranner to look forward to in my bed, lucky lass that I am."

The men chuckled.

Riggs's head spun with all she'd just said. Ari? A traitor? And for her to know the order in which she was to be raped, the men must have been talking, taunting her. She was taking it with pretended humor, but she had to be shaking with fear inside. His poor lady. Thankfully, it didn't sound like anyone had touched her yet. They were saving her for Bantus.

That sadistic shite wouldn't lay a hand on her. Nor would these maggots. Which meant he couldn't risk failure, especially since he was the only Maranner that knew about her other than the wounded messenger and the Valeworth barkeep. If he lost her tonight, there would likely be no rescue for her. Unacceptable.

"I'm more than happy to wait, sweet thing," the man at the woodpile said. "Long as Bantus and Commander Lance don't rough you up too much."

Riggs was going to kill that one first.

"What? Ari doesn't like it rough," Anya quipped. "Must be a Larnian thing, violence."

The men chuckled again, not denying it.

He had a stranglehold on his axe. This was intolerable, hearing Anya banter with men who would just as soon rape her.

A great distance behind him and to the left, it sounded like an ox was crashing through the trees. He tensed, turned his head. His ears pinpointed the direction of the sound, to the south just on the other side of the briar patch where good forest hare could be found. The sounds were too bold to be a wild animal. Must be one of the other trackers returning from a hunt. He relaxed his grip on his axe, shifting to peer through the thicket as the sounds grew closer.

A naked man with a dead boar piglet under each arm plowed through the underbrush and into the clearing. His face and torso were caked with blood. He must have just eaten the sow, a standard brown, coarse-hair variety, judging by the plain coats of the piglets.

Three men now, and Anya in their midst. Definitely not the right time to attack. He should slip away and go after the fourth tracker. If the man was hunting, he'd be naked and unarmed. Riggs could pick him off and start chipping away at those long odds. But the thought of leaving Anya made his stomach clench.

She looked up from the kindling and said to the new man, "I hope one of those is for me."

The man strode to her and tossed the larger of the piglets at her feet. "Only the sweetest meat for a lady so fine."

She snorted. "Fine as a lame mule with a bedraggled face. How do you ken your king is going to want me? Mayhap he'll slit your throats for bringing him somat so ugly."

The man squatted in front of her. He extended a hand to touch her cheek, but she swatted it away with a fierce scowl.

That's my lady.

"If I say you're fine, you're fine," the tracker said. His voice was low and dangerous, but he didn't try to touch her again. "And a pity it is you're so fine, because if you really were ugly, maybe Bantus wouldn't want you. Maybe I'd kill these lousy sods and keep you for myself."

"You could try," said the one who'd laid the woodpile. He

finished his task and scraped flint to start the kindling burning.

"Aye, fight amongst yourselves," Anya said, cheerfully. "Wouldn't Commander Lance be pleased to find you all dead at each other's hands and me ridden away on one of your horses, all while he was out hunting?"

So the one still missing was the commander, and he was, in fact, out hunting. Anya didn't seem to be in immediate danger, so Riggs snuck around to where the horses were tied, keeping an ear to the men by the growing fire. They continued their banter while he spotted the piles of discarded clothing at the tree line, confirming this was where the two hunters had left from. One pile had a brighter, newer looking war kilt folded at the bottom. The linen shirt on top was crisper.

He would have to come out from behind the tree to scent the clothing. He waited for an opportunity.

The one who had found the piglets took them to the bank to skin them. He disappeared around some boulders. Riggs focused on the other two.

"Bantus'll like this one," said the one leaning on the tree. "Feisty as a plucked hen." He shoved off and headed toward the horses, right toward Riggs.

Shite! He tucked himself tight behind the tree.

The tracker approached. Riggs heard the clinking of saddlebag buckles being undone. A minute later, the tracker's footsteps retreated back to the fire.

Riggs released the breath he'd been holding. After another minute, he peered around the tree.

"No fighting, then?" Anya said. "*Och,* I suppose I must make your tea, then, if I'm to be in your company for a while." She stood with a wince and limped to face the soldier, her hand outstretched for the teapot he must have grabbed from the saddlebag. By the moon, she was beautiful, even dusty from the road and with lines of strain bracketing her mouth.

"Women don't serve," the soldier said. "Ben'll make your dinner." He nodded down the bank toward the hunter skinning the boars. "I'll make the tea."

Riggs almost snorted. The Larnians couldn't conscience letting her make tea for them, but they had no problem taunting her and planning to use her in the worst possible way. King Magnus should have wiped out every last Larnian male while he had the chance.

"Where I come from, 'tis a grave insult for a lady to sit on her hands while a man fetches water," Anya said.

Both men near the fire had their attention on her. It was now or never. He tiptoed to the pile of crisp clothing, grabbed it up and returned to his hiding spot, heart hammering.

"Now give me the bloody teapot and let me do somat to keep my hands busy," Anya continued.

He heard the man with the teapot huff. "If you insist. Maybe I'll just put my feet up and watch you hobble about unnecessarily, yeah?"

Phew. He'd evaded the trackers' notice. As his pulse returned to normal, he buried his nose in the kilt and shirt, dragging the nose-ruffling scent of Larnian deep into his lungs.

"Funny one, he thinks he is," Anya muttered.

Riggs dropped the clothing and put his eyes on her one last time before leaving to take care of the commander. She took the teapot and tin of tealeaves from the tracker and carried them off to the river. He longed to have her in his arms. It would happen before this night was through.

Hang on, lady. I'll be back as soon as I can.

§

ANYA NIBBLED THE cooked boar for appearances, but she tasted nothing. Her stomach was in knots. Her hands shook. She pulled the sleeves of her shirt over them to hide the shaking. Also to protect herself. No matter how thoroughly she'd washed at the river, she dared not handle her food directly after harvesting roots of water hemlock to slip into her captors' tea.

Each of the three men had sipped their tea. The deed was done. No taking it back now. All she could do was wait.

It could take anywhere from minutes to an hour for the effects of the water hemlock to appear. Hopefully, none of the men would show signs of poisoning before their leader returned and helped himself to the tea as well. They called him Commander Lance or simply Lance, a fitting name for a man so coolly dangerous. If she'd had her way, she would have poisoned him first and taken her chances with the other three rather than the other way around, but fate had not given her such a choice.

Her gaze traveled from one man to the next. Across the fire from her was the one the others called Ced. A right cocky bastard, that one. Handsome, but with a cruel set to his mouth. Beside him, reclining on an elbow was the one she'd heard Lance call Gord. She hated him the most. Whenever he looked at her, 'twas with a leer that made her skin crawl. It had taken every ounce of effort she possessed to act casual with him—if she'd curled her lip the way she wanted to when addressing him, he might not have trusted her to make the tea. Nearest to her was Ben, the one who'd hunted and prepared the boar for her dinner.

Poor Ben. He wasn't a bad sort, but he wasn't courageous enough to go against his fellows. What they had planned for her, it bothered him. She could tell by the pity in his amber eyes when he looked at her. But the way his gaze shifted when she tried to meet it told her he'd not risk allying himself with her. Mayhap he would have helped her if she could have found a way to disable the others and spare him. Mayhap he wouldn't. This wasn't the time to take such a risk.

She had this one chance to escape. She'd committed to it and would see it through. For King Magnus and wolfkind. For Riggs.

She watched Ben carefully. He'd drunk the most. The other two sipped idly while murmuring amongst themselves, but Ben had drained his cup in a few minutes. He would show signs of poisoning first.

If the water hemlock acted on wolfkind as it did on humans and if they'd drunk enough, the men would fall to fits and expire soon after. She'd never seen it happen, but had learned all about which plants were helpful and which were harmful. Water hemlock looked a great deal like wild carrot, the seeds of which could be put in tea to keep a woman from catching a bairn. Many a poor lass had confused the plants and died when they'd merely intended to avoid dishonor.

Ben leaned back on a saddle and used his dirk to flick dirt from under his fingernails. She was close enough to see the striations in his thick, pointed nails, close enough to see his skin glowing with health in the firelight.

Come on. Come on.

Ben met her gaze. "You don't like it?"

She blinked. "What?"

"The boar? Is it not cooked enough?"

She shook her head. "'Tis fine. Thank you." She made herself eat some more.

He winced suddenly. Put a hand to his stomach.

Saints, it was happening. The water hemlock was taking effect.

He looked at his cup then at her, his eyes wide with alarm. He doubled over with a groan.

At the same time, a shout came from the tree line, near where the horses were tied. "To me! It's the Maranner filth who slayed my wolves!"

She recognized Lance's voice, and her heart lunged into her throat. She kent of only one wolf-slaying Maranner, and he should be dead.

§

DANU CURSE IT! Of all the foul luck.

At the sound of a shout behind him, Riggs whipped around to find the Larnian commander, Lance, charging out of the brush. Pale blue eyes set in a craggy face narrowed on him as the man advanced, still naked from his hunt.

In an hour of tracking the commander's scent, Riggs had found the carcass of his kill but not the man himself. Worry for Anya had hastened him back to the campsite. He'd hoped to intercept the commander upon his return and take him off guard, but it seemed he was the one to be taken off guard instead. The hunter had become the hunted. Now he would have to fight all four men.

So be it. Anya depended on him.

He got his axe up in a battle grip, but Lance lunged and buried his fist in Riggs's stomach, knocking the wind out of him. A surprise move. A dirty move. And it fucking hurt.

He curled around his stunned diaphragm, but brought his axe up at the same time to block a kick his opponent aimed at his face.

Rustling and jingling sounds from the clearing meant the other trackers were coming with their weapons. At least Lance wasn't armed. Riggs would take the small mercy, since it was all he'd likely get.

Turning his back to the unarmed man, he jumped through the brush into the clearing, poised for attack with his axe in one hand and his hunting knife in the other. The preemptive move should force the running trackers into defensive positions, which would give him a slight advantage if he could be quick on his feet.

Once he cleared the brush, he'd expected to find three men charging toward him. There were only two. A quick glance showed Anya by the fire with a man having convulsions on the ground.

He couldn't ponder that beyond a profound sense of relief she seemed unharmed.

With Lance's light footfalls closing in on his back, he threw himself at the smaller of the other two trackers.

If I fall, protect her.

As he swung his axe, it occurred to him that had been the first prayer he'd uttered in decades.

§

NERVOUSLY, ANYA WATCHED Ben try to gain his feet. His gaze followed Ced and Gord, but 'twas clear he'd not be answering Lance's call with his fellows. He managed to crawl a few paces before falling on his side. To her mixed horror and gratefulness, his eyes rolled back in his head, and his body went into spasms.

Keeping one eye on poor Ben, she watched the other two close in on the tree line, swords drawn. Before they could crash through the underbrush, an enormous form, large as an enraged bear, leapt from the forest. The snarling beast had wild black hair, blazing eyes, and in its hands were a hunting knife and a black handled axe.

Riggs!

His clothing was torn and bloody, his skin dirty, his face twisted with battle lust. But he was alive! She could scarcely believe her eyes.

Lance stalked from the forest behind him. He was naked and streaked with blood from his hunt, and he looked more vicious than she'd ever seen him. His pale blue eyes threw off sparks. They gleamed with violence. He was an animal. More wolf than man.

As Riggs swung his axe at Gord, Ced tossed his broadsword

to Lance, who caught the hilt easily.

Riggs's attack had forced Gord back a few paces. With darting gaze, he assessed Ced and Lance, keeping his feet moving all the while. He was doubly armed. But would it be enough against three soldiers?

Please let it be enough.

Ced had only the dirk he'd drawn from the sheath at his calf. The other two men had broadswords. Gord left his dirk sheathed, but 'twas there if he needed it.

Saints above, Riggs didn't stand a chance.

But her brave wolf-man didn't give up. He attacked Gord, his axe swinging from his side in a fearsome arc while pointing his knife toward Lance.

Gord used his sword to redirect the blow, grunting with the effort and managing to slice Riggs across his arm in the process. The axe embedded in Gord's thigh instead of his ribs. He bellowed.

While Riggs yanked his axe from Gord's leg, he thrust his knife toward Lance, but the shorter blade's reach couldn't match that of the broadsword. Lance's sword sank into his side.

No!

The wound wasn't near enough center to be immediately fatal, but it sank deep. When Lance pulled it free, it dripped blood.

Riggs curled around the wound with a snarl.

Ced swooped in, grabbed his knife arm and twisted it behind his back.

Riggs dropped the knife.

Ced grinned.

Riggs used the back of his head like a battering ram to break Ced's nose.

Ha! Take that!

Ced released Riggs to cup both hands over his bleeding face.

Riggs wasted no time taking another swing at Gord with his axe, but he was moving slower than before. Gord danced out of reach despite the blood pouring down his leg.

While Riggs wound up for another swing, Lance got an arm around Riggs's neck from behind. Ced and Gord closed in and unarmed Riggs. Gord tossed the axe away. It clattered to the hard-packed sand.

Her heart lunged into her throat to see Riggs without his axe, surrounded by enemies.

Ced and Gord held Riggs with his arms behind his back. Riggs struggled, but his growing weakness showed in the strained lines of his face and in the way his head drooped.

Lance moved to stand before Riggs with his back to her. He said somat she couldn't make out. Then he delivered two fierce punches to Riggs's stomach.

Riggs's mouth gaped open like a fish sucking air. He went down to his knees.

The two trackers held him while Lance rained blows to Riggs's body and face.

"I'll make you pay for my wolves, you goat fucker." This was followed by a vicious kick to Riggs's gut. "Those were prize trackers." Another punch. Blood flew from Riggs's mouth. "Make me come into fucking *Marann* to chase down what's rightfully ours!" Lance cocked his arm back for another punch.

"No! Stop it!" she shrieked.

The trackers all looked at her. With his cold, pale gaze locked on hers, Lance delivered a tooth-jarring uppercut to Riggs's jaw.

Riggs wobbled, but he didn't go down. Ced and Gord held him up, as if presenting him for more punishment.

"You're going to kill him!" She shook all over. This couldn't be happening. Riggs had survived the villagers at Valeworth, and he'd come all this way on foot—for her—only to have the trackers murder him before her eyes.

Lance dropped his eyes to the man who'd gone still by her side.

"What happened to Ben?" He abandoned Riggs to stalk toward her. Menace poured off him in waves.

She ought to think of some acceptable answer. She ought to scurry away and cower before this monster. All she could do was look at Riggs. His head hung down, blood dripping from his face. As if he felt her gaze on him, he looked up. It seemed to take all his effort.

One eye was already swelling shut. The other fixed on her. His gaze burned with regret. His mouth moved, forming a single, silent word. "Run."

As if she would even if she could. She would not flee like a coward while Riggs suffered.

Lance's shadow loomed over her as he came between her and the fire. Fear closed around her, making it impossible for her to think or move. She'd not flee, but she couldn't possibly fight. Could she? What could a crippled whore do against a man like this?

"What'd you do to him?"

Her heart pounded. "I—I doona ken," she stammered. "He fell ill."

A cruel hand fisted in the front of her shirt. He yanked her to stand belly to belly with him. Only her toes touched the ground.

His eyes burned into hers. Fear made her look away, down at Ben, anything to escape that icy blaze. Firelight winked on the polished hilt of the dirk strapped to Ben's calf.

Lance shook her by his grip on her shirt. "What. Did. You. Do. To. Him."

She craned her neck to look him dead in the eye. He was brawn and terrible grace glowering down at her.

"I killed him," she said, her voice as cold as his eyes. "And I'm going to kill you too." For what he'd done to Riggs. For what he intended to do to her. For the other women trapped in Larna.

Uncertainty flickered behind those cold, cold eyes.

A choked sound drew Lance's gaze off her and toward the men. Ced fell to the ground. He was seizing as Ben had done. Gord doubled over with his arms around his stomach.

She broke from his hold and snatched up Ben's dirk.

Lance appeared more concerned with Riggs, who threw himself to the ground and rolled, grabbing up his axe. In a heartbeat, he was on his feet. A single swing of his axe separated Ced's head from his shoulders. A second swing, and the axe blade embedded so deeply in Gord's back, Riggs had to rock it free. He'd ended them. He'd finished what the water hemlock had started.

Head down, her wolf-man raised his eyes. Sweat and blood dripped from his chin. He grinned at Lance. Death was written all over his face.

Lance went motionless, either frozen with shock or preparing to meet Riggs's challenge. He likely regretted not dealing a killing blow with his sword when he'd had the chance.

Taking advantage of his inattention, she thrust Ben's dirk forward, aiming at Lance's unprotected back, low and to the side—the place a former lover had told her was the best for disabling an opponent, if one didn't mind fighting dirty and attacking when a man's back was turned. She'd never minded fighting dirty, and now wasn't the time to start minding.

She put her shoulder into it, pushing the blade as deep as she could.

Lance stiffened and roared.

Riggs limped around the fire, whirling his axe through the air like the spinning sails of a windmill. The sound alone would have made her piss herself if she thought that axe was coming for her.

Lance tried to back up, but Anya twisted the blade in his back, making him arch and yell.

Riggs swung the axe, aiming high.

She turned away. The whistle of steel cutting through air was followed by a dull, wet *thwack.* Then the sound of a limp body hitting sand.

She turned to find Riggs pulling his axe free from Lance's neck. The man's head remained attached by the merest thread.

"Never asked you to drag your Larnian carcass into my country," Riggs said, and he spat on the tracker's still body.

Then he fell to his knees and into Anya's waiting arms.

Chapter 15

RIGGS BURIED HIS face against Anya's soft stomach and wrapped his arms around her waist. Her scent of flowers and hyssop enveloped him, replacing the metallic bite of his own blood and the stench of dead Larnian.

She bowed over him, trembling. Her small fingers gripped the hair at his nape. She rubbed her cheek over the top of his head like he'd done with her so many times. Marking him, comforting him. His heart swelled.

Anya.

No physical pain could match the soul-deep ache he'd carried all the way from Valeworth. Not a battered face, not a stab wound meant to be the first of many insults to weaken him before the deathblow. He would miss a lost limb less than he'd missed Anya. Her absence had diminished him in a way no physical injury ever could. Now he was whole again.

He raised his face like a flower to the sun, seeking something more than her nuzzling, though he didn't know what.

His lady knew. Her mouth alighted on his. Her cool hand soothed the hot swelling of his jaw. She ignored the blood and pressed her soft lips to his, moving them gently, tentatively.

A kiss.

The sweetest gift imaginable. He'd heard of kisses but never imagined he'd know the bliss of one outside his fantasies.

Her lips clung to his and released, clung and released, a rocking rhythm that his lips answered so naturally the wonder of it was like a blow to his gut.

Perfect. Complete. Anya.

Mine.

The soft pressure of their kiss shifted the tooth the commander had loosened with that last hit. The pain was nothing compared to the pleasure spinning through him. It heated his blood, soothed his soul. His eyes fluttered shut.

He tightened his arms around her, remembering when she'd told him he wouldn't break her. Had it really been just a few days since they'd left his cabin and he'd held her hand for the first time, helping her across a slippery log? He'd known her such a short time, but it felt like his life hadn't truly begun until he'd found her.

Against his mouth, her lips twisted into a grimace. She made a high-pitched sound. A protest? Was he hurting her after all? Had he done something wrong with the kiss?

He shifted her away with his hands on her shoulders. The fire had almost burned out, but there was enough light for him to see her scrunched-up expression. Her chin was dimpled and quivering and stained with his blood. Tears streamed down her cheeks.

Shite. He'd hurt her. Clumsy oaf! "What's wrong?" He ran his hands over her face, her head, her shoulders, checking for injury but also just to touch her, just to *be* with her. He wasn't sure he could stop, even if she demanded it.

"You bloody foolish man." She hiccupped. "You almost got yourself killed. Twice!" She grabbed his head and hugged it tight to her bosom. "I almost lost you. I almost lost you."

His stomach rolled.

"I'm here," he assured her, folding his arms around her again. Her heart beat against his ear. Her lush breasts cushioned his face. She felt like home. "I'm here now."

"*Och,* but you're bleeding like a speared boar. Lie down, let me look at you." She tried to back out of his arms.

He wouldn't let her go. He wasn't ready. He'd never be ready.

He held her tighter. "I'm fine." As long as she was in his arms, he was better than fine. "Come here." He sat back on his haunches and dragged her onto his lap, directing her legs around his hips.

Her body came to his willingly. Her silky hair cooled the knuckles of the hand he wrapped behind her neck. With his other hand, he supported her left leg, the one that pained her most, pressing it around him. Her slight weight bore down on his arousal, making him feel pleasurable pain. Her scent thickened with that heady spice that made him lose his mind.

Her gaze met his, and a feeling of deep connection snapped taut between them. Her eyes widened as if she felt it too. Her lips parted on a breath that smelled of cooked meat. For once the smell didn't bother him, because it came from her. It meant she'd been nourished tonight.

Protect. Love.

Keep.

Warm, dark possibility twisted through him. He racked his brain trying to think of a place secure enough to hide away for a lifetime with her.

"The commander stabbed you," she said, cutting off his thoughts. "You're no' fine. No one could be fine after what you've endured."

"I've had worse. I'll heal."

She wound her arms around his neck, bringing her sweet lips to the sweaty skin of his throat. "You better," she murmured there, making his whole body shiver with need. "If you die on me, I'll bloody kill you."

He smiled with a twinge of pain to his loose tooth and a deeper pain to his heart. There was no way he could keep this treasure for himself. No matter how badly he wanted her, he couldn't betray his king.

Gently, he eased her off his lap. Pain that had nothing to do with his injuries tore through him.

It's for the best. She's not mine. Never will be.

Even though he would always be hers.

Gripping her waist, he helped her stand, nice and slow—her legs didn't like quick changes in position. "Is the tea still hot?" he asked past his constricted throat. Addressing his thirst might help ease the sense of loss crushing his chest like a boulder.

Her eyes went wide. All color drained from her face. "Touch that teapot, and I'll skin you alive."

That's right. Anya liked to be useful. She'd want to serve him tonight. He felt himself grin at her feisty spirit. King Magnus was a damned lucky man. "Fine. I won't lift a finger. I'll let you serve me."

He sat back on the sand, memorizing the sway of her hips as she limped to the fire, the swell of her breasts as she bent at the waist over the notch in the woodpile where the teapot sat. The dying fire outlined those glorious orbs through the linen of his shirt.

"Hope it's good and strong," he said. "I could use a kick in my brew tonight. And see if you can find some poultice and bandages in the tracker's saddle bags after you pour me a cup."

Anya pulled her shirtsleeves over her hands to protect herself from the hot handle.

It would be nice to rinse the taste of blood out of his mouth with good strong tea. He licked his lips, so thirsty.

But Anya didn't pour the tea into a cup for him to sip. Instead, she hobbled to the bank and hurled the pot into the river with a cry.

Splash.

He blinked at the rings of water spreading around where it had sunk. Then he looked at Anya. She had both her hands clasped over her mouth.

He got up and went to her. Shite, he was lightheaded. He really could have used some of that tea. He'd have to settle for water, but not until he'd found out what was wrong with Anya.

"What is it, lady?" He put a hand on her shoulder.

She was trembling.

He gathered her into his arms and soothed her with long strokes over her hair. "Tell me. Did the trackers hurt you?" What else could upset her like this?

"I hurt *them*." She met his eyes. "I poisoned their tea. I killed them."

She'd poisoned the trackers.

It hadn't been Danu to miraculously help him when he'd needed it most. It had been his lady. No less a miracle for his rescue coming from mortal hands.

He'd thought to save Anya, but she had saved him. She'd saved them both.

Pride filled him. But *she* didn't look proud. Shite. He recognized the confusion in her gaze. He remembered his first time on the battlefield, the first time he'd buried his axe in a man instead of a straw dummy on the practice field.

She'd never killed before.

"I don't regret it," she said. "Does that make me wicked?"

He bent around her. "No. You're not wicked."

"What kind of woman kills without regret?"

"A brave one. A smart one." She appeared so fragile, but she was strong, his lady. He tipped her face up with a curled finger under her chin. "A beautiful one." He kissed her scars.

She closed her eyes, leaning into his kiss, making his chest puff up.

"You did what a good soldier would have done," he murmured against her cheek. "You fought. You saved my life."

She nipped her lower lip between her teeth. He couldn't help himself. He moved his mouth to hers and kissed those lush lips.

Sweet. So damn sweet.

Her fists curled in his shirt at his back. She clung to him.

He rocked his lips over hers the way he knew she liked.

She whimpered, a sound of helpless abandon. It heated him from head to toe, that little sound.

Then he did another thing he couldn't help. He thrust his tongue between her lips, between her teeth. He licked deep into her mouth as his lips sealed them together.

She gripped him even tighter and rubbed her tongue over his. That spicy scent of hers plowed over him. Pleasure tightened his stomach, made his blood sing with need.

The ground seemed to tilt under his feet. He thought it was the wonder of kissing Anya so intimately, but when a rush of blackness clouded his vision, he knew better. He'd lost too much blood. The wound in his side must be worse than he'd thought. He had just enough time to disengage from her before he felt himself go down and remembered no more.

§

"STUPID BLOODY MAN."

Anya scrubbed the tears off her cheeks as she stared down at a wolf-man in danger of bleeding to death on the coarse sand of a riverbank. He'd made her believe the stab wound in his side was nothing to fash over. Typical thick-skulled warrior, thinking himself invincible.

She'd almost believed him invincible, given all he'd withstood since they'd met. But he looked far from it now, sprawled on his back with his clothing tattered, his skin pale, blood staining his shirt.

Her chest tightened until it hurt to breathe. Why couldn't he be invincible?

"You'll die tonight over my dead body," she informed him.

Her lips still tingled from his passionate kiss. Her body still thrummed with desire. She ignored it all as she threw more logs on the woodpile to stoke the blaze brighter. Doctoring a wounded man in daylight would have been her preference, but if she had to do it at night, she needed better light than that of a dying fire.

Happy at last with the bright, leaping flames, she found a healing kit in the saddlebag that had belonged to Gord. Her gaze wanted to go to where his body lay near the tree line. *No. Don't look.*

Bloody difficult not to look upon a dead man—or tread upon one—when they littered the camp. She kept glimpsing a booted foot here, a dropped weapon by a too-still hand there. Each glimpse made her stomach contract with sickness.

"You did what a good soldier would have done. You saved my life."

She had nothing to regret. No reason to fash.

Putting it behind her, she hobbled to Riggs's side with the healing kit. She pulled his shirt from his trews and inspected the worst of his wounds. His torso was firm with muscle and thickly furred toward the center. Any other time, she would have longed to smooth her hands over that luxurious coat. Tonight her grisly task was to wash blood out of it so she could see what they were dealing with.

Using a clean rag and water from a skin, she uncovered a red gash about as long as her palm was wide. It cut diagonally through his hide where the hair began to thin at his flank. Blood dribbled from it freely, suggesting 'twas too deep to safely sew closed. She'd seen healers insert a hot iron into such wounds to stop the bleeding. Even if she had such a thing to heat in the fire, she doubted she possessed the courage to stick it into Riggs's body. The best she could do would be to dress it to staunch the bleeding. She hoped it would be enough.

After washing the wound with whisky she'd found in the

trackers' saddlebags and binding it with poultice-covered bandages, she turned her attention to the slice across his forearm. This she could sew.

A few more logs on the fire gave her sufficient light to thread a needle and mend Riggs's skin. Done with that, she inspected his face. He had an eye swollen shut and a wee cut over his red-hot cheek. His thick beard covered his jaw, but she felt the heat of blooming bruises through the coarse hair. His complexion would be darker than a stormy sky tomorrow, but none of these wounds were serious.

She fashed more about how pale he looked and how his eyes appeared sunken in his sockets. He looked like a man who hadn't eaten in days. Mayhap the last thing he'd had to eat was the measly meal of ferrets from the inn in Valeworth. And he'd traveled leagues since then, and fought hard. He needed food, but he couldn't eat while he was unconscious.

She'd make sure he had food close at hand when he woke—he *would* wake. She'd not tolerate him dying in the night. Death couldn't have him. He was hers.

The possessive thought came out of nowhere. But once she'd had it, she couldn't shake it away. No matter how ridiculous it was.

She understood that more than ever. There was no safe place for a woman outside Chroina. And she'd not endanger Riggs further by suggesting different.

Gathering up what was left of the cooked boar piglets, which was a substantial amount given her lack of appetite, she wrapped it and set it by Riggs. He preferred his meat raw, but if he was hungry enough, he'd be thankful for meat any way he could get it. Beside the meat, she put a full water skin and a flask of whisky, the latter in case he woke in much pain. She'd seen rounds of hard bread in the trackers' bags while searching for other supplies. She put some of those by Riggs as well, in case he refused the meat.

There. She'd done all she could.

The fire faded, allowing the cold night to close in. She'd not have Riggs freezing to death while his body worked to heal his wounds. She untied Lance's bedroll and unfurled it, skin-side down beside Riggs. Unceremoniously, she rolled him onto the soft fur lining, an event that left her exhausted enough to sleep for a week.

Before climbing in to share her warmth with him, she surveyed the camp. Four horses tied on a rope and resting by the tree line. Four dead bodies littered hither and yon. One unconscious wolf-man.

May he be well enough to ride for Chroina in the morn.

She wasn't sure to whom she prayed. The good Lord? Danu? Was anyone listening?

Likely not, considering Riggs's people had gotten to a state where their best chance at survival depended upon the barren womb of a crippled whore.

She ought to tell Riggs she couldn't be the one to save his people. But if she told him the truth, he'd never look at her again with fondness.

She'd nearly lost him. She couldn't bear to lose what affection he had for her, even if 'twas based upon lies. No sense spoiling their remaining time together by telling him things that would upset him. He'd bring her to Chroina, and when he returned to his cabin, he'd do it with hope in his heart. That hope would be her final gift to him.

Sighing, she lifted the flap of the bedroll and lay down beside him. Weariness dragged her to sleep the second she tucked the flap snug around them.

Chapter 16

HUNGER WOKE RIGGS with vicious gnawing at his stomach. He opened his eyes to the blue light of early dawn. The scents of forest, river, charred wood, and Larnian brought back the memories of last night in a blinding rush.

The trackers. The battle. The teapot. Anya on his lap. Anya kissing him, clinging to him. *Anya.*

Her scent was there too, flowers and hyssop and woman. He turned onto his side to find her soundly sleeping, pressed up against him in a bedroll that must have belonged to the commander, considering how the fur reeked of the man.

He ignored the unwanted scent and buried his nose in Anya's shining hair. She smelled sweet, smoky from the fire, and a little salty from perspiration. He couldn't keep from rubbing his cheek over her head, taking some of her scent, giving her some of his.

This is how he should wake up every morning, with his lady by his side.

No. Not his. He kept forgetting.

He made himself stop marking her.

His nuzzling hadn't woken her, but when he stopped, she shifted in her sleep, scooting tighter against him. Her slender arm went around his waist, drawing his attention to the bandages wrapped uncomfortably but effectively tight around him there. He reached up a hand to stroke her hair and noticed bandages on his arm too. His wounds ached, but with healing. He'd be all right. They'd be all right.

Thanks to Anya.

She slid her knee between his legs and burrowed her nose against his neck. Her breath heated his already overly warm skin. The hunger gripping his stomach transformed to a darker, more ravenous hunger. He felt weak as a newborn pup, but that didn't stop his body from rousing to the feel of this woman in his arms.

She nipped at his throat with her lips.

He closed his eyes against a wave of need. "Anya." He whispered her name to wake her.

"Riggs," she sighed, but her tone was breathy. Her eyes were closed. She was still asleep. But her body was rousing as surely as his. Her feminine musk thickened with that spice that drove him wild.

Shite.

She kissed his neck and moaned softly.

Another minute of this and he'd have her naked and joined with him no matter how weak and hungry he was, no matter how disloyal it would be to his king.

"Anya."

She started. "Hm?" She opened her eyes, blinked twice while focusing on his face, then smiled. Her smile was like the sun rising after months of darkness. She laid a gentle hand on his beard. "My wolf-man," she said, her voice as soft as he'd ever heard it.

Hers. Yes. He was hers. But he could not let his heart believe she belonged to him, no matter how badly he longed for it to be true.

"You came for me," she said.

He held her hand on his cheek then kissed her palm. That kiss would be the last he ever gave her. It had to be. Because it wasn't his place to give this remarkable lady affection. It was King Magnus's place. No other's.

Among all women she would be unique. She would belong to

one man. He refused to sully that by insinuating himself where he didn't belong.

He memorized the way her eyes sparkled with trust, the way her pillowy lips curled up in an almost feline smile. Her beauty stole his breath.

He was about to wipe away the tender affection on her face. It had to be done.

He cleared his throat. "Of course I came for you. You're my responsibility until I turn you over to King Magnus."

Her eyes dulled. She slipped her hand off his face and climbed out of the bedroll, slowly. Her legs always pained her in the morning. He didn't help her even though his hands clenched to do so.

Once she was on her feet, she said, "How do you feel?" All softness was gone from her voice. She wouldn't look at him as she dug a water skin out of a saddlebag and limped to the river.

It was better this way. They were traveling companions, nothing more.

He climbed out after her and found a full water skin, a flask, and a meal of cooked boar and bread beside the bedroll. She must have prepared all this for him last night. Of course she wouldn't have been able to hunt fresh meat for him, but she'd saved some of her own meat for him instead. Had she gone hungry to make sure he had something to eat for breakfast? His heart squeezed.

He washed down the lump in his throat with the contents of the water skin. So good, water, after being so thirsty. "Good enough to ride," he answered, wiping his mouth on his sleeve. He unwrapped the meat. She'd peeled away the charred skin, leaving him meat that was cooked, but still smelled of blood, deep in the center. He ripped into it, too ravenous to mind the dryness and changed flavor.

While he ate, he noticed Anya glancing sidelong at him as she knelt at the bank to fill her water skin upriver from where she'd tossed the teapot. He devoured every last morsel. It pleased him to show her his appreciation by consuming her gift. Also, he would have made a pitiful hunter this morning with his side zinging him at the slightest movement. Once again, Anya had helped him.

Now that he'd fed, it was time for him to make himself useful. He stood up and surveyed the camp. The body of the commander lay on one side of the charred spot where the fire had been. There was another body near the fire and two more near the horses.

"What do we do about the trackers?" Anya's voice brought his attention to her. She stood hands on hips, surveying the camp with a frown. She looked ready to work. He'd let her. Today, he needed the help. But he'd not let either one of them waste energy on burying Larnians.

"I'll drag them into the forest. Beyond that, the wild animals can have them."

She nodded and began searching the bodies. "No sense wasting anything of use. Will we take all four horses?"

"No. We'll travel light and ride hard to Chroina. Neil and King Magnus have to hear about those women. This could start a new war."

Anya stilled. She blew out a breath. "We need to help them. I doona ken how many there might be, but more than one, I'm cert."

He feared the same, judging by what he'd overheard.

While they saddled two horses, they traded information. They knew precious little about Ari and what his role might be, but they agreed he must have betrayed King Magnus.

"How do you suppose they're getting the women? I came through because of a meddling box. Mayhap they were brought over by magic as well."

He shrugged. "Who's to say? Jilken used magic eons ago to breed with wolves. You've got a magic gemstone that makes you speak our tongue. I imagine magic could be harnessed to bring people across realms."

He picked up the two rounds of bread Anya had left by their bedroll and put them in her hands. "Go on up to the cave," he told her. "Eat. Rest. We ride in half an hour." It was time to move the bodies. He didn't want her to see, or offer to help.

She looked like she wanted to say something, but she took the bread and limped away. She paused at the base of the hill where the cave sat and looked at him over her shoulder. Her mouth was a hard line. "Try no' to hurt yourself. There are no more bandages to hold you together." She started up the incline, proud as the queen she would no doubt become in a few days' time.

§

ANYA CLUCKED TO her black gelding and dug her heels into its ribs. The horse conceded to adopt a rolling canter but flicked his ears back in annoyance. Rounding a bend in the forest trail, Riggs came into view. He rode the dappled gray gelding that had been Lance's mount. Anytime she came within a few paces, he would urge his horse faster while hers would lose interest in making haste and slow to a bone-rattling trot. The same occurred now. Her mount slowed, and Riggs disappeared down a hill in the distance.

She growled in frustration, kicking the indolent lump of horseflesh beneath her. "Bloody infuriating beast!" That went for her horse as well as the man who seemed determined to avoid her.

Two days they had together before reaching Chroina. Two days! And apparently, he wished to spend it putting as much distance between them as possible. Even after he'd fought nearly to the death for her, kissed her with more passion than any man before him, and woken beside her with unfathomable tenderness in his gaze.

Her horse cantered again, slowing the moment she got Riggs

in sight. Again.

Argh!

Riggs had chosen the horses for the journey. Had he known this one possessed the spirit of a sluggard? If so, he must be congratulating himself on his selection.

Bloody cur.

The only things stopping her from giving him a tongue-lashing were the healing wounds he'd sustained for her sake. *Och*, not hers, King Magnus's. His words to her this morning made it clear as spring water. He'd fought for her out of duty. Nothing more.

Fine. He wanted to pretend a fire didn't burn between them? She could pretend just as well as he could. He wanted distance between them? She'd give him distance.

She'd grapple with her bloody lazy horse the whole way to Chroina and not say a bloody word about it to Riggs. She'd not say a bloody word to him at all. The time for conversing with him as a friend had passed. He'd forcibly closed the door on them being aught more than riders sharing the same road.

The road to Chroina. To her new home and her new position as broodmare to a king.

Defective broodmare.

According to Riggs, King Magnus would welcome her with open arms. But how welcoming would he be when month after month, year after year, she failed to give him what he most desired? Riggs would go about his life out near Larna's border. He'd continually hope for news of a royal birth. How many years would it take him to lose hope?

Her horse slowed again. She had to clench her teeth else they'd crash into each other with the jarring trot. Riggs disappeared around a hill. She didn't bother kicking her horse. She had no wish to lay eyes on Riggs just now. Instead, she let the beast lapse into an ambling walk.

Loneliness stole over her. She welcomed it. This would be her life from now on. A human alone in a world of wolf-people. A disappointment to a world that needed hope.

The forest thinned. Narrow trees with sparse late-autumn foliage surrounded her with dreary grays and browns. The overcast sky blocked out the sun, but the deepening gray light suggested it would be low in the sky. 'Twas mayhap half an hour from dusk. Far ahead, Riggs came into view then disappeared again as his horse descended a hill.

Several minutes later, she rode down the same hill. The forest came to an end as a vast hilly plain opened up before her. Long grass rippling like waves stretched as far as the eye could see. Riggs was little more than a speck as he rounded the nearest hill. While she watched, he reined his horse to a stop and looked back. Lifting his chin to acknowledge her, he rode on, not waiting for her to catch up.

His indifference was a bruise on her heart.

Whatever sadness tugged at her spirit, her horse seemed to feel the opposite. His ears pricked forward, and his gait sped to a lively walk.

"*Och*, like wide open spaces, do you?" Mayhap 'twasn't laziness the gelding suffered from but an aversion to forests. She gave him his head and touched his side with the barest hint of heel. He launched into a gallop and raced along the trail Riggs's horse had carved into the grass.

The wind ripped her hood free and tangled her hair behind her. She bent over her mount's neck and laughed, fingers curling in mane, feeling lighter than she had in a very long time. Never before had she ridden a horse as large and powerful as this one, let alone at a gallop. 'Twas exhilarating.

Grass-scented air heavy with the promise of rain filled her lungs. She whooped and reveled in the speed, the freedom, the land, so like her native Scotia yet a world away. All her fashing felt as if she'd left it behind with the trees.

She gained on Riggs.

He looked back, eyes wide with alarm.

As she barreled past, he shouted, "What in the low realm are you doing?" He urged his horse into a gallop and held pace with her, their legs nearly brushing. He grabbed for her reins.

"Hi'ya!" Her mount put on a burst of speed that left Riggs cursing.

He called after her, but his shouts grew distant as she and her mount cut their own path over the hilly plain. She cackled like a maniac to discover her horse was faster than Riggs's. Good. Let him see what it felt like to be left behind.

They flew, rider and beast as one, keeping to the low areas, gliding gracefully around the bases of gentle slopes and leaping narrow creeks. She watched for uneven ground and obstacles, but the horse proved to be as surefooted as he was fast. A warhorse, she realized. Her mount would be at home amidst a crowded, cannon-rutted battlefield. "You're an ornery lad, but I like you!" she shouted.

When his sleek coat began shining with sweat, she reined him in. It wouldn't do to be careless with him. After all, there would be no horse changes for them.

Her gelding bobbed his head as he prance-walked. He wouldn't mind running some more, but she was feeling a wee bit guilty for leaving Riggs so far behind. Even if he bloody well deserved it.

It took him a handful of minutes to catch up to her.

He passed her and angled his mount in front of hers, trying to force her to stop. Behind his bruises, his face was red and his eyes brewed with murderous rage.

Despite how spectacular he looked cloaked in anger, she tipped her chin in the air and steered around him.

He jumped from the saddle and grabbed her horse's reins,

yanking them to a stop. "Are you mad?" He spoke low and growly. His voice made her shiver. *Och,* she'd missed hearing it today.

She ignored the thrill and looked down on him. "Haud your wheesht. You said we'd ride hard today. I was merely doing as I was told."

"That wasn't riding hard. That was riding reckless. You might have been killed." He raked a hand through his wind-tossed hair, reminding her of when he'd been so concerned for her safety in Valeworth's inn. Where was this concern all day when he'd ridden so far ahead of her she'd assumed he'd forgotten she existed?

"I beg your pardon. I was merely in a rush to get to Chroina. I've got a king eager to plant a bairn in me. I doona wish to keep him waiting."

He grabbed her around the waist and hauled her down so quickly she yelped in surprise. Pinning her against his chest so not even her toes touched the ground, he said, "I don't care how fast we get to Chroina. I won't let you break your neck falling from a horse. You ride with me from now on."

She shoved at his chest. "Let me go, you great oaf! You canna ignore me all day and then yell at me for a few minutes of fun. I ken how to ride a bloody horse."

He wouldn't let her go. "You think this is easy for me?" he growled. "You think this is what I want? To give you to another man when all I can think about is—" He broke off and shoved a hand through his curls again, keeping her pinned with one arm. His nostrils flared. He quieted. "It's going to kill me to give you to him. Don't you know that by now? Imagining you in his bed drives me mad." A vein throbbed in his forehead, but his eyes went soft on her.

His confession was a blow to her gut. After all the distance he imposed between them today, he'd all but admitted he wanted her still. *"It's going to kill me to give you to him."* Didn't he ken it would kill her too?

A part of her she'd never been aware of before had risen to the surface in Riggs's presence. A hopeful part. A vulnerable part. A part that made her feel beautiful despite her scars and womanly despite her barren womb. That fragile, new part of her would wither and die when she watched Riggs walk away from her forever.

And he would walk away. There was no way around it.

If she kept her secret from him, he'd walk away believing in error she would save his people. He'd also walk away if she told him the truth, that her womb was as useless as a cart without a mule. Even if the king didn't want her, she'd have no choice but to remain in Chroina, the only safe place for women, and if Riggs wanted her, he'd have to stay in Chroina too. But what man in his right mind would abandon his land and livelihood for a woman who couldn't have bairns, especially when bairns were so desperately needed. *Och,* if she told him the truth, he'd be embarrassed by her. Or he'd pity her.

If she kept the truth to herself, she'd be showered with riches and honor, for a time, until her closed womb told on her. But Riggs would be long gone by then.

She had nothing to lose by keeping her secrets, and a few years of luxurious living to gain.

So why did her stomach contract when she imagined this night passing without telling Riggs everything?

"Put me down," she said. "Please." She needed stable ground under her feet to calm the shaking in her soul.

He rubbed his cheek over her head. "What if I don't?" The arm at her back flexed. He grabbed a handful of her bottom and used that to hold her tight to him.

It made her stomach flutter, being held like this. The strength it required, the possessiveness. It was too grand. She didn't deserve to feel this cherished.

She pushed at his chest again, and this time he let her go. The loss of his warmth and solidness left her feeling bereft.

Her horse had wandered to a wee creek, barely a trickle in the grass. She went to him and petted his neck while he drank. "Not too much, lad. Let's walk you some before you sate that thirst." She gathered his reins and walked him along the creek to cool him. Riggs didn't follow. Good. She needed time to steel herself for what she kent she must do. Only a coward would put it off any longer.

Dusk kissed the plain with cold gray light as she led her horse back to Riggs.

He was removing his mount's tack. "We'll camp here," he told her.

Surrounded by low hills, they were relatively well hidden, and there was water. 'Twas a good place to rest. As good a place as any to dash a man's hopes.

"I canna have bairns," she made herself say.

He froze in unbuckling the girth. His gaze bored into hers. They stood facing each other, watching each other breathe.

"My legs werena the only things broken in my fall. I havena had my courses since. I canna be who ye need me to be."

His eyes widened as he began to understand her.

She looked at her boots, unable to watch his admiration turn to disappointment. "I'm broken. All the way through, I'm broken." The truth chopped through her pride like the blade of an axe. It left her in pieces. She turned her back on him and limped away, hoping for privacy, because tears were about to fall.

He gave her what she needed by not following.

She found a pair of boulders and crouched between them, shaking. In the distance, she heard him tending to her horse. A little while later he spoke nearby. "I'm going hunting." His voice was gruff and quiet. "Unless you need me to stay."

She wiped her eyes on her sleeve. "Go. I'm fine. Go."

He went.

She wanted to shrivel into a ball and die. Riggs had thought he'd been in possession of a great treasure. Now he understood he'd gone to all this trouble for nothing.

§

RIGGS CROUCHED AT the top of a hill and gazed in the direction of their camp. Cold wind stirred his hair and the long grass around him. The moon hid behind a thick blanket of clouds, but he could feel exactly where it was. Its fullness called to his soul. There would be rain soon.

Anya knew it. Below, she was getting ready, pounding stakes into the ground with a rhythmic *tink-tink-tink*, using the trackers' supplies to make a tent for them to lie under.

He watched her wield a good-sized rock as a hammer. Her legs were crippled, but her arms were strong. He'd never been near enough to any female other than his mother to study their mannerisms, but men talked. Females liked the men to do everything for them, and the men dashed about to do it all. Not Anya. She liked to work. She wanted to be useful.

"I canna have bairns... All the way through, I'm broken."

He should be hunting. He'd never felt less like it. He sniffed the air, halfheartedly searching for a scent to pursue, but the salty scent of Anya's silent tears lingered in his nostrils.

Could he be mistaken about who she was? Was it a coincidence she resembled King Magnus's portrait? Did Danu have another delicate, chestnut-haired beauty up her sleeve?

The scent of plains hare tickled his nose. He didn't get up to follow it.

Anya began collecting bracken for firewood, cloaked against the cold, limping, piling her arms as full as she possibly could before delivering each load to their campsite. There were no large trees to provide fallen limbs, only bushes and dry, scrubby growth. Hands on her hips, she frowned at the pile she'd accumulated. It wouldn't burn long enough to cook that hare he smelled, let alone the feast he wished he could prepare her this night and every other. She eyed his axe, picked it up, tested its weight. When she took it to a shrub and began hacking awkwardly at the base, he felt himself smile.

The female King Magnus had dreamt about was supposed to have a paw print on her cheek. Anya's scars were jagged lines that could have been claw marks, but it had been rock to carve them into her, not a wolf. The female in the portrait wore a gemstone, a gift from the goddess, in a chain around her neck. Anya's stone was in her pocket, and had been given to her by a man, not a goddess.

He'd never seen the portrait with his own eyes, only heard about it from Vorish and that barkeep in Figcroft, then later in a report from the palace. King Magnus had described it so the entire nation would be watching for the savior Danu had promised them. One detail appeared in the report that he hadn't heard at the pub. The female King Magnus had dreamt about had been holding a baby, and on the baby's head was a crown.

The scent of the hare vanished on the wind. He plucked a blade of grass and twirled it between finger and thumb.

Anya couldn't have children. What could be more certain than that? She could not be the one King Magnus had dreamt about. She was not the savior Danu had promised.

He should feel sorrow. His people were still without hope.

He felt only hunger. For her. His arms ached to hold her. His body yearned to mate with her. His heart craved her devotion. He wanted to earn it every day for the rest of his life.

She didn't seem broken to him. She seemed whole and perfect. Perfectly lovely. Completely desirable.

Having given up on the trunk of the shrub, she chopped the thinner side branches, holding the axe far too close to the head to do any good. He purred with pleasure at her refusal to give up the lost cause.

She was everything beautiful and alive. She was the only thing worth living for. And there was nothing now to stop him from having her. It would not be disloyal. He would not face imprisonment. There was no penalty for mating outside of contract with a female past her time of breeding, as long as she consented.

Anya could not have children. That didn't matter to him. He loved her. He would have her. Tonight. Every night. Until the end of days.

He stood and strode down to his lady.

She heard him before she saw him. Her shoulders jumped. She spun around, her eyes wide with surprise.

He plucked the axe from her hands and tossed it away. Then he took her in his arms and covered her mouth with his.

Chapter 17

ONE SECOND, ANYA had been cursing under her breath at the surprising difficulty of chopping apart a bush with an axe—weren't the bloody things meant for cutting wood? The next, she heard stirring in the grass behind her, and her heart lunged into her throat. She'd thought it might be a wild animal or a villager sneaking up on her to take her away from Riggs again. When she'd whirled around to find Riggs bearing down on her, his eyes glittering in the night, she'd opened her mouth to ask why he wasn't hunting. But the question never made it out.

He'd ripped the axe from her grasp and sealed his lips over hers, effectively obliterating her ability to speak or think. Until she remembered she'd just taken away his hope. He shouldn't be showing her affection. He should hate her, or at least be disappointed in her.

Tension made her shoulders creep up around her ears and her hands fist in his shirt. She pushed at him, affecting no change in his posture whatsoever. She wrenched her mouth away. "What the bloody hell are you doing? Why are you wearing clothes?"

He buried his face in her neck and kissed her there, making her shiver all over. "Do you prefer me naked, lady?"

Aye, she did. A lass would have to be blind not to prefer Riggs naked, but she wasn't about to admit it. She'd admitted enough tonight. "*Och,* you ken what I mean. You should be finding our dinner."

"Later." He picked her up and carried her to where she'd

made a shelter from the trackers' bedrolls. "Unless you're hungry." He ducked underneath and laid her down. With his lips, he nipped her neck and shoulder. His big hands worked the fastening of her trews. "Are you hungry, Anya?" His voice was a low rumble. He wasn't talking about food.

Her head spun. What was happening? He was acting like a man intent on tupping when until this moment, he'd often been affectionate with her but never outright insistent.

Realization hit her like a kick from a mule. He'd resisted tupping her out of respect for his king. But now he kent she wasn't a fit gift for his king. Now he thought to use her as a whore was meant to be used.

So be it. She wanted this. And he had earned it. He'd fought for her, nearly died for her. What better price could a crippled whore ask for than such valiant protection? Let him have this. She was good at this. Good *for* this, even if she was good for naught else.

He worked her shirt out of her trews, the fabric lightly scratching. His palm was even rougher than the linen when he slid it up to cup one breast. *Och,* his touch there. 'Twas so much more than skin deep. It melted all the way through to her heart.

Doona let your heart feel this, lass. Enjoy it, but doona enjoy it overmuch or you'll regret it when he leaves you in Chroina.

He lifted her shirt and nuzzled her. The heat from his bruised cheek seared her skin. His beard scraped with delicious friction. Aye, this was what she'd been craving—tender intimacy with her wolf-man.

Och, there she went thinking of him as hers again, *feeling* as if he were hers. *Foolish lass.*

But how could she not *feel* when his affection poured over her like a flood? When he was who he was? Her friend, her rescuer, *hers.*

She couldn't lie to herself. Her heart was in this. Completely.

It had been since the moment she'd first laid eyes on him. She'd merely been afraid to admit it because the thought of his rejection had been too much to bear.

A groan rumbled from his throat. "So soft," he said. "So beautiful."

He wasn't rejecting her now. He wanted her. But for how long? Tonight only? For the first time in her life, it mattered if the man's wanting of her left off with the curing of his cock-stand.

She curled her fingers in his hair and yanked him up. "What are you doing?"

"Isn't it obvious? I'm going to mate with you." He parted her legs and settled between them.

A flutter of excitement spread from her stomach outward, but it wasn't enough. "Why? Because I'm good for nothing else? You'll take me here, tonight, and then what? We continue on to Chroina as if it never happened? You'll leave me there and return to your cabin."

He stilled. "Is that what you think? That I want you for one night, maybe two, then I'll leave you alone in a city where you know no one."

"That's precisely what you were planning to do an hour ago." An extremely practical plan, considering the state of his people. If she could be of use to his king, she would have gone willingly. For Riggs.

The sound of his breathing filled her ears. He cupped her head in both his hands, supporting himself on his elbows. "Anya. Sweet Anya." He sighed. "I will still take you to Chroina, because you won't be safe anywhere else."

She closed her eyes. 'Twas no more than she'd expected. But an inconvenient disappointment squeezed her heart.

His thumb stroked her ear. "But I won't leave you. Not ever."

She blinked. Searched for his eyes in the darkness. There they were, dark and near and earnest. Surely she'd misheard. "What did you say?"

"I won't leave you. I'll stay with you in Chroina. If you'll have me."

"For how long?"

"Always."

"But your cabin, your tanning." He'd leave it all behind? For her?

"I'll enlist as a soldier. I'll provide for you. Not as well as a king, but well enough. You'll want for nothing."

She scoffed. She cared naught about possessions. She cared about his happiness. "But 'tis where you lived with your da. 'Tis your home. Your land."

"You're my home."

Saints above. He stole her breath with his conviction.

"But there are laws. You told me exclusive pairs were forbidden."

"That only goes for women still having their seasons. Most of the women left are old. Many of them have taken a permanent lover, some more than one. When a woman's seasons are ended, she is free to choose her own men. Your time has passed. You are free to choose. Choose me. Pledge yourself to me. You have my pledge already."

His pledge? "You're speaking of pledgemates." Like in the story he'd told her about Aine and Gregor. It had seemed to her a wolf-man's version of marriage.

He nuzzled her cheek. "Yes."

He wanted her for his wife. He wanted much more than a tup. He wanted *her*. Her heart pounded. "But I canna give you bairns." What man of sound mind took a wife he kent was barren?

"If you could, I would be obligated to give you to my king. Since you can't, I can have you. By the moon, I want you so badly. Say yes. Say it."

A wee tremor went through his hands. He was nervous. He

thought she might say no.

She'd be a bloody fool to say no.

All her life her highest goal was to be wanted. She'd set her aim high, seeking the affections of her laird, and when he'd refused her, she'd seduced the Keith's war chieftain. If a powerful man wanted her, it would mean she was truly lovable. The love of a powerful man would be enough to erase the ache of her mother's leaving. Or so she'd hoped. Unfortunately, no amount of male affection seemed to fill that defect in her heart.

Riggs was not a laird or a war chieftain. He possessed no wealth or position. But he possessed her heart. And it seemed she possessed his. The enormity of the love between them eclipsed her mother's leaving until she barely felt the sting anymore.

Regardless of what she'd coveted in the past, the love of this humble tracker was everything she'd ever truly wanted. Dare she believe she could have him?

So many times she'd risked her pride and been cut down. But she'd never truly risked her heart. If she agreed to what Riggs suggested, it would give him more power over her than she'd allowed any other man. Could she trust him not to abuse that power?

The night was still. The air smelled heavy. The moon was hidden, but she felt it overhead more acutely than she'd ever felt it before, a lofty weight tugging at her chest.

"Say it," he urged.

He was Riggs. Her brave, strong, loyal wolf-man. He'd more than earned her trust.

She put her hands on his face. "If you want me—and I think you're daft for wanting me—then you shall have me. Take me."

His breath rushed out, as if he'd been holding it. His lips parted. He lowered them to hers.

His body was strung tight, but his kiss was soft. He nipped and moved his head in a gentle rocking motion, like he was making love to her mouth. She was the first woman he'd ever kissed, and he kissed better than any man who had done it before him. He kissed her with passion and honesty. He kissed as if her mouth was a gift, not something to which he was entitled.

Rain started to fall, pattering softly on the wool stretched over them.

Riggs's scent of forest and dusty dog blended with the fresh bite of wind-tossed field grass. His presence above her overwhelmed her in the best possible way.

He pushed her shirt up and over her head. Holding her arms like that, still tangled in the sleeves, he looked her up and down. 'Twas too dark to make out his expression, but she felt his gaze like a brush of lips along her chilled stomach, her breasts, her collarbones, her neck and face, back down to her breasts.

"Mine," he said, his voice even deeper than usual.

Aye. His.

The need to be one with him was a heavy, undeniable presence. Never before had emptiness felt like substance.

With one arm, he held himself above her. With the other, he shoved down his trews.

Aye!

Urgency made his movements jerky, but when he stripped her trews down her legs, he took great care. Patiently, he unlaced the boot on her right foot and eased it off, followed by the canvas she'd grown accustomed to, thereby freeing her good leg. Leaving her partially clothed, he pressed her painful leg, dangling trews and all, around his nude hip. The heel of her boot rested on his arse.

Och, *aye. Aye. Now.*

He paused.

With a tilt of her hips, she invited him to proceed. She'd never been more ready for a man.

He waited. What for?

"I pledge myself to you, Lady Anya," he said, and he stretched her in a single, slow glide that made her gasp.

He was large. And it had been so long for her. But her body eased his way. No oils needed for her wolf-man. She welcomed the mild sting and the bone deep pleasure that accompanied it.

When he was completely seated, he held himself still. "Feels so good," he murmured over her ear.

"Aye. It does." Even better was the ring of promise in his voice when he'd pledged himself to her. Holding him tight to her, she said, "I pledge myself to you, Riggs. Did I say it right?"

He made a noise between an amused hum and a moan. "Perfect," he said with a nip to her earlobe. Then he began to move.

Her wolf-man was not a gentle lover. Nor a quiet one. She couldn't have been more pleased. While he claimed her with his powerful body, he remained mindful of her. With one arm, he cradled her left leg, ensuring her comfort as he saw to her pleasure and his.

She held him possessively as they rocked together. The night air kissed her exposed skin with a shock of cold, but inside, she was molten hot. She was a forge, and her fire burned for one man, *her* man.

Riggs's breathing sped. He put his open mouth over hers as if for a kiss, but he was too far gone to complete the act. He moaned into her mouth as his stomach rippled against hers, and he found his completion.

She answered with her own moans as the pressure inside her burst, undeniable, quenching. Her fingers became talons in his flesh. Fire licked her body, and the burning was so very good, better than she'd ever known.

He cupped her head in his hand, forcing her nose to his neck. His scent drove her pleasure even higher. When it should have ended, her body continued to burn with delight.

Hundreds of times she had reached that carnal peak with a man. She was one of the lucky ones who could find her completion with almost any partner. It had made her valuable as a whore, and it had made working at the bawdyhouse bearable. But this went beyond all her experience. If ordinary coupling brought forth a pleasurable peak, this, with Riggs, was a blissful plateau that stretched on and on.

It felt impossibly grand. Was it because she'd given her heart? Because Riggs was wolfkind? No matter. She would not wonder at something so beautiful. Rather, she would rejoice in it together with her love, her pledgemate.

Waves of climax turned to gently lapping currents. Her body trembled. Riggs's chest heaved as though he'd run leagues.

He rubbed his beard over her head, roughly, sweetly. Was it her imagination or was his scent thicker than usual?

Her mind was too addled to find words, but she petted his back and shoulders, feeling his perspiration through his shirt, assuring him he'd pleased her greatly. More greatly than she'd ever imagined a man could.

"By the moon," he said at last, touching his forehead to hers. "Is it always like that with a woman?"

§

ANYA'S MIRTHFUL PURR rumbled through Riggs's chest. "I was about to ask if it was always like that with a wolf-man."

He pulled back to look at her. In the darkness, her skin took on a blue edge, like a sapphire reflecting moonlight. Her heavy-lidded eyes shone like onyx. Her lips curved in a sated smile. She was the most beautiful thing he'd ever seen.

He could hardly believe it. He'd mated a female.

Everything he'd ever heard about how to please a woman had flown out of his head the second he'd seen her breasts. He'd known only the urge to brand himself upon her. *Mine, mate, mine...* The litany pounded through his head as he'd pounded into his female. He should have been slow and gentle, should have made it go on much longer, should have seen to her pleasure before his own.

But she'd found her peak despite his distraction. No mistaking that. His chest swelled with pride at the memory of her cries and her clutching hands.

"What was that at the end?" she asked, her voice soft and alluring. She traced a finger down his clothed arm, causing his body to respond to her even though he'd just had her. "It went on and on. Is that what wolf-men do?"

So it had been unique for her too. "It's never happened before. But then I've never been with a woman before. Maybe we should try it again. See if we can repeat it." Still seated, he gave an experimental thrust.

"Aye. A grand idea." She grasped his arse and squeezed, urging him to continue.

He shook his head. This time, he'd do it right. He'd show her what a worthy pledgemate he would be. Ignoring her whimper of protest, he slid himself free and took his time undressing her.

Unclothed she was more striking than the full moon. He sat back on his heels and drank in her appearance. Her shape reminded him of an hourglass, small in the waist, generously curved above and below. Her thighs were pale as cream and soft, so soft. No experience in his life had matched the thrill of those thighs cradling his hips. Best of all were her breasts, smooth as rose petals and large enough to overflow his hands. He placed a reverent kiss in the tantalizing valley between them.

She writhed and said something that began with "*Och.*" He didn't understand the rest. Her gemstone. It was in the pocket of her trousers, no longer on her person.

"I don't know what you just said, lady, but I vow to bring you as much pleasure as you can bear tonight." He set to keeping his word. Speech wasn't needed for this communing of bodies.

While the rain fell upon their shelter, he explored his pledgemate. He played with her. He loved her with hands and mouth until he had her intoxicating scent and taste memorized.

Mine.

Her fingers curled in his hair, and she guided him up to kiss her.

He went.

After leisurely sipping at each other for long minutes, she pulled his shirt up and over his head and urged him onto his back. A submissive pose. He gave her his trust and did as she wanted, exposing his chest and wounded stomach to her. He allowed her to caress and kiss him there, exploring him as he had her. He watched until the pleasure of her touch made his eyes flutter closed.

They flew open again with a well-placed flick of her tongue on his chest. He found his pledgemate's gaze glittering with playfulness.

"Do that again," he warned, "and I won't be able to lie here passive a moment longer."

She did it again, the sparkle in her eye telling him she'd understood his meaning even without her stone.

His breath caught in his throat at her boldness, at her sensual teasing. He rolled her beneath him, and he took her again. He took what was his, and she gave. They gave to each other until they were coated with sweat and utterly spent. And like before, the ending went on and on, impossibly, wonderfully.

He fell asleep with deep contentedness filling his heart and with his pledgemate naked in his arms.

Anya. Beloved.

The cooing of pheasants in the grass woke him after a peaceful night. Dawn brightened the horizon with a lavender glow. The rain clouds had rolled away. The sky would be blue and clear today.

He nuzzled his pledgemate not to wake her, only to enjoy her. No longer was he in a rush to get to Chroina. Though it was still the safest place for her, their arrival was bound to be awkward. He'd done nothing wrong in pledging himself to her since she was barren, but that wouldn't be readily apparent when they entered the city. Their mating scents, however, would be.

It was a problem for later. For now, he drifted back to sleep with his hand splayed over her smooth stomach. Had any man ever known such bliss?

As he reentered the land of dreams, he found himself thanking the goddess he hadn't acknowledged in decades for the gift she'd given him. He could have sworn he heard the morning wind whisper, *"You're welcome."*

Chapter 18

AFTER AN HOUR on the plain, Riggs brought Anya two hares, the best two from a well-populated den. It was past midday. They'd dozed most of the morning, mated upon waking, and now they talked by the fire as the scent of cooking meat rolled over them.

Anya lifted a stick of cubed hare from the small blaze and blew on it. She glanced at him, and her lips curved into a secretive smile as she cooled the meat. He knew her secret. It was theirs. Theirs alone.

Mate. Mine.

He still couldn't believe it. He tucked her against his side, smelling her hair while she ate.

"What'll happen when we get to Chroina?" she asked.

"I'll take you to see my uncle first." Anyone else might think to arrest him when they recognized his mating scent all over her. His uncle would give him a chance to explain how she couldn't be the one the king had been waiting for. Then Neil could explain it to King Magnus. The king was fair and wise. He'd listen. He'd understand.

He also had to tell Neil his suspicions about the Larnians holding women captive and Ari being a traitor. "The king will want to meet you, I'm sure, but I'll bet the news about the human women will take precedence."

"Where will we live?"

"The women in the lottery all live at the *Fiona Blath.*" The five-story house was part of the castle grounds and was more heavily guarded than the castle proper. "But you won't be in the lottery. Women past their time of breeding are welcome to stay at the common house, but the ones who've taken lovers or pledgemates usually live in private homes. Under guard, of course."

Anya had stopped eating. She had a faraway look in her eyes. "What is it, lady?"

She looked up at him. Her mouth quirked. "You still call me lady," she observed.

"Mmm. It's how I think of you. *Lady*. Sometimes *Anya*, but usually *lady*." Or simply *mine*. He stroked wisps of hair off her cheek. "You went somewhere when I mentioned the ladies' living arrangements."

She shook her head. "It's nothing."

"It's something. Tell me."

She ate some more meat. "It's just, you called the common house *Fiona Blath*. That was my mother's name. Fiona."

"Tell me about her."

"No' much to tell. She left when I was six. Seona was eight."

"Seona?"

"My sister."

"Sisters." Two females born to the same sire. Incredible. But she'd already told him females weren't rare among her people. He couldn't imagine a world with equal numbers of males and females, let alone two females in the same brood.

Anya nibbled some more hare, but unenthusiastically. It took him a minute to realize why. Sisters. Male siblings were common for his people. He had two younger brothers, Garryn who served in the king's army and Jonoc who was still young enough to be a ladies' servant at the *Fiona Blath*. But to have a sister was highly uncommon. Most of Marann's esteemed ladies were the only children born to their parents. Everyone knew who Hilda and Neil were because they were born to the same sire and dame. They were one of three sets of mixed-gender siblings still alive in Marann. And they were close companions. If they were to experience a permanent separation like Anya had with her sister when she'd come here by magic, they'd mourn bitterly. It would be like having a loved one go to Danu's breast.

"You miss her," he said.

She nodded, picking at her meat. "I think I'll pack this so I can have it for dinner."

He helped her wrap the hare, wishing he could do more to ease her pain. Together they packed up the camp. He stood near her gelding, ready to help her mount up.

"You'll trust me to ride on my own today?" Her lips quirked with mischief. She no doubt remembered him commanding she would ride with him after her galloping stunt yesterday. He was glad she seemed over her spell of sadness.

He checked the girth. "If I put you on the horse with me, I'll end up mating you again. If we want to reach Chroina before the next full moon, we'll do well to ride separately."

She pretended a thoughtful expression. "Mating on horseback. I wouldna mind trying that. But I need a rest. You've tupped me sore."

Worry made him look sharply at her.

"Doona fash." She laughed and patted his chest. "'Tis a good kind of sore. Verra good."

He pulled her into his arms and kissed her deeply before putting her on her horse. They rode at a walk, side by side. He couldn't stop himself from reaching out on occasion to draw her to him for more kisses or to stroke his hand over her shining hair. She didn't comment on the fact they weren't "riding hard."

It was as if she understood things might be uncertain for them upon reaching Chroina. He would figure it all out, though. Everything would be fine. They were pledgemates. She was infertile. They'd done nothing wrong.

They stopped after a few hours for a meal of dandelion leaves and bread for Anya and just bread for him. He'd tried the mushrooms and leaves she liked, but aside from a garnish of dill weed or rosemary along with the salt he sprinkled on his bread, he didn't care for vegetation in his diet.

At the leisurely pace they were going, they wouldn't make it to the eastern forest before nightfall. He'd have to settle for plains hare again for an evening meal. Not much of a sacrifice considering how Anya seemed to enjoy the gamy meat.

They sat on the ground in the shade of a reaching yew tree. Anya leaned against him and traced a finger up and down his thigh. His prick made a tent of his trousers, as it usually did when she was near. Her light stroking crept nearer and nearer, but she didn't touch him there.

His pledgemate was teasing him again.

Tingles of pleasure followed in the wake of her touch. A woman was touching him playfully. His woman. He closed his eyes, enjoying her enjoying him.

He must be the luckiest man on the face of the Earth to have been blessed with her. Blessed. Hmm. Maybe he was beginning to believe in Danu again. Funny how hopeful he felt for his people even though he knew Anya wouldn't be their savior. If the goddess could bring one woman to them, she could bring another. She *would* bring another.

Anya climbed over his outstretched leg and knelt between his thighs.

He opened his eyes and looked directly into hers.

"I'm still hungry," she said as she unfastened his trews.

Definitely the luckiest man on the face of the Earth. "Far be it from me to let my lady go hungry."

"Fortunately for me, my pledgemate has provided an incredible bounty with which I may sate myself." She proceeded to make a meal of him.

His head fell back against the trunk of the tree. He lost himself in pleasure. It was like floating on a cloud, above all his cares.

When it was over, he wrapped a hand behind his lady's neck and told her he loved her.

Her satisfied grin melted into an expression of sweet surprise. Her eyes glistened.

"Come here." He dragged her onto his lap, pressed her face to his throat. "I love you, Anya." He'd tell her over and over again until it no longer surprised her to hear it.

She sniffed. "And I love you."

They held each other for long minutes, and then he stripped them both naked and laid her down.

"I thought we were to make haste today," his pledgemate teased. "We should be riding hard. Isna that what you said?"

Truly they shouldn't tarry any longer. But he couldn't resist rewarding her for the pleasure she'd brought him. He rewarded her well, causing her to cry out his name so loudly a bird took flight from the tree.

He didn't want to stop there. It was tempting to spend the rest of the afternoon mating, but he couldn't justify dallying any longer. She wouldn't be safe until they reached Chroina. They could make it by tomorrow night if they pressed on and rode 'til dark.

He stretched out beside her as she lay on her back, her breathing gradually returning to normal. "Are you ready to ride, lady?"

She rolled her head to give him an incredulous look. "You expect me to stay upright upon a horse after that? I think all my bones have turned to water. Better you drape me over my mount's back and let him carry me like a sack of grain."

Chuckling, he nuzzled her neck. He'd hardly ever laughed before meeting her. Not since his sire went to Danu's breast. Now, he laughed daily. He was happy. By the smile on Anya's face, he could tell he made her happy too. Of all he'd accomplished in life, he was most proud of that. He had a pledgemate, and he made her happy.

Anya drew circles on his chest with her finger. Despite knowing they should mount up, neither of them moved to get dressed. "Your peak was brief today, not like last night and this morning," she said.

He'd noticed. Wonderful as his finish had been this afternoon, when his pledgemate had used her mouth to please him, it had been over in seconds. When he mated with her in body, it took much longer and felt even more wonderful.

"Why is that, do you suppose?" She fondled his prick, examining it as though it held the answers she sought.

"I don't know. I've never experienced anything like it before. But I *do* know if you keep touching me like that, I'll need to have you again before we mount up."

"Hmm." She abandoned her exploration and straddled him. "Mayhap we should try to make it happen again."

Her hair fell around her face in chestnut waves. With a twinkle in her eye, she seated herself intimately upon him.

Ah. Yeah. So lovely.

She wound her arms under his to grip his shoulders from behind.

"Yeah. Yeah, hold on to me, lady. Just like that." He held on too. He gripped her hips and, mindful of her soreness, he took his lady for a gentle afternoon ride he hoped she'd never forget.

§

SITTING ASTRIDE A cantering mount after a night and a day of tupping was the cruelest sort of torture. Anya's privates burned with chafing. Her hips ached from spreading her legs around her pledgemate. Her lips felt bruised from their kissing. Mayhap she was mad, but she cherished every ache and pain. Never before had a man been passionate enough about her to take her so forcefully and so many times in such a short period.

Never before had a man told her he loved her.

She was wed.

She'd asked about pledgemating during the first leg of their ride that day. He'd told her there would be documents to file in Chroina, but that verbal pledges were honored among his people.

"But there were no witnesses," she'd said.

"Danu was our witness," he'd told her.

"You doona believe in Danu."

"Maybe I've changed my mind," he'd said with a smile so genuine the sight had tattooed itself on her heart.

"Leave it to a man to rediscover his goddess after a good tup," she'd said.

They'd both laughed. She loved the sound of his laughter, deep and full-throated, his eyes crinkling at the corners just so.

She'd never felt as alive as she did with Riggs, as free, as cared for. Her deepest desire, to be truly wanted by another, had been granted. Fate had finally smiled upon her. She could even think of her mother leaving without the usual worm of bitterness boring into her heart.

Riggs made her happier than she'd ever been. She was determined to do the same for him. He'd left his home for her. He'd called *her* his home. She would ensure he never regretted the decision.

She didn't care how sore she was. She would seduce him into tupping her every chance she got. Nothing she'd ever known in life was better than the look of helpless abandon on his face when he came for her. Nothing was better than kenning she was the first he'd given himself to. And she would be the last.

'Twas almost too good to be true.

Ahead of her, Riggs directed his mount up a gentle slope to

scout the plain. She urged her horse to follow, appreciating the powerful line of his shoulders. Even wounded and dressed in a stained and torn shirt, he inspired her confidence. 'Twas in the way he held himself, posture straight, chin confidently raised, eyes alert for danger.

Pride filled her. He was her pledgemate. Hers.

She drew up alongside him. The sun was behind them, dropping in the sky as they faced eastward, gilding the rolling plain that stretched for leagues. A dark patch far on the horizon must be the eastern forest Riggs had told her about. Kept stocked with prey, the forest served as hunting grounds for those who provided meat to Chroina.

"There." Riggs pointed to a glistening ribbon winding through a shallow valley not far away. "We'll camp by that stream tonight." He looked fondly at her. "We'll make the forest by nightfall tomorrow. I know a place we can rest where I'll be able to hear anyone approaching and get you away. We'll keep the horses saddled and make no camp."

The forest would be populated with hunters, Riggs had told her. They'd have to take great care not to be seen. Or heard by any sensitive wolf-man ears.

"You best get in all the tupping you want before reaching the forest then, since we'll do well no' to draw attention tomorrow night."

He grinned. "I'll never have enough of mating you. We'll just have to do it quietly."

A little shiver passed over her. It turned into a ripple of pleasure when Riggs cupped her behind her neck and kissed her.

His gaze tender on her, he let her go and started to ride down to the valley. His back went suddenly rigid. He reined his horse to a stop. "Shite."

She followed his gaze to the top of a hill a furlong away. A rider crested the hill, followed by another. Two riders became four. While they watched, the party grew. No less than twenty men rode into sight. The riders in front carried a banner. Even from this distance, she could tell it was crimson and gold.

"King Magnus," Riggs said.

"King Magnus? What would he be doing out here?"

"Don't know." His eyes were hard as he watched the king's party ride closer. There was still a great distance between them, but they would have been seen. She kent as well as Riggs must, there would be no running away to hide.

A sense of foreboding snaked up her spine. Her horse fidgeted. "What do we do?"

"We go meet them," he said.

She tucked her fingers into his hand and gave a squeeze. "Then let's go."

§

TENSION MADE RIGGS grip the reins too tightly. His horse tossed its head. This was happening too soon. He wasn't ready to face his king with Anya by his side.

He was afraid.

He'd done nothing wrong, but that wouldn't be apparent until he'd had a chance to explain. While they rode toward the party, he worked out what he'd say.

When they were the width of a practice field away, six riders broke off from the group and cantered toward them. He recognized the rider on the lead horse, not because he knew the man personally, but because of his royal regalia. King Magnus. He scanned the other riders, hoping to see Neil's war helm but not finding it.

His stomach dropped.

"Stay here," he told Anya. He'd been tempted to tell her to run if things went wrong—her horse was fast, she could escape these men. But that would be foolish. Where would she go? She'd be safer with the king's party than anywhere else. He should be thankful for this turn of events. Anya's safety was as good as guaranteed.

He just hoped he'd be permitted to enjoy that safety by her side. That was far from guaranteed.

A peek over his shoulder confirmed Anya had her hood up and her head down. There was no telling she was a female. Unfortunately, their shared mating scent was all over him. The riders approaching would recognize it. Unless Riggs could explain himself quickly, he would be asked to show his breeding contract. Having no contract permitting him breeding rights to Anya, a female obviously of breeding age, he'd be arrested.

Knowing what he needed to say, he tapped his horse's sides.

The king sat tall and commanding in his ornate saddle. He rode with imperial confidence and reined his horse to a stop neck to neck with Riggs's. Two of the other riders flanked Riggs and the king. Close up, he noticed the brooches pinning the wraps of their war kilts across their leather armor. The brooches depicted a golden lion within a silver crescent moon. These two were among the twelve Knights of the Crescent Moon, the elite guard serving the throne of Marann, the most loyal of the loyal, the best of the best. Their gloved hands rested on their hilts.

King Magnus removed his helm and shook out shoulder-length, golden hair. He was called the great lion king. The description was apt. Even sweaty and matted, his hair and beard resembled a lion's mane.

Riggs bowed his head low, taking care to keep both his hands in sight and far from the handle of his axe. Having this many men so close to Anya had his fingers itching for the feel of his weapon's handle in his palm, but he'd lose a hand sooner than he could touch his weapon.

"You may rise."

His show of deference was acceptable. He met the king's eyes briefly, respectfully, noting his irises were the yellow-amber color of hardened tree sap.

The king took in Riggs's battered face and torn shirt, his gaze moving with the quick alertness of a hawk's. This man would not miss much. Thank Danu Anya had washed the blood out.

Riggs dropped his gaze to the king's chin and waited to be addressed.

"Name and occupation." The king spoke like a man who knew his word was law.

Being addressed meant he had permission to look directly at his king. Riggs sat tall and made his voice clear. "Your Majesty, I am Riggs the trapper, son of Hilda. I live near the border west of Figcroft and have with me a female—"

"It's him, sire." One of the four guards who had hung back spoke over him. He'd been about to say, *female past her time of breeding,* but hadn't gotten the chance. "That's the name the messenger gave."

The other guards tensed and closed the circle tighter around him. The two nearest him, the knights, drew their swords.

King Magnus held up a staying hand. "I'll hear his version of events."

His version? Had news of Anya made it to Chroina? How? He tensed all over, waiting for the men to smell her on him.

The king addressed him. "A wounded messenger rode into the city yesterday. Claimed he witnessed a female captured by a Larnian patrol. Said a trapper by your name helped them." He peered around Riggs. "Who is your companion?"

Protect. Mate.

He couldn't stop the growl that rose in his throat. He cut it off, but it had to have reached the king's ears.

"It's her, isn't it? My miracle." The king's nostrils flared, as if he tried to scent her from where he was. He went very still.

Slowly, he turned those hawk-like eyes on Riggs.

"She's not your miracle," he answered. "She's past her—"

"He lies," interrupted the same guard who'd interrupted him before. Little shite. "It's her. It has to be."

"Silence," the king barked.

Riggs tried again. "She's past her time of—"

"I said silence."

Frustration had him growling again, but the king's intense stare made him clamp his jaw to keep from speaking again. Shite. This was bad.

The king inhaled again, this time with his attention firmly rooted on Riggs. His pupils shrank to the size of pins. "What have you done?" His voice was a menacing growl, the kind of voice a man used to strike fear into his enemies.

"She's past her—"

He flicked his fingers toward his knights. "Arrest him for mating with a female out of contract."

Danu curse it!

The king steered his horse out of the circle and rode toward Anya. The six men closed in.

He grabbed his axe to defend himself. He wouldn't hurt any of the king's guard, but nor would he allow himself to be arrested without explaining himself.

One of the knights shouted, "Stand down, trapper," and sent his sword in for a wounding blow. Riggs hooked the blade with his axe and directed it down. It nicked his leg but didn't come up again. The knight was experienced enough to know he meant only to protect himself. Thank the moon.

"No!" Anya's cry made the hairs on his neck rise. Her voice was too close.

He returned his axe to a defensive posture and spun his horse in a circle to keep the guards at bay. He worked to keep them all in view while searching for Anya. There! She steered her horse around the king's and rode straight for him.

She threw off her hood and tried to penetrate the ring of men around him. "Leave him alone!"

"Get back!" he shouted. There were drawn swords all around her! She'd get hurt!

The king intercepted her, his sword sheathed. He held out a placating hand. "Easy, lady. It's all right now. You're safe."

She drew her dagger. "Call them off. He's done nothing wrong. Call them off!"

When he didn't, she made a disgusted sound. She wheeled her horse to the side and rode around the king for the second time. Forcing her way in beside a young guard, she swiped at his armored arm with her blade.

Riggs recognized it for the warning it was. The guard didn't. He snarled and closed a hand around her wrist.

She yelped and dropped the dagger.

Rage was like a fist punching its way out of his chest. He roared, but could do nothing. There were four sword points at his throat, and a knight had just snatched his axe away.

"Stand down!" the king shouted. "Stand down! Release her! She's my miracle."

The guard released Anya like he'd been burned.

Anya shoved her way into the circle until her horse stood flank to flank with Riggs's. Their thighs brushed, and he breathed a little easier for the contact.

Her presence forced two of the guards to back off, leaving only two swords belonging to the knights at his throat. He trusted these two not to harm Anya, but still, the urge to get her safely away from this threat was a drumbeat in his veins.

"He's done nothing wrong!" Her voice rang with conviction. She faced down six armed men, one of them a king, fearless as a sow with a litter.

His chest swelled with pride.

"If you hurt him, you hurt me. He's my lifemate."

Silence fell.

Lifemate?

He tried to catch her gaze, but she kept it defiantly on King Magnus.

Except for the two knights still holding him at sword point, the others looked to the king as well.

The king's eyes blazed. His nostrils flared again as he took in their mating scents.

Is that why Riggs smelled himself more strongly on her than he'd expected? Is that the reason their finish went on so long when they joined together? Had he made her his lifemate? Was that even possible?

She wasn't wolfkind. He hadn't petitioned Danu for her. He didn't even acknowledge Danu. Or rather, he hadn't...until last night, when mating with Anya had forced him to believe in the divine.

It had been a full moon last night.

Wonder spooled through him as he considered the possibility.

"No," the king said, a fierce denial.

"Aye," Anya said with lifted chin. "A moment ago, you were ready to hear Riggs's version of events. I say you interview us separately. If we tell the same story, you ken we speak the truth. But I willna be speaking to anyone as long as my mate is under threat."

"I said, stand down," the king said quietly.

The knights sheathed their weapons.

"Fetch Neil," he said to one of the guards. "He can interview the trapper. The lady comes with me."

Chapter 19

ANYA SAT ON a boulder between two guards watching King Magnus wear a rut in the earth with his pacing. He was a tall man, though still half a head shorter than Riggs. Finely-worked armor protected his torso, forearms and shins, adding to his air of command. He wore a plaid of rich crimson and a cloak dyed black as night. The crest on the cloak portrayed in profile a golden lion reared up on its hind legs with one front paw resting on a book and the other turned upward to cradle an orb that might have been the full moon.

Here was the great lion king Riggs had extolled. With his mane of wild blond hair and amber eyes, he resembled the animal on his crest to alarming degree, especially with his agitated pacing and the brooding glances he kept flicking her way.

He was jealous. Of Riggs.

Probably because she'd blurted the first thing that had come to her mind that might get a half-dozen worked up men to take their weapons away from his throat.

Lifemates. As if such a notion existed outside of stories and legend. As if such a thing could occur between a wolf-man and a human.

But it had worked. The guards had put away their weapons. She only hoped she hadn't gotten herself and Riggs in too much trouble. Mayhap she should have stuck with the truth and said they were pledgemates. But seeing Riggs surrounded by those soldiers, her mind had reached for the most sensational thing she might utter to get their attention. It might have worked too well.

The lie sat like lead in her stomach. She had to confess it. Had to explain. The king had no reason to be furious with Riggs. She was not who he thought she was. She never could be.

At length, he stopped his pacing and faced her. Fists on hips, gaze boring into hers, he said, "Lifemates." His nostrils flared as he inhaled. His lip curled. "It should be impossible. Yet I smell the truth of it."

"I can explain—wait, you do?" How? Aye, a wolf-man's nose might be able to detect Riggs's seed on her, but according to the story of Aine and Gregor, the lifemate scent would be remarkable, unmistakable. 'Twould smell like more than mere mating scent. Surely the king, whom Riggs had told her took frequent lovers, wouldn't mistake mating scent for somat else.

The king went on as if she hadn't spoken. "I am repelled by your scent. It wafts off you like the pungent gas of a stinkflower. It's mating scent, but more. It's *him*." He waved an impatient hand in the direction Riggs had gone with the man who must be his uncle, the king's war chieftain. Then he motioned to her as if to indicate her entire person. "All over you." He curled his lip. "I should be drawn to you. You were supposed to be mine, and I don't even want you." He snarled and started pacing again.

She bristled and sniffed herself, smelling naught but her own mild scent and mayhap a bit of Riggs's forest-fresh musk. She didn't want King Magnus either, but no lass liked to hear a man describe her as repellent.

"*Och,* you're no' exactly appealing yourself, stomping about and havering over somat you ken nothing about."

He wheeled on her. Anger made fiery slits of his eyes.

She instantly regretted her manner. She needed to be more contrite. After all, Riggs's wellbeing rested in this man's hands. If he truly believed they were lifemates, he might imprison Riggs like the king in Gregor's time. Intolerable. She had to fix this.

"Forgive me. I—"

"Know nothing? *I* know nothing about lifemates?" He thumped a fist on his chest. "I have studied every word ever written about the topic so I would know how to do it when I found you. I waited fifty years for you. Fifty! I have stored up gifts to bestow upon you when I pledged myself to you. I have petitioned Danu every full moon since my coronation to bring you to me so I could make you *my* lifemate. It should be *my* scent marking you. *My* musk wrinkling the nose of every male in the camp. You were supposed to be *my* miracle, and you've gone and bound yourself to a trapper. A nobody!"

She launched off the boulder. Her legs protested, but her ire superseded the pain. "Nobody? Nobody! He's the one who saved me from being dragged off by a pair of Larnians when I first came here. He's the one who carried me halfway across your bloody country. He's the one who fought wolves for me, slew villagers for me, slew trackers who kept talking about bringing me to King Bantus. He's fought for me. Bled for me. Where were you?" She closed the distance between them and jabbed a finger at his armored chest. "What have you done for me? Why should I be yours when Riggs has given everything for me? Why should I belong to you when my heart belongs to him?"

King Magnus grabbed her by the shoulders. He towered over her, terrible, fierce.

She'd gone too far. He was going to kill her. Fear made a snare around her throat. Leave it to her to be killed by a man she'd angered. When would she learn to harness her tongue?

The fire went out of the king's eyes. His hands went soft on her shoulders. He expelled a harsh breath from his nose. "What have I done? Forgive me, lady. My anger is not for you. Never for you." He cupped her jaw with one hand and swept a thumb over her scars.

She jerked away from his touch. It should only be Riggs's

hands on her. Her pledgemate. Her husband.

She backed out of the king's reach.

His hand fell to his side. He was a handsome man. He had strong cheekbones, a straight nose, a luxurious beard. His skin was bronzed from spending time in the sun. He had lines of wisdom around his eyes. He appeared older than Riggs, but not aged. If he were human, he'd be early in his fourth decade, but Riggs had told her he was seventy-five. If she were not besotted with Riggs and missing his presence after less than a half hour apart, she might have been attracted to this fine specimen. He was everything she used to desire in a man—comely, important, powerful, and he desired her—or he would have if she didn't smell so offensive to his sensitive wolf-man nose. But she felt naught for him other than a strange sympathy. He'd thought he'd found his miracle when in reality, he'd merely found her.

She was no one's miracle. But she was Riggs's wife now. She'd given her heart and her body, such as it was, to the man who had earned them and earned them well. She would not apologize for it. Not even to a king.

His gaze roved over her, this time without the blaze of anger. He lingered on her scarred cheek. "You are not what I expected," he said quietly, as if he were talking to himself more than to her. "It should be a paw print, not claw marks."

"They're no' claw marks. They're from falling into a crevice in the rock. And they're no' all that's wrong with me. I can hardly walk. And I canna have bairns. I'm no' who you've been hoping for. If I were—if I ever could be, I would have gone to you. Riggs wouldna have taken me for his own. Please have mercy on him. He's done nothing wrong." It didn't hurt her pride one jot to beg for Riggs's wellbeing. She'd do anything to protect her pledgemate.

The king considered her with cocked head. Would he punish Riggs for supposedly making her his lifemate even though she was barren? Would Maranners near and far soon be telling the tragic tale of Anya and Riggs?

After a long while, he said, "The trapper's guilt is yet to be decided. Sit." He motioned to the boulder. To one of the guards he said, "Tell the men to make camp. When you return, bring tea for me and the lady."

The guard left. The other one positioned himself to the side midway between her and the king as she obediently resumed her position on the boulder.

"Start at the beginning," the king commanded. "Tell me everything."

He stood rooted to the spot with his hands clasped behind his back as Anya started with the moment dizziness had seized her at her da's cottage. He must have been a master at diplomacy, because his face gave naught away as she told her tale. Cool and immobile as a frozen loch, he was. Did he find her story credible, disturbing, bloody interesting in the least? The only indications he was listening were the occasional clenching of his jaw or flash in his eye.

"We took pledges to each other last night *after* I confessed to being barren. Then we continued across the plain, and you ken the rest since you found us soon after." 'Twas with great relief she finished and great trepidation she awaited his response.

His gaze bored into hers while silence built a wall between them.

She shifted. Her arse was half asleep from sitting on the boulder.

At length, he said, "So it happened last night. He petitioned the goddess for you, and she..." He blinked and looked away, not finishing. For the briefest moment a surprising softness passed over his face. Then he faced her again, and he was back to being the hard-eyed king. He held out his hand and said, "Show me the gemstone."

Of all she'd told him—the wolves, the villagers, the trackers—that's what he chose to discuss? She pulled it from her pocket. Somat about the glint in his eye gave her pause as she extended it to him, but how could she refuse? He was Riggs's king, her king now. She dropped it in his hand.

The hard line of his mouth relaxed as he examined it. He closed his eyes slowly, opened them and met her gaze. "It's the one."

"Which one?"

"The one the goddess showed me."

"What are you speaking about?" She glanced from his sober eyes to the gemstone, back to his eyes.

He handed the gemstone to a guard with enough gray in his beard to mark him as aulder than the king. Then he spoke to her.

She didn't understand. His speech was naught but a lilting jumble. Her heart beat faster. She suddenly felt vulnerable, sitting low on a rock before this hard-eyed man. Four guards loomed behind her. The one casting a shadow along her left side held her only means of communication. Her fingers clenched with the urge to take it back.

The king paused, judging her reaction. He spoke to the guard.

The guard stepped forward and said to her, "Did you understand any of what the king said?"

Glaring at him, she shook her head.

"His Majesty says Danu gave him a vision of a chestnut-haired woman with a paw print on her cheek and this stone hanging around her neck in a bejeweled necklace. In her arms, she held a baby. His heir. Your trapper would know this. Everyone knows it. He wonders why your trapper didn't tell you these things."

She gasped. They tried to make it sound as though Riggs had kept things from her. Aye, he had, early on. But he'd been honest with her at his cave. Mayhap he hadn't told her how closely she resembled his king's supposed vision, but he'd made no pretense about his intention for her to give his king an heir. So what if there had been a vision? The result was the same. What ought to concern the king more than Riggs's forthrightness was the very thing that had given him the freedom to take her for himself. She was barren, for heaven's sake! Had he not heard her the fifty times she'd mentioned it?

The king held out his hand for the stone, and the guard put it in his hand.

"He has not been completely honest with you, I see." Smug bastard.

"You're wrong," she said.

"You said he saw the stone. Between it and your scars, he would have known unequivocally, you are the one Danu promised to me. It is not I who am in the wrong. It is he. Your trapper is no more than a thief."

Speaking of thieves. She watched as he turned the stone over in his hand. Her pocket felt too light without it. She felt unbalanced. But more, she worried what the king intended to do to Riggs. "He's no such thing. He's loyal to you."

"Easy, lady." The king spoke over her. "Don't worry about your trapper." His voice was gentle, but his eyes were still hard. "You are lifemates. To separate you from him would be to hurt you."

There he went with the lifemate notion again. She kept from rolling her eyes with great difficulty. 'Twas best for now to let the lie stand since it seemed to discourage the king from punishing Riggs.

"I will never hurt you," he went on. "Your happiness has ever been my goal. Now, tell me your name and what breed you are. It is clear you are not wolfkind."

He'd already hurt her by taking away her gemstone. "I'll answer your questions when you give me back what's mine." She got up from the boulder with a rip of agony through her left knee. She swallowed down the pain and hobbled the two steps to the king.

He didn't so much as glance at her outstretched hand. "Not nice, is it? Having someone take what's yours."

"I was never yours."

"You will be. Danu promised you to me. Many years ago."

The certainty in his tone chilled her. He still thought to take her for his own. "But you promised you wouldna separate me from Riggs."

"And I won't. But hear this. I will have you. In my bed, carrying my heir. You *will* be mine."

"Why, you bloody arrogant—"

"Silence."

She hated him for wielding the kind of command in his voice that made her instantly obey.

"This is how it will be." He pinched the stone between his forefinger and thumb. "I will be holding onto this. Your lifemate will be held at Glendall in a guarded apartment. You will be permitted access to him, but his seed is not to touch any part of you until you give me an heir. At such time, I will grant him breeding rights to you and return this. Do you understand?"

Shock stole her breath. Riggs would be a prisoner. Until she could do the impossible and conceive an heir for the king. And he'd keep her stone, thus forbidding them from being able to speak with one another. "Aye, I understand," she said through gritted teeth. "I understand you're nothing like the wise, fair ruler your most loyal subject described to me. I understand all too well."

He stroked her cheek with the knuckles of one hand. "Such spirit," he said. "I would expect nothing less from the mother of my heir."

§

THE CIRCLE OF guards around Riggs parted, and a familiar warhorse and rider strode through. "Danu's tits, Riggs! What's this I hear about you fucking the king's lady?"

Brother of his mother, Neil shared Hilda's forest green eyes and dark hair, which curled from under his helm. His beard was longer than when Riggs had last seen him, and the lines in his weathered face were deeper, but when that face split into an exasperated grin, a bit of tension lifted from his shoulders.

Neil brought his horse nose to tail with Riggs's and they clasped arms as the guards closed ranks around them.

"She's not the king's lady. She's my pledgemate," he told his uncle.

Neil sat back in his saddle, an amused tilt to his mouth. "And then some. Lifemate, I heard. Is it true?"

He shrugged. "I don't know. Maybe." When Anya had uttered those words, it had seemed impossible. But the more he thought about it, the more it seemed to fit. Her new scent, their incredible mating, the way he felt like he was missing a part of his body being kept away from her like this. Lifemate. Anya. "Yes." He sighed. "I didn't mean to."

"It's true, sir," one of the guards said. "At least I think so. I was close enough to smell her."

Riggs glared at the guard. He was the same one who had interrupted him when he'd tried to explain himself to the king. A growl started in his throat.

"Easy," Neil warned. "What did she smell like?" he asked the guard, curiosity plain in his voice.

"Like mating scent but stronger. Tickles the nose. Like an insult. Makes me want to back away from her."

Smug satisfaction made Riggs's chest swell. *Mine.*

"I imagine it'll fade once this one's imprisoned." The guard smirked at Riggs. "The king's waited fifty years for her. He's not going to let a scent stop him from taking what's his."

Riggs growled and reached for the axe that was no longer strapped to his hip.

"No one's going to prison," Neil said. "At least not yet." His gaze grew sharp and sober. "You better have a good explanation for this. I'm your uncle, but I'm the king's war chieftain first. Sometimes he asks my opinion. Sometimes not. If he decides you're more trouble than you're worth..." He spread his hands.

Riggs got the message. Neil's first loyalty was to King Magnus. As it should be. If the king commanded his imprisonment or worse, Neil would see it done without question.

Good thing Riggs had an excuse. "She's barren," he said.

Some of the guards stirred.

"You can't know that," said the one who'd waxed eloquent on Anya's scent. "You were out of line, trapper. You never should have stuck your prick in the king's property."

Rage surged like fire in Riggs's veins. He dismounted, grabbed the guard by the front of his armor and yanked him off his mount. He punched him in his surprised face. His nose gave with a satisfying crunch.

The man staggered and fell on his ass.

Horses jockeyed all around him. Swords were drawn.

"Stand down," Neil said. He dismounted and stood over the fallen guard. "Next time you taunt a man with a lifemate, make sure to draw your weapon first. Go clean yourself up. You're dismissed until I say otherwise."

The guard swiped at his bloodied nose and led his horse away with a murderous look at Riggs.

He followed to lay the cocky shite out again, but Neil's grip on his shoulder stopped him.

"Barren?" His uncle's voice brought him out of a red-tinged haze of violence.

He forced his hands to uncurl. "You know I wouldn't have mated her otherwise."

Neil nodded. His brow creased as he looked past Riggs, in the direction where the king was speaking to Anya. His mouth turned down with disappointment. Like Riggs, he'd probably hoped she was the one. He sighed. "I know it. But the king doesn't. It's his opinion that matters. Why don't you start at the beginning. Tell me how you found her. I don't believe for a minute the messenger had the right of it. You'd have cut off your own legs before helping Larnians."

Riggs told his uncle everything, starting with tracking the marbled boar into Larna and hearing Anya's cries. He left out his suspicion about Ari and human women being held captive in Larna. He'd wait until he had Neil alone to share such sensitive information. He finished with, "I took her as my pledgemate last night. If I did more than that, I didn't mean to, but I don't regret it. I love her. She's mine to protect. Mine to love. Mine."

Neil looked over Riggs's shoulder. "Your Majesty," he projected with a bow of his head.

Riggs turned around to find King Magnus striding to stand toe to toe with him. Shite. How much had he heard? Between the sounds of the men making camp, and the direction of the wind, he'd had no warning the king approached. He cut a glare at his uncle. He might have let him know.

Neil's face was carefully blank. Some ally he was.

Riggs took a knee. "Your Majesty."

The king didn't tell him to rise. "What's his story?" he asked Neil.

Riggs kept his head bowed while his uncle summarized his story, spending more time on the points that would concern the king, especially the killing of the Larnian trackers at his cave. He wished his uncle would tell the king about Anya's bravery and resourcefulness. His lady deserved her share of the story to be told. While Neil talked, Riggs stole glances in the direction the king had come from, hoping to spy Anya. She was nowhere to be seen. His agitation rose with every minute of their separation.

When Neil finished, the only sound on the plain was the stirring of the grass in the wind. The whole camp had stopped to listen.

He didn't raise his head. Propriety required he wait for the king to address him. Instead, he fixed his gaze on the king's fine doeskin shoes. The wind shifted and Anya's scent teased him. The king had touched his mate.

He heard ringing in his ears. *Mate. Protect.* He curled his hands into fists to keep from strangling his liege.

"She tells the same story," the king said. "We'll discuss the dead Larnians further in my tent. They were within their rights according to the old treaty to track a woman brought across the border. If I'd thought they'd ever get their filthy paws on another woman, I would have dissolved the damn thing. As for you, trapper." He paused. The silence grew heavy. Everyone awaited his fate. "You may rise."

Relief rolled over him, even as he fought the urge to throttle the man. He stood and looked at the king's chin. *Don't lay hands on your king. Don't lay hands on your king.*

"Congratulations. You're the first man in a millennium to be blessed with a lifemate."

He chanced a glimpse of the king's eyes. They were hard, angry. But his tone was civil.

"And you'll be the first commoner in history to enter a breeding pact with a king."

The ringing in his ears turned to pounding. "Breeding pact?"

"It will be the first of its kind. Traditionally, children from a pact would legally belong to all pactmates equally. Bloodlines were not teased out, since it was often difficult to do so, as you can imagine. But, as king, it is imperative that my heir be of my blood. Therefore, I will have exclusive breeding rights to Anya until she gives me an heir. Then you'll have breeding rights until she bears a child for you. Then me again and so forth. Because you rescued her from the Larnians and delivered her safely to me, I will forgive your indiscriminate mating with her. That is, provided she does not get with child from it. If she does, the child will be yours when weaned, and you will forfeit all future breeding rights to her. You'll have a chance to read the pact before signing. My runner is drafting it as we speak."

The king wanted to share Anya.

All the air burst from his lungs like he'd been winded by a mace to the gut. Rage and confusion jumbled his thoughts, but he managed to spit out, "Why? Why do you want her? She's barren. Didn't she tell you?"

The king lifted his chin. "She's my miracle. What's a closed womb to the goddess who gave us life?" Challenge sparked in his eyes. The look was a double-edged sword. One edge rebuked Riggs for doubting the goddess the king had publicly devoted himself to since childhood. The other edge dared him to protest. *Give me a reason,* the look conveyed. *Say the wrong thing and I'll let you rot in prison while I claim sole rights to her.*

If he and Anya were truly lifemates, it would hurt them both to be separated. The king had the power to separate them, yet he claimed he wouldn't do so. Riggs bit his tongue until the taste of blood bloomed in his mouth to keep from giving the king reason to change his mind. "Of course, sire," he choked out.

"Be glad, trapper," the king said. "For, I have taken the lesson taught by Aine and Gregor to heart. Even though breeding rights will belong exclusively to me for the first term of the pact, your lifemate will be given access to you whenever I do not require her presence. However. If she comes to me with the scent of your seed anywhere on her person, I will consider it a breach of contract. You will forfeit all future breeding rights to her."

Riggs's throat felt thick. His face burned with indignation. Another man thought to tell him what he could and couldn't do with his mate. Intolerable! But to say so would be to damn himself and Anya. He swallowed the rage, forcing it deep, where it wouldn't offend his king, soon his fellow pactmate.

Acceptance numbed him like icy lake water. "May I see her?"

The king inclined his head, giving permission. "Of course." A smirk Riggs didn't understand tilted the king's mouth. Then he walked away with his guards, leaving Riggs with Neil and a half-dozen gaping soldiers that quickly found things needing their attention.

"He's not himself," his uncle said. "I've never seen him so vicious. Never. Tread carefully, son. Tread carefully."

He didn't need to be told he was on thin ice. What pissed him off was that there was no reason for it. None. The king shouldn't want her. Riggs had done nothing wrong, damn it.

He stalked away from Neil and rounded a low hill. Anya sat on the ground, her fists curled in the tall grass, her face angled downward. Four guards stood around her, two of them knights. One knight kept his eyes glued to her as if she might try to run. The other three faced outward, protecting her from attack. The salty scent of her tears stung his nostrils.

Ignoring the guards, he strode to her, met her there on the ground and hauled her up against him. The sight of her eyes swollen with crying, yet sparking with anger, undid him even as the missing pieces of him filled in with a glorious burst of sunshine to have her in his arms again.

"Oh, Anya, sweet Anya. What happened? What did he say to you?" Had the king told her about the pact? Was she so thoroughly bound to *him* that the thought of another man touching her upset her this much? She didn't deserve this.

She spoke, but he didn't understand her. Her gemstone. It was gone.

"Did the king take it from you?"

She shook her head, not understanding. Then she thumped a frustrated fist on his chest and pressed her forehead to his shoulder with a fresh wash of that salty scent.

He'd never had a treasonous thought until that very moment. He'd believed King Magus good and wise, but only a very cruel man or a very foolish one would steal from a lady he claimed was a miracle.

He held Anya tightly and soothed her with long strokes of her silky hair. Resting his cheek on her head, he glared in the direction of the king's tent.

You can make her yours on paper, but she'll never belong to you. You don't deserve this treasure.

Chapter 20

EARLY EVENING ON the second day of riding with King Magnus's party, Anya gaped at the stories-high wall of mortared stone stretching as far as the eye could see to the north and the south. It was the first thing she'd seen when they'd emerged from a thin, hilly wood onto a road lined with ruined buildings and abandoned mud huts like the ones she'd seen in Valeworth. With crenellated towers and iron spikes jutting outward like jagged teeth, the wall itself appeared impossible to penetrate. That was before she'd noticed the sun reflecting off a shining ribbon of water at the base of the wall. A moat.

"Does the moat go all the way around?" she asked Riggs. It boggled her mind that a wall would encapsulate an entire city, but where would they get enough water to fill a moat if it went all the way around as well?

He looked at her with raised eyebrows, not understanding.

Och, she ought to be used to it by now, but she still blurted things now and again, forgetting. Curse Magnus's eyes.

She'd stuck resolutely to Riggs's side since the king had taken her gemstone. Occasionally, she felt the king's gaze on her, but she never looked his way. Riggs did enough glaring for both of them. Her pledgemate was none too pleased with his king. His loyalty had been abused.

Did Magnus have any idea what a gift he'd tossed away by acting like a jealous cuckold? Likely not. The man didn't seem to consider much beyond his own pride.

Well, she had her pride too. Magnus might be the only man she could communicate with, but she refused to give him the satisfaction of going to him for any reason. She muddled her way through the simplest tasks with Riggs, making ridiculous hand gestures and using sticks to carve pictures into the earth when the party made camp in the evenings.

"Drayith," he said, pointing at the imposing structure they approached. *Wall.* He'd used the same word for the stone barriers demarking pastures they'd passed. He lifted his hand, pointing to one of the towers. *"Fornith."* The moat. *"Entieth laich." Laich* sounded similar to *loch.* It was one of the words their languages shared nearly in common. Once she heard them in isolation, they were easy to spot.

Their tongues were not all that dissimilar. Now that she'd gained an ear for it, she was learning rapidly. She could even say a few simple sentences.

I ride the horse was *Meh peehirath dorchlah.*

Give me more meat was *Hat feth brahnlach meh.*

Mayhap she ought to thank Magnus for forcing her to do this. She was mated into Riggs's kind now. 'Twas time she began learning the language.

She repeated the words after Riggs.

He grinned as he kept his eyes ahead, pleased.

Warmth suffused her chest. It shouldn't affect her so, making a man proud of her for somat so simple, but Riggs's pride meant the world to her. He meant the world to her. And she kent she meant the world to him. Her pledgemate had gone without meat the last two days because he refused to leave her side to hunt. No man, no person since Seona, had ever been so attentive to her, so steadfast. But even Seona had left, like her mother. Riggs would never leave her. She sensed it. She *felt* it deep in her bones.

Magnus likely sensed it too. 'Twas why he behaved so jealously.

The evening they'd met the king's party, his royal majesty of pulsating pustules had dragged her and Riggs into his tent and fairly forced them to sign his bloody pact. That was after he'd informed her that if she had come to him free of a lifemate bond with a commoner, he would have made her his pledgemate and queen. As it was, he couldn't even take her as concubine—her association with Riggs precluded any royal title. As if she'd want to be concubine to his royal highness of piss pots.

At least the pact allowed her to be with Riggs whenever the king did not "require her presence"—a clause open to bloody broad interpretation, but the king hadn't appreciated her pointing that out. He'd cited the case of Aine and Gregor and claimed he would honor the lifemate bond so as not to cause either one of them distress or to call into question that which Danu had blessed.

Och, she couldn't believe he'd bought it—lifemates! She wasn't even wolfkind. But she wasn't complaining. It was the one thing keeping Magnus from taking her for himself and leaving Riggs out in the cold, or worse, tossing him in a dungeon.

Riggs would be given quarters at Glendall, Magnus's keep. He would be given access to the king's hunting grounds so long as he exchanged his tanning services for the kills he made. If he chose to earn coin in the king's army, he'd be allowed. He wouldn't be as content as he would have been at his own cabin, on his own land, being his own man, but it was far better than being a prisoner, somat the king liked to remind them was within his power, somat he would execute without compunction if they should break the terms of the pact, mainly if the king ever scented Riggs's seed on her.

Because there could be no chance she might already be with child, a physician would examine her after a full moon cycle. If she was found to be with child, the pact would be dissolved. Riggs would take sole custody of the child when it was weaned. Anya would be permitted to visit with him and the child, but he would never again have breeding rights to her. Their visits would be under guard. Bloody waste of ink that portion of the contract was, since 'twas no way she could be with child.

"Make the most of your time with your lifemate," Magnus had told her just before he'd dismissed them. *"Once I know you carry no child, I shall require you in my bed every night, all night."*

So she was to be the king's whore. Until she did the impossible and bore him an heir.

Meanwhile, he forbade her from being with her husband the way her body yearned to be. The unfairness of it had her sitting stiff in the saddle. Her horse flicked his ears in irritation.

Forcing her concentration to the new words Riggs had just taught her, she said. *"Entieth laich"* and drew a circle in the air to indicate around. *"Chroina sumeth?"* *All Chroina?* If this city was to be her new home, she might as well learn about it.

Riggs restated the sentence the way it was supposed to go. She committed it to memory as a little thrill went through her at getting her meaning across.

"Ee-ah," he said with a nod. *Aye.* Then he said some things she didn't understand. But he gestured *around* and made a cutting off motion. Then he said land and sea, two of the many words she had learned in the last two days. Mayhap he meant the moat continued as far as the sea. So it would be seawater in the moat. Interesting. That explained the scent of brine in the air.

It wouldn't be long before they could speak easily to each other. Already, they were leagues ahead of where they'd been. That first night, after signing Magnus's bloody pact, Riggs had held her close in the bedroll, whispering unknown assurances to her and kissing her gently. Her body had burned for more, and the evidence of his desire had prodded her hip, but he hadn't tupped her, hadn't so much as touched her in an intimate fashion.

"Hinatha, hinatha. Chroina," he kept saying. *Soon, soon. When we reach Chroina,* she thought, but she couldn't be sure.

Did he mean he'd love her with his mouth, with his hands? With his cock, but not to completion? *Och,* to have another man place restrictions on that which should be theirs alone to enjoy however and whenever they wished rankled to no end. If Magnus had been anything but a king, she would have rebelled.

She dared not rebel, for she sensed Magnus's mood teetered on a precipice. If she pushed him, he'd make things even more difficult for them. Bloody jealous cur.

She'd thought fate had smiled kindly on her. Turned out, 'twas more of a cruel jape fate had played, letting her believe she'd found pure happiness only to yank too much of that happiness away.

As the party approached the moat, a great log and plank drawbridge lowered to welcome them. The horses' hooves thundered over the planks as they entered the city. The gate opened into a grassy bailey full of manicured trees, topiaries in the shapes of wolves and elk and other forest beasts, and curving paths lined with benches. Though lovely, the bailey was completely enclosed by tall stone walls. The only breaks in the wall were the drawbridge they'd just come through, a smaller gate directly across from it, and a passageway on each side just large enough for a pair of horses and a carriage. She understood why most of Riggs's people chose to live in Chroina. If the double walls went all the way to the sea, like the moat, enemies would have multiple barriers to overcome before breaching the city. She'd never seen a place so secure.

The second gate cranked open as the party approached. Beyond, the streets looked much like those in Inverness. Cobbled stone underfoot, markets and pubs stacked side by side with painted shingles she couldn't read. Men conversed in doorways, and did business at street carts. Everyone stopped and gaped at the royal party. Some bent their knee. Others lifted their chins in greeting. Some watched with nary an emotion on their faces, their eyes empty.

She watched all this from under the hood of Riggs's cloak, since riding while keeping herself covered had become habit. She didn't have to hide here in Chroina, where women weren't uncommon. Nevertheless, the thought of letting down the hood and inviting curious stares curdled her stomach. What would the people make of her? Would they be as disappointed in her as Magnus was? *Och,* it didn't matter. She wasn't who they all thought her to be.

As if sensing her unease, Riggs pressed his horse closer. They rode with their calves brushing. His nearness comforted her.

After a half hour's ride, the street opened to a large square lined with fine stone buildings. One had stained glass windows and a spire with an orb at the top. The full moon. She'd begun to associate the symbol with the goddess Danu. At the far end of the square, the buildings sat wide apart, and between them was a grassy vista that stretched toward a multistoried castle large enough to have housed Ackergill Keep five times over. Midway down the vista, a fountain as big around as a horse corral shot water into the air. The plume was perfectly centered between the two tallest towers of the castle. Atop the towers, banners of crimson and gold snapped in the breeze. Behind the castle to the north were snow-capped mountains. Behind and to the right was nothing but cheerful blue sky. The ocean lay that way, though it couldn't be seen from here. The visual effect should have been stunning, but she took it all in with dispassion.

"Glendall," Riggs said, eyes on the keep.

"Welcome home," she muttered.

Riggs pressed his horse even closer and took her hand. He twined their fingers and curled their joined hands to his chest. *"Hinatha."* Soon.

A shiver of anticipation went through her.

§

THE KING'S PARTY divided as they took a cobbled road around the keep to the stables in the back. Most of the soldiers turned off the main path and rode under an archway through which Anya glimpsed a green field scattered with hay-stuffed dummies and archery targets. That must be where the soldiers practiced. Mayhap they had their own stables. Four guards remained with her, Riggs, Magnus, and Neil. These four, all older men with shuttered gazes, were always with the king. His personal guard, mayhap.

As they approached the fine stone stables, the sun was sinking in the sky, making the shadows long and the hay in the outdoor troughs appear dull brown. There was more than a nip in the air. 'Twas quite cold, in fact. Without Riggs's cloak, she would have been shivering.

A dozen or so aged men in woad-dyed livery met them as they drew to a stop. Stable hands or servants or some combination thereof. One man appeared more distinguished than the others, his livery a crisper blue than the rest. The knotted linen at his throat was brilliant white. He wore a pin of fanned crimson tartan on his breast. All the servants had clean-shaven faces—they were the first clean-shaven wolf-men she'd seen—but the distinguished servant wore a neatly trimmed beard and moustache that framed only his mouth, leaving his cheeks bare. The king dismounted and began speaking with him, confirming her suspicion he must be the head of household. The servant's eyes wandered her way as he listened, but with her hood shadowing her face, he wouldn't be able to see her well.

Fine with her. She had no wish to be gaped at by Magnus's servants. Bad enough she'd had to endure the frequent sidelong glances and outright stares of the soldiers in their riding party for two days. Worse, though, were the looks the men had cast Riggs's way. They hated him. Most, she suspected, believed he'd made her his lifemate kenning she was supposed to be the miracle their king had been waiting for.

He'd brought her through his country determined to give her to another man despite wanting to keep her for himself, and he'd done it out of loyalty for his king. He'd only pledged himself to her once he realized she could not be Magnus's miracle. And *this* was his reward? Becoming the bane of Chroina? The unfairness of it choked her.

But when Riggs gazed upon her, there was no regret in him. She saw only love reflected in his gold-flecked eyes.

He dismounted and reached for her. She gladly trusted herself to his strong hands, and he lowered her to the ground slowly enough for her legs to adjust to bearing her own weight. She buried her face in his chest and inhaled his soothing scent. Since their pledging, his scent had a nearly intoxicating effect on her. She craved it, couldn't get enough of it. He seemed to feel the same about her. As he wrapped her in his tight embrace, he nuzzled her head and breathed deep, murmuring things she couldn't understand.

The keep represented uncertainty and fear. Foreboding stole over her as cold gray stone loomed many stories into the sky at her back. She did not wish to go inside. But Riggs's presence soothed her. As long as they were together, all would be well.

The clearing of a throat pulled her from the spell of security she'd found in her pledgemate's arms.

Magnus.

Riggs stiffened, but he didn't release her.

"Neil requests your company, trapper," Magnus said in his imperial voice. "When he's finished with you, my men will escort you to your new quarters. You've had two days to enjoy our pactmate. Now it is my turn. I require her presence for the evening."

After two days of gestures and learning new words with Riggs, two days in which the king never once spoke to her, suddenly being able to understand someone made her head spin. Then the king's words penetrated. He was dismissing Riggs, and it sounded as though she wouldn't be permitted to see him again tonight.

She clung to her pledgemate and narrowed her eyes at Magnus. "Two days we've had together, aye, but you've seen to it we'd no' be able to speak to each other. I'll go with you now, but I'll expect to be shown to my lifemate's quarters for sleeping."

Magnus's mouth made a hard line. "Of course, Lady Anya. In the meantime, I've instructed my head of household to prepare a bath and a meal for you. If a handful of hours puts undue strain on your bond, it is my hope that the gifts I plan to shower upon you will soothe the pain." His mouth tipped up in a strained smile. "Come. I'll show you your new home while the water heats." He extended a hand to her.

She had difficulty letting go of Riggs. They hadn't been apart since his brief hunting trip on the hilly plain the morning after their pledging. She commanded her hands to uncurl from his shirt and they refused to obey.

Riggs ran a hand over her hair and whispered *"Hinatha"* in her ear. He uncurled one of her fists and placed her hand in Magnus's. He was telling her to go, and if she translated the twinkle in his eye correctly, he was telling her not to goad the king while they were apart.

Och, she was acting like a lass with her first fancy. If Riggs could bear their separation, surely she could as well. How many times had he called her his brave lady?

Lifting her chin, she sent her own twinkle his way. *"Hinatha,"* she said, and she let Magnus lead her into the keep. Glancing over her shoulder, she saw Neil rest a hand on Riggs's shoulder. Both men watched her go with somber expressions.

§

ANYA DISAPPEARED INTO the castle with King Magnus and four of his Knights of the Crescent Moon. Riggs's chest snapped tight with longing. Being away from her caused him pain. Actual pain, like a constriction he could hardly breathe past that could only be eased by wrapping her in his arms again.

"Come on, son," Neil said with a pat on his shoulder. "She'll be indisposed for a while. Might as well come with me to the dungeon to interview Bilkes. Man lied about you. You have the right to be present when I read him his charges."

So the messenger would be formally arrested. Good. It was his fault Anya had been taken by the trackers, also his fault Magnus had intercepted them on the plain, wrecking Riggs's plan to explain himself to his uncle before bringing Anya to meet the king. He hoped they'd tossed the little shite into a dark cell deep in the castle's underbelly.

Neil led the way through the armory. It hadn't changed much since Riggs's days as an axeman for the king's army during the war. He followed Neil down the stairs into the tunnels that led to the dungeon. Neil was strangely quiet as they walked the underground corridors.

Shrugging, he let his mind wander to what he would do to his lifemate once they reunited. Though it left a bad taste in his mouth to know Magnus would provide for her from now on, he took comfort in the fact it would be *him* to bring her pleasure for an entire moon cycle before the king had her in his bed. In that time, he'd brand the feel of his hands and mouth on her. He'd give her his prick, too, but he'd be careful not to release in her per the terms of their pact.

A growl rumbled in his chest at the injustice of another man dictating how he loved his mate. He'd thought Magnus fair and wise, but the man had refused to listen to sense. Riggs had done nothing wrong, and yet the king punished him—and Anya—for becoming lifemates. He'd tried to shame Riggs with the implication that he lacked faith in Danu by believing Anya barren when, in fact, it was spending time with Anya that had restored his faith in the goddess. It was the king who lacked faith by assuming one chestnut haired miracle was all Danu was capable of.

He expected Neil to comment on his mood, but either his uncle didn't hear his growl, or his mind was elsewhere. Yeah, that made sense. As Magnus's war chieftain, Neil would have his hands full with the news Riggs had shared with him on the journey.

Riggs had taken his uncle away from the camp and shared how the Larnians Anya first ran into had assumed she had escaped from Bantus's harem. Then he'd told him everything he and Anya had overheard from the trackers. His uncle had frowned. "*I wish you hadn't discovered such things,*" he'd said. Riggs wished he hadn't discovered them, either. He wished there had been nothing to be discovered.

"What did the king say when you passed along my news?" Riggs asked as Neil nodded a greeting to two soldiers standing guard over a heavy iron door.

One soldier pulled a key from his shirt and unlocked the door. It squeaked on its hinges as Neil pushed it open and motioned Riggs through ahead of him. He had to duck and remain ducking since the ceilings were low beyond the door. He and Neil both had to bend their necks to keep from hitting their heads on the stones above. Behind them, the door shut with an echoing clang.

"Hm?" Neil grunted, as if he weren't really listening.

Riggs followed him down a narrow passage and around a corner. "When you told the king, what did he say? Will he send spies to Saroc to confirm there are women there? Will he invade?

What will he do with the women?" He couldn't imagine how the Larnians had managed to obtain human women. He ached for the human fathers missing their daughters.

"Oh. I haven't told him yet," Neil said as they approached another guarded door.

"What? Why not?" Wouldn't he and king Magnus want to start strategizing immediately?

The guards opened the door, and when Neil and Riggs went through, the other two men followed. It took Riggs a moment to make sense of what he saw. He'd never been in the dungeon before and had expected cramped stone chambers with damp floors and dark interiors. But when they'd stepped through that second iron door, the room he found himself in couldn't have been more different.

Fine furs covered the floor. Tapestries dressed up the stone walls. Warm light and the scent of burning oil came from lamps set around the large room on well-crafted pieces of furniture. The two side walls were lined with half a dozen stone arches each. Bars ran from the tops of the arches to the floor. These were the cells for holding prisoners, but from the open doors and the contents of the cells, Riggs could tell no prisoners had been kept here for some time. The cells contained couches or beds made up with fine pillows and luxurious furs.

Each cell had a curtain hanging from a rod above it. Most of the curtains were swept to the side and held open by braided ties. Some cells had their curtains drawn. From these came the sounds of men groaning, women moaning, and of flesh slapping flesh.

His stomach clenched. Those sounds plus the scent of mating musk in the air made it all too obvious what this room was used for.

"What in the low realm?" he started to ask, but the guards who'd followed him and Neil inside grabbed him. He reached for his axe, remembering too late it had been taken from him.

One of the guards put a dagger at his throat, effectively immobilizing him. The other used a length of rope to bind his wrists behind his back. Shock made him slow to react. Shite. Neil wasn't the ally he'd assumed. Shite.

"I'll have to have a talk with the Larnians about keeping their mouths shut. In the meantime..." Neil shook his head. "I wish you hadn't overheard all that, son. I really do. But there's too much at stake to let you blab to the king."

Riggs strained against the guard's grips, but the dagger cut into his skin, drawing blood, stopping shy of slicing his jugular. He stilled. "What do you mean, *too much at stake?*"

"The revolution is imminent," Neil said. "We've nearly got enough men to overthrow King Magnus. And not a minute too soon. His conservative ways will be the death of us. Can't have you cluing him in to the bribes that brought Bantus on board and ruining all our plans, now can I?"

"You're Breeding First," Riggs concluded. Breeding First was the political party that opposed the king at every opportunity. While Magnus held firmly that sires must be known, and thus women should mate with only one man per season, Breeding First held that women should mate with as many men as possible in a season to increase their chances of breeding. They must be bringing women to this chamber to mate with men other than those they were contracted to. And doing it behind Magnus's back.

He'd heard his uncle mildly criticize the king in private, but he never suspected him of being disloyal. Not only was he breaking the king's laws, he was also committing the worst kind of treason. "You're working with the Larnians," he said, disgusted. Riggs would rather his people perished than align themselves with a king who condoned the vilest abuse of women and animals.

"Only out of necessity," Neil said. "Don't worry. We've

bribed them with women, but like you suspected, not *our* women. Women from another realm."

"That makes it right? They're women like Anya. You trusted women like my *lifemate* to that perverted piece of shite and his lackeys?"

By the moon, Anya had almost known the same fate. If he hadn't chased that marbled boar into Larna, she'd be in Bantus's harem too. The thought made him sick.

"Out of necessity," his uncle said with his hands spread, as if the violation of human women were a reasonable price to pay to secure Larna as an ally.

"There's no excuse for working with that disgrace of a king," he said. "No need is that great. How do you plan to overthrow Magnus? By having the Larnians march here? Into Chroina? Shite, Neil, are you out of your mind? Our women are here. How do you know the Larnians will keep to Glendall and not make a run for the *Fiona Blath*?"

"Protecting our women is our first priority. We have a deal with Bantus. Ari provides him with the women from the other realm. If he follows through with his commitment to lend soldiers to the revolution, he'll earn the right to keep the women he has. If he fails us in any way, including harming any of Marann's ladies, Ari sends all the women back to the realm they came from."

Riggs shook his head. First off, he doubted the human women would be returned for any reason. Second, Neil was talking about the use of powerful magic as if it were an everyday occurrence. Magic came from the immortal realm, and legend held that immortals never shared their magic cheaply. What price did Ari pay for this power to take human women from Anya's world? What price would Marann pay?

"You're making a mistake," Riggs said. "How can you betray Magnus like this? He's been a good king. His family has always ruled fairly."

Behind Neil, beyond the fall of a drawn velvet curtain, male and female sounds of pleasure reached a crescendo that set Riggs's teeth on edge. Neil curled his lip and said, "This from the man who's being forced to enter a pact and share his lifemate? Most men in your position would be looking to help the rebels. But no. You're still loyal to Magnus, even though he'd just as soon toss you in the dungeon as look at you."

The curtain behind Neil opened, revealing an open cell door and a naked woman sprawled on a bed. Her hair-covered breasts rose and fell with panting breaths. Her face was flushed. A smile curved her lips. Her blond coat gave away who the woman was. Diana. The youngest female and the only one with hair so fair.

A man strode from the cell, wrapping his crimson war kilt to cover his spent prick. Sweat beaded his forehead, which was prominent due to him wearing his straight black hair swept back into a club. Ari. Magnus's second, who should be in Saroc keeping Bantus in line. Riggs knew him by sight, but had never met him.

Ari straightened his commander's sash and fastened his belt as he approached, coolly appraising Riggs. "Pacts and lifemates?" he said, inclining his head to Neil in greeting. "It seems I've missed quite a bit. I see Magnus's party has returned. Is this the one Bilkes warned us about?"

Bilkes. The messenger. So he was Breeding First too.

"Yeah," Neil said. He met Riggs's eyes with a sad shake of his head. "I can't say enough how badly I wish you'd minded your business out at your cabin. I would have made sure you got a chance to breed once the new regime was in place. Now..." He spread his hands again.

Cold dread made a fist around his bowels.

"Enough talking," Ari said. "Kill him."

Neil growled at Ari. "He's my nephew. No one's killing him. Use your magic stone. Send him to Saroc to be held with the resisting soldiers." Facing Riggs, he said, "When the revolution is over, we'll sort out the prisoners and release those not deemed to be a threat to the new regime. If you're smart, you'll keep your head down and not stir up trouble." His gaze became intense, as if he were warning Riggs about something.

He wasn't the one who needed to be warned. Neil and Ari, the two men Magnus held in closest confidence, were traitors. They planned a coup. Riggs had to get out of here and warn the king. He had to protect Anya. She wouldn't be kept out of harm's way in the *Fiona Blath* with the other women. She'd be in Glendall, where the coup would take place.

Ignoring the dagger at his throat, he reared forward, taking the guards holding him by surprise. At the same time, he kicked back, knocking the legs out from one of the guards. The blade bit further into his neck, but he let himself fall to the side and away from the dagger before it cut too deep.

"Disable him," Ari said.

The guards didn't give him a chance to regain his feet. One of them clouted him over the head with something heavy. Pain struck like lightning. He lost command of his body. He was yanked to his knees, but only remained upright because of the guards holding him. If they let go, he'd fall to the floor like a bag of sand.

"I'll send him to Saroc because he's your sister's son. But I make no guarantees of his safety," Ari said. "Bantus has an interesting idea of fun." He drew a jagged red stone from the pouch at his hip. "By the power of Hyrk, god of darkness, and for his glory, I call forth a door to the holding cell."

A glowing, swirling red light seeped from the stone and grew in size until a miniature storm churned in the middle of the room. "Give my regards to Bantus," Ari said, and the guards shoved him into the eerie light.

Chapter 21

"AND HERE IS the great hall." Magnus led Anya through two towering doors to a long room with vaulted ceilings and mahogany-lined balconies. Tables lined the walls, as if they'd been pushed aside for sweeping. At the far end by two fireplaces large enough for a man to walk into, male servants were laying rushes over the spotless flagstone floor. One of the servants was thin and fresh-faced. Unlike his fellow servants, he looked up and fixed innocently curious eyes on her. He smiled, and his cheeks turned pink. Aye, just as she'd expected. He was quite young, a lad not quite into manhood.

He'd be rare, this young man, if the birth rate was so low. Yet he served. Interesting.

Oblivious to the servants, Magnus strode ahead of her and spun in a circle, arms spread. "The oldest part of Glendall. In the old days, this served as throne room, kitchen, dining room, and dance hall, and the balconies served as sleeping quarters. Today, it's used for dining and entertaining only."

He looked at her with eyebrows raised in expectation, as if to say, *Go on, tell me how wondrous you find it all.*

"It's lovely," she said without enthusiasm, wondering when the tour would come to an end. She didn't mind the walking after days of riding, but she was eager to reunite with her pledgemate. Riggs's promise of *soon* was turning to an interminable delay. How furious would Magnus be with her if she requested to skip the bath he had planned for her so she could find Riggs instead?

Or if she asked to share the bath with Riggs? *Och,* she kent better than to ask for the latter. Judging by Magnus's tenuous smile, she'd do well not to mention Riggs's name at all. Standing before her was a man who was working hard to be content with his lot.

"I've saved the best for last. This way, Lady Anya." He led her out of the great hall.

She cast a last look at the young servant before Magnus's guards closed in behind them and blocked her view. "That one servant," she said. "He looks quite young."

Magnus beamed at her, the most genuine smile she'd received from him. "That's Julian," he said with a proud puff of his chest. "He's twenty-two. Many of my servants are young men. I honor the youngest citizens of Marann by giving them prized positions in my household. The very youngest receive the greatest honor of all. They serve in the *Fiona Blath.* You know of the common house?"

She nodded. Riggs had told her all about the building that housed Marann's women of breeding age. It was the most secure place in Chroina.

"All except Travis, that is," Magnus said. "You'll meet Travis soon." His lips twitched with a secretive smile as he threw open the doors to a vast room.

There was marble everywhere. The floors were marble. The walls were marble interleaved with tapestries. Marble columns ran the length of both sides of the room. A marble dais occupied the far end. Upon the dais were two thrones, a large one and a smaller, less ornate one. Fascinated with the opulent room, all thoughts of children and servants flitted from her mind.

Magnus walked her down a crimson carpet. "The throne room." His voice echoed off the marble as he gestured grandly. When they neared the dais, he left her facing the thrones and walked to the side of the room. There he pulled on a long braided cord. The crimson curtains behind the thrones parted to reveal two portraits.

The one over the large throne depicted Magnus in what must have been his finest clothing. He held a bloodied spear and posed over the carcass of an enormous boar with mottled hide, like the one she'd seen when she'd first arrived in this place. With his chest puffed up and his eyes ablaze with pride, he reminded her of Laird Steafan. Thinking of her former laird and would-be conquest no longer thrilled her deep in that place of womanly longing. That place was now filled to overflowing with love for her humble wolf-man, a man who killed beasts like the one shown in Magnus's portrait with his bare hands instead of a spear because he wouldn't want to mar the hide, a man whose most prized possession wasn't a throne but a ring given him by his mother.

Her gaze wandered to the portrait over the smaller throne. Recognition plowed over her. Her face went cold. Her whole body went cold. Ringing filled her ears.

She felt Magnus's attention rooted on her. She couldn't look away from the portrait.

"I dreamt of you the first time when I was a young man," he said, his voice punching through the ringing even though he spoke quietly. "Newly crowned after my mother, the queen, went to Danu's breast, I had this commissioned to restore faith to my people. The paw print is wrong. And I see the dream misled me in a few other details as well. But still, the likeness is quite good. You see now why I believe you will give me an heir."

The weight of his gaze pressed too close. It was too intimate. He gave a single slow stroke down the length of her unbound, wind-tangled hair, and the warmth from his hand left a trail down her scalp and the space between her shoulder blades.

Only her pledgemate should touch her like this. Still, she couldn't look away from the portrait.

"This wasn't just any dream," he went on. Another slow

stroke. He was standing so near. "It was from the goddess. The high priest confirmed it. Danu gave me a vision of what was to come. She gave me a vision of you as my queen—or at my side, at any rate, holding my child. Our child."

In the silence that followed, the ringing finally began to fade. She tore her gaze from the portrait. "It's no' me," she said. Her voice sounded far away, as if the ringing had left wads of wool in its place. "It's no' me." Her knees felt like water. She collapsed, and Magnus caught her.

He laid her gently on the crimson carpet. "Lady? Lady Anya?" He patted her cheek.

A commotion at the entrance made them both look that way. Neil was rushing toward them shouting somat she didn't understand. Bloody Magnus thieving her bloody gemstone! "Stop slapping me." She shoved his hand away and sat up, reluctantly accepting the help of his arm behind her shoulders.

He squatted at her side, new tension pulsating from him. He frowned past her. "How? When?" he asked Neil.

Neil sucked air. His chest heaved and sweat dampened his hair, as if he'd run a great distance to tell the king whatever news this was.

"What's he blethering about?" she demanded. "And help me stand, will you?" Bloody undignified being laid out on the floor.

A pleat of concern formed between Magnus's brows. "Perhaps you should remain sitting for the moment. He says your trapper has fled."

"Fled?"

"He says they were interviewing him when he suddenly became violent, disabled a guard, and ran away."

Ran away? She'd never witnessed Riggs run from anything. No, her courageous and capable wolf-man always ran *toward* trouble, facing it head-on with honor. Besides, he'd promised, *"Hinatha."* 'Twas not the sort of promise a man would make if he planned on running away.

"He wouldn't," she said, but the men went on talking in urgent tones, not listening.

"What's being done to find him?" Magnus asked as he stood with her cradled in his arms like a child.

Neil responded, but of course, she didn't understand him.

She squirmed. "Put me down. I can stand. What did he say?"

"He says they've sealed the city gates. That means he's still in Chroina. Don't worry. We'll find him." He didn't put her down but strode from the throne room carrying her. Neil kept pace at his side.

Magnus shot off orders like arrows. "Send a unit into my hunting grounds. Have another scour Glendall. Go to the stables and see if any horses are missing. Ask the stable hands if they've seen him. He can't have gone far."

To his credit, he seemed shaken by Neil's news and intent on finding Riggs. If readiness and action hadn't rolled off him in palpable waves, she might have wondered whether Magnus had arranged to remove Riggs from the pact by foul means. But he hadn't. His fashing was genuine. He believed she and Riggs were lifemates and separation from him might cause her to fade away like Aine.

A few days ago, she would have scoffed at the notion of bonding so closely with any man that his absence would cause her to fade away. She wasn't scoffing now. As it began to penetrate that Riggs was missing, some vital part of herself seemed to wither. It felt like her soul was curling in on itself, protecting itself from the horrible possibility of a lifetime without her wolf-man.

No. She would not give quarter to such ridiculous notions. Lifemates. Bah. Legend and folklore were making her overly sentimental. She wouldn't swoon and mope that Riggs was gone. She'd bloody *do* somat about it. She'd not soak in a warm bath and trust others to locate that which belonged to her.

Riggs might not be her lifemate, but he was her pledgemate. He was her love. *Hers.*

Think, Anya.

She started with what she kent. She'd last seen Riggs standing with his uncle as Magnus took her into the keep. Not an hour later, Neil had come running to the king to claim Riggs had fled, which was a bloody lie if she'd ever heard one. Neil had been the last one to see him and was also the one to report him missing.

Words from a lifetime ago came to her. *"Where ye last saw 'tis where it shall be found. Look harder, child. Our treasures doona fade into thin air like magic."* She didn't have many memories of her mother, but that was one. She'd lost her favorite figurine and had given up all hope of finding it. But her mother had refused to let her give up. She'd listened to her mother and returned to the last place she'd seen it. Sure enough, a more thorough search revealed the porcelain doll under some shavings near the woodpile. But she'd had to get on her hands and knees and brush the shavings aside. She'd had to look beyond what was plainly visible.

Still carrying her, Magnus turned into a carpeted corridor with lower ceilings and fine pieces of furniture on display, a residential part of the keep. He and Neil were discussing their strategy for finding Riggs. She studied Neil. His gaze shifted a mite too often. He nodded too enthusiastically when the king dictated commands. He struck her as more distracted than he ought to be, as if his mind were in two places at once. A sense of wrongness made the skin at the back of her neck prickle.

What have you done, you sly mongrel? What are you hiding?

If he'd hurt Riggs, she'd gut him. Slowly.

They turned another corner and Magnus brought her into a lushly appointed suite that smelled of orange blossoms. A copper hipbath steamed in front of a crackling fire. A delicate table laden with breads and cheeses stood next to the bath. 'Twas a paradise amidst chaos. She wanted no part of it.

"You're no' leaving me here. I'll help search the castle." The shaking in her soul demanded action.

Magnus set her on her feet and pressed somat into her hand. "I should not have taken this from you. I acted rashly. Here."

She looked down. Her gemstone! She closed her fingers around it.

"I will be busy searching for your lifemate," Magnus said. "I would not have you unable to communicate your needs to Daly. And I would have you secure here in the chamber that adjoins mine." He motioned toward a closed door across the room. Between the door and a marble fireplace, standing still as statues, were the distinguished ageing gentleman she'd noticed earlier, and a young lad with a mop of blond hair.

She blinked at the wee ane. He appeared no more than eight or so. But Riggs had told her the youngest child had been born eleven years ago. Could this be…

"Travis," Magnus said reverently. "He's the youngest of us, the Pride of Chroina. He helps care for the ladies when they come to visit Glendall. Now he is your servant exclusively. He and Daly will tend you. Ask of them anything, and if it is within their power, they will see it done."

The distinguished servant inclined his head in greeting. The lad beamed at her, showing a great deal of pearly white tooth.

"I won't rest until your lifemate is found," Magnus said. "This I swear." He started to leave.

"Wait!"

Magnus paused in the door. Neil watched her over his king's shoulder.

"A private word," she requested. "Please."

Neil frowned.

"Go. Find the trapper," Magnus said to Neil. Then he shut the door on the man and the guards. "Quickly," he told her. "There is much to be done."

"Your war chieftain lies," she said. "Please tell me you can see it."

His mouth made a hard line. His gaze was intense on hers, but while she watched, it softened, grew weary. "Your lifemate would not have fled. No force on Earth could make a man abandon his lifemate. Unless everything I've read on the topic is false."

She didn't bother correcting the lifemate notion. The point was Magnus believed her. Riggs wouldn't have run away. Neil was hiding somat. A horrible thought struck her.

"Did Neil tell you everything Riggs and I learned about the women in Larna?" Riggs had taken her and Neil a short distance from the camp and told him their suspicions. Riggs had trusted him to share the news with the king. They'd both assumed he would do it right away.

Magnus's eyebrows snapped together. "Women in Larna?" He had no idea.

Och, she'd been too concerned with Riggs's wellbeing when she'd told the king her story to bring up the other women at that time. Then, once Magnus had taken her gemstone, she'd been too angry with him to fash about those women. She'd been selfish not to make sure he kent about them.

"Bloody lying traitor that one is." Fury rolled over her at the thought of Riggs's uncle deceiving him. She clenched her fists until the gemstone tried to carve itself into her palm. "I willna take the time to tell you how I ken it, but ken it I do. There are women being held captive in Larna. Human women like me." She spoke urgently, kenning action must be taken immediately to find Riggs. She also spoke quietly, aware Neil could have his ear pressed to the door. Valeworth had taught her never to underestimate a wolf-man's hearing. "If not for Riggs, I would have been added to their number and no one in Marann would be any the wiser. The Larnians I had the misfortune of meeting referred to the women as Bantus's harem. There's more that Riggs and I overheard from the trackers. Suffice it to say they confirmed our suspicions. If Neil didn't share all that with you then he must be involved. And he's the last one to have seen Riggs. What if he did somat to him to keep him from telling you about those women?" Her hands shook with concern for her pledgemate. She'd never fashed this much over another. She'd never even fashed this much over herself.

Magnus had gone completely still. His eyes blazed. "Women," he said. "Human women? In Larna?"

"Aye."

He straightened. 'Twas his turn to clench his fists.

Poor Magnus. He'd kent nothing of this. She watched emotions pass over his face like clouds over the sun. Rage, betrayal, guilt. Finally, he said, "I've suspected for some time my second has been moving against me. Now I know Neil is in it too. But why would that involve women of your kind?" His jaw clenched and unclenched as his gaze went unfocused on her in thought.

Och, a plot against Magnus. What had she and Riggs stumbled into? A flare of sympathy penetrated her fashing. It had to be difficult enough to rule a nation almost depleted of women without one's closest councilors acting against one. "Doona ask me what they're up to. I just hope you have some powerful allies to counter having your second and war chieftain against you."

"Do not fear, precious one." He laid a hand on her shoulder. "I am not without supporters. I had just hoped I wouldn't have to call on them so soon. Keeping women in secret is a violation of our treaty with Larna and grounds for war. But before I gather my faithful and march for Saroc, I vow to exhaust every possible resource to find your lifemate."

He faced a political plot against him and still, he made finding Riggs a priority. She wouldn't let him shoulder this duty alone. Riggs was *her* pledgemate. She'd help find him. "The bailey where we dismounted, that's where we'll begin our search. Someone must have seen where his uncle took him."

"That's where *I'll* begin *my* search. I can't look for him effectively if I'm worried about your safety on top of a duplicitous war chieftain and a second who thinks to steal my throne. You'll stay here with Daly and Travis and with four of my most trusted men at the entrances. You are not to leave under any circumstance."

A retort rose in her throat, but she bit it back. He made sense. From what he said about Neil and Ari, it sounded as if her safety was far from guaranteed. Turned out Chroina wasn't half as safe as Riggs had assumed.

Riggs. Her heart tore with longing to lay eyes on him. *Don't let him be dead.*

"Fine," she agreed. "Well. Go on with you. Find Riggs and you'll have one more ally, and a strong one at that." She waved him to the door, eager for him to begin his search, aye, but also eager to question Daly, who had seen Riggs outside the stable and might ken where Neil had taken him.

Magnus put his hand on the latch. "I will, precious one. Stay here, and do not fear." He stepped into the corridor.

"Thank you for the gemstone," she said as he pulled the door closed.

He paused. "You're welcome," he said with a wan smile, and then he was gone.

Only after the door had closed did she remember how Neil had interrupted them before she could explain her reaction to the portrait over the smaller throne. Magnus had said the likeness was good. She agreed. Quite good. But the likeness wasn't hers. No. The lovely face rendered in expert strokes was that of another chestnut-haired Highland lass.

The portrait was of her sister, Seona.

§

RIGGS FELL FOR what seemed a long way before hitting a hard surface. The landing knocked the wind out of him, but he hadn't hit as hard as he'd expected. That eerie red light disappeared, leaving him surrounded by the darkness of a narrow stone cell. Now this was what he'd expected to see when Neil took him down to the dungeon, only he never expected to end up on this side of the bars.

A small, barred window set high in the wall let in the scent of brine. A different part of Glendall's dungeon? But Glendall wasn't situated close enough to the harbor to account for such a strong ocean scent. What had Ari said before the soldiers shoved him through that strange light?

"Give my regards to Bantus."

Ari had spoken with Neil about sending him to Saroc. Could it be? Could he be more than a week's journey from Anya, way up at the northern tip of Larna? The possibility alone was enough to make his heart pound with terror.

He tried to sit up, but his wrists were still bound behind him. Tightening his abdominal muscles, he got himself upright. Too fast. His head throbbed with pain. He was lucky he hadn't lost consciousness from that blow. The dagger wound in his neck had soaked his collar with blood, but it wasn't too deep. It'd scab over by morning. It was the non-physical insults that would evade healing. His uncle's betrayal, not just of him, but of Magnus. The separation from Anya. Both twisted like knives in his gut.

Grunting with effort, he got to his feet and stood at the bars along the front of the cell. The light was meager, but he could make out the dark gray, almost black color of the stone making up the walls. There was only one place black rock was harvested and used for building. Northern Larna. He was in Saroc. In Blackrock Castle, Bantus's home.

Ari had sent him here using a magic stone. He'd called on the name of some dark god.

Shite.

And Ari was in Chroina. With Neil and Anya.

He roared and banged his shoulder against the bars, trying to break them. They didn't give.

Maybe if he could get his hands free he'd have a chance. He searched the cell for any loose or protruding pieces of rock he could use to cut through the rope. A turn around the barren space revealed nothing sharp enough. He tested the bonds. Too tight to wriggle out of. Too strong to break. Damn.

A distant rattling sound like a key in a lock made him hold his breath to listen. The shriek of a heavy door on rusted hinges. The stomping of several pairs of shoes descending some stairs. If he wasn't mistaken, there were three shod men and one with bare feet.

"Bull, go on ahead and prepare the play room." A voice so deep, it was almost distorted.

"Yes, sire."

Sire? Must be Bantus. Great.

One set of footsteps shuffled ahead of the others. They grew closer as "Bull" came toward Riggs's cell.

He shrank back into shadows before a man in a faded blue war kilt and worn work shoes lumbered past carrying a lantern. The Larnian soldier had arms the size of tree trunks and a chest like a boulder. Riggs could see how he'd gotten the name Bull. The soldier never glanced in his direction. His footsteps continued down the hall and turned down another.

Scuffling and whimpering sounds came from the direction Bull had gone. It sounded like several frightened animals cowering together. The whimpers reminded him of when he'd first heard Anya's cries in the Larnian forest.

The human women. They were being kept in a cell not far from his own.

Bull's heavy footsteps paused. "Yeah," he said in his grating voice, "you know what's coming, don't you? Who's it going to be tonight, huh? You, pretty thing? Yeah, you with the big tits. I hope so." He grunted and moved on. Riggs heard him unlock a door beyond the women's cell. Then he heard nothing but feminine whispers in a language he didn't know.

Fucking bastard, stopping to taunt the women. Danu help him. Riggs's worst fears about what could be happening in Larna were being confirmed right before his eyes. He had to get out of here. Had to stop this.

Unhurried footsteps approached his cell from the direction Bull had come. Three more men.

"Any requests, gentlemen?" Bantus's voice.

"Whatever pleases you, sire," said one man.

"Can I have a turn?" said another. "It's been so long since I've had my pleasure with a female."

"*Tsk, tsk.* Have you learned nothing, Myre? Those who request anything but their king's pleasure get the beam. Reddick, when we get in the play room, hang him up and strip him."

"Yes, sire."

"No! Not the beam! I'm sorry, I'm sorry. I only desire your pleasure, sire!"

A cold chuckle. "Too late, Myre. Too late. Reddick, hang him facing away from the festivities. For being a sniveling ass kisser, you lose the privilege of watching."

Festivities. Bantus spoke of abusing women as if it were sport. Maybe he could provide a different kind of sport to distract him and spare the women tonight.

When the men came up along his cell, he stepped up to the

bars. "Larnian filth," he spat. "King Magnus should have wiped you all out while he had the chance."

The men stopped. He instantly knew which one was Reddick and which was Myre. Reddick was tall and lean with piebald stubble covering his head. He had a craggy face and cruel, orange eyes. Myre carried a lantern and a ring of keys. He was smaller, scarred, and hunched with shame. The third man was King Bantus.

Though Riggs had been in Blackstone before as a spy, he'd never had the displeasure of meeting the lord of the castle. But he'd heard of him. Rumors abounded of a pale king as cruel as he was tall. If his height was anything to go by, Riggs was not looking forward to sampling the man's cruelty.

Dressed in a pristine blue war kilt and nothing else, not even shoes, Bantus stood at least seven feet tall—the first man Riggs had ever met taller than him. Blond fur covered a lean, muscular chest. Straight, silver-blond hair hung over his shoulders. He faced the cell, hands clasped at his belt, and smiled a toothy smile. Like most Larnian nobles, his teeth were sharper, more wolf-like than Maranners', a remnant of Jilken's magical breeding with wolves.

"Look, gentlemen, we have a new guest." That too-deep voice was like mud in Riggs's ears. He wanted to shake it out, never hear it again. He was not to be so lucky. "What's your crime, soldier? Or are you a soldier?" Bantus appraised his common clothing with eyes the white-gray color of an overcast sky. "Hmm, a commoner. Why would Ari send me a Maranner commoner?" He clapped once. "Ah well, no matter, I'll see to your comfort once I've had my entertainment for the night. Myre, I'll allow you the pleasure of fetching Fluffy before I hang you from the beam. Bathe her and prepare her for me." The men started to walk away, toward the cell housing the women. Unacceptable.

He pressed his face to the bars. "Is Fluffy one of your she-wolves?" he called after them. "I heard you Larnians had grown desperate since you failed to hang on to your own women. But desperate enough to mate wild animals?" He scoffed. "King Magnus should have put you all out of your misery twenty years ago."

Bantus stopped. He came back to face Riggs. "Do you know what separates a strong ruler from a weak one?" He didn't wait for Riggs to answer. "A strong one grabs hold of the opportunities fate gives him. A weak one squanders them. Do you know what your golden lion is?"

"A brave warrior. A wise leader. A champion of women." For all his personal anger with Magnus, he recognized the good his family's rule had done in Marann. Especially when compared with Larna's rulers.

"A squanderer. And do you know what I am?"

"A maggot. A flea-infested, shite-covered—"

"An opportunist," he interrupted. "I'll have Magnus bowing to me before the next full moon. I'll have you bowing to me before morning." He snapped his fingers. "Myre."

The smaller man jumped. The keys on his belt jingled. "Yes, sire."

Bantus inclined his head to the guard without taking his eyes from Riggs. "Count your blessings. I've found someone to hang on the beam in your place."

Myre's face lit up. Then his brow furrowed. "What about Fluffy?"

"Leave her. For now. I have a new pet to break in."

This was going to be a long night.

Chapter 22

A BATH WAS the last thing Anya wanted at the moment, especially a hot one when her legs would prefer a cool soak. But she consented to let the lad, Travis, help her undress and step into the copper hip bath, tasks he performed so smoothly 'twas clear he'd been serving ladies a long time. Daly had discreetly left and returned carrying an armload of silk dresses once she was submerged in water made cloudy with copious perfumed oils. The sunny, sweet scent of orange blossoms bloomed around her, but she detected notes of vanilla and lilac in the olfactory cocktail. If she weren't fashing to distraction over Riggs, she would have appreciated the silky texture and relaxing scent of the bath if not the temperature, which was just shy of scalding and turned the swelling in her left knee to tight throbbing.

She hadn't a stitch of clothing on, so she kept her gemstone tucked tightly in her fist. After Magnus's jealous stunt, she was loath to be parted from it again. Besides, she needed it. When the trackers had taken her from Valeworth, Riggs had come after her. It was her turn to find him. She didn't have his nose nor his strength and endurance, but she had her wits. And she had two servants at her disposal. If she'd learned anything from her gossipy associations with Laird Steafan's servants, 'twas that very little occurred within the walls of a keep that the staff didn't ken about. If Riggs remained in Glendall, a servant would have heard about it by now.

Gritting her teeth against the pain in her legs, she said to Daly,

"So you're to be my servant, aye?"

"Yes, lady Anya," he replied while hanging the dresses inside an armoire enameled in white and trimmed with gold inlay. Like Magnus, his accent was more cultured than Riggs's. After straightening the dresses, he faced her with hands clasped at his belt. "It is my great honor to serve you."

"Mine too," said Travis, nodding enthusiastically. He moved behind her with a pitcher and began rinsing her hair and lathering it with soap smelling strongly of orange blossoms. His massaging fingers distracted her from the pain in her legs. She kept her eyes on Daly. 'Twas he who had seen Riggs with Neil in the bailey by the stables.

"'Tis *my* honor to be served by the king's head of household and the youngest person in the world." Wouldn't hurt to butter them up a wee bit. "He said I could ask of you anything."

Daly raised his eyebrows, a cautious invitation.

She chuckled. "*Och,* 'tis merely information I seek."

"What information is that, lady?"

"You heard the king, aye? My lifemate is missing."

He nodded, his brow pinched. "I am sorry, lady. This is a travesty of the worst sort. I'm sure King Magnus will do all in his power to restore your lifemate to you."

"He ought to be worried about himself," she said, tipping back her head for Travis's rinsing. "Tell me about this uprising he faces. His second is involved, aye?"

Travis's hands froze in her sudsy hair.

Daly's gaze darted to the door, then back to her. "My job is to see to the king's comfort, and now yours. If any who keep council with the king are plotting against him, I am not privy to such things." She couldn't help but notice how he didn't bother lowering his voice. Any guards outside the door would have heard him easily. He came closer and stooped to put his mouth by her ear. He smelled of shaving soap and cloves, and he had creases around his eyes that showed he smiled often. "His second heads a party called Breeding First," he said quietly. "Have you heard of it?"

She tried to shake her head, but Travis was wringing water out of her hair with surprisingly strong hands for a child. "No," she whispered, "but I can guess from the name what their objective is. Wouldn't it be the king's too? To breed?"

Daly nodded. "Of course," he whispered, "but Magnus holds to the old ways, the ways established by Danu. Sires must be known for the blood to be strong and blessed. Breeding First has been striving to change the lottery so multiple men can win breeding rights to a single lady within the same season."

Interesting. "That wouldn't necessarily help," she said, mindful to keep her voice quiet. "If the problem is with the women, no amount of seed is going to make them conceive. If 'tis truly a curse on your people, doing the opposite of what your goddess decries seems a foolish measure."

Travis moved around to her other side. "That's what the king says."

She frowned at him. "*Och,* arena you too young to ken about breeding?"

It was Daly who answered in hushed tones. "Everyone talks about it. The children can't help but hear."

"I know a lot about breeding," Travis whispered earnestly while he ran a soft sponge over her arm and shoulder. "Like I know my sire isn't really the noble who was contracted to my mother at the time I was conceived, even though my certificate says otherwise."

She felt her eyes widen.

"My sire is Ari," he said, looking less than proud. He lifted one of her arms to wash away her natural musk. "Breeding First thinks he should be king because he sired a child when King Magnus hasn't been able to." Finished with her underarm, he moved around to the other.

"But you disagree." She gathered as much from his tone.

He nodded so vigorously his blond curls bounced. "Magnus is a good king."

She kept hearing that. If he hadn't behaved so jealously when she and Riggs had run into his party, she might actually believe it. "Does he ken you're Ari's get?"

"Everyone knows, but no one talks about it. I look like him, see? I have my mother's hair, but everything else is Ari's, especially my eyes."

The lad's eyes were stormy gray with flecks of lighter gray, like clear skies trying to break through the clouds. She kent little about Ari, but if these were his eyes, he must be a striking man. "If Ari was with your mother when she was contracted to another man, isn't that illegal? Shouldn't Ari be in prison?"

Daly said, "Such a thing can't be proven, especially since Ari was supposed to have been in Larna at the time Travis was conceived. It wasn't until the past year or two that Breeding First started whispering about Travis looking like Ari. A man can only be imprisoned if there are witnesses to him taking liberties with a woman out of contract or if mating scent can be detected on both man and woman. No one has come forward as a witness, and it's far too late to detect mating scent."

"*Och,* what a difficult situation for Magnus. Was that how he realized Ari was against him?"

Daly nodded. "I think so. There were clues before, but I don't think His Majesty wanted to believe his cousin would betray him." He stood and said crisply, "Let's get you out of the tub now, lady, and see which of these gowns might fit you. Of course I'll bring in the king's own tailor tomorrow, and he will create a wardrobe worthy of you."

"Some of the guards are on Ari's side," Travis whispered by way of explaining Daly's sudden increase in volume.

Daly winked at her and whispered. "The king trusts the guards he placed at the door, but one never knows. One never knows."

Saints above, what did all this mean for Magnus? For her and Riggs?

From the sounds of it, Ari had been sneaking around gathering support so he could take Magnus's throne. But how had he managed such a feat from Larna? More importantly, what did all this have to do with Riggs? Why would anyone want Riggs out of the picture? Was it because of what he'd overheard about the Larnians keeping human women? She'd overheard things too, and Neil kent as much. Did that mean she was in danger too?

Travis lent her his hand, which was larger than a human child's would be, and helped her stand up in the tub while Daly busied himself in the armoire.

She stood with a groan and leaned heavily on the lad to step from the tub. Water streamed down her legs, soaking into a sheepskin mat near the hearth. The fire kept the chill at bay as Travis toweled her dry with a linen blanket.

He was careful not to ogle her, but his gaze paused on her bare breasts. Must be an odd sight to him after helping wolf-women bathe; Riggs had told her how they had as much hair on their chests as he did, and that the ladies groomed their coats fastidiously. Travis would likely have assisted in this since he routinely served the ladies who stayed in this chamber, the ladies King Magnus had tried to breed with.

The thought brought no jealousy whatsoever. She was beginning to respect Magnus, but she had no desire to visit his bed. In fact, the thought left a cold pit of dread in her stomach. As she remembered his treatment of her and Riggs the night he forced them to sign his bloody pact, anger made her clench her teeth. 'Twould take more than returning her gemstone for him to earn her forgiveness.

Yet she had to rely on him to find Riggs, it seemed, since she was stuck in this room. Nevertheless, she would do her part to help. Daly and Travis had proven more than willing to talk about private matters with her. Time to ask some possibly touchy questions.

Daly approached with a garment of silk the color of ripe peaches. "A dressing robe for you, my lady. To wear while you dine and while Travis combs your hair."

She slipped into the robe. It felt like a gentle breeze on her skin. "Thank you, Daly." Lowering her voice, she said, "Tell me about Neil. What's he doing in all this? Why would he want Riggs out of the way, and where might he have put him?"

Daly seated her at a dressing table with a costly glass mirror framed in gold. Some of the whores in the bawdyhouse kept rudimentary ovals of brass for applying their rouge and pinning up their hair, but never had she seen such luxury as this: an entire piece of furniture simply for viewing one's reflection!

While she marveled at the extravagant furnishings, Travis crouched to fit silken slippers on her feet. They were too long for her, but they'd keep the chill off her toes.

Meanwhile, Daly set a tray of breads and cheeses at her elbow.

She could get used to palace life, she mused as she popped a ball of moist, white cheese in her mouth, but not without Riggs at her side. She'd rather have a simple cabin and her pledgemate than all this finery and a gaping hole in her heart.

Travis set to combing out her wet hair while the flavor of tangy cheese, salt and herbs burst over her tongue. *Och,* she hadn't had cheese in ages! But she wouldn't let the fine meal distract her from her mission. She grabbed up some more cheese and a slice of bread but fixed her gaze on Daly, awaiting his answer.

"I wish I knew, lady," he said. "I saw them standing together in the bailey, but left before they departed. Didn't see which way they went."

"There were other servants out there," she said. "Stable hands, household servants. Surely someone saw somat." Two men the size of Riggs and Neil, who stood of a height with his nephew, didn't escape notice, especially since rumors of Riggs taking her as his lifemate would have passed through the halls of Glendall like wildfire. "Can you summon servants for me to question?"

"I think I know where the war chieftain took him," Travis said.

She twisted on the couch to find the lad peering at Daly with a blush rising in his cheeks.

Daly looked stunned.

"Where?" she and Daly asked at the same time.

Travis cleared his throat. "There's a room in the old part of the castle, in the dungeon." He gently turned her to face the mirror and began working the comb through her hair. "I see guards and nobles go in. Everyone who goes there is Breeding First. They stay there for an hour or so and come out smiling. Sometimes I hear people laughing in there. Or—" He swallowed. "Screaming, but not like they're scared. Sometimes it sounds like they have women in there, but I've never seen any of the ladies going in or out. A few times, I thought I heard my mother in there."

She and Daly exchanged a look. What Travis described sounded like a bawdyhouse. This room could be where Breeding First carried out their mission, all behind Magnus's back.

"How do you know of this room?" Daly asked.

"Me and some of the other pups like to explore the tunnels." In the mirror, she saw Daly nod, as if he kent what tunnels the lad meant. "There are passageways off the tunnels that run above the lower hallways. You have to crawl through them. There are grates where you can get in and out. One of the grates looks over the door to that room. There are always guards there. The war chieftain goes there a lot."

A thump at the door made them all look that way. Men's voices could be heard. They escalated in volume.

Travis's hands grew tense on the comb.

A man outside shouted. There was a sound of two swords clashing.

Daly gripped her arm and encouraged her off the couch. "This way, lady." He directed her to the door that adjoined Magnus's chambers.

"What's happening?"

"I don't know, but the king gave me specific instructions if we should hear any disturbance at the door." He spoke urgently, no longer keeping to a whisper. "Travis, take her through the tunnels to the north wing." He pulled open the door to Magnus's rooms. To her, he said, "You're to barricade yourself into the storeroom and not open the door to any but His Majesty." To Travis, he said, "Once you see her to the storeroom, find the king. Tell him of this room in the dungeon and show him where it is." He pushed her through the door. Before he closed it, she saw the glint of steel in his hand. *Och,* did the aged head of household think to fight to give her time to get away?

She started to protest, but Travis dragged her along the wall of an opulent solar. Midway along the wall, he lifted a tapestry and pressed a stone. A passageway opened with a scraping of rock on rock. Sounds of a fight filled the chamber they'd just left.

"Come on, lady, hurry!" Travis tugged at her hand.

She hobbled after him fast as her legs could carry her, but they were on fire from that bath. The tunnel was dark as night, but Travis seemed to ken where he was going. After many minutes, her legs wanted to give out.

"I canna go any farther," she panted.

Men's voices echoed behind them.

"You must," Travis said. "Hurry." He pulled her along until

her muscles cramped and her left knee buckled.

She cried out.

"There!" a man's voice said. "Did you hear that?"

"She won't get far on those legs," said another. "Hurry."

They were close. And they were right. She couldn't run any more. She couldn't even walk, not until she'd tended to her legs.

"Go," she urged Travis. "Away with you. Find Magnus and tell him of this."

"I won't leave you."

"You must." The men's running footsteps were nearly on top of them. "Quickly," she whispered. "No arguments. Go."

Travis squeezed her hand, then let it go moments before the men arrived. Their heavy footfalls disguised the soft scampering of the lad as he ran away.

"I'm on the ground," she told the men. They stopped before her. "Don't tread on me. Help me up, will you?" She held up a hand.

One man clasped her wrist and helped her up.

"If you plan to take me somewhere, you'll have to carry me. I've done all the walking I'll be doing tonight."

"My pleasure, lady," the man holding her hand said. Big hands banded her waist and lifted her.

She obliged by winding her arm around a beefy neck with hair grown over the collar. Mayhap these men kent where Riggs was. Her own welfare was naught compared to Riggs's. If she could save him, she'd gladly sacrifice herself.

"I'll do as you ask. But if I find you've harmed my lifemate, I'll gouge your eyes out with your own daggers."

Both men chuckled.

"Legs don't work, but she's got a fine spirit," the man holding her said.

"What's Ari going to do with her?"

The man holding her shrugged. "Let's find out. Come on,

lady. We're taking you to see the man who will be king of Marann by tomorrow morning."

§

TRAVIS FLATTENED HIMSELF against the tunnel wall, breathing silently and becoming one with the darkness.

Two guards had found Lady Anya. The scent of fresh blood rolled off of them. He worried about Mr. Daly. The old servant had been ready to fight when Travis had dragged Lady Anya into the tunnels. He hoped he was all right. Who would see to the running of Glendall and the care of King Magnus if anything happened to the head of household?

He recognized the guards' voices. From his hiding spot in the crawlways, he'd heard these two making conversation as they'd guarded the room he'd told Lady Anya and Mr. Daly about. The tunnel was too dark to see them now—good thing since if he could see *them* they'd be able to see *him*. But he remembered what they looked like. They were Breeding First. Like his sire. Ari.

They'd said he would be king of Marann by tomorrow. That meant they were planning something tonight. He had to warn the king. But first, he'd follow the guards to see where they took Anya. He had a sinking feeling he knew where they'd go. He hoped he was wrong.

Chapter 23

RIGGS HAD NEVER known such pain. Bull and Reddick had sliced the rope from his wrists only to bind them with iron manacles. The manacles were welded together, forcing his wrists to make an *X*. A heavy chain ran from the manacles to an eyehook the size of a cart axle which someone had screwed into a thick wooden beam in the rafters. It was from this chain he hung, his feet barely touching the dirt floor, his bare back against a wall of damp black stone. Manacles on his ankles prevented him from kicking his persecutors. He was strung up like a gutted boar, and he was minutes from losing consciousness.

A few more ounces of blood, a few more burns from Bantus's hot irons, and he'd pass out. Then Bantus would no doubt turn his attention to his other "pets," the women he'd heard in that other cell. Judging by the filthy mattress atop a pallet against the other wall, Bantus entertained himself in even more despicable ways with the women.

He had to hang on. For as long as he could. As long as Bantus played with him, he wasn't hurting a woman.

If only it weren't so blazing hot in this Danu forsaken dungeon! A fire crackled happily at one end of the high-ceilinged room. That was where Bantus liked to heat his irons. He also had a pot of water heating over the fire. Riggs cringed at the thought of what he planned to do with that water once it was boiling.

Let it be me he intends to scald, not any of the women.

Exhaustion had his head hanging. Sweat burned his eyes. The

oppressive heat tempted him to give in to the dark oblivion of unconsciousness.

Bantus's bare feet moved in front of his wavering vision. What torture did he have in store for him now? Whatever it was, he'd grit his teeth and take it. To spare the women, he'd take it.

By the moon, he hoped Anya was safe with King Magnus right now, that she'd never know anything even half as dismal as this dungeon.

He raised his head to look Bantus in the eyes. "Hope you've got something worth my time, you piece of royal shite. Stop playing around with tickling me."

Bantus grinned. "Oh I've just begun, Maranner. I wasn't speaking idly before. I'll have you bowing to me and calling me Your Majesty before morning." He paused to stroke his beard. "I think it's time to start pulling teeth. Myre. Bring the tongs."

Myre brought the tongs.

Bantus squeezed them in a snapping motion inches from Riggs's face. "Do you know the best way to break a man's spirit? You'd think it would be to take his stones. Not so. First, you remove his teeth so he can no longer eat meat. Then his tongue so he can no longer take bread. Then his hands and feet so he can no longer work. That is how you break a man. We'll see how far I get before you swear fealty to me."

Fear flooded his mouth with bitterness. But determination puffed his chest. "I'll never swear fealty to you. You're a blight on the face of the Earth. You've brought your country to ruin, and you destroy all you touch." He mustered enough strength to spit, hitting Bantus square in the chest. It would likely be the last victory he ever knew.

Bantus's face darkened. "Bull, hold his head."

Danu, give me strength. Send help for the women. Take care of Anya for me.

§

As soon as the guards carried Anya through the iron door, she kent where she must be. The room in the dungeon where Travis had heard men and women carrying on. Old cells had been converted to tupping chambers, complete with fancy beds and couches done up with fine linens and bedfurs. Curtains could be drawn for privacy. Tapestries hung from the walls, making the stone room a warm and comfortable retreat. Oil lamps filled the space with soft light.

Neil paced before one of the open cells, listening to a man in a red plaid with black, clubbed hair. The unfamiliar man stood near a bed and rubbed the back of a stately woman in an emerald silk dressing gown like the one Anya had on, but trimmed with lace. The woman sat on the bed with her arms crossed. The robe gaped enough for Anya to glimpse the blond coat covering the woman's large breasts. The three seemed to be having some sort of conference.

"Here she is," stated the guard holding her. "Where do you want her?"

The man and woman looked up.

Neil stopped pacing and faced her. His mouth made a grim line.

"*Och,* I'm no' a bloody piece of furniture. Put me down, ye great oaf!"

The guard huffed and set her on her feet. Her legs nearly didn't hold her, but she gritted her teeth and locked her right knee, taking all her weight onto her stronger leg. She gripped the gemstone in her hand. "What have you done with Riggs?" she asked Neil.

His jaw worked. His forest green eyes burned with anger, but she had the feeling it might be directed at the other man, not at her. "You're about to find out," he bit out. "I'm sorry, lady. I wish there was another way."

"Another way for what?"

"Is this supposed to be the female Magnus was to take as queen?" The woman stood from the bed with liquid grace. She was almost of a height with the dark-haired man, who was shorter than Neil, but likely of average height for a wolf-man. She cinched the satin belt of her robe and slinked past Neil to frown down her slender nose at Anya. "Doesn't look like the portrait to me. I thought she'd be taller. And prettier." Her emerald eyes roved over Anya's scars.

The dark-haired man came up and put a hand on her shoulder. "Don't worry about her, Di. She'll be gone soon. No one will sit on the second throne but you, and you'll be there tomorrow. I vow it."

Di must be short for Diana. This was the youngest wolf-woman. Travis's mother. And the dark-haired man must be Ari, the man who thought to take Magnus's throne. Tonight, it seemed.

"I've heard of you," Anya said to Diana. She looked at her flat belly. "I thought you'd be with child. Aren't you supposed to be the most fertile woman in the world? How long has it been, eleven years since you've had a bairn?"

Diana's hand flew. Neil caught it before she could slap Anya.

"You'll not raise a hand to her," he growled. Turning sad eyes to Anya, he said, "She'll face enough violence at Bantus's hands. Promise me she'll be the last." He looked to Ari.

"She'll be the last," Ari said. "We make our move tonight. Then it will all be over."

"You'll get those women out of Larna once you sit the throne?" Neil spoke of the human women.

"As soon as possible. Once we have the loyalists under submission, there will be no need to keep Bantus as an ally."

"There'll be no reason to keep him alive," Neil said with a

decisive nod.

"What are you waiting for?" Diana said, sidling up to Ari. "Contact Bantus. Personally, I'll be surprised if he accepts this latest gift. Maybe you shouldn't count on him coming through tonight until he sees those scars."

Diana spoke as if they meant to give her to King Bantus, as if they'd given other human women to Bantus in exchange for an alliance with Larna. But how could such a thing be possible? How was Ari here when he ought to be in Larna? Her understanding had to be faulty. She squeezed the gemstone. Mayhap it wasn't working properly.

"He'll come through." Ari pulled a jagged blood-red gemstone from his sporran. "By the power of Hyrk and for his glory, open a door to Bantus the Terrible."

A red light expanded in the air before them and began swirling. 'Twas like an angry sky given motion and turned on its side.

Anya jumped back from it only to find herself engulfed by the arms of a guard. "What the bloody hell is that!"

No one answered her. The swirling madness continued to grow until it was oval-shaped and large as a door. The center of the oval became a shimmery surface, like a gently rippling loch. An image of a man came into focus. A very tall man with long pale hair. He had on a plaid in some dark color—'twas difficult to tell because of the red tint. He was facing away from them, but half turned with a look of surprise on his face. He held some sort of tool, as if he were about to stoke a fire. Dark liquid had spattered his hands and arms.

Could this be King Bantus? Did this oval give them a window of sorts into Saroc? She'd witnessed magic in Gravois' camp, but this felt different. A subtle wind shifted her hair like the scrape of a bony hand. "This is evil," she said. "You are committing evil."

Diana rolled her eyes. "By the moon," she muttered, nudging

Neil's elbow with hers, "I hope Bantus takes her."

Neil ignored Diana. He was glaring into the oval, grinding his teeth. Somat had him even more angry than he'd been.

Ari started to address the man in the oval, but the man spoke first.

"Bad timing, Ari. I'm busy with the new pet you sent me. Come back later." The man's voice was so deep it made her skin crawl.

"It's time for you to honor your bargain, Your Majesty," Ari said. "Gather your two hundred men. I open a door to your great hall in exactly one hour." Aye. This was Bantus the Terrible, the king Riggs hated with all his being, the one who had abused wolf-women and been defeated by Magnus, the one descended from the vile King Jilken.

They meant to give her to this horrible man.

Fear gripped her insides. She pushed at the guard's arms, but he held her fast. "You're all mad!" she yelled. "Let me go!" She did not want to go into that red oval. The guard clapped a meaty hand over her mouth and held her so tightly she couldn't even bite him.

In the oval, Bantus shifted, revealing another form behind him. A large man strung up by his wrists. A man with dark liquid dripping from his downcast face. A man with black curly hair. *Riggs!* That's where he'd gone! He was in the hands of Larna's king!

Had Ari sent him through this oval earlier? Was he even alive? The way he hung, she couldn't tell. *Och,* she couldn't tell.

She screamed and thrashed, to no avail. She had to *do* somat, but she was completely helpless. Where was Magnus? This was his bloody keep. Didn't he ken this wickedness was going on beneath his feet?

She looked to Neil, but he avoided her eyes. He turned from the oval and resumed his pacing. *You did this!* she wanted to shout at him. *You gave your own kin to that monster!*

"You said the coup would take place after the lottery drawing," Bantus said. "That's not until next week."

"It's in two days, actually," Ari said. They bickered like fat bloody hens while she struggled with the guard. "But I intend to be on the throne by tomorrow morning. Magnus has found out about our arrangement. He's gathering his supporters now. We must act swiftly or risk being outnumbered. Your new plaything can wait."

Bantus handed the tool to someone out of the frame. He stroked his beard. "Well, my new pet has just passed out on me. And after only a single pulled tooth. *Tsk, tsk.* I had higher hopes for this one. I suppose I can finish breaking him after the coup. It'll cost you, though. What do you have for me?"

"You mean besides Magnus to hang from your beam before sunrise? How about this?" Ari dragged her from the guard's hold and pinned her to his chest with an arm across her throat. The constriction prevented her from giving him the verbal lashing he deserved.

Bantus eyed her scars. "Someone's played with her already."

"Yeah. Your own men. This is the one the Maranner behind you found while trespassing on your land. Isn't that right, Neil?"

"Leave me out of this," Neil growled.

Bantus raised his eyebrows. "Trespassing?" He turned and punched Riggs in the stomach so hard it shook the chain he hung by. Riggs didn't react.

Agony ripped through her to see him abused so. She tried to call his name, but Ari's hold choked her.

"You'll pay for that, Maranner," Bantus told her unconscious pledgemate. "No one trespasses on my land. No one. No one steals women from me." His voice rose until it broke. He was mad. Saints above, Riggs was in the hands of a madman, and she would be soon as well.

Och, enough. Rage surged though her like boiling water. She turned the gemstone in her fist and gouged it into Ari's forearm.

He released her neck with a shout.

She spun to face him, snatched his cock and bollocks and gave a wicked twist. Tried to wrench them clean off his body, she did.

He yelped and doubled over.

Before she could do more, the guards were on her, pulling her off him.

"Riggs! Riggs, wake up!" She fought the guards until she could see into the oval again.

Riggs didn't move. This was intolerable!

"Magnus! Help! Help!" Remembering Valeworth, she screamed, pushing her voice as loud as it would go.

"Silence her!" Ari shrieked, and a guard clamped a hand over her mouth too quickly for her screaming to do any good.

Ari's face was red. He couldn't stand up straight. 'Twas the least he deserved. She hoped he never stood straight again. Diana rubbed *his* back now, staring daggers at Anya.

Framed by the oval, Bantus was bent double too, but not in pain. He was laughing. Joyously.

"Rumor has it these two are lifemates," Ari ground out. "If you really want to break him, you'll mate her while he watches." He glared at her as he said it. Payback.

Neil stormed out of the dungeon. Coward. He was war chieftain. If he wanted to put a stop to this he could.

"But it'll have to wait," Ari said, hands on his knees. "Two hundred men. In your great hall. One hour. Once I hold Magnus's crown, you get the female, and you can play to your heart's content."

"Send her now or you get nothing from Larna." Bantus's eyes gleamed with excitement.

"There's no time," Ari snarled.

"I want her now." Bantus stamped his foot.

"Your word you'll gather your two hundred."

"Just for that last sight, I'll make it two hundred five and twenty."

Ari nodded at the guard. Before she kent what was happening, she was shoved into the oval. She fell. And fell. Too far. Then she hit a hard floor.

The air changed. It became suddenly moist and sweltering hot. Sounds of a fire crackling filled her ears. Large hands hauled her up.

Stunned by the fall, she blinked and met a pair of eyes so pale they reminded her of snow. Bantus.

He inhaled, then grinned, showing a lot of tooth. "Freshly bathed. Perfect. Reddick, put her with the others while I gather my generals. Myre, make the bed and wake up the trespasser. Bull, come with me. As for you, my new pet," he said to her. "I will be back shortly. I have only an hour before I must go to battle. If you sate me well, I will bring you back the head of a king." He kissed her scarred cheek and handed her off to another man. Terror had such a hold on her she could think of no retort.

As the second man carried her from the dungeon, she peered over his shoulder at Riggs. He raised his head an inch, enough that she could see how badly his face had been beaten, enough that she could see blood staining his lips. His nostrils flared as he inhaled. He opened his eyes and fixed them on hers.

Then a doorway blocked her view.

Her heart pounded. She'd found Riggs, but they were sorely outnumbered. They were prisoners. Pets. At the mercy of a mad king.

The man carrying her, Reddick, unlocked a barred door, put her on her feet, and nudged her through. She dug in her heels, but it only earned her a shove that made her fall to her hands and knees.

The door closed behind her and Reddick stalked away, leaving her in a cell smelling of piss and stale blood and lit only by the meager light coming from that cursed dungeon room. She couldn't help it. She began to cry.

"Hush, now, lass. It'll go worse for you if ye let them see your tears."

She started at the soft, alto voice. 'Twas painfully familiar. "Seona?"

A gasp. "Anya? Is that you?"

"Aye." Her voice wavered.

Arms went around her, more slender than she remembered, naught but skin and bone.

She wrapped her arms around her sister's skeletal body. Her heart rent to feel the bones of her ribs, the bumps of her spine. She cried harder, needing to squeeze her sister tight, but afraid to hurt her.

"Hush, Anya, hush," Seona whispered frantically. "I meant what I said. You doona want to show them tears."

She gulped back her sobs and brought her galloping heart under control. Pulling back, she gazed into her sister's eyes, lighter brown than her own, but the same shape. They were sunken and rimmed with purple shadows. Poor Seona was starving.

She touched her sister's face, assuring herself she was real. Her fingers found a rough patch on her cheek.

Seona's hand clasped Anya's to her face. "It's his mark," she said, her eyes sad. "We all have it." She motioned behind her, and Anya noticed at least a dozen sets of eyes fixed on her and Seona. The human women. She'd found them. She'd found her sister. And she was powerless to do aught about it. "You'll wear the mark too. He'll brand you before he tups you. It hurts like bloody hell, but it'll heal, Anya dear. It'll heal."

Did she mean the branding or the tupping? Anya shivered.

There were some things that never healed. She feared these women were scarred in ways that had naught to do with Bantus's paw-print brand. Judging by the way Seona dropped her gaze when she tried to offer comfort, she was more broken inside than her pride would allow her to admit.

Anya was going to kill Bantus. For Seona. For the other women. For Riggs. She didn't ken how, but she would find a way. If it took the rest of her life, lived out in the squalor of this cell, she'd bloody well find a way.

Chapter 24

ANYA SAT ON the cold stone floor arm in arm with Seona. The woman with her forehead pressed to hers was her sister but not. Her eyes darted nervously. She refused to speak of the horrors Anya feared had been visited upon her by their mad captor. She would only answer the most rudimentary questions, and even then, 'twas like baiting a hook and reeling in each bit of information a word or two at a time.

Roughly half an hour had passed since Reddick had put Anya in this cell, and all she'd managed to learn was that Seona had been lured from the bawdyhouse in Thurson by a man matching Ari's description. *"Told me I'd belong to a great king. I'd never have to work again. Ha!"* She'd begun laughing hysterically, and the cackling had raised the hairs on Anya's arms even as it rent her heart in twain. None of the other women paid Seona any heed. Or Anya, for that matter. Chained in their own thoughts, or divorced from all thought. Hard to say which.

Had they all been lured away from the Highlands by Ari? Or were they from different places? Was anyplace safe from him when he held that red stone?

Once she found a way to kill Bantus, she was going to set her sights on Ari. She'd string him up by his gonads and beat him until *he* cackled like a lunatic.

A clang echoed in the passage outside the cell. Footsteps approached. A palpable tension descended over the women. Some of them scampered to the shadows.

"I hope you've had a chance to rest, lovie." Bantus and Reddick appeared at the cell door. "Because it's time to play."

She reached for Seona's hand, coveting her sister's support, but Seona was no longer by her side. Anya peered around and found her hunched and shivering in a corner.

She hated her sister in that moment. For being a coward. At the same time, she ached for her. This should not be. None of this should be.

She squared her shoulders and faced Reddick as he unlocked the cell. When Bantus grinned and motioned her forward, she limped to him and looked him in the eye, craning her neck to do so.

He hummed with approval. "A brave one, Reddick. How long do you think she'll have the courage to meet my eyes?"

"Not long, sire."

She would not show her fear. Riggs had awoken when Reddick had carried her from the dungeon earlier. She would be brave for her pledgemate. Lord knew he'd suffered enough this night. She would do naught to add to his suffering.

And if the Lord saw fit to rescue them soon, she'd welcome it with open arms.

§

"WAKE UP, MARANNER." *Slap.*

The wretched guard, Myre, tried to wake Riggs, but he was already awake. If one could call the fuzzy consciousness he clung to wakefulness.

He ignored the guard. Instead of giving him the satisfaction of opening his eyes, Riggs rotated his wrists in tiny increments this way and that, exploring the range of movement of his bonds. He flexed his arms, lifting himself so his weight left his feet and was completely sustained by the beam overhead. The soles of his boots remained touching the floor, but only barely. He did all this subtly, so as not to alert Myre to the fact he was working out whether he might get free.

The moment he'd scented his lifemate and opened his eyes to find her present in Bantus's dungeon, he'd called to Danu from his moonsoul. He'd paid the goddess little heed through his life. Had never worshipped or prayed to her as his father had. Why should he? If she existed at all, she'd abandoned wolfkind, a people of her own creation, to a slow but sure death.

He'd called to her moments ago. He'd called to her in desperation. He'd called to her in faith. She would answer. She must, because it was Anya at risk. *Anya.*

Danu would help, but he had to do his part. So he tested his bonds, searched for any little bit of give he might exploit. Where was the weak point? Where must he focus his strength so he could save Anya from a horrific fate?

Myre slapped him again.

He fluttered his eyelids to get the guard to leave him alone. It worked.

Myre moved away, muttering.

Sounds outside the dungeon punched through his concentration. He recognized the baritone rumble of Bantus's voice. And the lilting cadence of Anya's steps.

She was walking to what she must know would be certain torture. And with no hesitation in her gait. Brave lady. But then he'd known that. He'd witnessed her bravery many times over.

He wouldn't fail her.

Danu wouldn't fail her. Anya was not to be the salvation of wolfkind, but she was *his* salvation. She was his life.

He didn't open his eyes when he heard her enter the dungeon with Bantus and another man who was likely Reddick since the footsteps weren't heavy enough to belong to Bull. He stilled his explorations, rested. He would need all his strength for what he must do. And some of the goddess's too, if she would lend it.

He breathed deep. Waiting. Praying.

"Good. You have the fire nice and hot." Bantus. "Myre, heat the brand."

Those words should send him into a panic. They didn't.

Breathe. Rest. Wait.

"Reddick, you know what to do." Bantus spoke to his guard, but he was standing in front of Riggs, facing him with breath smelling of wine.

He fluttered his eyes again, pretending to come to.

"Wakie, wakie. Time for a treat, pet. Do you enjoy the symphony of a woman's screams? I do." Behind him were sounds of movement. Then a struggle.

"Get your bloody paws off me!" Anya. Furious.

His heart beat faster. They were manhandling her onto the bed Myre had just prepared with fresh linens.

Wait. Wait. Not yet.

"Clean her cheek. Yeah, the smooth one. Don't want my mark lost amidst those scars."

Anya's protests became muffled. They'd either gagged her or someone had a hand over her mouth. She was frightened. He could tell from her rising pitch.

Wait. Wait. Breathe.

Clinking by the fire. Bantus was pulling the iron from the flames.

Riggs slivered his eyes open. The Larnians in the room all had their eyes on the glowing paw-print-shaped iron in their king's gloved hands.

Anya had her eyes on Riggs.

He opened one eye to let her know he was with her, then closed it again to concentrate. Before darkness wiped out that glimpse of her, her gaze had darted to the dagger strapped to Reddick's calf. The man was sitting on the bed with her between his legs. With one hand he held her wrists behind her back. With the other he clasped her jaw, forcing her head to his shoulder so her smooth cheek was presented for branding. Her chest rose and fell with her rapid breaths beneath the peach silk dressing gown she must have been given at Glendall.

Bantus turned from the fire and began moving toward the bed. *Now.*

He took a deep breath and flexed his feet, tipping his toes up, using the manacles around his ankles as an anchor. He tensed every muscle in his legs, abdomen and back. Lifting his chin to align his neck for maximum power, he poured every ounce of strength he'd ever possessed into pulling down on the chain.

When the eyehook had been screwed into the beam high overhead, it had gone in slightly off-center. During his testing, he'd found the slightest bit of wiggle and had worked it to make a bigger defect. He exploited that defect in full now.

No longer trying to remain inconspicuous, he roared with the strain. When his muscles and joints protested, he demanded even more of them.

Bit by bit the screw eased from the beam until with a mighty snap, the eyehook broke free.

The men all wheeled on him with wide eyes.

He pinned Bantus with his gaze. The man stood at the foot of the bed, iron in hands, inches from searing his mark forever into Anya's eggshell smooth skin.

Like with the wolves, time seemed to slow down. Splinters rained down from the beam at a fraction of their expected speed. The chain began to fall, chinks collapsing into each other. With it came the heavy eyehook. It would all land in a pile on his head if he didn't do something.

Whipping his arms in a circle over his head, he threw the chain like a whip, directing it toward Bantus.

Danu, let this work.

There! The chain hit its mark, collaring the vile king.

Without the chain to keep him upright, he fell forward. Using the momentum of the fall, he twisted his shoulders midair and yanked the chain. It tightened around Bantus's throat. A final jerk of the chain as he hit the floor and it tightened enough that Bantus dropped the iron to clutch at the links.

It wasn't sufficient to choke him, but it made a nice distraction. There was one at the ready who'd been waiting for such a distraction. Anya.

She had not been idle when the men had turned to gape at him. She had been stealthily slipping Reddick's dagger from its sheath.

With a growl as fierce as any she-wolf, she broke free of Reddick's hold and lunged at Bantus's back. She clung on like a monkey with one arm locked around his throat. In a single swift move, she brought her other arm up and sliced across his neck, just under his jaw.

Blood poured over the chain and the peach silk sheathing her arm. It ran like a river down the king's chest. The wound gaped like a gruesome smile. Larna's king would bleed to death in moments.

Anya had dealt the fatal blow.

Pride and wonder rushed through him, but freedom was not yet theirs. Reddick was still a threat. Not Myre. He huddled in a corner, whimpering. But Reddick's orange eyes darkened. When Bantus began falling forward, Reddick plucked Anya from his back. He held her by her throat and shook her.

Rage shot through Riggs's limbs, but lying on the floor with his wrists still bound and his ankles chained to the wall, he was next to worthless.

Wait. The hot iron Bantus had dropped. Riggs twisted to find it lying beside the fallen king. He grabbed it, ignoring the heat of the handle, and pressed the business end into Reddick's calf.

He howled and released Anya, who fell to her hands and

knees and immediately crawled to cup Riggs's face in her hands.

"Riggs! *Och,* Riggs!" Her reddened face appeared over him. So lovely, even though she'd nearly been choked to death. Her touch was like quenching water to the fire of his pain. But there was no time to savor her closeness.

Reddick had limped to a wall full of items Bantus had referred to as "toys" and pulled down a flogger tipped with nails and shards of glass. He had his gaze fixed on Anya.

"This is for killing my king!" he cried as he advanced. "You think you're scarred now. Wait 'til I'm done with you!"

Red light flooded the dungeon. One of Ari's magic doors opened, but it wasn't Ari who charged through, sword aloft. It was Magnus. And behind him was a horde of crimson-kilted soldiers.

§

ANYA WAS STILL catching her breath from Reddick's manhandling when he came at her wielding a flogger. She pushed away from Riggs to draw Reddick away. She could take a flogging, but Riggs had been abused more than enough tonight. *Och,* if the bruises and burn marks covering his torso weren't bad enough, the gaping hole where his eyetooth used to be left her nigh speechless. Her poor wolf-man. Her poor pledgemate.

If she ever made it back to Chroina, she'd gut Ari personally for his treachery. Neil deserved just punishment, too. But first she had to survive Reddick and snatch those keys from his belt so she could free Riggs and the other women.

Before she could figure out how she might accomplish such impossible feats, the dungeon filled with a fearsome roar. She whipped around to see what had made the sound and came face to face with King Magnus, surrounded by a halo of red magic.

His eyes blazed with golden fire as they quickly took in the dungeon. She watched him catalog her presence, the blood on her sleeve, Riggs on the floor, Bantus dead, Reddick snarling and charging her.

She threw herself to the floor, meaning to lay herself over Riggs to protect him from the fighting that was about to take place, but her wolf-man was quicker than she was.

He scooped her 'neath his battered body and made an impenetrable shield around her. The scents of blood and sweat surrounded her, but peeking through were the scents of pine and loyal dog and somat else that spoke to her on a visceral level. 'Twas some woodsy nuance to his musk that carried a hint of *her*. A sense of completion swelled in her breast.

He's more than a pledgemate, and you've kent it all along.

'Twas a knowledge so deep, it seemed she'd kent it from birth. Lifemate.

The sounds of running feet multiplied. There must have been dozens of soldiers spilling from the red oval. Most exited the dungeon, but several stayed to engage Reddick and Myre. Would the Maranner force be enough to overcome the one Bantus had been gathering in the great hall?

A body fell. Then another. Bantus's two guards.

Riggs pushed himself up with a groan. "Anya? Are you all right?" He feathered his fingers over her head and shoulders. She rolled to face him. His hands found her face, awkwardly, for his bonds forced his wrists into an X. "You are well?"

"Aye, love. Aye. You?"

He nodded. His mouth opened in a grisly smile. He tongued the spot where his tooth had been. "I've been better, but I'll heal." His brow furrowed. "You can understand me?"

She sat up and opened her left hand. The fingers ached. She'd had a death grip on the bloody gemstone the whole time. "Magnus returned it."

Riggs glanced over her shoulder. At Magnus. She kent 'twas

him without turning by the approving twinkle in Riggs's eye. Returning his attention to her, he raised his arms with a wince and lowered them again with her inside the circle of safety and brawn. *Och,* she'd never forget the sight of those arms flexing and bulging until the veins stood out and a bloody *beam* splintered to set him free.

She clung to him and buried her face in his neck. Tears of relief slipped from her eyes. "I almost lost you," she sobbed. "Again! Don't you e'er give me reason to fear like that again."

"I vow it." He rained kisses over her head and face.

She was tempted to sacrifice her wits to this sweet relief, but this battle was not over. She turned in Riggs's arms to find Magnus staring down at them with nostrils flared.

"*Och,* doona stand there like a jealous cuckold. I heard that bloody tyrant say he would have two-hundred five and twenty men in the great hall and that bloody traitor, Ari, was going to bring them through to Glendall within the hour."

"I got a confession from him. My men are on their way to the great hall now. My guess is once they see Bantus's head, they'll desist." He nodded to an aged but fit soldier, who raised an axe and brought it down to sever Bantus's head from his body.

She swallowed, sickened, as the man lifted the head and carried it from the dungeon.

Magnus crouched to face her on a level. "I must see to the great hall, but first I would know this: did Bantus hurt you?"

"Nay. He tried, but thanks to Riggs, I slit his throat before he could do aught."

"*You* slit his throat?"

She raised an eyebrow. How dare he doubt her?

He grinned and palmed her cheek. "Brave lady."

Riggs's arms tightened around her.

She remembered her sister. "Before you go, you must ken there are a dozen women down the way in a cell. Humans, like me. And if I'm no' mistaken, your promised one is in there. I tried to tell you the woman in your portrait isna me. Now I ken for cert. 'Tis my sister. Her name is Seona, and she's been in this horrid place for more than a year." Her voice shook.

Riggs breathed a curse in her ear and rubbed his cheek on hers.

She drew strength from her lifemate. "Go, tend to what a conquering king must. But ken you this, those women arena well and will need much healing. Of body and of mind. Seona's in no state to become anyone's queen or bedmate or aught else. Do you understand?" Her voice had become steel, and she made no apology for lecturing a king.

Magnus's jaw went rigid. Even through his thick beard, she saw the muscles work. He said naught, but rose slowly and strode from the dungeon with a curt nod to one of his guards.

The guard blocked the door to the dungeon, protecting them, while another swooped in with the keys from Reddick's belt to unlock Riggs's manacles. A third got the keys from Myre's body and ran after Magnus, mayhap to free the women.

"Your sister," Riggs said, cupping her face in both hands. "You found her?" Deep cuts in his wrists bled freely. He'd suffered so much, yet his concern was for her.

"Aye," she answered. But she feared the Seona she'd found was much different than the one she'd lost.

Fate had returned one thing to her that was as it should be: Riggs. As ever, he was steadfast, loyal, and bursting with love for her. She pressed her lips to his. "I'm sorry your uncle betrayed you."

"It's not me he betrayed, but Magnus. He'll get what's coming to him."

"Aye." She'd see to it, just as she'd see to it Ari suffered for what had happened to Riggs. "Now, where's that tooth? Your body seems to heal everything else, why not that too?"

Chapter 25

Anya rinsed Riggs's tooth in a pot of heated water by the fire and slipped it back into its socket. It went in surprisingly easy, but it wiggled precariously.

"You'll need to keep your tongue pressed to it, I suspect," she said.

One of the guards standing watch over her and Riggs crouched down and inspected the tooth. "Seen a man lose a molar once and put it back in like that. It healed, but he had to bite down on a wad of linen for a week. Here." He pulled a bandage from a sporran-like pouch he wore next to his scabbard. After cutting a smaller strip, he rolled it and handed it to Riggs. "Clamp down on that and try not to move it."

Riggs did so and nodded his thanks.

The guard helped Riggs stand then guided him to the bed. He inspected Riggs's wrists. "Name's Maedoc." Broad-shouldered with gray in his beard, he had shrewd eyes that didn't miss much and a kind manner about him. Jerking his thumb at the other two, he introduced them as well. Anya recognized them. Four guards remained always with Magnus, but she'd learned there were more than four who shared this duty. They did it in shifts. These must be his most trusted guards, and he'd left three of them with her and Riggs. 'Twas a great honor. These men were the best of the best, the most loyal of the loyal. Some of their fellows had been guarding her door when she'd been with Travis and Daly as well. Had any of them fallen? She started to ask, but Riggs spoke up.

"Tend to Anya first," he said past the wad 'tween his teeth.

"I'm no' injured," she protested. "You, on the other hand have fared better." She motioned for Maedoc to continue.

He did so with a friendly crinkling of his eyes.

She missed the press of Riggs's hand when Maedoc began bandaging his wrist, but she made herself useful by removing Riggs's boots. Bruises darkened the skin of his ankles. They looked sore but didn't require tending, so she reluctantly turned her attention to his torso. She'd been avoiding looking too closely, kenning she'd find evidence of things she never wanted to imagine happening to her lifemate.

Blackened burns from what must have been a fire poker dotted his skin. The edges of his days-old sword wound were red and swollen, as if someone had been prodding at it. Fresh blood trickled from the site, but not enough to truly worry her. It had to have been painful, though. Very painful. "I doona suppose ye have any salve in that pouch?" she asked Maedoc.

He shook his head. "We'll get him fixed up in good time."

'Twould have to be enough.

Where Riggs wasn't burned, he was bruised. He'd been beaten with somat that left bruises of frighteningly uniform definition, a heavy stick or a mace? She refused to scan the wall of torture implements behind her. She didn't need to ken what had done this to Riggs. If she dwelled on aught, it should be that Riggs lived, and he would heal.

"*Och*, Riggs, how did you break free? I've never seen such a feat of strength." Not even by Metawuli, the strong man of Gravois' camp. The glimpse of Riggs roaring and ripping that enormous eyehook from the beam high above would live forever in her memory. She'd wanted to gape like the Larnians, but she'd made herself look away and steal Reddick's dagger. And good thing, too, since it had taken both her and Riggs to bring down that bloody despicable king.

"Wasn't me," he said, removing her hands from his body and pulling her to lie in his arms. His face was battered...again. His eyelids drooped with weariness. But he had a gleam in his eye that proved he was with her, he loved her. "I called on Danu, and she answered."

"You're a believer now, aye?"

He grinned. The wad of linen made his cheek round. "Yeah. Batty as the king, I suppose." He guided her head to his shoulder, and she was content to rest like that with him and trust Magnus's guards to protect them.

While they waited for word on the battle, she inquired about Maedoc's fellow guards, the ones she'd heard fighting when Travis had dragged her into the king's chamber and then the tunnels.

The guard shook his head. Anger clouded his features. "There are twelve of us, yeah? The king's Crescent Knights. Turns out one of us was a traitor. In bed with Breeding First."

"Eogan," spat the guard Maedoc had introduced as Drustan.

"Yeah. Eogan," Maedoc said darkly. "Because of him, Justus is in hospital. Wounded badly. He'll live, but it'll irk him to be out of this fight. It were him and Eogan at your door, lady. Should have been two against two, but Eogan turned to make it three against one."

"What happened to Eogan?" she asked.

"King Magnus had him imprisoned. He'll deal justly with him later. And with Ari. Turns out some of the ladies were in on it too. Don't envy the king's decision on what to do with them."

"What of Neil?" Riggs asked.

"You're his nephew, yeah?"

Riggs nodded against the pillow.

Maedoc leaned in. "You know the pup Travis, yeah? He comes racing into the practice yard, where the king was lining up his men to stand firm against Breeding First, not knowing what they had planned, only that they had something going tonight. 'They have Lady Anya!' the pup shouts. 'They have Lady Anya!' Well, the king gets down on a knee and asks the pup to start at the beginning. 'There's no time,' the lad says. He's out of breath and beside himself. Can barely string two words together. That's when Neil comes striding toward the king. 'I'm in it, sire,' Neil says. 'But don't want to be anymore. Ari's about to send your lady through to Saroc.' While the king sprints to the dungeon, Neil tells him all about how Ari's been using this stone of his to go back and forth between Saroc and Chroina and using it to cross the veil into a different realm, one where women abound." He shook his head.

"The king arrives with all his men at his back, and Ari knows he's outmatched. Magnus signals Faolan—" Here he nodded toward the third guard, who stood with his brawny arms crossed over his chest. "—to hold Ari's arm down upon one of the fancy tables in that secret room and without warning, the king brings down Faolan's axe and relieves Ari of his right hand. 'Care to confess or shall I take the other as well?' the king asks, cool as a snowcap. Ari confesses, hands over the stone. The king summons his high priest to bless it, then he tries the incantation Ari told him about, only using Danu's name instead of that god Ari was worshiping. It works. We all come through in time to see the last of that shite-king's blood run from his body and to help you and the lady."

So Travis had done as she'd asked and reported what had happened to the king. And Neil had turned himself in. "What'll happen to Neil?"

Maedoc looked grim. "Don't know. Maybe he'll get some sort of deal if he reveals everything he knows. His career in the king's army is over. That's for cert."

Riggs sighed, his face troubled. "He brought it on himself," he said at last.

She agreed.

It took the rest of the night for Magnus's men to subdue the Larnians and secure in place leaders who could oversee Larna's transition from independent country to vassal state. The guards escorted her and Riggs from the dungeon. When they walked past the cell that had held the women, she saw it now held men in tattered trousers and faded blue plaids. Resisting Larnians. Many more cells held Larnians as well.

"Where are the women?" she asked the guards.

"Taken to Chroina. They're safe."

She hoped so. She didn't ken how deep the conspiracy against Magnus had gone, but with both his war chieftain and his second against him, it must have gone very deep indeed. She itched to ask Magnus, but he would have much to deal with at present. From the snippets of conversation she overheard from the guards and soldiers, it seemed he had made the care of the human women his top priority. That pleased her. She would give Marann's king much grace and trust him to root out the conspirators in his own time so long as those women were out of danger.

The guards brought her and Riggs to a great hall with towering ceilings crisscrossed with more of those heavy beams like the one Riggs had been strung up beneath. The aged wood against the black stone should have made for a pleasing sight, but kenning this keep was the home of such a vile king, she took no pleasure in its beauty. Along one side of the great hall, arched windows let in the pink light of a new dawn. The scent of brine was thick in the air.

The hall bustled with Maranner warriors in red plaids. They moved swiftly but without urgency. Dozens of cots held the wounded, who were being tended by their fellows. A red oval the size of a door glowed on the dais. Several guards surrounded it.

She gulped as the king's guards led her and Riggs that way. Under her hand, Riggs's arm stiffened.

"Can we not take horses and ride for Chroina?" Riggs asked.

"Fear not, trapper." Magnus's voice brought their heads around. He strode to them from the direction of the wounded men, looking strained but hale. "I had Danu's high priest bless the stone. It is the goddess's power that holds it open. She has blessed us with this miracle, but I don't know how long it will last. So, let's get you through. I refuse to abuse Danu's blessing or take it for granted. We use it this day for as long as she allows. Then the high priest will guard the stone in the temple. It will be used again only at Danu's bidding."

A wise plan. When Magnus offered her his arm, she took it, but without letting go of Riggs. She stepped up onto the dais that way, between the man she belonged to in heart and the one who had made her his with a contract.

Red light from the oval shaded the dark blond of Magnus's hair. He smiled ruefully at them. He changed his grip to hold her hand between both of his. "I will publicly apologize to you both, but ceremonies will have to wait until Larna is stabilized. For now, I offer you, Lady Anya, and you, Riggs the trapper, son of Hilda, my sincere apology. In my misplaced jealousy, I have caused you both much pain. As soon as I am able, I will have the pact between us dissolved."

No more pact? She and Riggs could be as they were? Pledgemates. Lifemates. Free to love each other as they wished. 'Twas too good to be true. She'd believe it when she saw it done.

"I accept your apology, Your Majesty," Riggs said, extending his arm.

Magnus clasped it.

She eyed Magnus. "I'm no' as quick to forgive as my lifemate. I must think on it."

"Of course, Lady Anya. In the meantime, you have my word that none of the terms of the pact will be binding." He surprised her with a wink and gestured toward the light. Maedoc, Drustan, and Faolan herded them closer to the magic portal while Magnus issued instructions. "Have Daly settle them in the apartment in the North Tower. Make sure Travis has rested. Then send him to tend Lady Anya. Once the physicians have finished with the women, bring one to tend to Riggs." With a final nod in their direction, he strode away.

Passing through the oval was like stepping into a weighty nothingness. Her heel met the flagstones of what turned out to be Glendall's great hall even as the toes of her other foot touched the slate floor of Blackstone's great hall. In between were leagues of distance that pulled at her like a heavy stone. She hurried through with Riggs's arm firm around her, where it remained all the way to the North Tower. He limped, but not as badly as she did, and never did he lay any weight on her. His touch was one of comfort alone. *Och,* they made a fine pair, both lame and bedraggled. At least Riggs's ankles would heal and he'd be hale again soon. Her wolf-man had more than earned a chance to rest.

"Will you be able to eat with that tooth?" she asked him.

He shrugged. "I'll take broth today and try some bread tonight, if I can get some."

"I'll have some sent up," Maedoc said. "And whatever the lady wants as well."

Riggs clapped the guard on the shoulder then lifted Anya into his arms to carry her up a curving staircase. The North Tower. The apartment they entered on the third landing was much grander than she'd expected. With its upholstered couch, curtained four-poster bed and enameled armoire, it reminded her of the bedchamber adjoining Magnus's apartment. Rather than smelling of orange blossoms, it smelled of vanilla and fresh herbs. A tray of potted plants in the wash of sunlight coming through the window explained the herbal scents. She spotted an aloe plant and grinned. She'd heard all about the prickly "miracle plant" rumored to grow in India and southern climes, but had never been fortunate enough to find any extract from it for sale. Leave it to a king to have an entire plant sitting on a windowsill in his castle. Her fingers itched to break open those long, waxy leaves and make a poultice from its oils for Riggs's wounds.

"Some of the ladies would like to stay near the king when contracted to him," Maedoc explained. "Others, like your mother," he said to Riggs, "preferred privacy when the king didn't require their presence. He kept this room for them."

A muscle ticked in Riggs's jaw. He winced and said, "Damn tooth."

Och, it hadn't occurred to her Magnus might have tupped Riggs's mother, but it made sense. Riggs had told her Magnus had bedded every woman of breeding age trying to get an heir. His mother was no longer of breeding age, but she would have been in the earlier days of Magnus's rule. Did Riggs long to see his mother now that he was in Chroina? Would he want Anya to meet her? *Och,* concerns best left for another time.

Maedoc left, and Riggs barred the door. They were alone.

He hauled her into his arms with a silent sob. For a long time they just clung to each other and breathed. Tears slipped from her eyes. She let them dampen Riggs's chest.

"I suppose that torn up shirt of yours is lost forever," she said with a shaky laugh.

"Good riddance," he said, and he rubbed his cheek over her head. Gently, so gently, he touched his lips to hers. "I want to mate you, but to do it justice, I should rest first."

"Aye, love." She could use a long sleep herself. "And a bath wouldna be amiss." Her silken robe was ruined, stained with blood and torn from her struggles. The stench from that horrible cell clung to her. "For both of us."

Until Travis could come to them, they'd have to make do with the pitcher and ewer on the chest. Riggs consented to let her wash him first. She took her time, scrubbing the places where he wasn't wounded, dabbing delicately at his burns and other wounds. While the fire dried his rich coat of manly hair, he slipped her robe from her shoulders and washed her slowly. They were both hungry and exhausted, but they ended up on the bed in each other's arms nevertheless.

Riggs entered her slowly, took her with a quiet, determined passion. When they shared that special finish she'd missed since their private moments on the hilly plain, it quenched her body and soul.

"My lady," he whispered, and he fell asleep, still inside her.

§

RIGGS WOKE TO a dim chamber, the sounds of a flickering fire, and the hearty scents of broth, seasoned bread and the unique mating scent he shared with Anya. Pain licked him from head to toe, but his mouth lifted in a smile. They were safe. Bantus was dead. Magnus was bringing his foes under control. Anya was his. *All* his. And he was hers. Forever.

He opened his eyes to spy her through the parted bed curtains. She stood at the partially opened door, whispering with a bright-eyed young pup. Propping up on his elbows, he caught the pup's eye.

"Travis?" he said, remembering Magnus saying he'd send Marann's youngest citizen to tend Anya. His king honored them greatly by doing so.

The pup grinned. "You're the one who rescued Lady Anya."

Anya laughed, a throaty sound that brought a certain non-injured body part awake beneath the bedcovers. "Aye, lad. The verra one. Riggs the trapper, the champion of Anya." Meeting his gaze with her twinkling one, she said, "How many times have you rescued me, now, love? Four, I think."

Facing Travis again, she ticked off her fingers. "Let's see.

There were the Larnians near the border, nasty blights those, the wolves that nearly tore us limb from limb, the four trackers at the cave—and that's no' counting the six villagers who tried to waylay him, and now he's rescued me from the heart of the enemy's lair. Yanked a great eyehook straight out of a mighty beam. You should have seen it. The eyehook was big as a wagon spoke and made of iron. The beam splintered and rained down shards of wood on him, and then he used the chain as a whip and wrapped it around Bantus's neck."

He huffed with amusement and laced his hands behind his head, watching increasing states of wonder pass over the pup's round face. How beautiful the child was. How compact and expressive.

"Are you going to tell stories all evening or share some of that food with me?" he asked Anya. The chest was spread with a linen cloth and covered with trays of bread and cubed meat, some cooked as Anya liked and some fresh for him. He wouldn't be able to eat it. Not yet. He didn't trust his loose tooth with more than broth. Tomorrow he'd try bread.

"You really did all that?" Travis asked.

"He did," Anya answered. "And I'll tell you all about our adventures in due time, but first, my lifemate needs a good soak. Have you a hipbath you can bring for him?"

"Yes, lady." He loped away, and Anya closed the door after him.

"You have a talent for speaking with children," he told her. Personally, he found Travis intimidating. Oddly, he craved the pup's attention but feared it at the same time. He'd have to adapt to having the pup around since he was Anya's servant now. She seemed at complete ease with it all.

Glowing with contentment, she limped to him with a cup of broth and a goblet full of wine. "Wee anes are wee anes. Human, wolfkind, they all love a hero's tale. He'll be spreading it about

Glendall without a doubt. By morning, the servants will all ken what a brave man I have for a lifemate."

Her words made his chest fill with pride. He sat up and took the broth in both hands, letting her set the wine on the table beside the bed. He'd never slept in a bed so large. The straw mattress was softened by down ticking and was long enough for him with a hand to spare. The bed was broad enough to sleep five men shoulder to shoulder. Velvet curtains, when drawn, would block out the light and keep in the warmth he and Anya created. Immaculate skins of long-haired goat draped the foot of the bed.

Anya deserved luxury like this, but he wouldn't be able to afford it on a soldier's salary. Definitely not on a trapper's income. Ah well. He'd provide for her as well as he could. She was his. *His.* Completely. Irrevocably.

She nestled against his side with a trencher of bread, meat and cheese and nibbled happily. "How's your tooth?"

"Hurts," he admitted, sipping the hot, salty liquid carefully. "Your sister?"

Her smile fell. "Travis tells me she willna eat. I'd like to go to her, but I didna wish to leave you while you slept."

He was grateful for it. He would have worried if he'd woken to find her gone. "We can go together after we eat."

She brightened. "Aye. I'd like that." She slipped her gemstone from the pocket in her robe. "Riggs, I'd like to give this to Magnus. Those women, they canna understand what's happening to them. Travis tells me they're frightened. Some fight the physicians rather than let them do their work. It doesna help that all who tend to them are men. They doona understand how this world is. Or why they're here. Only that they've been abused by a terrible man. Magnus has tried to speak to them, but he frightens them as well. If he had this, mayhap they'd listen. Mayhap 'twould help them. Could you bear to go back to how 'twas after the plain? When we could hardly understand one another?"

He put down his broth and cupped her face in his two hands. "For those women, for your sister, I'll more than bear it. I'll embrace it. I'll teach you my tongue, and then once you know mine, you can teach me yours if you like."

Her eyes grew shiny. "*Och,* you're a fine man, love. A fine man."

"Luckiest man in the world."

She kissed his mouth, her lips as gentle as the brush of flower petals. "And I'm the luckiest woman."

Chapter 26

THE WINTER CHILL nipped Anya's face and hands as she walked down the stone steps that spilled into Glendall's rear gardens. She held on to Magnus's arm for ceremony but not because she needed him to steady her. Daly, who had suffered naught but a bump on his head during his scuffle with the rogue guards, had devised a pair of shoes for her in which the left sole was built up with cork to overcome the difference in the length of her legs. When she wore the shoes, she no longer limped, and the pain in her legs and back was largely diminished. She'd kissed his cheek after her first turn around the room in them, and had scarce taken them off since except to sleep…and to tup, both things she and Riggs did frequently as they recovered from their brief but strenuous time in Saroc.

Three weeks had passed. Winter had set in with its overcast skies and damp, cold air, which she hardly noticed when tucked away in the warm private retreat she and Riggs made by drawing the curtains of their bed. But she wasn't in bed now. She was outdoors in a gown of burgundy brocade and a cloak trimmed with the surprisingly soft hide of marbled boar. Despite the heavy fabric of the gown and having the hood of the cloak up for warmth, the cold sank into her body and revived the ache in her left knee. The pain didn't dull her joy. Nor did the mild sickness she'd woken with this morning or the weariness that seemed always to drag at her eyelids. Nothing would dull her joy this eve. 'Twas her wedding day.

After returning from Saroc, she'd requested an audience with Magnus and given him the gemstone to aid his communication with the rescued women. He'd accepted it graciously with the promise she could ask to borrow it at any time. So far, she hadn't felt the need. She was learning Riggs's tongue rapidly. That evening, Magnus had invited her and Riggs to sup with him. During the meal, he'd asked them to make Glendall their permanent home and had set this day as the date to publicly confirm their pledging.

Now her king led her toward the bower where she would oft sit upon a bench with Travis to enjoy an hour or two of fresh air while Riggs, now fully healed, trained in his new role as axeman in the king's army. The lad liked to read her stories to help her learn the language, and she enjoyed spending time with him when she couldn't be with her lifemate.

Gravel crunched 'neath their soles as they walked a path lined with bare bushes and a few ornamental trees proudly clinging to their green leaves. The low murmuring of a gathered crowd grew in magnitude as they neared the bower.

"*Och,* how many have you summoned to bear witness?" In her beloved Highlands, a few close family members on each side would do for a proper handfasting. Only men and women of note invited the entire clan and then more commonly for the feast, not the vowsaying. Then again, she and Riggs seemed to have become notable among the citizens of Chroina, in which case a small crowd was mayhap understandable.

"Only a few hundred."

She gasped. "A few *hundred?*" How would they all fit? There were only six benches lining the bower.

Magnus grinned down at her. "Nervous, Lady Anya?"

"Doona be ridiculous. Of course I'm no' nervous." She'd long since stopped fashing over his calling her lady. All the men did it, and none could be dissuaded. But there was one man she never discouraged from calling her lady, one man who would call her such and make her toes curl in her shoes every time. That man came into view as she and Magnus rounded a hedge into the intimate space paved with flagstones and lined with closely packed trees that made a canopy of winter-bare branches overhead.

Riggs.

Her heart leapt to see him standing at the head of the bower beside the white-robed high priest of Danu's temple. His broad shoulders filled the crisp linen shirt he would don each morning as part of his military garb. His plaid, well fitted if faded like the rest of the low-ranking soldiers', fell in an immaculate sweep across his leather armor and past his knees. A rabbit fur sporran draped his hip in front of the flap that covered the deadly head of his axe.

The benches had been pushed aside. Lanterns of beveled glass hung all around, making the dusk sparkle with golden light. Hundreds of standing wolf-men and a few wolf-women packed the space nigh to overflowing. But her eyes fastened on Riggs's. To her mind and body, they might as well have been alone for the sweet peace that filled her. Eager to reach his side, her pace quickened.

Magnus chuckled in her ear. "Patience, my dear," he chided, bringing her through the center of the quieting throng. Heads turned their way. Bearded faces split into broad smiles. Shaggy heads bowed out of respect for their king.

Near the front of the crowd, Magnus stopped her before an ivory-skinned, dark-haired wolf-woman in a gown of sea-blue and a cloak of sable fur. "Lady Anya, I present Hilda, mother of Riggs, mother of Garryn, and mother of Jonoc. Lady Hilda, I present Anya, lifemate of Riggs, sister of Seona, slayer of Bantus the Terrible." He'd introduced her as such before, but the list of her accomplishments still sounded strange to her ears, especially the part about Seona. Magnus believed she would be queen one day, and thus Anya's relation to her was notable. Considering the few conversations she'd had with her sister, Anya feared Magnus's faith was once again misguided.

Riggs's mother regarded her with forest green eyes and the restrained warmth Anya had learned was proper for public gatherings in noble society. The tall woman had only a few streaks of gray in her hair and only a few lines on her lovely face. She was one hundred and four.

Magnus released her arm so she could clasp both of Hilda's hands and kiss her right cheek while Hilda kissed hers in return, a greeting between women she'd learned from Travis.

"My pleasure to greet you, Anya," Hilda said in a cultured alto voice.

"And mine to greet you," she said in the language of Riggs's people.

"Come visit me once your mating week is ended," Hilda said. "Bring your lifemate," she added with a wink.

Riggs had last seen his mother shortly after their return from Saroc. Anya had abstained from the meeting since Riggs had gone to bring Hilda news of Neil's sentence for his treason: incarceration for life. Though a far cry better than the sentence Ari had received—a swift and public death—the news had sent Hilda into a period of grieving. Anya understood. She'd grieved when she'd been separated from Seona. She still grieved, because though she had access to Seona in body, her sister was no longer the same in mind.

"How can you love one of them?" she'd sneered. *"They're beasts one and all. They're vile. I'll find a way home, Anya. You'll see. I'll find a way out of this hell or I'll die trying."*

She felt her smile become strained and released Hilda's hands. Magnus led her to the front of the crowd. He placed her hand in Riggs's.

Her lifemate's warmth and confidence twined with her being and swallowed up the sadness brought on by thoughts of Seona. He bent to her ear and whispered, "You look beautiful." The low rumble of his voice and his familiar scent wrapped her body like the most treasured of cloaks. Her cheeks warmed at the heated look in her lifemate's eyes. She could not wait until the feast was over and they could divest each other of their fine garments in the privacy of their chamber.

The priest stepped to the side while Magnus took the prominent place at the center of an arch made from braided vines adorned with colorful ribbons. "Esteemed ladies and men of Marann," he began. "We gather this eve to bear witness to the confirmation of two pledgemates. Riggs, son of Hilda, champion of Anya and Anya, sister of Seona, slayer of Bantus the Terrible."

Beside her, Riggs's chest swelled. She stole a glance at him and found him gazing proudly at her. *Och,* he was a handsome man. And a good man, through and through. And he was hers.

She still struggled to rest in this happiness she had found at his side. 'Twas too good to be true. And yet, if 'twas all a dream, she'd not woken from it. She hoped she never did.

"I have wronged these two brave souls." Magnus's voice yanked her attention firm to him. She heard him in her own tongue, an effect of the gemstone he carried with him always. But words of humility and repentance from a king struck her as altogether foreign. Catching her eye, Magnus inclined his head, a gesture of sincerity. He did the same to Riggs.

"Every citizen of Marann in this gathering should consider himself blessed beyond measure, for we stand in the presence of the first lifemates in one thousand years. When I found them and heard their story, one that I hope I can encourage Riggs to tell at the feast tonight—" He smirked at Riggs, who paled, causing the king to huff a good-natured laugh before he sobered. "I reacted with a hard and jealous heart. Rather than wait on Danu and trust in her promise, I tried to insinuate myself into the union she had created. I committed a grievous blasphemy. Riggs, Anya, I should not have forced your consent in a pact when Danu had already blessed your exclusive union. I beg your forgiveness."

"I forgave you already," Riggs said, and he clasped arms with the king.

They both looked at her. "*Och,* if I doona forgive you, I'll look like a spiteful wench."

Magnus grinned. "A king learns how to secure what he desires. I desire your forgiveness and will sink to any depth to obtain it." He spoke just to her now, no longer projecting his voice. His grin smoothed, and he adopted a serious air. "I have learned much through this. Patience. Faith. Fairness. Not only do I ask your forgiveness, but I thank you for teaching me these sound lessons."

She'd had little to do with it. Luck…or Danu, mayhap, had been on their side when they'd found Seona. Would Magnus have dissolved the pact if they'd never found her? Would he honor Anya's wishes by not pestering Seona while she recovered from all that had happened to her in Saroc?

The crowd was silent. Magnus looked expectant. She didn't like being coerced into forgiveness, especially on her wedding day. On the other hand, in the past few weeks, Magnus *had* proven himself a compassionate guardian of the rescued women, housing them all in a previously unoccupied wing of Glendall and treating them every bit as well as he did the wolf-women of Marann. Despite his army and court being in disarray after the failed coup, he'd taken time to arrange for this fine wedding. He'd invited her and Riggs to live in his home and he'd allowed her to keep Travis as her personal servant, a great honor.

Speaking clearly for the benefit of the crowd, she said, "A Highland lass trusts carefully and forgives slowly. But when she sees goodness in a man, mayhap she can forgive more quickly than is her wont. You have my forgiveness." She lowered her voice and added privately, "But I ask that ye tread carefully with Seona. If you have truly learned patience, you'll give her the time she needs to heal."

"You have my word." Lifting his gaze to Riggs, he said, "Riggs, son of Hilda, champion of Anya, you have proven yourself among the very best of men. Loyalty, honor, and strength are yours in abundant measure. Your service as axeman in my army is appreciated. But I have a new calling for you. As all know by now, I lost one of my twelve Knights of the Crescent Moon. One of my twelve proved a traitor. The opening must be filled, and I would have it filled by you. Do you accept this duty and this honor?"

Riggs expelled a great burst of air, as though Magnus's request had knocked the wind out of him. His hand tightened around hers. He cleared his throat. "I accept, Your Majesty."

Pride straightened her spine. Joy brought hot mist to her eyes. She couldn't tear her gaze from her wolf-man. He stood tall and proud and looking every bit the respected knight he'd just become.

Magnus beamed at them both. He motioned the priest forward to start the ceremony. While the priest took his place, Magnus withdrew from his rabbit-fur pouch a golden necklace. "I had this made for Lady Seona. I will give it to her when the time is right. It is yours to borrow until the end of your mating week." He held it up with one side of the open clasp in each hand. The chain was fashioned from gold links done to look like woven cords. Rectangular amethysts interleaved with octagonal emeralds marched along the sides. The sizes of the gems increased as they drew the eye to the centerpiece, the amethyst gemstone Magnus had begun calling the Translation Stone. Wee diamonds surrounded it in a dazzling display. It looked exactly like the necklace in the portrait in Magnus's throne room.

He gave her the gift of comprehension so she could enjoy her husband this week without constraints. And he trusted her with the precious gift he planned to give her sister should she ever accept him as he hoped. One thing was for cert. Seona could do far worse than a generous king who was humble enough to admit his fault when necessary and wise enough to recognize and promote greatness when he saw it. He'd more than earned her forgiveness in the last five minutes. "Thank you, Magnus."

He fastened it around her neck, kissed her cheek, and went to stand beside Hilda and two of his knights. The priest then prayed over her and Riggs and confirmed their pledging and their lifemating with trembling voice and tears in his eyes.

When it came time to repeat their pledges, Anya had difficulty holding back her own joyful tears. She managed it with the determination of the Keith and the dignity of Scotia.

It had been a long journey to this place, and far from an easy one. Now that she was here, at Riggs's side, she vowed in her heart to embrace her new home, honor her new king, and show her wolf-man what it was to be loved by a Highland lass.

Epilogue

RIGGS OPENED HIS eyes to a blade of sunlight peeking past the seam in the bed curtains. He stretched his toes to the end of the bed and rolled his head to crack his neck, careful not to wake Anya. He was stiff from cradling her in the same position all night, but he welcomed the mild discomfort since she'd had a peaceful night. Normally, he wouldn't worry about shifting and waking her, but lately, she'd been more tired than usual and prone to feeling ill in the mornings.

He pressed a soft kiss to her temple, pulled her scent of flowers, hyssop and woman deep into his lungs. It was four days into their mating week, a moon cycle from the eve they'd become lifemates, and he was happier than he'd ever imagined a man could be.

He almost felt guilty about closeting himself in this posh apartment with his beloved. His duties as a Knight of the Crescent Moon awaited him when he and Anya emerged from their mating chamber. He was eager to begin his new career, but not so eager as to lament the fact he had three glorious days left to do nothing but nuzzle and kiss and mate with his woman.

Speaking of nuzzling, Anya began rubbing her nose on his neck. She kissed him there, under his ear, where the sweet press of her lips made his blood heat. Then she sucked in a breath, the way she did when sickness took hold of her.

"My poor lady," he murmured against her hair. "I will have Travis summon a physician for you as soon as he brings our morning tray. You'll not refuse me this time." He indulged her too much. It was time for him to be firm. No more risks where her health was concerned. This had lasted long enough that he was well and truly worried.

"As you wish, love."

Something serious was wrong with Anya. She'd just given in to a demand she'd previously refused. He felt her forehead. She was warmer than normal. "You have a fever." He sat up and threw open the curtains. In a flash, he had his civilian trousers on. "I'll have the guards fetch a physician."

Anya dove past him and ran for the privy screen. He dashed after her to find her retching over the chamber pot.

His heart jumped into his throat. She was very sick. He ran for the door.

"It can't be," she whispered.

He stopped with his hand on the bolt. She didn't sound distressed. Her tone was one of wonder.

"Anya?" He turned to find her sitting back on her heels. Her night rail pooled around her knees. The king's necklace lay against her chest, the amethyst gem settling just above the valley between her breasts.

Eyes unfocused, she ladled water from the ewer into a cup. After drinking deeply, she wiped her mouth on the back of her wrist. When her arm lowered, she had a broad smile on her face. "I doona require a physician, love," she said. The glow in her cheeks didn't fit with the sickness she'd just experienced.

"Enough arguing. It's time we find out what's wrong with you." He started to open the door.

"Naught is wrong," she said on a laugh. She leapt up and limped to him, her stride quick and light as air. Reaching him, she went up on her toes and wrapped her arms around his neck. "I'm with child, Riggs."

He blinked. He must have heard her wrong. "What did you

say?"

"I'm with child. *Your* child. Your seed has quickened in me. It's a miracle."

He forgot to breathe. "Truly?"

"I think so. I'm no' certain, but I'm showing all the signs. I canna believe it took me so long to realize. Illness at sunrise, weariness during the day, tender breasts. *Och,* do they feel larger to you?" She parted her dressing gown and put his hands on her breasts.

He dutifully weighed them. By the moon, touching her like this made him want to mate her. He shook the thought away. How could he think of mating at a time like this? He trained his attention on the feel of her smooth mounds. They did seem larger. Heavier. Her nipples were a deeper shade of pink. His mouth watered. "They do feel larger," he made himself say.

"We're going to have a wee bairn." Awe filled her voice.

Wonder filled his heart. Anya carried a child. *His* child. His *child.*

She removed his hands from her and kissed his fingers. Then she drew him down and kissed him soundly on the mouth. She tasted of cool water and his beloved Anya.

When she pulled back, her eyes shone with joy and love. He'd never seen her so happy. And he'd seen her very happy in the past weeks. "Did you hear me, Riggs? We're going to have a bairn."

"I heard you." A slow smile stretched his cheeks. "We will be the first parents to welcome a child into the world since Travis's birth." Elation sang through his blood. He picked up his lifemate and swung her around. Then immediately regretted it. "I didn't hurt you did I?"

"Of course you didna hurt me. I'm no' an invalid. I'm with child. I'm with child!"

He was going to be a father.

Hope for his people lifted him like a refreshing wind. A child.

Half wolfkind, half human. The birth would be celebrated by all Marann. No, by the whole world.

Boy or girl, it didn't matter. The child represented hope. Maybe this was the turning point they'd been longing for.

The world would be revived. Because of Anya.

He'd thought Danu had blessed him above all men for giving him such a brave, beautiful, passionate woman. If the goddess's blessing was an iceberg, he had the feeling he'd merely experienced the tip.

The servant pup came through the door with their morning tray.

"Travis," Riggs said. "Go get Magnus. We have news to share."

A note from the author

Thanks so much for reading *The Wolf and the Highlander.* I hope you enjoyed it. This novel is the second in my Highland Wishes series. Next is *The Highlander's Witch,* due out in 2015.

Reviews make my day. Whether positive or negative, reviews help an author immensely. Please consider leaving an honest review at Goodreads and/or your favorite retailer.

About Jessi Gage

Jessi lives with her husband and children in the Seattle area. She's a passionate reader of all genres of romance, especially anything involving the paranormal. Ghosts, demons, vampires, witches, weres, faeries…you name it, she'll read it. As for writing, she's sticking to Highlanders and contemporaries with a paranormal twist (for now).

Jessi can often be found having coffee at one of the many neighborhood coffee spots she frequents, or indulging in sweets with The Cupcake Crew, her wonderful critique group. The last time she imagined a world without romance novels, her husband found her crouched in the corner, rocking.

Find Jessi at the following online haunts:

Website http://jessigage.com/
Blog http://jessigage.wordpress.com/
Facebook https://www.facebook.com/jessigageromance
Twitter https://twitter.com/jessigage

To send her an email, visit her website and use the contact form at http://jessigage.com/Contact.html

To receive email updates when new releases become available, subscribe to Jessi's newsletter at http://jessigage.com/

73342316R00214

Made in the USA
San Bernardino, CA
04 April 2018